LUCY LE EY

LUCY LEIGHTON'S JOURNEY

Genevieve Lyons

PAN BOOKS

This edition published 1999 by Pan Books
an imprint of Macmillan Publishers Ltd
25 Eccleston Place, London SW1W 9NF
Basingstoke and Oxford
Associated companies throughout the world
www.macmillan.co.uk

This first world edition published in Great Britain 1996 by
SEVERN HOUSE PUBLISHERS LTD of
9-15 High Street, Sutton, Surrey SM1 1DF
First published in the USA 1996 by
SEVERN HOUSE PUBLISHERS INC of
595 Madison Avenue, New York, NY 10022.

British Library Cataloguing in Publication Data
Lyons, Genevieve
Lucy Leighton's Journey
1. English fiction – 20the century
1. Title
823.9'14 [F]

ISBN 0 330 39651 X

Typeset by Hewer Text Composition Services, Edinburgh
Printed and bound in Great Britain by
Mackays of Chatham plc, Chatham, Kent

This book is for my dear little
Aussie friend Lynette, with my love
And Michele

Chapter One

Hardly anyone came to the funeral. In the big echoing church the coffin stood, candle-lit in solitary splendour on the catafalque and there was only Lucy. There was only one meagre and mean wreath, isolated on the polished lid.

The church was empty except for Lucy, the vicar and the men from the funeral parlour who seemed like gaunt shadows lurking in the darkness, hovering like vultures near the coffin. Mercedes Marchant had drawn her smallest crowd ever. She would have been mortified.

Not that Lucy expected a crowd. But she could think of a few neighbours who should have bothered, local people who might have made the effort. In the event no one turned up, and she, and the men from the undertakers shivered in the vastness of the vaulted grandeur of St Luke's Methodist Church. Her mother, Lucy had to accept, had not been a popular woman with the few she saw during her last days. She had not, to be fair, consorted much with the locals. She had mainly kept the neighbours at arm's length deeming them inferior. "They're my *audience* darling," she would tell Lucy. She had been frosty with the greengrocer, cool with the chemist, arrogant with the girls in the supermarket, and positively rude to the woman in the off-licence. She considered them *hoi polloi* and far beneath her.

Lucy's mother had been on the London stage. She had shone brilliantly, a big name for a time and since then Mercedes Marchant tended to get her status slightly out of proportion.

In those far-off days stage stars were goddesses, worshipped and adored. They were the idols of their time, revered and courted and Mercedes Marchant had glittered brighter than most. That was before actresses ceased to be glamorous.

Lucy sighed in the cold church. She had only the most faded memories of her mother in her grander days. Her pre-multiple sclerosis days. Mercedes Marchant had reached the height of her fame in the late Fifties and early Sixties. Lucy was born in nineteen sixty-eight. The halcyon days of Mercedes' adulation, her champagne days at the Ritz, *foie gras* in the Caprice, dancing in Annabels or Tramp were well and truly over when Mercedes began to show signs of her illness which struck in actuality when Lucy was thirteen.

Lucy blamed herself, albeit obliquely, for her mother's demise from popular star to helpless invalid, even though she knew quite well it had nothing whatsoever to do with her. Nevertheless she felt guilty in the presence of that piteous decline and the flashes of anger that shot every so often like poison darts from her mother's eyes.

Sadly for Lucy she had not known the shining woman in the sequined strapless figure-hugging ball gown in the blown-up *Vogue* portrait that hung on the wall of their house in St John's Wood. Lucy could not imagine her mother as that exquisite goddess. The mother she attended had a slack-muscled, square body, sexless and helpless. Her sagging face, her crippled limbs were familiar to her daughter and bore no resemblance to the beautiful noble-faced girl, slim as a reed in the photo of her in lawyer's robes as Portia. Or the proud figure in tights as a radiant and mischievous Rosalind in *As You Like It*. Mercedes Marchant was to Lucy a loved mother certainly, but a woman prematurely aged by pain, someone who had to be handled tactfully, for the agony of multiple sclerosis had made her temper uncertain and her body a tormented battlefield.

Yes, Lucy had looked after her mother from the age of thirteen. She had been nurse, minder, cleaner, cook and carer as her mother's strength declined slowly but surely into total dependence on her daughter. Lucy nursed her willingly, almost with relief. She was a shy girl, fearful of life, its demands and responsibilities and she found her sick mother a convenient excuse for opting out. When faced with the challenge of growing up she hid behind the role of minder and avoided the experience entirely. Her mother had to be looked after and it was Lucy's duty to do so.

Her dedication to the task had forged a resilient

spirit, a character both courageous and patient and yet someone totally ignorant of the world. Lucy Leighton was, at twenty-eight, as innocent as a Victorian maiden yet wise as many a learned sociologist or Sister in charge of a geriatric ward. She was prematurely older than her years yet in some respects guileless and trusting as a nun.

Now her mother lay dead and she was on her own. A merciful release, Dr Wilton had described it. But Lucy had been too busy arranging the funeral according to her mother's wishes to sort out her feelings then. She had put the announcement in *The Times*, gone to the funeral parlour of her mother's choice and talked to the vicar of St Luke's where her mother wished to be buried. She had managed, as usual, entirely on her own.

She had been her mother's only child. Brent Leighton, Lucy's father, had deserted them when Lucy was only three years old. He claimed that with the advent of Lucy the romance had gone out of his life with Mercedes. He said he could not compete with a baby, so he had left them. He had also broken Mercedes' heart and she never divorced him.

A dramatically good-looking actor of mediocre talent, he had run away from the shackles of family life and the very high standard of acting on London's West End stages. He fled to Rome and Cinnecitta and got small parts with Fellini, de Sica and Antonioni, ending up in Spaghetti Westerns in Spain's Andalucia. He had a sudden heart attack on the set of a Western and died there under the klieg lights with a hundred extras dressed as Red Indians and Cowboys around him. Mercedes had wept all night – the only time Lucy had seen her mother cry.

Lucy had thought that some relative, some long forgotten aunt or uncle might pitch up for the funeral having read the obituary in *The Times*, but no. So she was alone in the church, the vicar droning on about 'eternal Life' and 'crossing the great divide' and 'ashes to ashes, dust to dust' in an emotionless voice that revealed a familiarity with death bordering on the monotonous.

She felt uncomfortable in the black suit, bought for the occasion. She wore a hat, which she hated and her scalp was itching unbearably underneath it and she could not reach up far enough under it to scratch, so she shifted uneasily in her seat and the Funeral Director and his men and the vicar all glanced at her as if she was a time bomb about to go off. What were they expecting of her? Dry-eyed she stared back at them.

As Lucy sat there, she was trying to understand her emotions which, to add to her discomfort, seemed to consist primarily of a mixture of relief and excitement and not the grief of loss that she had expected, and that she felt would have been more appropriate.

Lucy stared at the vicar's nose which glowed red against the white of his cassock and felt strangely elated. It suited her that the day was so rotten, the church so cold. It made her feel less guilty about the surges of excitement that coursed through her like electric currents.

She felt that morning as if she'd been released from bondage and although it was a frightening sensation it was exhilarating as well.

Not that she hadn't loved her mother. On no, Lucy had absolutely adored Mercedes. She had been glad to devote her life to her mother, without reserve and with unstinting generosity. Her exhilaration came from the realisation of a job well done, a job she had completed to the very best of her ability and which was now over.

People in this psychologically oriented age had tried to foist upon Lucy feelings of resentment and the shadow of exploitation. Some insisted that she was 'in denial', saying that she should, if she was normal, *hate* her mother. They insisted that her mother had spoiled her life and she had every reason to loathe her. She *had* to be damaged, they said, repressed and deprived, but she shrugged off their psychoanalysing which at best was amateur and told them she had *chosen* her path. Her mother had always made it clear to her that she would cheerfully go into a home if necessary; it was Lucy who insisted that she wanted to do the job. It made her happy. It was what she wanted to do. Any other course would have made her miserable. The so-called experts sighed, shook their heads and left her alone.

Lucy had felt no desire to break loose from the bonds of love and duty that held her to her mother. She had rarely yearned for the umbilical cord to be cut and had perplexed those people, eager to categorise and pigeon-hole, who felt that the least she could do as a teenager was to rebel. But Lucy didn't. She had no desire to rebel. In her quiet accepting way she had early on decided that it was her duty to look after her mother and although she was no long-suffering saint she actually enjoyed her usefulness and the fact that her mother found her essential.

"She looked after me," she told anyone who tried to sort her out. "All those years, without help from my father. She put me through school when she was sick, when the illness must have been debilitating and exhausting. She never let me down. I am only too proud and honoured to look after her now that she needs me. It's the least I can do." They shook their heads and babbled clichés. If she wanted to give up her young life to care for an ailing mother then who were they to stop her?

The vicar was nodding to the Funeral Director and four of his assistants were shouldering the black coffin. The Funeral Director removed Lucy's wreath from the coffin and a shower of petals billowed to the stone floor leaving ugly brown dead-heads amid the greenery. The flowers could not have been fresh. She frowned. She thought 'I'll have to complain', but in her heart knew that she wouldn't.

The vicar indicated that she should follow as they proceeded to the closed doors of the church. Then, as with most funerals, there followed a moment of comic relief. As they waited in front of the closed doors a soft snore broke the eerie silence in the church. The verger had been dozing near the door and now they all turned to look at him. The vicar prodded him and he snorted awake, leapt to his feet, shook himself and as they waited he began to open the door under the frowning gaze of the Funeral Director with a huge old-fashioned key. He obviously found it difficult to manage and kept dropping it as he glanced around fearfully at his impatient boss and the little cortège at the doors.

Lucy felt a giggle rise. She was not a giggly person and at first could not identify what it was that tickled her throat and she had to swallow hard to suppress it, deciding in her own mind that it must be hysteria, not laughter that had overcome her. She pressed her handkerchief to her lips as they waited and the poor verger wrestled with his keys and the vicar tapped his foot and the undertakers' men sweated and hoped they would not drop the casket.

The funeral cortège finally emerged into the grey day.

Lucy blinked her eyes. It was classic funeral weather: howling winds that sucked umbrellas inside out and moaned through the trees like a banshee. It cut like a sharp knife slicing into Lucy's cheeks. The driving rain slanted towards the graveyard at the back of the church, turning the leaves all in the same direction, pale side out. It drove the cat out of the cemetery into the parsonage and the warmth of the blazing fire and the vicar's wife's lap.

They walked with dignity to the open graveside and Lucy watched as the men lowered the coffin into it. She shivered. It was an awe-inspiring moment and sudden tears darkened her eyes. There was no sound except the vicar's drone and the tattoo of the rain on the foliage.

A wave of sadness hit her. It was the emotion she had expected to feel but had up to now eluded her, leaving her perplexed. Now, looking into the clayey recepticle her mother's coffin was going to be neatly tucked into, the space having been marked out years ago, and paid for, Lucy felt an overwhelming sense of loss and horror and grief at the reality of it all. Gone forever. The end. Finito. She pressed her handkerchief to her nose, which was watering in the wind and glanced up at the dancing branches of the trees.

As her eyes descended she realised that there was someone standing beneath the chestnut tree over to her right. A tall man, coat collar turned up, he was trying to shelter from the drenching rain and wind. He was hatless, silver-haired, distinguished and handsome and she wondered who he was. He was, she deduced, obviously someone paying their last respects to her mother for he was facing the grave and looking directly at her. She met his eyes and saw in them a responsive sympathy, and as their glances held, her attention was caught by a movement, another on the other side of the tree, near a lichen-covered tombstone.

They could have been brothers; maybe they were. They seemed reflections of each other, mirror images. They both wore camel coats and were good-looking men, well-groomed, middle-aged, probably pushing sixty, and they stood facing the little group at the graveside: Lucy and the undertakers' men.

Another movement to her right caught her attention and there in that grey day, in the sleeting rain was yet another, this time a fedora-hatted elderly gentleman sheltering under an umbrella that he was desperately trying to hold on to in the raging wind.

And there another, a little behind the fedora-hatted man, this one holding a bowler against his chest. He had a swatch of silver hair carefully draped across his bald pate but as she looked it rose and stood up like a flag, vertical in the wind. Lucy reflected idly that he really should not have taken his hat off though he had obviously done so out of respect for her mother.

She knew they were her mother's friends and reason told her that they were probably old theatre buddies, but how odd, she thought, her mother had not been in contact with any of the old crowd for years.

The thunk of the sods on the coffin brought her attention back to the ceremony. "Ashes to ashes, dust to dust . . ." *Again*! Oh the dreary old words to comfort but rather terrified the mourner. The inevitability of one's own mortality. The vicar intoned the unarguable words and the wind increased in velocity, whistled and screamed around the church belfry and black blankets of clouds scudded across the stormy sky like angry barges intent on war.

She looked to her left, averting her face from the fierce bite of the wind and to her amazement saw at least four or five other men, all elderly, all dapper, though revealing in their garb varying degrees of prosperity. They were standing about under the trees and around the tombstones and she glanced over her shoulder and there, behind her, stood yet another group. So her mother had not been forgotten after all.

"Amen!" The vicar looked at her deeply and with great sincerity He pressed her hand and murmured, "She's at peace now." How on earth did he know that? His nose was dripping and his eyes watering and he was obviously torn between the desire to do his duty to the best of his ability while filled with an overwhelming longing to go home.

She nodded. "Thank you," and looking about added, "why don't you go home. It's all over now."

He nodded to her and went. The undertakers' men were drifting, trying not to rush *too* eagerly to the limousines. The Funeral Director was sitting in the hearse smoking surreptitiously. The strange groups of elderly gentlemen were dispersing. Lucy hurried over towards the first man she had spotted who was also the nearest.

"Excuse me! Excuse me." She touched his arm and he glanced at her. "Do you mind me asking, who you are?"

"Eh?" He'd looked away from her towards the bleak landscape and the new grave. The trees were bending over it in the velocity of the wind as if making obeisance to her mother.

"My turn soon," he murmured.

"Oh nonsense!" Lucy cried in the brisk nursing voice she'd used to curb her mother's worst excesses of self-pity. "You're hale and hearty. It will be a long time yet."

He shook his head and to her horror replied, "No my dear. They've given me, maximum, a year."

She pressed her gloved hand to her cheek. "Oh gosh! Oh I'm so sorry."

He smiled. "Don't be. You couldn't have known."

"It was tactless though, really gross of me."

He smiled again at her. It was a charming smile, a practised smile, a professional smile. "No, no. But let it be a lesson to you. Enjoy life while you can. It's a gift and it's a crime to waste it."

"Who are you though? I hope you don't mind my asking, but . . ."

"You're wondering what I'm doing here?"

"Yes. And the others. It's so odd . . . I . . ."

"I'm Barry Brocklehurst. An actor. The others too. Theatre folk."

"But it's been years since Mother . . ."

He smiled again. "Oh we never forget. Certainly not *her*. Not Mercedes. You're her daughter I take it. Most of us knew you when you were a baby. Most of us are members of the Green Room Club. An actor's club. Private." He grinned. "Oh it sounds very grand but it is really a place where us old pros can meet and jaw over the good old days. Word went around there of Merry's death. Someone read it in *The Times*."

She frowned. "Merry?" She could not imagine her mother being called Merry. Not in a million years. The pale ghost of a woman, bitter and in constant pain was very far away from such a diminutive.

"Yes. We called her Merry. Well," he waved his hand, "we all came to say, 'Farewell, let flights of angels sing thee to thy rest'." He gave her a wry glance and pulled his coat closer around him adding, "Though the demons of hell seem to have been let loose this ghastly day."

"How kind of you all," she said.

The man with the bald head and the fluttering flag of hair had replaced his bowler and was gesturing to Barry Brocklehurst Some of the others had joined him and he was mouthing something about a jar and miming quaffing a drink.

Barry said, "I'd ask you to join us, only the Green Room Club is all male. Women are allowed only on sufferance. Mind you, I think it is still that way in this day and age because no woman in her right mind would want to join or spend time there." He looked at her quizzically. "Let me take you for a drink before I join the others. I take it there's no wake?"

She shook her head. "I didn't expect anybody," she murmured helplessly, feeling she'd somehow let her mother down though she could not think how or why. She could not have expected such an abundance of gentlemen at the graveside and, even if she had, she doubted if they'd have wanted to return with her to the St John's Wood house. Still, she felt guilty.

"Of course not," he replied.

One of the other gentlemen had come up to Barry. He stood beside him clearing his throat. "Look old fellow, we're off . . ."

"This is Merry's girl . . . em . . . I'm afraid I don't know your name?"

"It's Lucy. Lucy."

"Lucy this is Errol Armitage, actor and gentleman." She smiled at him. He was in his early fifties, amazingly attractive and distinguished looking. Lucy felt sure his face was familiar and thought she'd seen it on the box. It drew to mind a period piece; an ambassador? A rather grand father? A commanding officer? Or perhaps all of those images. His expression switched in an instant from a good fella indicating to his pal that a drink was in order to a *terribly* sympathetic mourner at a funeral. His face was devastatingly grave.

"My dear, I'm *so* sorry. *So* sorry. You must be lost! How sad. How very sad! Parting is such sweet—"

"Don't say it Errol, just don't say it," Barry Brocklehurst admonished. "I'm taking Lucy for a drink before I join you lot in the Green Room."

"Mind if I join you?" Errol Armitage gave Lucy a huge smile. "Stanley is tending to cling this morning and I don't think I can bear him till he's had at least three drinks in him."

Barry Brocklehurst shrugged good-humouredly. "Fine, old chap." He turned to Lucy. "See the chappie in the bowler? Well that's Stanley Stoddard. Magic actor but one of the great bores of all time. He gets very maudlin over Merry. He's in a state about her dying though he hasn't seen her for *years*! But he says she reminds him of his youth. 'Struth Errol, fine lot of old codgers we are." He linked her arm in his and they began to walk.

Errol on her other side asked, "You all right Lucy?" and Barry stopped a moment saying, "Watch out for this fellow. He's a dire lady-killer. Don't fall for his charm."

"The pot calling the kettle black," Errol laughed.

It was all harmless fun. There was something innocent about these men Lucy thought. It was as if they had lived life in a hothouse, in some way protected from the real world.

The one called Stanley, who was the one with the streamer of hair, stood shivering on the outskirts of the group. His hands were deep in his pockets, pushing them down to his knees. "You coming?" he shouted as they neared him.

"Oh Stanley, this is Merry's child. Lucy."

"How do." The man called Stanley was obviously too cold to care who she was. He nodded at her, shivering, and she could see his hands clench and unclench in his pockets.

"Nice to meet you," he said, then added, "You coming?"

Barry called, "Stanley, we're taking Lucy for a drink. You go ahead with the others. I'll see you there in an hour or two." Stanley waved a hand, hurrying away, pushing his head down into his collar and replacing his hands in his pockets.

Barry Brocklehurst looked at Lucy. "Shall we go?" he asked. Then as she made as if to look back at her mother's grave he added, "No. Don't do that. It won't help. Let's get out of here."

Errol Armitage had gone over to the grave and stood, his back to them, staring down into the gaping muddy wound. His coat flapped in the wind and his shoulders drooped.

"Come on Errol, we're off. It's an appalling day. Only place to be is the pub." Errol nodded. Lucy thought, when he joined them, that he seemed to have been weeping, but then, it might have been the wind. He too tucked his arm into Lucy's free one and thus, arm in arm the three of them left the bleak place, not looking back, looking forward to a drink.

Chapter Two

The pub was directly opposite the cemetery gates and they hurried into it as if pursued by demons. Breathing sighs of relief the three of them clustered around the fire which burned merrily in the wide fireplace. It was only after a while, when they were settled in comfortable wooden cottage chairs, that Lucy realised it was actually a gas fire; a cunning imitation almost impossible to decipher from the real thing. Nevertheless it was a cheery and warming focus for the three of them.

Lucy was beset every now and then with an overwhelming desire to giggle. She had a vision of herself flanked by these two silver-haired ridiculously good-looking actors with their full and rounded diction and for some reason she found the picture funny.

However, the men were both easy to talk to, friendly, and sympathetic. They wanted her to like them and they obviously liked her. The pub, sepia-shadowed, mellowly lit was warm and relaxing after the shrill wind and whiplash rain outside. Lucy felt very comfortable and if she thought the situation faintly silly she did not show it.

"Your mother was a wonderful woman Lucy," Barry Brocklehurst told her. He had ordered her a brandy saying, "It is medicinal Lucy, and no matter what you think you must be feeling shocked."

Errol Armitage added, "It's a very dark experience, the burial of someone you love." He glanced at her. "It can make you weep or giggle hysterically, depending on your temperament."

Both men drank beer and a chaser, and it seemed to Lucy their habit, something they often did together.

When Barry spoke about her mother, praising her, lauding her talent, rhapsodising about her beauty, and Errol nodded his head in agreement, Lucy felt they were talking about another woman, not her mother. This woman they discussed was nothing like the mother she had nursed for the last fifteen years.

"Half the men in London wanted to marry her," Barry said. "It was the fashion. You *had* to be in love with either Vivian Leigh, Margaret Leighton, Fiona Campbell-Walter or Mercedes Marchant."

Lucy stared wide-eyed back at Barry and glanced at Errol who confirmed this amazing statement with a nod. She noticed that whereas Barry rattled on, slowly drinking his beer and every now and then taking a sip of his Johnny Walker, Errol, on the other hand, remained silent and seemed to scrutinise her when he thought she did not notice.

Barry, on closer inspection, did not look a well man. His skin was sallow and there were dark circles under his eyes. Errol, conversely had that pinkish glow to his skin under a light tan and clear bright blue eyes of the very healthy.

"I wanted to marry her myself," Barry was saying. "I plagued her with proposals, I really did." He shook his head, remembering. He must have been gorgeous back in those days, in his prime Lucy reflected, looking at him now in the golden light from the fire. So handsome. He was still remarkable looking. He did everything with a flourish and sawed the air with his hands as Hamlet had specifically asked the actors *not* to do. Any fool could tell he was an actor but Lucy could sec that underneath the elocuted tones, dramatic gestures and flamboyant façade there was a frightened and kindly man.

"Did you act with her?" Lucy asked him. She was enjoying herself in the cosy pub in the company of these men, the fiery brandy sliding warmly down into her stomach. Every now and then she was seized by alarm, an urgency she was so familiar with. It was the warning she had lived with for so long, the reminder that her invalid mother was waiting for her alone at home. She might need Lucy. There might be an emergency. It was the tie that prevented her from ever relaxing. She had never been free, not her own mistress to stay or go as she chose.

Only now, for the first time in this pub she could shrug it off, remind herself that her mother no longer needed her ministrations, that her mother was dead. As she sat there and listened to Barry a moment of pure panic and desolation overwhelmed her. Suddenly she felt rootless, lost and terribly alone.

Errol, who had been watching her patted her hand, holding it a moment in his and smiling at her, chasing the blues away and she felt a flood of relief and relaxation, and a realisation of a freedom she had never experienced before.

Barry was assuring her, "Dear me yes. I was privileged. So was Errol here. Yes, I played Bassiano to her Portia. And I played many another role opposite her. I was very lucky." None of this meant anything to Lucy. All she knew of her mother's career were the portraits in costume on the walls at home. She saw Errol's eyes flicker as he gazed into his beer. Barry continued, "Errol here played the servant to her Miss Julie, the Strindberg play. He was very young, younger than Merry. Younger than me."

Errol glanced up at her, his blue eyes intense. "She was my first love," he said softly. "So beautiful. So beautiful." He sighed and looked back into his beer.

"It was a very romantic time," Barry said. "We held each other when we danced and tunes had wonderful lyrics that you could hear. We brought flowers or chocolates when we took a girlfriend out and we wooed the ladies."

"You sound like an old fogey," Errol remarked.

"I *am* an old fogey Errol. I don't delude myself."

There was a silence. The fire hummed just like a real one and a group in another corner laughed loudly. The laughter died quickly, then rose again.

They were obviously telling stories, dirty ones by the sound of it. The bartender read the racing page of the *Standard* and crinkled his eyes up against the smoke of the cigarette between his lips.

"It was Merry, you know, who broke the connection." Errol looked at her again and Lucy was startled by the sadness in his eyes. "In case you thought we deserted her."

"We didn't," Barry said stoutly, "we tried to keep in contact but she wouldn't have it." He stared into the fire. "I was hurt at first. I was such an old friend. We'd been through so much together. We thought she was too absorbed in you," he smiled at her, "but then we found out about the MS and we were shocked. The others too. We understood. She couldn't bear us to see her disintegration." He sighed. "We wanted to help," he looked at Errol who nodded, "all of us. Lots of people wanted to support her through it but she wouldn't let us."

Errol concurred. "Not just men either; women too, although Merry was a man's woman. We wanted to help, show solidarity, but she wouldn't have it. She shut us out very firmly, told us we were not wanted. It was her choice."

"We tried very hard at first," Barry mused. "We talked a lot about it at the Club. Stanley was the most persistant. You met Stanley, he was there today. Oh and Josh. But it was all to no avail."

Errol looked over at Barry. "Maybe we should have tried harder. It was all left to you my dear wasn't it? The nursing, the cheering up, everything."

Lucy shook her head. "No matter how hard you tried it wouldn't have done any good," she reassured him, "Mother was a very obstinate woman." The two men laughed.

"Yes she was indeed," Barry agreed.

"But it must have been very hard, stifling all that talent," Errol said. "Sitting on it. Not using it."

"She was brilliant, a faultless actress," Barry agreed.

Another silence fell. There was no strain in the lull, just a warm peace. Lucy felt half asleep.

"So what are you going to do now?" Errol asked her.

She shrugged. "I don't know." Then frowning, added, "What I *hoped* was to travel." She gazed at the two men her eyes bright as stars. "You see I've never been *anywhere*. Never left this country, looking after Mother. Oh and I so want to see the world. So much." She was ardent, like St Joan talking about her voices Barry reflected. "I thought I'd sell the house . . . I don't need—"

"You mean the house in St John's Wood?" Lucy nodded. "It's a mansion as I remember," Barry said. "Should bring in a nice price."

"Yes," Lucy agreed eagerly. She had never confided this dream of hers before to anyone. Saying it aloud excited her. "I could go on those Classic Tours you see advertised. You know, visit places like Capodocia and Padua, Acapulco and Petra. Oh you know, places I've read about, dreamed about." Her eyes glowed, shining with her dreams and for the first time she looked very like her mother. The two men smiled at her enthusiasm.

"Sure you can," Barry cried.

"Sure you must," Errol affirmed.

Barry then looked at his watch. "We must get on," he said. "Will you be OK?"

"If I had my car I'd drive you back," Errol said, "but we came in a cab."

She shook her head. "No, I'm fine," she protested. "I'd rather take my time. I have an appointment to see Mr Crabbe, our solicitor. I said I'd call in today."

"Whereabouts is he?" Errol asked.

"Lincoln's Inn."

"Well we can take you as far as the West End," Errol said and they stood up preparing to leave.

"Here's my card," Barry said.

"And mine," Errol echoed. "I still have the number in St John's Wood, would you believe."

"Call us if you need a chat," Barry added.

"Call us anyway," Errol told her. "I'd like to talk over the old stuff sometime maybe, that is if you'd like."

She nodded. "I'd love to," she told him, meaning it.

"Well do. Don't just think about it. Promise?"

"Promise."

"Well let's go then," he said and they put their coats back on and very reluctantly left the cosy warmth of the pub and ventured forth into the wild wet day in search of a cab.

Chapter Three

Anthony Crabbe sat behind his desk which was piled high with documents, papers, invoices, letters, old-fashioned wire in and out trays and a computer. The room in Lincoln's Inn Fields was postage-stamp small and had been occupied by a Crabbe since 1824. Anthony's father often said that if you searched hard enough behind the wall-to-wall files you would probably find documents from the sixteenth and seventeenth centuries. None of the Crabbes explored those files unless it was absolutely necessary as in the case of disputes about estates or lands, etc. The Crabbes dealt mainly in land and property. They were kept very busy and like most lawyers were very prosperous indeed.

The crowded old-fashioned office, far from discouraging clients in fact had the reverse effect. Its antiquity reassured people.

Lucy had left Barry and Errol in Regent Street with brisk assurances that she was perfectly capable of making her own way from there, and she now sat on a chair in the offices of Crabbe, Appelbe and Winston in front of the ancient desk groaning under its weight of paper-work despite the shiny technologically advanced computer.

"I wanted to see you a.s.a.p.," Anthony Crabbe told her. Lucy did not know what a.s.a.p. meant. Anthony realised she didn't, and smiled a trifle condescendingly. "As soon as possible," he amended.

"Oh! Why?" Lucy asked calmly, staring at him.

Anthony Crabbe was not particularly good-looking. What he was was well-groomed, well-fed, well-cared-for; cosseted even, so he had that fat-cat look that the wealthy upper classes often had and that a poorer childhood never gave off in adulthood, no matter how good-looking the person might be or how far they advanced socially. He had that patina, that glow that the privileged often have and which comes from a constantly healthy diet, regular dental care of the best sort, the gentle tan that Switzerland and skiing painted in the winter and Barbados in January and that cruising round the Med on a yacht in summer bestowed. A face that had never been vulgarly exposed without protection to the sun. He wore a pink sea-island cotton shirt, a Savile Row pinstripe three-piece suit, a dark blue Valentino silk tie and hand-made brogues.

He looked at Lucy Leighton a little apprehensively. It was not good news that he had to deliver and he hated breaking bad news to girls. He positively *enjoyed* breaking bad news to men, but not to girls, or gels as he called them. They were a truly foreign species to Anthony for he had been sent to public school aged six and his dealings with his Mamma or indeed any other female except the matron had been minimal.

He had married a jolly girl called Davina Rathbone-Clyde five years ago and had expected a peaceful existence afterwards. He had been led to believe that she would know her place. She would run the house in Wilton Crescent, the small villa in St Raphael, give him a couple of brats who would be carbon copies of Davina and himself. The boys would go to Westminster and Cambridge his old alma mater, and the girl to Roedean. Davina's family were the right sort of people and he had thought he had everything worked out in the stage-management of his life, but to his horror his wife turned out to be stroppy rather than jolly. Anthony, a hopeless judge of women had read her wrongly. Davina was not the biddable spouse he had hoped for. She was headstrong, (his words), had, worse luck, ideas of her own and in general gave him a hard time. She exasperated him for he failed completely to understand her point of view.

She did not want to start a family just yet. To his consternation she ignored the fact that her biological clock was ticking rapidly on, and he pointed out to her that the best age for women to breed was in their twenties. "After that, sweetness, there can be complications. After all I don't want you to be forced to make decisions you might find traumatic."

"What decisions?" she asked him pointedly, blinking her eyes furiously in a manner he detested.

"Well you know, have to have an ecto—"

"If you think I'd agree to an abortion because my child was going to have problems, Anthony, you're wrong. I'd deal with it. Besides I doubt it will come to that."

He was appalled by this information.

She did not like the villa in St Raphael, saying the place was impossible to run and she would prefer an all-mod-con apartment in Marbella. The notion horrified him. Marbella was full of rich Americans, and, good God, film stars!

He was not a happy man just at this moment – Davina, having pouted at him over the breakfast table this morning when he had once more suggested the possibility of starting a family, had adamantly refused to entertain the thought.

And now he had to break this bad news to the Leighton girl. Not his day!

Lucy Leighton frightened him a little. She was, after all, a woman, an unpredictable emotional entity that disconcerted him and made him distinctly uneasy. He watched her as one might watch a wild animal in the zoo, safe behind his desk but wary.

Still he could not help but admire her as she sat before him having just come from her mother's funeral in her neat black suit and hat. She was made of the stuff true Englishwomen were supposed to be made of: uncomplaining, dedicated to duty, biddable and respectful of the opposite sex. Davina could take a leaf from Lucy Leighton's book. Lucy Leighton, he felt sure would run his houses without making a song and dance about it. She would not complain about St Raphael. She would breed dutifully and not give him a hard time about Marbella and flat stomachs ruined by childbearing backed up with complaints about lack of freedom and civil rights. *Civil rights* for God's sake!

But then one wouldn't *marry* Lucy Leighton, certainly not in the position she was now in, that was for sure. Whatever else, Davina's dowry had been substantial.

He gazed at Lucy across his desk, wondering how to begin. She was pretty with thick mahogany-coloured hair tucked in under her hat, wide dark marmalade-coloured eyes and thick lashes, little freckles across her nose and a soft, tender loving mouth.

Anthony Crabbe sighed. Why, oh why had he gone by appearances and not given Davina the same careful assessment he gave his clients? He had taken Society's and his mother's opinion of his wife and thereby got himself in deep shit. His own stupid fault. He had to resign himself to the fact that he was lumbered for life with a stroppy female. No getting out of it. Divorce was out of the question. Davina would strip him clean and he would be left high and dry with nothing. Davina's daddy was a High Court Judge.

Anthony cleared his throat. "Lucy, how are you bearing up?" He began uneasily. "This is indeed a tough time for you."

Lucy was suddenly alarmed. Something apprehensive in his attitude alerted her to the fact that all was not well. She sensed bad news. How that could be she did not know, could not guess, but she could feel in her bones that things were not as they should be. Anthony Crabbe looked very uncomfortable indeed.

"You wanted to see me?" she asked. Anthony cleared his throat again.

"Er . . . yes." He leaned forward clasping his hands over his fountain pen. No use beating about the bush as his tutor in Cambridge used to say. Get it over, just get it over. "You see Lucy, your mother died broke."

He waited for Lucy to digest this news but she seemed relatively unconcerned.

"Well I knew she'd . . . *we'd* used up her savings. I did not expect any money." Lucy hesitated, then continued, "I thought I'd put the house on the market. I should get a good price for it and the sale will give me some independence." She noticed the expression on Anthony's face which, she thought, registered disapproval. "Oh I know it's not a sellers' market but I can't afford to keep it up and I'll need the money—"

"Lucy the house is not yours to sell." Anthony's voice was firm. Lucy gazed at him perplexed, then with growing alarm. "The bank own it. In fact, to be blunt your mother would have been evicted had it *been* a sellers' market. She died just in time to save a very awkward situation."

"I don't understand!"

"I did my best Lucy and the bank have been very patient. In fact they could have foreclosed ages ago." He smiled wryly. "They have behaved very well actually and allowed your mother to die in peace when in truth they could easily have chucked her out to die in the street. See, Lucy the truth is your mother ran completely out of funds about a year ago, maybe longer. The last bond was sold, the last payments made. She had nothing left. No way of paying the mortgage, the *second* mortgage I have to tell you. The property, lock, stock and barrel belongs to Coutts."

"You mean I'm homeless?"

He clenched his jaw. It was difficult to meet those large and troubled eyes. "Yes Lucy. Oh the bank say they'll let you stay until the end of February. That's a month. I persuaded them. They've agreed. It was kind of them." He smiled again. "They've been amazingly co-operative and they're not usually so . . . shall we say accommodating."

"What will I do?" she asked helplessly. "How will I live?"

He shrugged. "Get a job I suppose, like anyone else."

"But I've no training. I wouldn't have a clue."

"You have enormous experience in nursing the sick," he said.

"But no credentials."

"You could study nursing. Get a grant." He knew how pitifully small students' grants were, but after all it was better than nothing. Did they give students grants any more he wondered? No. He thought they had to get bank loans. Would a bank give twenty-eight-year-old Lucy Leighton an unsecured bank loan? He doubted it.

But she was shaking her head. "No, no, no!" she cried. "I *hate* nursing, everything that goes with it."

"But you were so good with your mother," he protested.

"Yes, but I *loved* my mother. I adored her. Don't you see?" She gazed at him wide-eyed. "I did it because of that, not because I liked nursing."

He nodded. "I see," he said.

He wished now that she'd go. He felt acutely uncomfortable in the presence of her dilemma and his inability to help her. His upbringing had ingrained in him a sense of responsibility to the weaker sex, as he called women. He was the big, strong male and he ought to be able to offer an answer, wise advice, succour and help, and he knew he could offer none of these things.

She rose abruptly as if she'd read his mind. "I better go," she said. "This is not your problem." She shook her head, then smiled. "Of course you are right. I'll get a job. It can't be *that* difficult and there must be something I can do. Thank you Mr Crabbe."

"Anthony, please." He felt a wave of sympathy wash over him in the face of the situation. A pretty girl, a dead mother, no one to help or guide her. "If there is anything I can do at any time please don't hesitate to call me."

"You are very kind Mr Crabbe – Anthony."

"I'm just sorry I had to be the harbinger of bad tidings, on this day of all days"

"It's your job," she said. "And I'd rather know sooner than later." She held out her hand. He took it, shook it, then pressed it between his own.

"Any time. Remember," he assured her and watched as she left the room.

She descended the steep worn wooden flight of stairs, nearly hitting her head on the low beams. Outside the rain had stopped, the day was dull and grey and dripping. From trees and leaves and eaves and gutters, drip, drip, drip. She shivered, looking around her. It was so quiet in the square. The grass was very green after the rain. She could hear the hum of traffic in the distance, from Holborn and Chancery Lane. There were some sparrows cavorting and splashing about in a puddle. They shook their wings and ruffled their feathers joyously.

Lucy went and sat on a bench near them. The bench was damp but she didn't notice, she was still trying to absorb what she had just been told.

She sat there thinking for ages. She felt bemused, numbed. Anthony Crabbe, when he left his office much later saw her there, sitting under the bare dripping branches of the sycamore and hesitated. The droop of her shoulders was forlorn and defeated, but when he stood before her she looked up at him with strangely sparkling eyes.

"You can't sit here in the cold and damp," he said irritably. "It's foul weather."

"It's stopped raining," she said absently. "It was raining at the funeral."

"Sorry," he said. "Sorry. But I mean . . . you can't, can you?" He sounded sweetly reasonable. "You'll catch a chill. You have to go home."

She nodded emphatically. "Yes," she said with sudden decision, rising, "Yes. I must. You're right Mr Crabbe—"

"Anthony!"

"You're perfectly right Anthony. I'll get a job. I'll get the *Standard* on my way home."

"Can I hail you a cab?" he asked, waving a rolled umbrella.

She giggled. "No thanks Anthony. I've no money, remember?"

He blushed. "Oh yes! Sorry. Righto."

"Goodbye Anthony, and thank you."

He was taken aback by her lack of resentment at his role of bearer of bad tidings. He was used to clients being angry with him on receipt of such news, but she smiled at him, that warm generous smile, the dark marmalade eyes glowing. He said, moved by the sweet expression, "*Do* get in touch for advice if you need it. Don't hesitate."

"I won't. And if you get an idea you'll let me know. I'm pretty clueless you see." He nodded, regretting this renewed pledge to help already, but knowing he would not – could not even if he wanted to – forget. He walked away from her through the misty square. She watched him go, then made her way to Chancery Lane, to the tube station.

Chapter Four

On impulse and because it was the sort of thing one does when one's world falls apart, Lucy called in on her only friend on her way home from Lincoln's Inn to St John's Wood. Vicky Ledbury lived near Marble Arch and although they had not been in touch for about three years, Lucy suddenly got off the tube, bought herself a newspaper from the kiosk outside the station and turned down the Edgware Road and right into the residential warren behind the Odeon Cinema. The houses, neat as pins, were cheerfully painted a variety of colours. There were window-boxes of red geraniums in the front of Vicky's house and Lucy rang the bell.

For a moment she wondered what on earth she was doing there. She was worn out by the events of the day: the funeral, her meeting with Anthony Crabbe, the fact that she had not eaten but had had several drinks.

Vicky opened the door. She looked surprised when she saw Lucy and glanced up and down Montague Street before drawing her friend inside.

"Well Lucy, what brings you here?" Her greeting,

Lucy felt, was less than warming. "It's *ages* since I've seen you." Then looking Lucy squarely in the eyes, "You should have phoned. I'm expecting someone."

Lucy gulped, but, used as she was to her mother's briskness and an honesty that veered on the unkind, she apologised for the intrusion and said she'd leave.

"No, no. Now you're here, come into the kitchen. We'll have a cuppa."

The kitchen was small and delightfully appointed. Chrome and wood, stainless steel, smooth surfaces, glittering copper pots and pans. There were pots of geraniums everywhere and ropes of onions hanging from the wall. A cosy place, and Lucy sat on the stool opposite Vicky as the latter chopped onions and herbs, red, yellow and green peppers and sautéed them in a black pan.

"You won't mind if I get on," she asked and Lucy shook her head.

Vicky Ledbury was slim and fair and wispy. They had been friends all through their schooldays. Vicky had felt sorry for Lucy because of her mother's illness and Lucy felt sorry for Vicky because *her* mother had run off with a pop singer and her father married their au pair girl, a flirtatious Parisienne younger than Vicky and who she hated with all her heart.

All through secondary school they consoled each other in the playground and sat side by side at lunch and in class and swore undying friendship.

When they left school, however, their friendship

faltered and wavered and they both took very separate paths. They realised that they were growing further and further apart. Lucy stagnated (according to Vicky) looking after her mother and Vicky fell in love and married the first man who proposed to her. To get out from under her father's feet, she told Lucy. To escape from the au pair from hell. Lucy asked her mildly if that was a good reason to marry and Vicky tossed her head and told Lucy to mind her own business.

Their real falling out, which because nothing much was said was really more of an estrangement, came about because of him: Gordon Ledbury. He was, in Lucy's opinion, sharp as a razor, slick, an opportunist and when he made a pass at her with Vicky in the next room Lucy could not conceal her disgust. She asked Vicky if she *really* loved him; Vicky pouted in fair imitation of her stepmother and launched into a defiant defence of her fiancé. Lucy learned the lesson that if you wanted to keep a friendship you *never* voiced derogatory opinions about your friend's other half.

"You still looking after your mother?" Vicky asked now, spooning freeze-dried coffee into floral mugs. She too had alienated her friend by criticising Lucy's decision to nurse her mother. She said Lucy's devotion was excessive. Lucy always felt that Gordon put her up to it. Gordon was full of glib psycho-babble, knew all the latest labels and mindlessly quoted the buzz jargon.

"Mother died," Lucy answered. Vicky put the kettle down abruptly.

"Jeez! Oh Lucy, I'm sorry. I didn't realise."

"It's OK. A blessed relief in some ways."

Vicky nodded. "Yeah. Well now Lucy, maybe you can get on with your own life. Gordon says that sacrifice makes doormats of us and God knows you've sacrificed everything to that mother of yours."

Lucy wondered for the first time whether Vicky was perhaps jealous of her friend's closeness to her mother. "Gordon says nothing is gained by that. He says we must live our own lives *selfishly*. He says we have to put ourselves first. He says in the end if we're happy doing our own thing, then those around us are happy too."

How typical of Gordon, Lucy thought. Twisting philosophies to suit himself. She said, "But Vicky, my mother *was* 'my own thing' as you call it."

Vicky tossed her head impatiently. She didn't like to be disagreed with. "Oh we'll never see eye to eye about that Lucy. *I* believe, *we* believe that you've wasted the best years of your life looking after a sick old woman who probably never thanked you for it!"

Lucy saw in her mind's eye her mother's face, her eyes those last weeks, the gratitude there. The look of love and tenderness for her daughter, there with the pain and the despair. That look had made Lucy's heart swell with emotion. That look which she carried with her all the time filled her being with a profound peace. How good it was to feel you'd done your best. How good to feel you'd lived up to the demands life made of you.

She knew Vicky would not understand so she said nothing, glancing at her friend as she talked, noticing Vicky's pale discontented face, the disapproving curve to her lips, the anger deep in her eyes.

"People can be very small-minded Lucy," she was saying. "We all have to do what we have to do and no one has the right to stop us." She was talking just like Gordon, and Lucy wondered if he'd used that reasoning to get himself out of a hole. Maybe Vicky had found out about an indiscretion and Gordon had excused himself with some of the platitudes Vicky was now spouting so mindlessly. Lucy thought about bringing the crime angle into it, then decided against it. It was not worth the trouble.

"Who are you expecting?" she asked, more to change the subject than anything else.

"Oh a friend. Someone I talk to." Vicky was evasive. "Look, I'd love to chew the fat, ask you to stay, but . . ."

"No Vicky, I perfectly understand. I called because I wanted to ask you something. A favour."

"Well, fire ahead," Vicky sounded impatient.

"I've lost the house."

"In St John's Wood? Oh Lucy how ghastly!" But her eyes were on the kitchen clock and her sympathy insincere.

"My mother, through our solicitor, had it mortgaged up to the hilt. So I'm penniless. And I wondered . . ."

Vicky was staring at her apprehensively. She had that 'I hope you're not looking for anything from me' look, but Lucy continued, "Do you know of any jobs going? Are there any vacancies in your or Gordon's—"

Vicky's hoot was involuntary. She burst into incredulous laughter. "Gordon? Me? We're fighting Lucy to keep *our* jobs. Ask anyone these days. God Almighty!"

Vicky was a beauty consultant and Gordon was an Investment Advisor to a big insurance firm.

"Oh I wouldn't care what I did," Lucy protested. "How humble it was. I'd happily be tea-lady—"

"They have machines now!" Vicky said tartly. "Look Lucy, people are being made redundant *everywhere*. You can't just walk into a job these days you know." She shook her head. "Jeez! Where you been?"

"Well thanks Vicky." A despondent Lucy rose and went to the door. "Thanks for the coffee." They both looked at the full mug for Lucy had not drunk a drop. "I'll see myself out."

"It's OK. I'm sorry Lucy. Look . . ." Acknowledging her lack of helpfulness Vicky tried now, as Lucy prepared to leave, to modify her refusal to be of assistance. "Look Lucy, if you do a course, get a certificate, I'll do my best to help with interviews." She shrugged. "But it's pretty hopeless at the moment."

She kissed Lucy on both cheeks at the door. Her embrace was perfunctory and automatic. There was not even a small squeeze of sympathy. "Bye Lucy." She did not say call again or I'll phone you.

"Bye Vicky." Lucy thought that she was probably saying goodbye to her old friend for good.

Once again Vicky stepped into the street and once again her eyes raked right and then left. She waved as Lucy called a final farewell and stepped back into the house and closed the door.

Lucy stood a moment trying to rationalise her erstwhile friend's lack of support, trying not to mind. After all she had not been in touch recently with Vicky. She had neglected her friend during the last three years of her mother's illness, when her mother had become *completely* dependent on her. It was nobody's fault; friendships die unless they are nurtured. How could she expect Vicky to suddenly care about what happened to her old friend? But in her heart Lucy knew that if the situation had been reversed she would not have treated Vicky so cavalierly.

The young man bumped into her . . . or rather *she* bumped into him as she turned to go to the bus stop.

"Oh sorry!" she cried.

"No,no, beg your pardon. My fault."

He had a nice face, twinkling eyes and he blushed. She walked on, then glanced back over her shoulder in time to see him ringing the doorbell of the house with the geraniums outside. Vicky's house. The door opened and he vanished inside and Lucy went home.

Chapter Five

The next few weeks were very depressing for Lucy. It was, she said afterwards, lucky for her that she was an optimist. Otherwise she would not have survived. She had always before felt needed in this world and now all of a sudden she was made to feel distinctly superfluous. From being essential to her mother's very existence she was now one of the vast army of out of work hustlers.

No one wanted to employ her. She was considered too grand by prospective employers for casual labour. She spoke too well and for some reason they felt that a disadvantage. And she had no qualifications for skilled work. She wrote over a hundred letters, received five replies of a positive nature, and sixty rejections, wherein she learned that she was 1) not suitable, 2) unqualified, 3) too old (at twenty-eight) and 4) not what they were looking for. The five positive replies turned her down on interview, which did nothing for her self-confidence. She had not realised it would be so difficult.

She went into every shop advertising for help in the window, but failed each time to get anything.

Mostly she was turned down for lack of experience and the baffling phrase that she 'was not what they were looking for'. If you didn't fit into a category you were lost and it seemed she fitted nowhere. She was not a drop-out looking for casual labour neither was she professional. She was in no-man's-land.

She did not enjoy going to and from interviews. She had to travel around the city for the first time and she sensed an anger, an aggression in the crowds milling around her. Was it her imagination she wondered that people in London were not content? Were they as near the boil as she felt them to be? Their body language ordered others not to approach, to keep away. They sent off messages of wariness, belligerence and hostility.

She did not enjoy her interviews either. The other applicants returned a frozen face to her friendly smile and the secretaries or receptionists were cool, aloof, superior and unhelpful and Lucy usually returned home deeply discouraged and depressed.

Perhaps other girls had a mum or dad, a sister, brother or some loved one to support them but Lucy came home to an empty house. She felt utterly isolated and alone. There seemed no opportunities for oddities like herself. Even to baby-sit needed references and she had none.

In one shop where she had casually asked for employment they gave her a trial, but displayed no patience, expected her to pick up everything in one day, and sacked her for inefficiency. "You are clumsy and obviously know nothing about selling," they told her and dejected she left.

People were neither kind nor sympathetic she discovered. They were brisk and matter-of-fact, showed no interest in her as an individual and employed little tact in their rejection of her. Most days, returning to St John's Wood, she spent the evening alone in the vast emptiness of the house, sobbing. She walked through the rooms twisting her handkerchief between her fingers, hiccuping and shivering, afraid to turn on the heating for fear of bills she would not be able to pay.

The house was big. She had never consciously realised how big until now. It was set back from the road, the front door reached by a gravel driveway, then a flight of stone steps guarded by two stone lions *couchant*.

The hall was circular and dark. The walls between the doors that opened into the drawing room, study, living room and dining room were decorated with six-foot portraits of Mercedes Marchant in the various parts she had played: as Portia, Rosalind, Lady Macbeth, Strindberg's Miss Julie.

They had converted the front drawing room into a bedroom–cum–living room for Mercedes in the last years of her life, and off it, the dining room had been where Lucy, ever alert to her dying mother's needs, lived. The grand staircase to the upstairs had not been used for many a year, and Lucy spent most of her time in her own little room now, fearful, terrified of the future, subconsciously waiting for her dead mother to call her. It was a waiting room, her room, a place where she rested between bouts of dutiful activity. A nurse's room. Only now she had nothing to do, no duties to perform. She was redundant.

She felt so alone. There was no one she could turn to. Oh Anthony Crabbe and Barry Brocklehurst and Errol Armitage had been extravagant in their invitations but she was only too aware of how impulsive people could be and how reluctant they were when push came to shove to actually *do* anything. The road to hell is paved, they say, with good intentions. Lucy had discovered that during her mother's illness the only help she could rely on was the help she paid for.

She lay wide-eyed in her bed night after night and prayed that something would turn up. Anything. But she prayed without real hope, only too well aware that her position was dire.

She did not go into her mother's room. The door between the two rooms remained closed. The thought of entering it and her mother not being there alarmed Lucy so she stayed out.

And wrote more letters. And received few replies. And had interviews that ended in, 'not suitable', 'Sorry, we don't feel you are the person for this particular job,' and '*No* qualifications? Oh dear! Well, sorry, you understand.'

It began to dawn on Lucy that perhaps the world would be better off without her. It was a gradual realisation, this feeling of being totally unnecessary to life itself. It was compounded of rejection after rejection, friendlessness, isolation and the loss of her mother.

Her mother had been the pivot of her life, the *raison d'être* and after her demise and the first flush of freedom Lucy felt utterly abandoned. There was nothing for her to *do* any more, no reason for her to live.

She missed her mother dreadfully: both the loss of her love but perhaps more as an occupation. There were no routine chores any more, no schedule to be followed scrupulously. In her dawning despair, her loneliness, her sense of uselessness, Lucy knelt down one miserable day towards the end of February and demanded God's help, or else! She had a bottle of her mother's sleeping pills clutched in one hand and a glass of water on the bedside table. She shut her eyes tightly and tried to imagine the God she invoked. "This is your last chance," she shouted at Him.

God who made the world must be kind. It was such a beautiful world and all she ever wanted was to see it. Experience it.

Since she was a child Lucy had dreamed of travel. She had fantasised about foreign places. The names in the Bible had intoxicated her. Phrygia and Syria, Damascus and Sinai. Egypt and the plains of Mamre, Uz and Persia. Judah, names that sang. And Shakespeare had given her Padua, Antioch, Venice, Arden, Verona and Athens, names that sent her senses reeling. She devoured the poets,

John Masefield inspiring her dreams as he talked of Nineveh, Ophir and sunny Palestine. W.B. Yeats rhapsodising about Innisfree and Coleridge of Zanadu. The magic-sounding names of foreign lands thrilled her to the marrow of her bones.

But travel had been denied her. She had never complained, but she had never given up her dream. She had not begrudged her mother her time and the curtailment of her freedom. She had never blamed her mother that she could not do the thing she wanted most: to travel. She knew it was not her mother's doing. And always in the back of her mind was the plan. She would sell the old house and go, man, go. Take off. Travel the world.

But that plan had been nipped in the bud and she had been cast out into the wilderness, jobless, soon to be homeless, friendless and alone. Despairing.

She clutched the bottle and prayed, eyes tight shut. "You made a beautiful world God. A rose would be enough. Or a tree. Or a tiny mouse. A bluebell. Dear God what do you want me to do? I just don't know so I need your help. HELP ME NOW! PLEASE!"

The telephone rang. At first Lucy did not stir but kept her eyes screwed up tightly closed. I'm imagining it, she thought. Then the ringing penetrated, shrilly insisting on being answered. She tossed the little brown bottle of pills on the bed and ran to answer it. It was probably that damned solicitor again.

It was.

"Hello?"

"Hello, Lucy?"

"Yes."

"Lucy, this is Anthony. Anthony Crabbe."

"Yes?" What on earth did he want. Probably telling her she had to leave the house instantly, that it had been sold or something. Lucy sighed. Her luck was beyond belief!

"Look Lucy, you've been on my mind. Er . . . have you had any luck? Jobwise I mean?"

"Nothing. Nothing Anthony." She managed to sound quite cheerful. Her voice was so light, so carefree, when deep in her heart a profound darkness lay.

"I was afraid of that." He cleared his throat. He had a habit of doing that she thought, inconsequentially, and wondered if it came with the territory. Legal people had to think very carefully before they answered.

"Em . . . look here Lucy, my wife, er Davina, has an aunt. A dear dotty old thing who also happens to be a brilliant journalist. Thing is, she's looking for someone to work with her. She's got this project. It's an article she has to do on some writer chappie and she needs someone to type her notes. Says there may be a book in it."

"Look Anthony, I'm self-taught," Lucy protested, "I'm not very good at typing." She could imagine a journalist needing rapid results. Someone who spoke a certain jargon. She knew she typed very well and accurately, but *professionally*? She had been turned down at so many interviews when they timed her typing and found out she knew nothing about computers.

Anthony chuckled, "That's just it Lucy. She doesn't *want* some human dynamo. She likes you to take her notes away and type them up in your own time. Within reason of course." He laughed again. "Thing is Lucy, she *won't* work with computers. That's the snag. She wouldn't need anyone if she would just listen to me and take a course. She's very stubborn. And that's why I thought of you. She's advertised but all she gets is gels who work with computers and think she's from the stone age when they find out she doesn't. And gels who are so efficient that they scare her silly. That's why I thought of *you*. Dear old Auntie needs someone exactly like you. Someone she can trust. An intelligent gel. Not an idiot. A nice sort of gel who'll type her notes and be a help to her when she travels. An intelligent, literary companion who'll travel with her and make all the arrangements."

"Travel?" Lucy's knees felt weak. She sat down abruptly on the chair by the phone.

"Yep. That a problem?"

"Oh no. No. *No.*"

"Well good. Thing is, she'd like to meet you. Says you sound the right sort. You interested?"

"Oh yes, yes, yes."

"She is a dotty old bird. Not the easiest person."

"Oh Anthony, I don't care if she's Myra Hindley—"

"Hey, steady on—"

"I don't care. I'm so grateful."

"You know how difficult creative people are."

"Mother was creative," Lucy said.

"Oh of course. Of course. I forgot. So I take it you're interested?"

"Absolutely Anthony. Definitely."

"Then can you meet her for tea at the Savoy tomorrow at four o'clock?"

"Certainly."

"In the tea lounge."

"Yes. How will I know her?"

"She'll know you. Besides you'll pick her out. I'm certain."

"OK."

"OK Lucy. Good luck."

"Thank you Anthony. Thank you so much."

"Oh rot. Don't thank me yet. You may hate her."

Oh no I won't, Lucy thought. I won't. I know this is going to be right for me. I *know*. I hate computers too.

"Bye Lucy."

"Bye Anthony."

What was it her mother used to say? In the old days before she was completely disabled she used to tell Lucy, don't give up ten minutes before the miracle. So many people do. Lucy did a little twirl in the dark emptiness of the hall and then looked up and out through the stained glass panel in the hall door, gazing at a tree tossing its branches outside.

"Thank you God," she whispered. "Whatever, whoever you are. Thank you."

Chapter Six

Lucy had never been into the Savoy Hotel. She caught a bus to Oxford Street and then took another to the Strand. The fountains in Trafalgar Square danced brightly in the pale yellow February sun. The old grey stone glittered and the tourists crawled all over the lions, their cameras clicking. They wore anoraks and sneakers and queued up the steps of the National Gallery. On the steps of St Martin in the Field Crypt vagrants lay, unshaven, their clothes multi-layered and grotty. They sipped cider and God knows what make of cocktail from brown-paper wrapped containers. The bus swept past Charing Cross station and up past the theatres where Lucy alighted and crossed the road to the hotel. The doorman smiled at her as she entered. The foyer embraced her with a welcoming and soothing hush. She was suddenly glad that she had worn her smart black funeral suit. It fitted in here.

All was calm. People moved more tranquilly. Bell-boys seemed the only ones to hurry and even they had a cheerful briskness rather than the aggressive purposefulness one met in the streets.

The waiters glided with majestic efficiency and a pianist tinkled on a piano in the lounge, 'Smoke Gets In Your Eyes'.

Lucy spotted her immediately. Clarissa Bourke-Rathbone, Davina Crabbe's auntie.

She had a large body; a lady with an autocratic manner. As Lucy descended the steps to the lounge she could see her waving her hands about and saying something to the waiter about the egg sandwiches.

"I *never* have egg sandwiches in the selection," she was saying in a firm but kind voice, like a headmistress speaking to a recalcitrant pupil. "You should know that by now. Please take them away and bring me a double helping of cucumber."

She wore a Queen Mother outfit that demanded attention: a pale grey waistless dress in a light material with matching coat. She was decked out in pearls; pearls at her neck, in long strands over her ample bosom, pearls snuggled in her soft plump earlobes and around her wrist. She had a diamond clip on the lapel of her coat, a silver fox wrap over one shoulder and she wore a turban over her thin fine hair. Not a politically correct lady at all Lucy decided.

Clarissa Bourke-Rathbone looked up and saw Lucy standing at the other side of the low table on which the tea things lay scattered.

"My dear, you must be Lucy Leighton. Yes, yes, I can see at a glance you'll do. Perfect. Old-fashioned gel. Anthony, bless him, didn't say you were so pretty. But then he wouldn't. I like pretty young things. So easy on the eye. Come,

come, sit down my dear and let's get to know one another." She patted the sofa seat beside her and Lucy sat down. She smelled strongly of Chanel No.5 which Lucy found unexpected in a woman of her age. She appeared to be in her sixties. "Anthony is a selfish boy, narrow-minded, dull. A conventional chappie. But people have this habit of surprising one. This is a stunningly good idea, giving you to me. The best idea he's ever had. If not the only one!" She laughed. "Apart from marrying my niece that is. Now, as he probably told you I am Clarissa Bourke-Rathbone."

"How do you do Mrs—"

"No, no, Clarissa please. Never Rissa or Clarie or any diminutives. Intimacy is fine but it *can* be overdone. Then it palls. The Americans do it all the time!" She smiled at Lucy. Her smile and her laughter were warm and comforting and Lucy fell under the spell of her large embracing personality.

"I feel we're going to be the best of friends, aren't we? I always know instantly," she continued. "Don't you?" She had the same soft transparent skin as Lucy's mother but she lacked her mother's fine-chiseled beauty. Her large face was a mish-mash carelessly arranged but with two of the kindest eyes Lucy's had ever met. She felt the sudden pin-prick of tears behind her lids at the loving sweetness and sympathy so unexpectedly beamed upon her.

"What kind of tea would you like?" she was asking. "Assam? Earl Grey? Darjeeling? Or do you prefer China? Or herb? Peppermint? Vervain?

Camomile?" She's giving me time, Lucy thought. "You don't look the herb sort . . . still one never knows, does one? People are so unpredictable. Like Anthony. It affords me such amusement. Everyone has a totally unexpected side to their character. It's what makes my job so fascinating." She had been nattering on, Lucy felt sure, to give her time to recover her equilibrium. She had sensed Lucy's rush of emotion and was being tactful.

"I'm a writer, as Anthony probably told you. Mainly journalistic stuff. But I have written two novels." She glanced up at Lucy and the girl was struck once more by the wonderfully kind and loving warmth in the depths of her eyes. The colour was indeterminate, the setting baggy and wrinkled, but the expression would draw out the secrets of one's soul without any effort at all. Lucy could understand how she might be a very successful interviewer.

"Your mamma died I believe." She patted Lucy's hand. "I adored her. Never missed a performance of hers. Hers was a rare and brilliant talent." She twisted the ropes of pearls between her fingers. "I'll never forget her Rosalind," she said.

"Everyone says that," Lucy remarked, "but I never saw it so I don't know."

"How very sad." Clarissa's hands were plump and marked with liver spots but the short nails were painted a cheerful crimson.

"I'm very inexperienced," Lucy ventured. "I taught myself to type. I'm not that terrific."

"Don't underestimate yourself," Clarissa told her,

"I don't want an expert. I loathe computers as no doubt Anthony explained. Technology leaves me cold!" She glanced at Lucy. "I did purchase one – a computer I mean, but it ate a disc and got a virus and I kept getting side-tracked. I'd have written two books, the time it wasted."

Lucy had typed at home on the electric typewriter her mother had got for her, or rather told her to get for herself. Lucy wanted this job so badly that she felt she would give her all to get it but she was not going to get it under false pretences.

"But I'm an amateur," she said.

Clarissa laughed. "Bless you. Do you know what amateur means?" Lucy began to answer but Clarissa pre-empted her, "Amateur means, one who cultivates a thing because they *love* it."

"I thought it meant unprofessional," Lucy said.

"That's the negative view I suppose," Clarissa replied. "I prefer the dictionary meaning." She leaned forward, fixing Lucy with intent eyes. "What I want Lucy, what I'm looking for is a *person*." She patted Lucy's hand. "You see I want someone with whom I can have an exchange. I'll give you my notes to type and then it is up to you to get them done. If you're up half the night typing them you'll speed up the old 'words a minute' I guarantee. There's nothing like a deadline to promote efficiency. You can tell me if anything I've written seems obscure to you. What I want Lucy is someone just like you. A pleasant person. Someone intelligent. Someone who does not exaggerate. You are honest I can tell. You did not pretend to me, you spoke the truth about yourself. That's rare these days. You are sensitive. I saw that when you sat down and realised that I liked you. So you see you are perfect for my requirements."

"So I've got the job?" Lucy could not believe her luck.

"Yes my dear."

"Tell me exactly what I have to do please."

"What I want is for you to type my notes each afternoon or evening. I write in the morning. I want you to be a companion on my travels. I want you to look after the travel arrangements. I want you to keep me in order, see I've got what I need and get to where I want to go. I want you to give me your opinion but only when I ask for it. I want you to eat with me when we're away. I want someone I like and I like you."

The waiter came and Lucy ordered Darjeeling. She told Clarissa she needed a strong cuppa. Clarissa waved her hand. "Have you a notebook?" she asked. Lucy had. Not a proper notebook but some pages she'd been scribbling job possibilities on. She fished them out of her bag. The waiter handed her a biro.

"Good girl," Clarissa said, then to the waiter, "bring her tea. And sandwiches. And scones. She's starving I can tell." Then as the waiter left she told Lucy, "Write down, 'bring tea-bags'. They often don't have tea in Italy. Or give you one bag for a pot!"

"We're going to *Italy*?" Lucy breathed, hardly

daring to believe what she had heard. Shakespeare. Padua. Verona. Venice.

"Yes dear. Capri. We'll need tea-bags. Bring your favourite sort. I'm not fussy, as long as it's tea and as long as it's strong. The Italians make the best coffee in the world, but they are totally ignorant about tea. Still," she twinkled, "they'll have boiling water so it will be no problem."

"Capri," Lucy whispered enchanted. "Capri."

"It's where this fellow I'm after lives. Conrad Morheim. I want to try to interview him. Do a piece on him. The paper has asked me; well, I suggested it to them, and they leapt at the idea. Mad keen for me to try. He's been a recluse since the middle of the Eighties. Oh I'll tell you all about him by and by. But first dear you have to book us on a flight to Naples—"

"Naples!" The name was magic.

"If you want to keep my esteem Lucy you'll stop echoing everything I say."

The keen eyes pierced her with a look so commanding that Lucy felt a shiver down her back. Clarissa Bourke-Rathbone had not reached the top of her profession and stayed there without a devastating authority.

"I'm sorry, it's just that I've dreamed of these places all my life," Lucy said in a small voice.

"They're a let-down Lucy I'm afraid," Clarissa said matter-of-factly. "Don't live up to expectation. Never as pretty as the pictures." Her eyes softened again. "Still, I expect you might enjoy the novelty."

The waiter brought another silver pot of tea. He had a cake-rack laden with goodies for Lucy: sandwiches, scones, butter and jam. Lucy suddenly felt very hungry. She hadn't eaten properly for days. She tried to masticate slowly, take small bites in a ladylike fashion but the tiny sandwiches vanished down her throat, the scones after them and she discovered to her horror that she had consumed every last crumb while Clarissa Bourke-Rathbone talked to her, explaining her duties, giving her dates and data. She either did not mind Lucy's voracious appetite or did not notice it.

The pianist was playing 'Lady Be Good' and the light outside was darkening "I hope you grasp the general duties I'll expect you to perform Lucy," Clarissa said. "It's not all comfy-cosy stuff. Booking flights and hotels is, for one, boring beyond belief. But you have the list?"

"Oh yes, yes I have. It's all stuff I think I can do."

"As I said, it's not the job, it's the *person*."

"Yes. I'll certainly do my very best."

"That's all I ask." She contemplated the girl before her. "You know Lucy, I admire you. Anthony told me how you looked after your mother all these years, how you cared for her. I can't tell you how much I admire you for that."

"But I loved her." It was Clarissa's turn to feel the prick of tears behind her eyes. The affirmation was made so simply, so sincerely that the older woman was strangely moved. "It was not difficult at all."

Clarissa looked into the young girl's face. It was a very pretty face, but more than that, it was an open face.

Clarissa Bourke-Rathbone thanked her nephew that evening on the phone and told him he was not as stupid as he looked. "She's perfect," she said.

"I thought she would be," he replied in a self-satisfied way that irritated her. Then he infuriated her by adding, "Gosh Aunt, you've no idea! It's a load off my mind. I can tell the bank they can foreclose now."

She put down the phone abruptly. What on earth had happened to human nature? she wondered, then put it out of her mind and retired to bed feeling the day had been a great success.

Chapter Seven

Lucy was kept busy over the next few weeks. They were to leave for Italy in late March so Anthony Crabbe persuaded the bank to allow Lucy to stay on in the St John's Wood house until the departure date. He had no difficulty at all getting them to agree, in fact they were quite happy to have the house occupied. "We've no intention of putting it up for sale just yet. The market just now is dire!" Stephen Rutter the young bank manager told Anthony. "She's welcome to stay a while." He frowned. "See, we worry about squatters and if you board up windows etc., the neighbours object. Say it's ugly – an eyesore. So it suits us that she's there. As long as she understands that she's on borrowed time. Until a buyer suddenly pitches up. But that's not likely just at present."

A buyer didn't pitch up and Lucy remained there until she left London.

She did not see much of Clarissa Bourke-Rathbone, as her employer mainly conducted their business over the phone. "Won't have anything for you to type just yet," she told Lucy, "but you'll be kept very busy with travel arrangements and the packing."

Lucy could think of nothing she'd rather do. Even to enter a travel agency caused her heart to beat a little faster, and making arrangements to go off into the wild blue yonder filled her with unbearable anticipation.

They had one last meeting before the day of departure. Lucy was summoned to tea in the Savoy once more. This time she was far more relaxed. She had gained some assurance over the weeks since she got this job. Clarissa Bourke-Rathbone was good for her morale. She relied on Lucy and made her feel needed, just as her mother had done.

Lucy entered the Savoy nonchalantly this time and walked confidently into the lounge. There she was, this time in powder blue, sitting at the same table, being served by the same waiter. This time, however, there was a young man with Clarissa. Such a handsome young man, a little older than Lucy, chatting nineteen to the dozen to her employer, who turned as she arrived. "Oh Lucy, there you are! Come, sit down." She patted the seat beside her on the sofa, the same place Lucy had sat before. The young man, who had been lounging in a comfortable armchair at Clarissa's right, rose now with alacrity.

"This is my son, Adrian. Adrian, this is Lucy Leighton, the girl I was telling you about."

Her son! Though she was *Mrs* Bourke-Rathbone Lucy had never thought of her employer as a married woman. It had not entered her mind. Now she looked at her handsome offspring and smiled. He must take after his dad. Tall, fair-haired, rangy, he seemed to bear no physical resemblance to his mother, being more or less the opposite in every possible physical way. What he certainly had inherited from her was the keen kindly expression in his eyes and the warm smile.

"Good God Ma, you never said she was lovely!" he exclaimed. He took Lucy's hand in a firm grip and looked at her intently with those brilliant eyes as he spoke. "You are, you know that? I have to say it's jolly brave of you, taking on Ma. But you look as if you can cope."

"Sit down Adrian, there's a dear. I won't have you putting Lucy off. She's a treasure so you stop alarming her. Can you believe, she doesn't *mind* travel agents!"

"My mother," Adrian stated, standing until Lucy sat down, then re-seating himself, crossing his long legs, "is the most outdated person you'll ever be likely to meet. She lives in the Middle Ages. I recommend you order what you want to do your work on and don't mind Ma. She cannot bear the modern world at all. Don't let her restrict you Lucy. She'll have you rubbing sticks together to make fire, given half a chance!"

"Nonsense Adrian." Clarissa smiled fondly at her boy. She obviously adored him and he her. "Lucy is an old-fashioned girl and suits me down to the ground," Clarissa said.

"I could never work complicated new equipment anyway," Lucy assured him. "I'm afraid I'm not very professional."

"The dear child has never been out of England!"

Lucy blushed. She wished Clarissa would not make her out to be gormless. But then, she thought ruefully, she was helping her employer to convince Adrian that she was a complete rustic, totally unsophisticated and for some obscure reason she did not want Clarissa's son to think badly of her.

"Neither had I until I was eighteen," Adrian said, making her feel better at once. "Ma wouldn't take me with her on assignments and we always holidayed in Southwold. Dear old Suffolk! So you see, you are not the only one to start late."

"Oh abroad, as they call it, is wasted on children," Clarissa insisted. "And it is a let-down. Exotic places never come up to scratch, and you have to contend with nasty bugs. Mosquitos!"

Adrian winked at her, eyes twinkling. "Ma is a martyr to mosquitos. They think for some reason she's delicious. The *plat du jour*."

"And the *plat du nuit*!" Clarissa laughed. "God how I hate the nasty little beggars."

"But they love you Ma," Adrian joined her laughing. "Put down on your list of essentials: insect repellent. Get a couple of sprays. Boots does a good roll-on. See you bring plenty," he warned.

"I've remembered. They're already packed."

While Adrian went to settle up the bill, Clarissa

handed her an envelope. "Here's your cheque Lucy," she said.

She was paying Lucy the basic rate and all expenses, which, she told Lucy, the paper were covering.

"Oh thank you Clarissa." Lucy took the envelope and stared at it. Her first pay cheque.

"Don't let Ma diddle you," Adrian remarked, returning to the table.

"It's all quite correct," Clarissa protested. "I'm not being overgenerous Lucy," she warned her employee, "but then, you are not overqualified."

"Gracious Clarissa, I'd do it for nothing," Lucy cried and Clarissa tutted. "What a very rash statement Lucy," she remarked. "I wouldn't, if I were you, go around saying things like that. People might take you at your word. No, I'm paying you what a junior would get, a girl Friday. I've got a good deal. But you've not got experience. That that does not matter to me is neither here nor there." She thought for a moment. "And remember, you're on call twenty-four hours a day. But you'll find me fair. You'll have lots of time off, never fear."

And she did. Clarissa let her do all the booking, shopping, in her own time, and except for that one tea in the Savoy with her son, they did not meet again until the departure date in March.

The week before she left for Italy Barry Brocklehurst telephoned her and asked if she would like to have dinner with him and Errol Armitage. "We thought it might cheer you up you know, take your mind off things. As you haven't called us, we're calling you." He chuckled into the receiver. "Besides we liked you. Do say yes."

She said yes.

They met in the Groucho. Errol and Barry were propping up the bar, looking, Lucy thought, like leads in a high-class comedy film. They were projecting, reaching their audience, which was their main objective; to let the young whipper-snappers here know they'd been there, done that, seen it all. There were a lot of designer-stubble torn-T-shirted slashed-jeaned and black-leather-jacketed media personnel sitting at the tables in the bar, puffing on fags, supping their beer, laughing loudly and showing off. At the same time they were trying to hear what Barry and Errol were saying while endeavouring to give the impression that they were totally indifferent. Lucy felt that she was in a garden of peacocks, all posing, squawking loudly, each and every one trying to prove that he was big-shot No.1, top-gun, cock-o'-the-walk. She decided they were all, including Barry and Errol, little boys.

They went upstairs to eat and Lucy felt warmly entertained by her two companions. It was all very well to sense that these theatrical people were a trifle immature but they were also extremely good company. She did not have to work. The men did all the talking and reminiscing. So much of it was amusing and interesting, the rest baffling. It seemed to Lucy that it would be a shame to interrupt the flow and she was obviously the audience they needed.

They spoke a lot about her mother. They told her of Mercedes Marchant, her past glories, the stage-door Johnnies. They talked of waltzes and foxtrots and cha-cha-chas, of cocktails and tables for two in dark corners of the Savoy and Claridges. They spoke of evening dress and dance cards and afternoon tea in the Waldorf Astoria. They chatted about long forgotten times and drew her into their world of Morris Minors and Rileys, no central heating, big fires and no TV. They laughed about touring and theatrical digs and the landladies, of rep and Ralph and Larry, Johnnie Mills and Pat Roc, Maggie Lockwood and Kay Hammond.

And Mercedes Marchant.

Lucy listened to the tales of her mother's exploits, her professional and emotional journey with wide-eyed interest. She might have felt anger and jealousy only it never occurred to her. While in her twenties her mother had had a glittering career, had taken lovers, led an incredible life while she, her daughter, had spent that period in her own life nursing her.

But Lucy did not crave fame or fortune and the Mercedes she had known was a far cry from the glamorous star these men talked about.

She enjoyed the dinner. They ate a rocket salad followed by devilled kidneys, then plum tart. Barry, she noticed, looked very tired and drawn. When he excused himself to go to the men's room Errol, as soon as they were alone, leaned across the table. "He's going downhill fast," he told her, his blue eyes worried. "He's not got much longer."

She did not know what to say so she said nothing.

"I'm very fond of him," he said. "We've been friends a long time. I was married to his sister."

"Oh. Is she . . .? is she . . .?" Lucy felt awkward and did not know how to phrase her question. But if there was a Mrs Armitage around it was odd that Errol had not mentioned her.

"She's passed on," Errol told her. "A smashing lady she was. A leading lady of note. Great comedy timing. Like Barry. His timing is impeccable." He glanced at her. "It can't have been easy for you," Errol said.

She shook her head. "Oh it wasn't too bad," she said brightly.

"I think you are very brave," Errol insisted.

Tears sprang suddenly into her eyes, tears that stung like bees but did not fall. "Oh if you knew me you wouldn't say that," she cried. "I was so often impatient with her. I often hated what I had to do. Sometimes I let her see that. I often cried into my pillow." The tears shone, filming her eyes like a curtain. "And sometimes I was *glad* my mother was sick. It meant that I got sympathy. It meant that I had an excuse. It meant that I did not have to go out there and get involved. Life's battles could pass me by. I could opt out of life altogether."

He covered her hand with his. She blinked and the tears vanished. When she looked up at him her eyes were newly-washed. "So you see, I'm not brave at all."

Errol smiled. "Oh I still think you are," he said softly. "I think you are being hard on yourself. All of us have unworthy thoughts about our loved ones. No one's thoughts are noble all the time." He looked up. "Ah, here's Barry."

Barry returned to the table. "Lucy, how selfish we are," he said glancing at Errol, shaking his head. "We haven't asked you about yourself. Have you sold the house? When are you off on your world tour?"

She told them what had happened, about Anthony Crabbe and the house, about Clarissa Bourke-Rathbone and her job.

She realised now that Errol had set the direction of the conversation in order to entertain Barry, amuse *him* rather than her. It was touching, she thought, how subtle he could be.

When she had finished he said, "I know Clarissa. She's a brilliant, quixotic journalist. She gets to the heart of the person. She's very intuitive." Then he laughed. "But her novels! Purple prose! Amazing! Passion rampant! Wonderful!"

Barry was frowning. "I remember Conrad Morheim," he said slowly. "Amazing mind. Bit dark, you know, gloomy for me. He suggested that we were on a self-destruct course. The world, I mean. Maybe he's right."

Errol was looking intently at Lucy. "If you ever need anything, please don't hesitate to ask. Money or help in any way." And as she opened her mouth to protest, "No, no. I mean it Lucy. We were thwarted in our efforts to help Mercedes, so please, if you need us, give us the chance to help you."

Barry agreed. "We're two ageing actors. I'm divorced. Errol lost—"

"I've told her," Errol said and Barry continued. "Our children are grown. Married now. So we've nothing better to do than live on our dreams of past glory. Give us the privilege of helping Mercedes Marchant's daughter, if you are in any kind of need."

She nodded, deeply touched and promised. "Enjoy yourself," they told her and she said, "Please look after each other until I return."

Outside in Dean Street they kissed her on both cheeks and looked sadly at the grey London sky. There seemed to be no stars, or if there were, they were invisible. A moon hung, fragile, sickly-pale over the Post Office tower. Pulling their identical coats about them, turning their immaculately groomed silver heads in search of a taxi, they waved at her and she turned and hurried away towards Oxford Street.

Soho had come alive in the time they had been eating. Garish red lights indicated sex for money. Flesh for sale. The restaurants were open. Chinatown pulsated with life. Sleaze city jostled side by side with cosmopolitan eateries and gift shops.

For some reason Lucy's mother's death seemed more real to her at that moment than when she found her cold in her bed, or at the cemetery. Perhaps it was the energy of sexual immediacy all around her, the affirmation that life is to be grabbed at all costs, that made her feel like that. A grip of pain squeezed her heart and she walked faster, hurrying when there was no need to rush. Then she saw in an Italian restaurant a poster for some town in Italy. Amalfi. Her heart lifted. Life was, could be beautiful. Her mother was dead and now it was her turn to live.

Next morning she decided it was time to pack. She took only one suitcase with her. She had no idea what she'd need in a place like Naples, or Capri. She decided that two pairs of jeans and her white cotton and chambray shirts, her chino shorts, her red Professor Higgins cardigan and her navy blazer would be all right anywhere in the world. They would, she decided, *have* to be. They were all she'd got.

She packed her black suit and a light button-through floral dress, her toiletries and her books. Some tapes, her cotton socks, pants, bras and half a dozen notebooks from Rymans and she was ready to take off. She sat on her case in the big dark hall and tried to still the beating of her heart. She stared at the cobwebs that veiled the corners of the ceiling and thought, I'm going to Italy. I'm *really* going to Italy. I'm going to Italy!'

She took the portraits of her mother from the walls and a few books and mementos and she put them in storage. The bank owned all the rest, and when the taxi came at last to the St John's Wood house on a pale yellow day in March, Lucy Leighton left the home she'd lived in all her life without a backward glance. The past lay behind her now, a past of service and ill-health and sacrifice. The future beckoned so enticingly. Naples. Capri. Names to enchant. She was off on an adventure and it seemed so strange to her that she felt as if she was someone else. Someone quite different. Lucy Leighton had begun her journey.

Chapter Eight

She met Clarissa Bourke-Rathbone at the appointed time at the check-in counter. Adrian was with her.

"How nice to see you again," he greeted her, his face sunny. He was very helpful. He insisted on buying them a drink after they'd checked in and before they went through passport control. Lucy, who was in a rush to get going, who wanted to be up, up and away, hardly noticed what she drank. She was in a fever of excitement and amazed at the others' blasé attitude.

"Lucy you look perfect," Clarissa told her. "What you are wearing . . . it's an Italian uniform my dear. All the girls wear it. Jeans, white shirt, pullover and blazer. All you need is a scarf and you could pass for a gel from Florence or Rome. They all dress like that."

"I think she looks just lovely," Adrian said. Clarissa glanced at him, surprised at the wealth of admiration in his eyes and astonished when he leapt to his feet, hurried over to the Hermès counter and returned moments later with a scarf which he draped around Lucy's neck.

"For good luck," he told her.

"You look terribly Italian now my dear," Clarissa said. "Come Adrian, I'm afraid we'll have to go."

They said goodbye to Adrian at passport control, and like Barry and Errol, he kissed her on both cheeks, and like them too he told her to let him know if she needed anything. She felt cared for and liked the feeling. She was so used to doing the caring.

Lucy was in charge of the papers and passports but far from feeling nervous on this, her first trip abroad, she felt adventurous and once through passport control a powerful elation seized her. I could tackle just about anything, she thought.

Clarissa bought Lucy a bottle of perfume at the duty-free. "I always indulge," she told her young companion. "Feel I'm getting a bargain. I *love* a bargain." The perfume was Christian Dior and Lucy sprayed it liberally over herself. She loved the scent and kept sniffing her wrist, breathing it in.

She watched the crowds as they waited for their flight to be called. The people seemed to her to be stressed, anxious and angry. She could not understand why and decided it must be the accepted way to behave travelling. She herself had never been so happy.

On the journey Clarissa told Lucy about her commission. About Conrad Morheim, the man they were on their way to meet.

"He is, or was, an extraordinary man. He was virulently opposed to the Thatcher regime and all it stood for. He was appalled by what he called the Western world's descent into greed and corruption, the loss of integrity and honour. He found the demand for instant gratification demeaning and thought what we were doing technologically and ecologically to the world we lived in, atrocious. He was hated by the Establishment but the intelligentsia adored him. My dear departed husband thought he had a great mind." So, Lucy thought, Clarissa was a widow. "He married a beautiful Italian film star called Mara or some such name," Clarissa continued. "I'd better check it. They had a child, a little girl called Leah."

"He was a writer wasn't he?" Lucy asked. She'd looked him up in the library. There was a portrait of him on the back of one of his books: a thin aesthetic face, bony, large accusing eyes Lucy thought, angry eyes, dark and bottomless. Thick dark hair falling down over a deep pale forehead, an uncompromising mouth. This man, Lucy felt, would be slow to forgive. He would not put up with half truths or compromises. For him black would be black and white, white. She would not, she decided, like to be judged by him.

"He was a journalist, a poet, a novelist. A very inspired . . ." she searched for the word, "em . . . *dark* writer. He wrote very controversial stuff." She closed her eyes for an instant. "Re-reading him recently though," she added, "I've discovered that he was correct about so much, although we thought him a wee bit extreme at the time."

"For instance?"

"Well, he says in one scathing article that members

of the government and leaders of industry were greasing each other's palms. The big industries were into all sorts of skulduggery with the connivance of government officials, including arms dealing and insider trading. This was long before the Guinness and Lloyds catastrophies. He was castigated for the stuff he wrote then, but now, well, it was all true, wasn't it?"

"What happened to him?" Lucy asked. "I mean why did he leave England?"

"He always said he would. Threatened to. He'd been lionised you see and he hated that. He was so popular in the Seventies with his philosophy of peace and love and back to nature. When the Eighties came and it was every man for himself, ruthless ambition rampant, success at all costs, nothing mattered and everyone had *carte blanche* to do as you wished as long as you were not found out, well he wrote about that and was dropped by the in-people, and the Establishment turned their backs on him which did not worry him at all. Only the intelligentsia did too, all his old friends and he was left without support. The papers plagued him, calling him the Prophet of Doom. I think he became sickened by it all. He had a breakdown, left England and moved to Rome where he met and married Mara (by the way her name I'm sure is Mara) and he finally settled in Capri. The press hounded him for a while but eventually gave up and he became a forgotten man. His wife died. They said he adored her and never recovered."

"And you're going to dig him up?" Lucy asked.

"Funny way of putting it, but yes, I suppose so."

"Is that kind? Suppose he doesn't want to be dug up?"

Clarissa shook her head and clicked her teeth. She wore a soft wool turban and it had slipped askew over one eye. It made her look tipsy. "Golly you're naïve," she said pushing the turban up. "It doesn't matter to me whether he wants to be 'dug up' as you put it, or not. He's of interest because he made loud and vociferous noises in the Seventies and Eighties when he *wanted* to be interviewed, when he cultivated notoriety. Anyone who publicises their opinions with the uncompromising frankness that he employed is going, metaphorically speaking, into battle. He cannot complain then when the other side engages. At all events I'd like to ask him how he feels about being so right in his predictions. It's time we found out how he feels about that."

Clarissa folded her hands in her lap and closed her eyes and dozed off. Lucy relaxed and gazed out of the window. She stared at the banks of pristine white cloud beneath them, at the Madonna-blue sky above, and thought the whole experience stupendously exciting. The British Airways plane was crowded with holidaying families, children running about and crying as their ears popped. People squashed together like sardines in a tin was, to most of the passengers, an endurance test, but to Lucy it was a magic carpet, a fairy-tale chariot bearing her to exotic places.

The miracle of it astounded her. Here she was, high in the blue, blue sky being carried in the belly of a silver bird to a far-off land, to Italy. She thrilled to the efficiency of it, the navigational skills it took, the mechanics. She thought Clarissa all too dogmatic about technology. Her employer, she noticed, derided progress but nevertheless took advantage of it when it suited her.

Lucy glanced at her companion who had dropped off to sleep, her mouth ajar, her hands tangled in her pearls and thanked God that she *was* so prejudiced against all things technical. If she was not, she, Lucy Leighton would not be on this floating magic carpet, being wafted across the seas, being served delicious drinks by smiling hostesses in smart uniforms.

Who could have believed such exciting things could happen to her? She smiled happily to herself and tucked the blanket around her employer's legs and turned her face to the sky.

Chapter Nine

Lucy was to feel even more entranced when they left the plane in Naples. Emerging from the cabin, the atmosphere hit her so that she stopped for a moment taken aback by the strangeness. She was wrapped around by the warmth and the powerful scents: of flowers, of sun, of unfamiliarity. It hugged her in an overwhelming embrace. It was such a *foreign* feeling, unexpected and sultry; heat and stillness like a towel on her forehead, on her hands, on her cheeks. And then, on their way across the tarmac to passport control she heard it: the seductive sound, the liquid beauty of the Italian language.

"*Grazie Mario.*"

"*Roberto . . . Roberto Sbrigati*!"

"*Sto facendo il possibile*!"

"*Caio bene.*"

"Come along dear, don't let's lose our place." Clarissa turned and beckoned her on. "Keep up dear, keep up." Like the rest of the passengers Clarissa was short-tempered. Lucy had stopped bemused, and was staring at the Italian faces, listening to the words, captivated. The baggage men on their carrier-carts, the groups of groundsmen, laughing, talking in this incomprehensible and seductive dialect, bewitched her for a moment and it was with reluctance that she moved hastily to catch up with her employer.

They boarded a bus for Sorrento after they'd been through passport control and Lucy had collected their luggage and piled it on a trolly whose wheels insisted on going in the opposite direction. They set off after a short wait on a ride that, if she had been entranced before, simply lifted Lucy on to another plane entirely. It transported her into a dreamworld of beauty that left her drunk with delight.

The colours! The flowers! The scenery! Was such abundance possible? Gone were the primrose-yellows, the mauves, the greys of London. Here colours vibrated; they were intense. Cerise, purple, vermilion, flaming orange, emerald green, dark indigo and vibrant blue that picked up the reflections of sea and sky. A brilliant peacock.

Flowers in banks crawling over everything, sprawling everywhere, over walls, over roofs, over houses, over mountain sides in riotous profusion. Bourgainvillea, wisteria, oleander, hydrangea, hibiscus, a glorious abundance so luxuriant that it was almost excessive.

The sea, jewel-green splashed with sapphire, glittered and danced and twinkled as if scattered with diamonds. The luscious mountains, the ragged coastline, the jetty rocks and fertile vineyards; never in her life before did Lucy imagine that there could be such a profusion of breathtaking beauty so vibrantly alive and fecund. Oh she'd always been sensitive to the glories of nature around her, but this, this was *lavish*! As if the Creator had been filled with such joyous elation that He lost all control and coloured this part of the world wildly, fashioning it as extravagantly and lushly as possible.

They eventually reached Sorrento as the sun set over the bay of Naples but by that time Lucy was in no condition to appreciate the glory of it. Sated by the sights she had seen on her journey there, she was incapable of absorbing any more and the sunset was not fully appreciated, a golden haze seen through half-closed eyes.

But the delights of the day were not over yet for Lucy, tired though she was. The hotel they were booked into was of the Grand variety, a lovingly refurbished relic of the Edwardian era, palm-courted with a grand staircase leading upstairs and a huge Venetian glass chandelier.

There were bell-boys to whisk their luggage to their rooms, pretty maids in uniform, busy with towels and soaps and dusters in the corridors.

There was a vast dining room resplendent with glittering chandelier, pristine damask napery, pink blossoms in cut-glass on the tables and a huge flower arrangement on a marble surface near the wall. There was a funny little orchestra, a quartette on a stand at the back of the room playing, 'O Sole Mio' and 'Come Back to Sorrento'. A fat tenor with greased-back hair sang his heart out as they silently dined on pasta and veal cutlets and ice-cream.

Both of them were half asleep but basked in the care and attention they were receiving and not for the first time Clarissa reflected that the Italians were the best waiters in the world. It all slipped past Lucy in a dream and more than ever she felt unreal. Exhausted by her travels, the excitement and the onslaught to her senses of so much beauty, such grandeur and magnificence, the girl's eyelids kept drooping and her head kept dropping, and she was almost asleep on her feet when after supper she at last reached her bedroom and fell on to her bed fully clothed and sank into a deep sleep.

Sometime in the night she undressed and slid naked between the sheets and slept soundly until the first chorus of birds awakened her.

Chapter Ten

Opening the window on to her balcony next morning, letting in the birdsong and the sunshine, Lucy rubbed her eyes in delight. It had not been a dream after all. The bay was there, embracing the land in a garment of peacock-blue shot with currents of green. Little black islands bathed in the shimmering morning sun. Fishing boats left and returned to the harbour below. Pleasure cruisers prepared to make their first trips of the day and to her right and left the cerise and purple, the rose-madder and emerald green, the cobalt and sapphire blues, the buttercup yellows and all the reds: cardinal, crimson, maroon, scarlet, vermilion and wine of the flowers splashed their splendid colours across the face of the land.

Lucy sighed contentedly and breathed in the warm scented air. Life could be perfect.

"Well, you're up at last child," Clarissa's voice startled her and she turned. Her employer sat at a table on her balcony sipping tea and scribbling. She wore a flowery satin *robe-de-chambre* whose colours rivalled the intensity of the bourgainvillea and oleander around them. It was wrapped around her large frame and a matching turban was twisted over her head. There were croissants on the tray and tiny pots of Tiptee jams.

"Join me Lucy. Last night you were far too travel-weary to order breakfast, but it *is* one of your duties. Tell the concierge what time it is to be served and give him our order before you go to bed each night. All right?"

"I'm so sorry Clarissa, really sorry. Of course I will. I don't know—"

"Oh hush up. Come, join me."

Instantly contrite Lucy vaulted over the low iron partition and sat opposite Clarissa. "I don't know what happened last night. I just passed out. I was so excited."

"That will soon wear off," Clarissa said dryly. "Each night order breakfast before you retire. A pot of boiling water for me," she sighed and glanced up at Lucy from her notes, "it's just not the same as scalding the pot and having real tea leaves. Ah well, I unpacked the tea-bags." She smiled at Lucy. "You're quite a treasure you know. I found everything neat and labelled. It was a delight."

Lucy had put the various necessities in polythene self-sealing food bags and carefully labelled them all. "I ordered coffee for you Lucy. You like coffee, don't you?" Lucy nodded. "Italians really know how to make coffee," Clarissa remarked, then more to herself than to Lucy, "Italians know how to cook. Italians really are very talented in the kitchen." She smiled to herself, "And on the cat-walk," she added and began to write. "And with fashion. With design. With architecture. With wine. With music. With opera. Ah, Italians are masters." She was scribbling furiously and when Lucy tried to speak she waved her hand for silence and continued writing.

Lucy took a warm croissant from under the napkin that partially covered the bread basket, smothered it in blackcurrant jam, poured herself some coffee, added the warm milk and settled to enjoy her breakfast in the glorious setting. The sun was warm on her face and the smell of the pine and cypress trees around her, the scent of the flowers and the gentle shush-shush of the sea below, all lulled and reassured her. She felt wrapped around in beauty and utterly content and when Clarissa at last put her pen down and looked at her across the table Lucy smiled such a beatific smile that the startled Clarissa said, "You look as if you'd died and found yourself in heaven Lucy."

Lucy giggled. "I feel that way," she replied.

"Well I'd prefer to be in dear old England, a little rain outside. There's something so therapeutic about rain I always think." She glanced at Lucy. "I'm sorry to interrupt your bliss Lucy, but there's work to be done," Clarissa said briskly. "I need you to pack for me while I shower."

Work! This wasn't work. Work was emptying a bedpan, washing a helpless broken body covered in bed sores, feeding someone whose face muscles had ceased to function. Work was hoovering a dark house and endlessly dusting where you'd dusted the day before and the day before and the day before that.

"We need to pack up and be on the ferry to Capri within the hour." Clarissa stood up. "I'm going to shower now. You get everything ready and meet me in the lobby a.s.a.p." Lucy knew now what that meant. Clarissa took a credit card out of her bag. "Pay the bill with this. I'll sign it when I get down."

Lucy was happy to comply. It was no hardship putting Clarissa's silver-backed brushes, her toiletries, the clothes she wore yesterday travelling and her night things into their cases. It was all delightfully easy and Lucy wondered for the first time in her life what she had missed all these years tending her mother. Did others take all this for granted? Were people in general free like this? Why did the people on the plane complain all the time when they were surrounded by miracles? She glanced through the window every now and again, pausing to take in the beauty of the world outside as she packed sweet-smelling garments and bath-salts and perfume. Was it only illness that smelled so stale and foul and made one want to hurry through life? There had been no time to pause and stare in St John's Wood and no such sweet scents to bemuse her.

The warmth hit them as they left the Grand Hotel and were taken by a mini-van down to the harbour. Their luggage was piled into the van by dutiful hands and Lucy discovered that travellers like Clarissa *and* their secretaries (as Clarissa dubbed her) never actually *carried* baggage. There was always some helpful hotel minion with his hand out ready to do it for them.

The sea was calm and enchanted; the waters Ulysses and Julius Caesar sailed in, the island nearing all the time as the boat cleaved the smooth water like a knife. It seemed to Lucy as if Capri moved towards them, not the other way around. She sat on the azure and indigo sea, a towering rock, dotted with little villas drowsing in the sun.

They reached the Marina Grande and once more the hotel bell-boys were waiting for them at the harbour; white jackets stiff with starch, faces wreathed in the sincere smiles of staff who expect a large tip. They knew that travellers, anxious and in a strange place, would be so reassured to see them there, waiting to transport them to the comfort of their hotel, that they would tip them generously. They would show their gratitude in a delightfully mercenary way.

Their bags were piled on to another little buggy and the ascent to the hotel began.

Clarissa, who did not like heights and had kept averting her eyes from the sheer drop of cliff on the road from Naples and in Sorrento, now commended her soul to her Maker and firmly shut her eyes as the little mini-bus climbed up the winding road without the protection of windows, or it seemed anything between them and the spitting gravel with the plunging fall beside the hurtling buggy. And all the while, the Vespas zoomed past them at breakneck speed, usually ridden by glorious young men without helmets and a girl holding on behind.

But Lucy was enthralled. She leaned out of the speeding van at the sights rocketing past her until Clarissa pleaded, "*Lucy*. You're giving me heart-failure doing that. Sit back immediately! *Please*!"

At last they were settled. The hotel, or *pensione*, perched on its cliff above the Piazzetta and the church of Santo Stefano, had once been the summer villa of a noble Florentine family. It was modest compared to the Grand Hotel in Sorrento but delightful just the same. And it was family run.

The little island, ringed by an indigo sea, drenched in the shimmering light of the spring sun, opulent in beauty, luxuriating in garlands of gaudy blooms, was to be her home for a while and Lucy, a bemused and eager visitor, drunk on the lavish glory of the place, settled down in a haze of wonderment.

Chapter Eleven

It seemed to Lucy, as the days went by, that all life paused in the middle of a wonderful summer day. It was always just afternoon, warm and sunny, a delicious meal on the verge of being served *al fresco*; everything perfect, perfect, perfect.

Clarissa fussed. She rampaged. She fumed. She fretted in her anxiety to find and interview Conrad Morheim. She was like a battering-ram systematically beating at a closed door. "He's like the bloody Scarlet Pimpernel," she cried in a frustrated gasp. "*I seek him here, I seek him there* but he's always just out of reach! Damn, damn, damn."

They had gone up in the funicular and broached his villa, the Villa Azura. Everyone said he lived there, it was his address. He was supposed to *be* there. Clarissa had had Lucy telephone the villa but no one ever answered. Irritated Clarissa telephoned herself, but with the same result. Undaunted she then insisted on going up there uninvited. "I want this interview, so I'll get it, you may be sure," she told Lucy, who was startled by the determination of her employer. Lucy had never in her whole life forced herself on anyone.

When they reached the Villa Azura, high up on the island, the gates were firmly shut and no one answered the bell. "It seems to me they're all deaf!" Clarissa announced angrily pulling at the bell-rope violently.

"Round here." Clarissa, eager as a terrier scenting prey, circled the walls that surrounded the villa. "Here. We'll get over here."

She'd stopped where the wall was low, the ground high and she indicated to Lucy that she was going to climb it. Lucy stared at her in astonishment. She had never imagined Clarissa would go to such lengths. It was a precarious thing for a woman of her age and build to attempt but she did not feel she could say that to her boss. Clarissa hauled herself over, rather like a seal flapping up the rocks and tumbled down the other side. Lucy followed reluctantly.

They stumbled through the undergrowth to emerge into a small vineyard. The grapes were unripe and Clarissa blundered on, having lost her hat and torn her dress. If they did beard Conrad Morheim in his home, he would not be at all impressed at the spectacle they presented. The sun glared into their eyes and Lucy was deeply uncomfortable at the situation. Clarissa seemed unaware for once of the little clouds of bugs that hovered under the trees in the heat and who were lunching off her white arms in spite of the repellent so liberally and optimistically applied that morning.

They came upon the house suddenly. It was pink-walled and built on several levels, open to the elements with arches encouraging the breeze from the sea to cool and scent the interior. It was a peaceful place, sleeping in the sun.

Clarissa went boldly up the flight of stone steps at the side of the house, to what was obviously the main entrance. Lucy, embarrassed and trying not to show it, followed her reluctantly. She absolutely hated this kind of intrusion and dreaded the anger of the owner who had not struck her as a tolerant man.

The door was wide open and nothing daunted Clarissa who entered and beckoned Lucy to follow. The two women found themselves in a polychrome marble hall which was open to the sky. The walls were alcoved and in each curve a Greek or Roman bust rested, exquisitely carved, beautiful to behold. There were urns of ivy and in the centre a fountain splashed in the quiet stillness.

Lucy gazed around her, moved by the tranquil beauty of the courtyard. Arched passageways led off it in three directions and the fourth revealed a breathtaking view of the island below them and the sea. How magical to sit here, she thought, in this cool and elegant place and think and dream and simply be. The bees hummed and the birds sang and all else was quiet and for a moment Lucy felt as if time itself had stopped and stood still.

The man and the dogs came upon them silently, taking them by surprise. Clarissa and Lucy, drawn by the breathtaking view had moved towards the arch through which, it seemed, the glorious world lay at their feet.

Lucy heard it first. Like a far off roll of thunder. Someone or something was right behind them. They turned. Clarissa defiant, prepared to hold her ground and Lucy, embarrassed beyond belief, wheeled around and there they saw, first the dogs, two great black mastiffs on leads, lips pulled back, snarling softly in their throats, every sinew and muscle alert and quivering with contained energy barely held at bay, held in check by a square, heavily built man of oriental appearance. He wore a white jacket and was obviously a servant. He was also obviously unwelcoming, even threatening.

"Sorry to intrude," Clarissa said facing the man squarely, though Lucy could tell she was nervous. Lucy lurked behind her trying to pretend she wasn't there. "We've come to see Signor Morheim." God, she's got a nerve, Lucy thought. The man said nothing but stared at them expressionlessly and then jerked his head towards the open door through which they'd entered. Clarissa did not move. "We've come a long way," she said, sounding Lucy thought, faintly melodramatic. Climb every mountain! Ford every stream!

The man jerked his head again and as Clarissa did not budge he let the dogs go. The dogs did not leap up or attack them as Lucy felt sure they would. Instead they moved, still tense-muscled, towards the two intruders, snarling softly at them, circling around them, growling at their heels. Lucy could *feel* the hot breath on her ankles. The dogs nudged them, pushing at them, rounding them up like sheep, barking menacingly when they didn't move until Clarissa and Lucy were out in the sunlight.

But Clarissa had not, even then, given up. She tried again once more. Lucy could not but admire her persistence. "Why are you behaving so inhospitably *signor*? *Per favore*, I have to see Signor Morheim. He'll not be at all pleased when he finds out you turned us away."

The servant stood, massive, unmoved and unblinking, blocking the doorway. The dogs, now facing the ladies, as if they'd received a signal raised their voices and began barking ferociously. They removed their attention from Clarissa's and Lucy's ankles and the women found themselves looking into bloodshot angry eyes and in that moment Lucy knew that if they did not go the dogs would certainly attack. And they hadn't a leg to stand on; they were trespassing.

"Will you tell Signor Morheim that I'm here," Clarissa tried one last time. She held out her hand with her card in it.

The dog nearest to her snapped his jaws and, she said afterwards, if she had not pulled it back instantly he would have bitten it off. Her card fluttered to the ground and the dogs barked and strained forward and Lucy and Clarissa hurriedly descended the steps, and trying not to run, walked briskly away from the villa. The man stood flanked by the black dogs, quiet now and watched them go. He had not said a word and did not bother to follow them.

When they got to the gates they had to climb back over the wall much to Clarissa's disgust. A hotel mini-bus full of tourists came hurtling up the road as Clarissa, skirts up at her waist, plump legs in the air came reeling over the side. They hooted out of the windows, jeered and made ripe and unflattering comments, shouting lewd and ribald remarks at Clarissa who, face bright red with fury, fell into the hedgerow with a sensational lack of dignity.

The journey back to the hotel was punctuated by Clarissa's angry comments about Conrad Morheim, dogs in general, black dogs in particular and the ingratitude of interviewees. The dogs drew from her: "Think they're the bloody Hounds of the Baskervilles. Out of a Hammer Horror movie. Should not be allowed!" The oriental servant: "Fu Manchu eat your heart out! James Bond here we come! What pretension! Kashoggi at his worst!" And people who thought they were above journalists. "Who made them in the first place? Where would he *be* without people like me? I'll tell you – living in obscurity in some tower block in Surbiton!"

"I don't think there *are* any tower blocks in Surbiton," Lucy murmured.

"Don't get sassy with me girl," Clarissa hissed, marching down the little road, pushing at her hair which, turbanless, was decorated with bits of grass and bush. Her shapeless cheesecloth dress was stained with the juice of some nameless purple berries met in her collapse into the ditch.

She was cross and disgruntled. "They are desperate for publicity when they start," she complained, waving her arms like the vanes on a windmill. "That's what fame *is* for God's sake! Fame is being in the papers and magazines so everyone *knows* who you are. That way they can sell their wares: their films, books, plays, paintings, whatever. Then they make their money. Money to buy houses like the one we've just been refused entry to. *Then* they get all uppity. They disappear behind high walls built by the wealth *we* helped them to make. They vanish into huge houses protected by wire and electric technological bibs and bobs and *dogs*!" She spat the word out in disgust. "They don't realise it but they are prisoners. That's what they are, prisoners of their own making."

Shaking her head she padded on down the hill tired and worn out. Buses passed them but did not stop, and the walk was long. Poor Clarissa was exhausted when eventually they reached the hotel and she dived speechless into her room and Lucy left her to recover her equilibrium.

Chapter Twelve

Clarissa's luck *vis-à-vis* Conrad Morheim seemed to be out. Not that it bothered Lucy. She did not care too much whether Clarissa ever found him or not. In fact the longer he remained out of reach the longer they could stay in this paradise.

They settled into a comfortable routine; well comfortable for Lucy who refused to allow Clarissa's frustration and therefore ill-humour to disconcert her or spoil her wallowing in the glories of this Mediterranean island. Her experience with her mother helped, for Mercedes had always had to assert herself over her illness by picking on Lucy in a disgruntled tirade first thing in the morning. Clarissa did exactly the same thing. However, Lucy had long practice over the years learning how to ignore it, letting it pass over her head and not trouble her spirit.

After her morning grumps over a fruit, croissant and tea-bag breakfast on the balcony of the *pensione*, Clarissa made her way to the Piazzetta, Lucy behind her, down the little via of boutiques and small shops, the walls of which were drenched in purple bourgainvillea and filmed with ivy and wisteria. Everyone met there, drank coffee, read the papers, worked. Everybody that is it seemed except Conrad Morheim who proved constantly elusive.

Clarissa knew a few people there and before long, through these contacts, she knew everyone. Except Conrad.

There was an old newspaperman called Buffy Casswood who had obviously shared a past with Clarissa and they often swapped memories of the 'good old days' in Fleet Street before the ghastly move to Wapping, God help us! Buffy was constantly topped up, alcohol oozing from his pores. They met through Buffy, an American writer, Cliff Benedict. It appeared Clarissa had known him briefly in Paris, also, to Lucy's amusement, in 'the good old days' when Paris was Paris and not the mess it had become with the Pompidou building disfiguring the landscape and that frightful pyramid in front of the Louvre.

There was also a woman friend of Clarissa's, dauntingly overdressed and over-made-up for the place and her age. The Contessa d'Olavena was a French woman who had married an Italian count, now deceased, and who lived on the island. She arrived just after them to the Piazzetta each morning and joined them for a coffee.

Clarissa, when they arrived, would pay a fortune for yesterday's *Times* in English from the news-vendor at the corner of the square. She would then choose a table on the square. She would order their coffee by raising a hand to the gossiping group of white-jacketed waiters.

She would sit, drumming her fingers on the table. The waiter would bring the coffee with a flourish, tear the bill across and leave it under the ashtray. Clarissa would take out her notebook, which never left her handbag and jot down in it every now and then.

The Contessa would arrive dressed to the nines, as if she were strutting down the Champs-Elysées or the Via Veneto. She wore Chanel or Lacroix with all the trimmings, looking weirdly out of place here in the shimmering sunshine, on a sea-lapped island. Her make-up was heavy – purple lipstick, hair and eyebrows dyed jetblack, a lot of jewellery: gold chains and pearls and glittering ear-rings. She also wore inappropriate high heels and carried a toy Yorkie with a bow in its carefully groomed hair. The bow matched her colour of the day: red or blue, black or green. This Yorkie reposed in his mistress's arms and lay inert with eyes half-closed, and rebuffed any attempt at friendliness from strangers with a vicious bout of soprano barking and a gnashing of alarmingly sharp teeth. Clarissa, after her experience at the Villa Azura viewed Chi-Chi with distaste and alarm.

Clarissa and the Contessa greeted each other with no attempt at a pretence of real affection. It was obvious that the Contessa deplored Clarissa's taste and thought of her as an English frump. In fact she often said so commenting loudly, "Ze English have no style. None!" waving her inch-long nails and lighting her cigarette which she smoked through a long holder. Clarissa would wink at Lucy and the Contessa would glance with distain at Lucy's jeans and shirt, the sleeves of her pullover tied over her shoulders and at Clarissa in one of her two-piece dress-and-light-matching-coat outfits, her exotic turbans, her pearls.

"Egg-cen-tric. The English. Taste-less! One should *not* let go of one's standards in zis kind of place. Wan should, at all times be elegant." She would glance around the little square as if she was in the Black Hole of Calcutta.

Clarissa told Lucy that the Contessa's late husband had been a Fascist, a powerful figure in the Mussolini government. When the war was over he had fled to Argentina until feelings had cooled down, and only his great wealth had protected him when he returned to Italy in the late Fifties. And the fact that he had kept a low profile. He had been discreet. He had not tried to reinstate himself in Roman or Florentine society, sticking to the less condemnatory south: to Naples, and eventually to Capri.

The Contessa despised Capri and looked on the island with the contempt a big-city dweller has for the unsophisticated rural backwater. Yet Valentino and St Laurent had boutiques here Lucy noted, and wondered at the woman's inflexibility. Lucy felt it sad that she had not been able to relax into the beauty all around her, that she seemed unable to adapt.

There was a curtain over her eyes which looked inward all the time, never outward.

The morning after their visit to the Villa Azura they were joined by the Contessa as usual, and, as usual, Clarissa asked impatiently if her friend had managed to see Conrad Morheim. All her friends were charged with the same request: to get a hold of Conrad Morheim.

"No I 'ave not seen 'im," the Contessa replied, sitting down and flicking her ruby talons at the waiters. "I 'ave tried *ma cheri* truly I 'ave. But 'ee is not, ow you say . . . available."

The waiter brought the coffee instantly. He did not want one of the Contessa's lectures in vile Italian, complaining about the ghastly service in Capri as compared to the service in Place St Michel.

"Good Lord, he *must* be available *sometime*," Clarissa protested. "This is a small island. He's got to surface now and then. Surely?" she appealed to them.

The Contessa shrugged eloquently, greedily sucking in the smoke from her cigarette through the ivory holder. Looking at it made Lucy feel sick. Ivory was elephant tusk and she shuddered. It was funny, she reflected, that her mother, so ill, incontinent and helpless, never disgusted her, while the Contessa with her inward looking eyes, her greedy smoking, her ivory holder and inappropriate clothes did.

"No 'ee does not," the Contessa insisted firmly. "The point of the island *cheri* is that one can go up, up, up and never come down. You stay where you want and there is no need to move. No one bothers you."

"Which you know all about Contessa," Clarissa, who could never forgive the Contessa for her German sympathies during the war, could not help remarking. "To your advantage," she added.

"You are unkind Clarissa," the Contessa complained. "'Ow can you blame me for Alphonso's politics? I am, after all only his wife!"

"Oh come off it Risa," Clarissa hooted. "Come off it!"

"But it is true," the Contessa insisted. She had probably convinced herself by now Lucy thought. There was a pause while they drank coffee and Clarissa scribbled.

Then suddenly the Contessa spoke. "There are no straight lines on the island," she said, "the paths twist and turn."

"What has that got to do with anything?" Clarissa asked irritably.

"Well, it is silly don't you see." The Contessa sounded touchy. "You cannot here drop in on people. You just cannot! They can see you coming."

Lucy glanced at Clarissa, recalling their visit to the Villa Azura. Clarissa glared back at her then shifted her attention to the Contessa who continued, "Apart from anything else, if they do not wish to see you they can escape. All visitors can be seen approaching from a great height. So, you leave your villa and go into the hills for a walk or simply retire to your room and send a servant to say you are not available."

Lucy glanced again at Clarissa who avoided her gaze and kept her attention on the Contessa who tapped the side of her nose, a sudden light in her eyes. "Aha! So that is what you did! You tried to beard the lion in his den! A servant put you out. It will have been Han Su." She burst out laughing, then seeing

Clarissa's furious face she stopped. "Ah Clarissa, you will not get to Conrad like that. If 'ee does not want to receive you, you will not find 'im."

Clarissa bit her lip in vexation. "Have you told him I want to see him? That I'm *very* sympathetic to him? That I'm willing to meet him on any ground? Agree to any conditions?"

The Contessa looked up at the church. The bells were ringing. Lucy glanced at her watch. It was eleven o'clock.

"I 'ave got to go *cheri*."

"I'll get your coffee." Clarissa put a finger over the bill and drew it out from under the ashtray.

"I 'ave not seen 'im or talked to 'im," the Contessa said. "But I will keep trying. And then there is the concert at Signorina Gianocco next weekend. He would not miss that."

Clarissa was watching her with rapt attention and Lucy could see that the Contessa was enjoying Clarissa's forced kow-towing. "Please Risa, oh please can you get me invited. It is so important to me. Please."

"I will try *cherie*. I will do my best," the Contessa remarked tranquilly.

"Who is she?" Lucy asked.

"You 'ave not heard of her? *Mon Dieu*, what ignorance! She is, well *was* a great opera diva. Divine voice. She gives a dinner every so often (she has a place here) and sometimes she sings for us. The lucky ones." She smiled at Lucy. "It is an experience not to be missed."

"Will an invitation be difficult?" Lucy asked, earning from Clarissa a grateful glance.

"It should not be. For some reason she likes the English. I'm sure I cannot think why! She says she was very 'appy in Covent Garden. I will ask 'er. It is the best I can do."

"I will be very grateful," Clarissa said, mollified.

The Contessa rose, her cigarette in its ivory holder between her teeth, barely missing Chi-Chi's ear, and brushing down her skirt, waved cheerily at them and took off towards the boutiques.

Lucy repressed a shiver at the thought of the ivory holder and the fact that she had been sipping coffee with an erstwhile Nazi, and Clarissa met her eye and read her thoughts. She shrugged as if to say the end justifies the means and set again to her notes.

This was their daily pattern. After the Contessa had gone to make a nuisance of herself in the boutiques, Clarissa would begin to scribble and Lucy would wander away to explore the island, go for a walk or look at the shops.

She often took the funicular railway to Anacapri. She had explored the sights the first week: the Blue Grotto, Villa Jovis, the Belvedere and San Michele. She had gazed at the rock formations and the wonderful natural arches. She had been seduced by the sheer black protuberances rising from the shimmering indigo sea. She had puttered about on the Marina Grande and the Marina Piccola and gazed at the Faraglioni from the public gardens where the profusion of flowers made the senses reel. She spent the time dreaming sensuous imaginings, sun drenched fantasies, allowing her body to unbend to the sun, to relax and flower in the heat.

She often crossed the enchanted island to Anacapri where the most glorious views of all defied description. Spending time until lunch like this filled her with joy, left her breathless at the sights and sounds and scents all around her. She had acquired a golden glow from the sun. Her cheeks were tinted with a rose-petal blush. Gone was that lost anxious look in her marmalade-bronze eyes. The whites now were clear and the eyes looked out brightly and expectantly at the world. Gone was the crease between the eyebrows, the unhealthy pallor of those permanently indoors.

When she returned to the Piazzetta, Clarissa, looking up from her writing, could not help but notice the vitality that her young charge radiated. Pleased, she would close her notebook and arm in arm they'd go and eat fresh fish at a restaurant in the Marina Piccola or the Marina Grande or one of the many delicious little eating houses in between.

In the afternoon, siesta time, Lucy rested and read, then typed Clarissa's notes while her employer slept. In the evening they returned to the Piazzetta and had drinks with acquaintances. They met people, as Clarissa said, and mingled. Then they would find a place to dine. Sometimes they would go to the mainland, to Positano or Sorrento. The boat trip enchanted Lucy and finally they would sit watching the sun go down and the stars come out shimmering in fistfuls across the velvet sky.

Lucy kept in the background as much as possible, partly because it was her nature and partly because Clarissa and her friends seemed overwhelmingly capable of monopolising the company. They were all flamboyant characters and Lucy felt no match for them. The only time she had contributed to the conversation they had all turned and stared at her and she had felt an idiot so did not repeat the attempt.

Lucy liked Cliff Benedict best. He had a roguish twinkle in his eyes, a sort of faded Rhett Butler *savoir faire*. He flirted outrageously with all women, young and old, that he came in contact with but most of all he flirted with Clarissa. He was kind, Lucy could tell, but was incapable of being serious about anything, which was tedious if it continued, as it did, day after day, night after night. She certainly found it trying to keep up a continuous banter but Clarissa obviously thrived on it.

Buffy Casswood on the other hand rarely spoke. He limited himself to monosyllables in the American Cinema vernacular. Yup! Nope! Mebbe! This monosyllabic repartee was invaluable to Buffy when he got drunk, which he did every night, and Lucy realised quite quickly that after ten p.m. any conversation with Buffy was strictly one-way traffic.

It was one morning at the beginning of their second week on the island and a week after their fruitless trip up to the Villa Azura that Lucy, pottering about, semi-comatose in the sun, met the stranger.

She was in her shorts, sitting on a rock in the sea at the Marina Piccola. She sat, blissfully dangling her feet in the water, idly watching the waves break in a flurry of white foam against her knees, when looking up she saw a tall dark shadow between her and the sun.

The silence, the peace, was suddenly shattered as the voice barked a command. "Hold still! Don't move!" Then as she started, "God-dammit I said don't move!"

She froze. Used to instant obedience, used to reacting to commands and emergencies, she obeyed and sat immobilised.

A hand plunged between her legs into the sea. The hand held a rod, a piece of piping. Whoever it was agitated the rod violently about in the sea.

"Pull your legs out *now*!" Again a harsh command which she instantly obeyed. "Quickly!"

Both of them had fixed their attention on the rod which the stranger now drew from the water. Wrapped around it, sliding off it, was the largest jellyfish Lucy had ever seen.

"It would have stung you," the stranger said. "Hundreds of quills. They turn poisonous. You have to get them all, every single one out. It can be very painful."

"Oh gosh! Thank you."

"You're welcome. I'm sorry if I startled you though. I had to. I saw it clearly from up there.

Curling nearer and nearer your legs. Be careful in future." He pointed to a narrow flight of stone steps just behind her. "Good thing I caught it in time. They're lethal," he said.

"What a pity. It's my favourite thing. Dangling my feet in the water," she told him, feeling foolish as she said it.

"Well don't do it. There is always something evil lurking beneath the most innocent of pleasures." The man was talking as much to himself as to her.

She could not see him for he stood back to the sun and now he turned and all she saw was his silhouette. Rod in hand he was disappearing away from her up the steps.

"Thank you, I will," she called after him. "Keep my feet out I mean."

He turned his head and looked over his shoulder at the sound of her voice. His brown hair fell over his forehead and he had the most intense gaze she had ever encountered. He nodded to her then sprinted up the remaining steps two at a time and was gone, moving swiftly out of sight up a small pebble-stoned path and around a corner.

She had recognised his face from the dust-jacket of his book in the library.

It was Conrad Morheim.

Chapter Thirteen

She did not tell Clarissa about the encounter and she did not know why. It was certainly not because she was afraid to. It was, she eventually figured out, because it seemed to her a little bit like cheating.

Clarissa was on a single-minded mission to interview Conrad Morheim. She intended to intrude into his life uninvited whether he wanted it or not, and Lucy did not feel that in her role as secretary she had that same mission. She felt it would be a kind of betrayal. The man had saved her from a very unpleasant ordeal. She owed him. She had heard people talking about those stings. Buffy said his whole foot became infected by the quills which, because of the wine, he had not felt. He had left them to work their own way out and he'd nearly lost his foot. He said he would have done so, only he'd been so full of alcohol that he was disinfected. Conrad Morheim had instinctively come to her aid and she could not betray him.

Besides what could she have done? She could hardly have lassoed him and frogmarched him up the hill to Clarissa, although she had a nasty feeling that her boss might have expected her to do just that.

That evening in the Piazzetta in the twilight, sitting with a very tipsy Buffy, Clarissa and Lucy sipped wine and chatted in that desultory way that people do when they are hanging out together, not going anywhere in particular. Lucy gazed at the stars and sadly acknowledged that the first tiny blot had appeared on her landscape; the first deception, the first betrayal of trust. She had met Conrad Morheim and she had withheld this fact from Clarissa. Carrying this was a burden.

Oh how good a clear conscience feels! How uncomfortable even a small evasion is. Twice she nearly gave the game away, once when Buffy muttered something about Conrad being a small man, she nearly contradicted him and cried, "Oh no! He's very tall", and when Clarissa remarked that the last person who'd interviewed Conrad ten years ago said he never smiled she almost said that he had a lovely smile. So she decided to keep her mouth shut that evening until the memory of the meeting faded and she could trust herself not to slip up.

Buffy's linen jacket was crumpled and stained. Sunk as he was in his alcoholic haze he did not notice Lucy's reticence but Clarissa did. "Life in foreign parts beginning to lose its flavour Lucy?" she asked. "Capri beginning to pall?" Lucy shook her head and did not reply.

"I *long* for England," Clarissa continued. "I absolutely identify with Browning, 'Oh to be in England, now that April's there.'" She shrugged. "Why I travel all the time I do not know. It's like a disease."

At that moment the Contessa arrived with Chi-Chi snuggled in the crook of her arm. She was not alone and she sashayed across the small crowded square in her stiletto heels and Chanel two-piece with that slightly suggestive hip-swinging strut that women who feel they're admired use to attract even more attention. Clarissa muttered, "How misplaced is her confidence!"

The Contessa had two boys with her, young handsome men. Clarissa leaned over as the Contessa hip-swung over to them and explained that Nucio was Risa's lover and not to show surprise. Lucy gulped but took it in her stride. Nucio was about twenty-four to the Contessa's sixtyish, and that was giving the Contessa the benefit of the doubt.

"The make-up ages her, if only she knew," Clarissa whispered to Lucy and added, "Poor woman! She's so afraid of old age."

"And death?" Lucy asked.

Clarissa nodded. "Yes. And death." Then she sighed, "But then, who isn't?"

Just behind Nucio another young man of approximately the same age hovered, waiting to be introduced. He seemed ill-at-ease. There were candles on the tables protected by glass storm-globes and the only other light came from the star-strewn sky and the shimmering moon. The young man was pushed into a seat beside Lucy by the Contessa, who introduced her escorts at last, having kept them hovering whilst she greeted Clarissa and Buffy like long-lost friends. "As if she hadn't seen us just this morning," Clarissa remarked. Nucio had been about to seat himself next to Lucy but the Contessa swiftly retrieved him and put him firmly between herself and Clarissa. Then she introduced the other.

"Luciano Lorenzi, this is Lucy Leighton, Clarissa Bourke-Rathbone and Buffy you know. Grappa all round. Garçon, *per favore*?"

Luciano turned his enormous dark eyes on Lucy. They were the most amazing eyes she had ever seen on man or woman. Brown as molasses, soft as pansy petals, they were fringed by thick black lashes both top and bottom. Lucy was used by now to the beauty of the young Italian male but Luciano took her breath away. He was from a painting by Raphael, a Leonardo, a Lippi. He smiled at her, flashing perfect teeth and pushed his hand through his thick dark hair, but his wonderful eyes were curiously guarded, remote and indifferent.

"You are visiting Capri?" he asked her politely.

Lucy would have liked just to sit there and stare at him as she would at a spectacular painting or the view from the Belvedere. She would have liked to gaze, absorbing the perfection of such beauty but she replied as politely as she could, "Yes. Visiting." Then as he went on staring at her she added, "I'm also working," she nodded across the table, "I'm Clarissa's secretary."

"Oh!" He did not sound very interested. He took out a crumpled pack of cigarettes and shook it with a proficient little twist of the wrist so that one shot out. He offered it to her, then when she shook her head he put it between his lips and drew it out of the pack. He took the storm-globe off the candle and bending forward, lit it. The light flickered on his sculptured cheekbones, on his flared nostrils, on his smooth milk-chocolate skin.

"Couldn't you just eat him?" the Contessa whispered behind his back to Lucy who shook her head.

"Oh no!" she cried, but, she thought, I could sit here all night watching him.

Yet she felt a coldness from him, a preoccupation as if he was physically but not mentally there. He smoked the cigarette leaning back in his chair.

"My dear Nucio, will you light mine *si vous plait*. Your friend has no manners." The Contessa leaned the other way towards her companion, her Gitane between her lips.

"I'm so sorry," Luciano said but did not sound as if he meant it and he made no attempt to correct the error.

Buffy was nodding off and Risa and Clarissa were talking. Clarissa was as usual speculating on the possibility of meeting Conrad Morheim sooner rather than later. "Do we have to wait for the Diva's party to get to him Risa?" she queried plaintively.

"Be thankful that I got you an invitation at all," the Contessa said.

"But I've got to get to him soon Risa. *Tempis fugit* as they say, oh *tempis* is bloody *fugit*!"

Lucy felt a twinge of guilt whenever they talked about Conrad but she kept silent. It was too late now to talk of what happened days ago.

"Don't be impatient *cherie*. Time here does not exist. It is, how you say?" The Contessa patted Nucio's wrist, then began to play with his fingers. His hand was beautifully manicured, smooth and young, hers was clawlike with liver spots and long red nails. The contrast was incongruous. Luciano glanced occasionally at the hands on the table, his expression inscrutable. "Suspended," the Contessa finished triumphantly. "That is it. Time here is suspended."

Luciano suddenly pushed his chair around to face Lucy, turning his back on the Contessa and his friend. He looked sulky.

"Do you live here?" Lucy asked him, shy for some reason.

"Here? Oh no! I live in Roma. I am down here to see old friends." He threw a glance over his shoulder at Nucio. "Shit, friend? I am not so sure any more." He looked over his shoulder again at Nucio and the Contessa playing with his fingers. "I thought I knew him. But agh . . . It is disgusting, don't you think." His voice was low but violent and he squashed the cigarette out in the ashtray. "When he said *older* to me I thought he meant . . . oh, like Sophia Loren maybe, but this . . . this is *old*!" His voice dripped with scorn.

"Nucio seems, well, willing enough. He doesn't seem to mind," she said gently.

"Nucio is doing it for the money," Luciano replied contemptuously. "Agh! It is disgusting!"

"If he doesn't mind, it's not up to you, to us really, to condemn him, is it?" Lucy protested.

He focused on her properly for the first time. "I suppose not," he said doubtfully and began smoking another cigarette in silence. Then he looked at her under his lashes. "Your name is Lucy?"

"Yes." She smiled at him, drinking in the handsome face, the perfect alignment of bone and sinew and hair. After a pause she asked, "What do you do?"

"I paint."

At first she thought he meant he painted houses, then he said, examining her closely, "I would like to paint you. Your face is so . . . different."

Her hands flew to her cheeks. "How? Different?"

He laughed. "Oh don't look so worried. It is lovely and gentle. Very gentle. So English. Not at all Italian. Italian women are beautiful, voluptuous, passionate. Strong." He mused, speaking slowly, scrutinising her intently. "But you, your face is pure. Virginal. Innocent. Without guile. Are you a virgin?" He asked the question lightly, out of curiosity and without thinking she nodded. He stared at her then struck his hand against his forehead. "*Mamma mia*! That is why you look like that. It is a book that is not written in yet. But no! It is not possible, is it?"

She nodded again, looking distressed. He bent near her.

"Don't look so sad little one. You have the look of a Lippi Madonna. It is not something to be ashamed of."

"What are you two whispering about?" Clarissa asked.

For a terrible moment Lucy thought Luciano was going to tell them all what she had said, make a joke about it, but he did not. She knew that any of the others would have, it was just the sort of thing they'd find funny. Except perhaps Clarissa.

"I've just asked your secretary if I may paint her," Luciano said swiftly to Clarissa and Lucy shot him a grateful glance.

"Of course Lucy. Why not? As long as it does not interfere with my requirements. Not that there's too much for you to do at the moment, me not being able to find the Goddamn man. Let Luciano immortalise you. Who knows, some day you may hang in the Tate." Clarissa leaned across to the Contessa.

"Is he any good?" she asked.

"He is considered very talented," she replied. "The Academia Italiana rates him highly."

"He is considered a most brilliant portrait painter," Nucio added.

"His talents lie in a different direction to yours Nucio," the Contessa said roguishly.

Clarissa stood up. "Come along Lucy we must retire." Lucy could see that she was bored. She rose dutifully. Luciano rose too.

"Tomorrow then?" he asked. "I'll call your hotel."

Lucy nodded, staring at the beautiful face. Then she turned away, linked arms with her employer and the two of them walked back to the hotel through the warm star-filled night.

Chapter Fourteen

When Lucy came across Conrad Morheim a second time her discomfiture at not telling Clarissa about these accidental encounters became acute. She felt she was leading a double life, deceiving poor Clarissa who had saved her from homelessness and poverty. Lucy was not at all used to lies and deception and found the garments uncomfortable to wear.

She also felt that Clarissa, in her bull-headed way, was barging heedlessly into all the wrong places, looking in all the wrong directions, but she thought it would be presumptuous of her to try to enlighten her boss.

The following day some post arrived from England. Clarissa had told Lucy that the Italian post was notoriously bad but Lucy did not expect anyone to write to her. However, in the pile of mail for Clarissa, there were three little envelopes for Lucy. She was very surprised for she had not imagined she would get any.

The first was an engraved card in an envelope. On the top of the card was printed, '*Compliments of Anthony Masters Crabbe. Solicitor*', and in a scrawl underneath Anthony had written, '*Hope all is well. House sold. All debts cancelled.*' There was a PS which said, '*Give regards to Aunt Clarissa.*'

The next one was a proper letter on notepaper from Errol.

'Dear Lucy,

Barry passed away two days ago. Very peacefully, in his sleep. It was how he wanted to go. He dreaded becoming too ill to look after himself so I cannot but be glad that he did not suffer too much. The announcement will be in *The Times* next week. He rates two columns.'

Then he'd added, '"Do not stand by my grave and weep. I am not there. I have gone."'

He'd ended, 'So many of my friends have died recently Lucy dear including your mother and I miss them very much. I miss you also though why that should be I cannot think. We only saw each other twice yet you made an indelible impression on me. You have a rare and lovely quality of sympathetic understanding and you *listen*, really listen, and you know what they say; the greatest gift you can give anyone is rapt attention.'

The last was a notelet with a spray of roses on it and it was from Adrian.

'How are you bearing up under Ma's single-mindedness, or shall I call it ruthless obsessiveness? Keep your cool Lucy. If she stays another month I may pay her a flying visit. Chin up. Adrian.'

She was glad to get the news from all of them, touched that they had bothered to write.

True to his word Luciano telephoned the hotel and Lucy, having caught up on all her work, asked Clarissa if she could sit for him. Clarissa smiled absent-mindedly and told her to go ahead. "I'll be working on the notes I have here and I have to read some old newspaper articles and do some research this afternoon. On top of that I don't feel a hundred per cent." How could anyone not feel well in this climate? Lucy wondered.

Clarissa continued, "I'll have some pasta in my room. So if I'm not in the Piazzetta at lunchtime you better fend for yourself. I'll see you at dinner, perhaps. But I warn you, there'll be a lot of typing to do tomorrow." She glanced at Lucy and added seriously, "Be careful Lucy, of Luciano. He could lead you into such pain!" she warned.

Lucy was well aware of the danger of beautiful young men like Luciano. She'd consumed and digested the contents of women's magazines of the cheaper sort during her long nursing life and knew the inevitable consequences of falling in love with glamorous foreigners in exotic lands. She waved to Clarissa and set off.

Luciano was staying in a *pensione* in Anacapri. The house was high up on a hillside and the room he inhabited was high up in the house. One whole wall facing the sea was glass, and the view, all mauve haze in the morning sun, was a feast for her eyes.

Luciano came up behind her as she stood looking

out. He put his arm over her shoulder and Lucy left it there. "It's so beautiful it makes you want to cry," she said.

"You are beautiful," he told her and she laughed and shook her head.

"Ah no!" She smiled up at him, remembering Adrian Bourke-Rathbone. "No, I'm *pretty*. Lovely even. But I'm not beautiful. *You*, now, *are* Luciano. You are beautiful. It is different." She had turned and faced him and was amused to see that he was discomfited. She had taken his line away from him.

"Where shall I sit?" she asked.

"Here," he indicated a stool and she sat, hooking her foot on one of the bars near the bottom of the stool. She was wearing her jeans and a fresh cotton blouse, open at the neck, Adrian's scarf carelessly knotted at her throat.

"Are those your paintings?" she asked, indicating piles of canvasses against and on the wall opposite her.

He shook his head. "No. The studio is rented by a friend of mine, Dmitri Papadorou. He is in Greece at the moment. He lends it to me when he's away."

"His paintings are . . . depressing," she remarked. They were reminiscent of Francis Bacon, grotesque figures with stomachs slashed open, entrails hanging out.

"Yes," Luciano laughed. "He's *very* successful. Much more so than I am." He grinned at her. "People today like gore. In paintings, in movies.

Spilling their guts." He laughed again. The phrase, she knew had quite a different meaning, but she did not enlighten him.

He had placed a canvas on an easel and went now and produced a portrait which was lying face against the wall. "This is one of mine," he told her. He examined it in a detached way, staring at it as if it had been painted by a stranger. He turned it towards her so that she could see it. She drew her breath in sharply.

It was the Contessa and it was startling in execution and style. He had caught accurately the travesty of the woman, the garish make-up, the mutton-dressed-as-lamb; but he had caught too the fear in her eyes, the desperation and the vulnerability at her heart's core. It was both bold, cruel and yet tender and compassionate.

"It's . . . brilliant!" She spread her hands. "Wonderful. I'm not at all sure I want you to paint me now!"

"Why not?"

"Because of what you might see in me. Make me see too."

"I told you, you are an unwritten page." He frowned. "It will be difficult," he said.

"Why?" she asked.

"The Contessa was easy. She's has the world's experience on her face. You . . ." he threw up his hands, "well, well we shall see. A challenge. Quite a challenge."

He turned her this way and that until she was sitting

exactly as he wanted, looking out over Anacapri, one foot on the floor, the other hooked on the rung of the stool, her hands clasped loosely in her lap.

He worked silently, the room so quiet that Lucy felt suspended, almost in a trance. It was as if all the world paused. She could see no one, hear nothing from the outside, the sound was cut off by the glass. The leaves moved languorously, stirring in the soft breezes from the Mediterranean, but no gentle breeze entered here. A bird, a seagull she thought, flew across the sky and fluffy little cirrus clouds hovered on the horizon as Luciano worked and she sat quietly stewing in the hot room. She could feel her body baking in the heat and beads of sweat dewed her brow. Her hands in her lap felt wet and tendrils of her hair stuck to her neck. Yet she rested there content.

She felt his intense concentration on her. She did not meet his eyes but knew he was probing her, examining her very soul, scrutinising her with a fierce razor-like intent, but also with impartiality that did not embarrass her. She found, to her surprise, for she had always thought of herself as a very private person, that she did not mind at all.

At last he sighed loudly, yawned, put down his brushes and stretched. "That's all for today," he announced.

She let her head fall forward, then stretched it back, then saw he was standing before her. He was looking intently at her as if searching for the answer to some puzzle. She stared back at him and knew he was going to kiss her. She waited breathlessly.

She had only been kissed once before; well, twice if she counted the incident in the chemist shop.

The shop had been closed and she had had to pick up a prescription for her mother and Mr Patel, the chemist, had tried to embrace her. He had been het up and it had been a fumbling and awkward encounter, Mr Patel breathing heavily, panting like a dog, trying to kiss her and she turning her head from side to side, lips squeezed together struggling to get away, to avoid that fat mouth at all costs.

She had escaped (the silly man had not locked the door) and no harm was done. She had scrubbed her mouth fiercely in the bathroom when she got home.

The only other time had been Jimmy Mulvany behind the bicycle shed at school and Jimmy pressing hard tightly-closed lips against hers and she wondering how she was supposed to feel, knowing that what she *did* feel was acute discomfort.

There was nothing hard about Luciano's kiss. It was soft, insistent and intoxicating. Her body seemed to disintegrate. She felt like ice-cream melting, it was so sweet, so tender, so thrilling. Lips on lips, feeling the sensitivity of nerve and tissue and Lucy felt the sweet sensation course through her from head to toe. She had often watched curiously men embracing women on TV and in the movies and wondered how they felt. Now she knew.

Then he let her go. She nearly fell but he did

not try to continue. He watched her, waiting for her reaction.

What might have happened next was anyone's guess, but the door opened and Conrad Morheim came into the studio.

He stopped still staring at them, the sun shining through the wall of glass into his eyes.

"Good Lord! Who are you? Where's Dmitri?"

"He's away," Luciano said, "in Greece. I'm—"

"Oh yes. We met before. His friend from Rome. Luciano Lorenzi, is it not?"

Luciano nodded and Conrad's eyes went swiftly to Lucy. "And you?" He's like a headmaster she thought. "You're the girl with the jellyfish. In the harbour."

"I am painting her," Luciano muttered. He sounded bad-tempered and Lucy wondered if perhaps the older man irritated him. He certainly talked to him as if he was a schoolboy.

"I'm Lucy Leighton," she said and held out her hand.

"English," Conrad said. "You have to be. With that skin, that paleness, that handshake!"

She laughed. He was quite charming now, perhaps because of Luciano's truculence.

"I'm sorry to intrude. I wanted a word with Dmitri."

"Well he won't be back till June."

Conrad Morheim standing in the doorway somehow made Luciano seem juvenile. There was about him an energy, like his dogs Lucy thought, a harnessed energy. The dark eyes were restless and anger lurked there just as in his photograph on the dust-jacket of his book. The skin, taut over the harsh-hewn bones of his face, was tanned and the composition gave him a rough-diamond look, yet the broad brow was the forehead of a thinker. As before he wore chinos and a pale blue polo shirt.

"OK. Well." He stood a moment staring at her and she felt once more that her very soul was being scrutinised. Yet his look, unlike Luciano's made her uncomfortable. It was somehow much more personal. Perhaps, Lucy decided, it was because he was focusing on her innermost being directly, whereas Luciano examined her more objectively, as a subject to paint.

She squirmed under his gaze. Was it because it was so fierce, so personal? she wondered. Luciano's had been much more impartial; an artist assessing his subject. Under Conrad's dark eyes she felt emotionally exposed. She crossed her arms over her breast in a gesture of self-protection.

"You remind me of someone," he said.

She did not reply. Like a rabbit caught in the headlamps of a car she gazed back at him unblinking, dazed.

He shook his head then as if to clear it, frowned at her and repeated, "You remind me of someone." Then he turned to Luciano and the mood was broken.

"Tell Dmitri I'm looking for Leah," he said.

"I won't see him. At least not for a while,"

Luciano replied, unconcerned. Conrad nodded and then he had gone. Disappeared. Lucy could hear him descending the stone steps outside.

Luciano smiled at her, came nearer and touched her cheek. “Lunch,” he said. Then he began to put his paints away. “Will you tell Clarissa you’ve seen him?” he asked as he cleaned his brushes. She could smell the turpentine and she wrinkled her nose. It reminded her of the rubbing alcohol she’d used on her mother.

“No,” she answered him.

“I didn’t think you would.”

“Do you think I’m wrong?” she asked.

He shrugged. “I don’t think you have any choice. It would not, after all, get her to see him and it would irritate her to death. She’d take it out on you. Suddenly it would be your fault.” He turned and looked at her. “He is very dangerous you know,” he told her.

She laughed, remembering that Clarissa had said the same thing about Luciano. He took her laugh for derision and added earnestly, “No, Lucy he is. Dangerous. He changes people. Brings them down. He destroys. That’s it . . . he is a destroyer. He destroyed his wife they say. And his daughter. Some say he killed his wife and I know he ruined Leah. I know because I saw.”

“You know Leah?”

He nodded. “I know her well.”

“Will you tell me about her Luciano?” she asked.

“At lunch,” he answered, then taking her arm, steering her out of the room he continued, “*Andiamo*! *Andiamo*. Let’s go. I’m starving.”

Chapter Fifteen

Clarissa was not in the Piazzetta when they got there and Luciano, who had held Lucy's hand in his on the way across from Anacapri, suggested they go to a quiet little *trattoria* he knew in one of the side streets off the square. "Is better there. Not so tourist," he explained solicitously. "You are so hot Lucy. It will be cool there."

"Oh I'm sorry," she said, not really feeling apologetic.

"Is all right. *I'm* sorry. The studio is like a – is *molto caldo*."

She enjoyed being with him. There was no tension between them. In his presence she felt relaxed and happy. She was not worried what his opinion of her was, she did not feel she had to prove herself to him or impress him. She felt comfortable and at ease in his company.

He took her to a small place with fish in a tank, a peculiar little aquarium that she hoped profoundly did not contain her lunch. The water looked murky and the fish, in so far as she could tell about fish, seemed exhausted but, it turned out that she would not be expected to choose one for her meal. They were the proprietor's pets.

The interior was cool and dim and very pleasant after the noonday sun. The food was wonderful. The roasted peppers were to die for and the canneloni the tastiest she had ever sampled. The owner, fat, a bit greasy, jolly and welcoming with a spectacular gold filling in his front tooth, was right out of Central Casting.

Over lunch Luciano told her about Conrad Morheim's daughter. "She's a mess Lucy. You don't want to know. Leah Morheim! Oh God!" He stared into the middle distance and she sat and waited, admiring him. He was so good to look at; so perfect.

"I only met her father once before today. I met Leah in Roma. Through Dmitri. Dmitri is my friend. Well, sort of. He's a difficult guy to know. He's the one who owns the studio here."

"I remember," she said. "The paintings."

"Yes. He's Greek. He studied art with me," he shrugged, "not that you can teach painting. Not really. It is a gift. But you can help with the technique. Encourage direction. Bring out talents . . . what you say?"

"Latent. Latent talent," she supplied.

"Ah yes. But Dmitri . . . he is a wonderful painter. But a wild man. I am a careful portraitist. He is inspire . . . inspire . . .?"

"Inspirational."

"*Si Si*. Anyhow we hang out together in Roma.

Then one day Dmitri brings home Leah. As soon as I saw her I thought, this one is trouble. She is sulky and, such a wild thing too. She is on drugs. I know. I can tell. Dmitri is no good for her. His personality, like her father's, sets out to destroy."

"How do you mean?" Lucy was not sure she understood all this talk of wildness.

"They meet someone. They beguile them, hypnotise them, then begin to control them, manipulate them. So bit by bit they lose their personality. They change. They get like the one who is doing this to them. Their thoughts become like his, their ideas similar. They become subjugated. Then these people Conrad, Dmitri, they discard the one they have dominated. It is like an enchantment only unlike the fairy-tales they are thrown away, not married and don't live happily ever after."

"And this was what happened to Leah?"

Luciano nodded. "Yes. I think so. I do not understand all of it, but it frightened me."

"Tell me," she said.

"Well, I shared an apartment with Dmitri. In Roma. He moved Leah into his room. I did not like it."

"You did not like *her*?"

He shook his head. "No, no. I did not like her *being* there. It was our studio. We worked there. Another kind of girl might have been all right. But not Leah. Because of the drugs. When you have someone living with you who is messing about with drugs you have a . . . how you say . . . a loose cannon. Messy all over the place. Jittery. Dishonest." He paused and sighed. "She stole my money," he added. Lucy's eyes widened. "One night I awoke and she was in my room, naked, going through my pockets. She took my wallet and all the *lire* and left."

"Didn't you stop her?"

"No." He looked over her shoulder at the fish. "I was afraid of her," he said. "I am not ashamed to admit it." Lucy looked puzzled and he explained, "She had a knife."

Lucy laughed. "You were afraid of her?" she asked in disbelief.

He nodded. "Oh yes! Of course I was. I am not a *macho* fool! She stabbed a friend of Dmitri's once. Nearly killed him. He has a scar on his chest, will never go away. She attacked Dmitri many times. Violently. He would laugh. He liked it. Said he'd tame her. But there was about her a lack of . . ." he frowned, "a lack of . . ."

"Restraint?"

"Ah yes! She would go mad. Lose all control. Break things. Fight. Yet she obeyed Dmitri like a lamb once he'd dominated her. She did everything he told her. Followed him about. And he played games with her, I think to see how much control he had. Once he told her to make love to me. There in the studio. He would watch. 'You do this for me,' he told her. She nodded. Like a slave. As if it gave her pleasure to do what he told her. As if she had no will of her own."

Lucy was agog. This was not the kind of thing she

was used to hearing about. A sort of sick excitement battled inside her with disgust. How humiliating that must have been; for a woman to be asked by her lover to sleep with his friend in front of him. How degrading. Yet she was fascinated by the situation.

"Did you . . . did she . . .?"

She paused and he looked at her startled. "*Mamma mia* of course not! What do you take me for?" He was angry with her, glaring at her.

"I'm sorry," she said meekly.

"You always say that . . . stop it!"

"I didn't mean—"

"Don't keep saying I'm sorry."

"Well I am!"

He shrugged. "Is all right," he replied, recovering his good humour. "You could not know." He gave her a sweet smile. "I have no problem with women," he informed her calmly. "I do not need to do that kind of thing."

She could well believe it. Women would throw themselves at this Adonis, this beautiful specimen of manhood.

"I told Dmitri to piss off. 'Scuse me. I told him to find someone else. I don't like that sort of thing. I like to make love with girls, not go in for weird . . ." He shook his head in disgust and lit a cigarette.

They drank their espressos in silence, Lucy digesting not only the lunch but the information she had received. "Do you mind if I tell Clarissa about this?" she asked eventually. "As she is writing about the father?"

He shrugged. "Why should I mind? Everyone knew about Leah. It was no secret."

"And what happened?"

He shrugged again. "I don't know. I left for England. I had been given a scholarship to the Slade. I was to study there in London for a year!" A smile flitted across his face as if what he was remembering was very pleasant. "The English girls were . . . great fun. I liked it there." He smiled at her. "Did well too. The English have a talent for portraiture. It is what they do best. Except perhaps for Turner. I was helped a great deal."

"And Dmitri?"

"He came to England to see me. He was alone. I had a room in Earl's Court. I let him stay. Sleep on the sofa." He looked at her and laughed. "But he had many girls in England. Each night a different girl. Dmitri is very selfish and cruel. Maybe because he is Greek. The Greeks are very . . ." he clicked his fingers together, then said, "Ah! Uncompromising! That is what they are. His mamma adores her son. You know, spoils him. He is God!"

"Doesn't your mamma adore you Luciano?" she smiled at him. She could imagine a mother doting on a boy like Luciano.

He laughed. "Oh yes!" he cried fervently, "but she stands no nonsense. She hits me here," he pointed to his right temple, "if I am . . ." he sought the word.

"Cheeky?"

"Yes. If you say. If I am not a good little *bambino* do as she says." He laughed again, then serious, leaned across the table towards her and took her hand in his. "I adore women Lucy. I love the way they feel, the way they smell, the softness of them. I love every bit of them. But one thing, to me, is very important. I have respect." The large liquid eyes met hers, their expression earnest. "I love to make love to them, but I only want what they want. Dmitri! He dominates them."

"So you never found out what happened to Leah?"

"Tell the truth, I forgot about her. I remembered only when I saw Conrad Morheim today." He frowned. "I wonder what did happen to her?" he mused.

A decision was forming slowly but surely in Lucy's mind. She had missed so much in life and she knew that if she stayed in England she might never do the things a lot of girls had already done in their salad days. She'd not been in the *habit* of 'doing things' in England. But here it was different. She was being handed an opportunity on a plate and she decided that the time had come to seize her chance. If she returned to England without taking her fate in her hands the chance might never be given to her again. Oh she'd probably meet some nice guy and get married. Be happy, as such. Sort of compromise with life, but wonder every now and then what other men were like. She would become used to her husband's love-making and perhaps ponder what others did and how they did it, but having no experience would sigh and accept the fact that she would never know.

Well, fate had set her down here on this enchanted island, surrounded her with exotic flowers that perfumed the air and seduced her senses. The gods had put her in an atmosphere that was warm and relaxing and placed in her pathway a glorious man.

Lucy smiled mischievously to herself. She would go to bed with Luciano. The decision had been creeping up on her over the day. It would be easy, she knew, to get him to make love to her, rid her of the burden of her virginity. There was a bond between them, an easiness, a relaxed affinity and she wanted to experience what everyone in the world of her age, except perhaps nuns, had experienced and that only she, again except the nuns was ignorant of. She had thought about Luciano physically since she met him. She surprised herself by realising that her body wanted his. In this dozy, languorous climate, this seductive atmosphere, the beautiful young painter with his unselfconscious and affectionate personality had become irresistible to her.

She was not in love with him, she knew that. This had nothing to do with love. It was a drowsy need, a dreamlike lust. Her body had, it seemed, awakened, like the Sleeping Beauty in this lotus-eaters' land, this blossoming world and was calling out to be caressed and loved, petted and made love to.

But only by this safe young man, this beautiful being. Not by anyone else. There were men out there, like this Dmitri Papadorou who were frightening, who would demand a knowledge of her that she was not prepared to give, participation in her life that she was not prepared to share, emotional exchange that she was not prepared to bestow on anyone yet. No, Luciano could dally with her and she with him. He would not ask her for more than she could give.

"Let's go back to the studio," she said, turning her hand upward, palm-to-palm with his. "If Clarissa is not in the Piazzetta, let's go back."

It would be a sign. She would gamble. If Clarissa was there she would take it that it was not meant to be. If she was absent, then that gave her permission to go ahead.

She watched the sudden dawning in Luciano's eyes as he read her purpose, her invitation.

"Yes. Let's," he said and clicked his fingers for the bill.

"And this time lock the door," she suggested, smiling.

He smiled back at her. "Don't worry *cara*, I will."

Chapter Sixteen

This time he did lock the door. In the drowsy heat he took her clothes off slowly, so slowly.

"Have you any protection?" she asked, feeling odd about it but firm in her inexperience and in the knowledge gleaned from her magazines. It didn't happen in the movies but she was a sensible girl, not given to stupidity.

She guessed he would have protection. Luciano in his softly sensuous way would always be prepared. He did not disappoint her. "Of course," he said.

He undressed her tenderly, kissing her, leading her and she relaxed under his caresses. She did not tense up at this first invasion of her modesty and wondered at herself that she succumbed so ardently to his embraces. She blossomed under his touch like an exotic flower slowly opening up under the sun.

It was thc island, she decided, this warm and mellow place, the light so pure, the heat so relaxing, the utter strangeness of the place, its total un-Englishness that helped her lose the inhibitions that had held her captive at home.

He was even more beautiful naked. His body was

like a perfectly sculpted bronze statue. He was totally unselfconscious and showed such intense admiration at the sight of her nudity that all her fears vanished and she was drawn by him into the cocoon of his sensuality. She felt herself come alive, every tiny nerve focusing between her legs in waves of tingling sensation, so acute that she closed her eyes and opened her mouth under his soft kisses and moaned gently at the pleasure of it.

He was sweetly urgent in his love-making, arousing every bit of her so that she responded warmly. He was not fierce or harsh in his passion but slow and infinitely voluptuous. He gave himself up to sensation and drew her into the powerful and slow rhythm of his erotic river of arousal that when he at last sank into her she only gasped softly and felt her body cry out for a fiercer rhythm, a more urgent need, until there came to her a desperate little climax, sharp and sweet and a little elusive.

"It will be better," he said, trailing his finger across her face.

"It was pretty good," she told him, a little smile on her face, thinking, now I'm a woman. Thinking, so this is what it is all about.

He laughed. "So English! Pretty good! What a way to talk about love."

"I better go," she said, sitting up. She wanted to be alone to think about what she had experienced, assess her emotions. But she told him, "Clarissa will be looking for me."

"So soon? I thought we'd do it again."

"Now?" she asked naïvely.

He laughed again. "It will be better for you," he told her.

She shook her head. "No. Dear Luciano, I have enough to think about for one day." She smiled at him tenderly. He was so beautiful. She felt so comfortable with him, so natural.

"Oh dear, there is blood on the sheets," she said.

"Not much. Just a little."

"You've bedded virgins before!" she exclaimed.

A fit of giggling seized him and he curled up on the bed laughing. "*Mamma mia*, you are funny!"

She slapped his smooth round buttock. "Stop it. Stop it Luciano!" she cried, but she was not really angry. "Oh stop it!" He was like a friendly animal, a brother, a best chum.

He turned over on his back. "Bedded! It is like Shakespeare!" He pulled her towards him. "Yes, I have bedded virgins before," he told her, "but none as enchanting as you." He smiled into her eyes. "And others, not virgins. What does it matter? What does it have to do with anything?"

"Nothing Luciano," she laughed. "Nothing."

"And the washing machine is there in the little kitchen."

"Yes Luciano," she said meekly, and then as he began to kiss and touch her, "Oh my God! Oh, oh, oh!" she gasped.

He began to make love to her, this time more fiercely. Her body felt soft as cotton wool and as pliable and he played on her senses until she was swooning and it built and built inside her, boiling up and then exploding, slowly, infinitely dynamic, a long shudderingly-sweet orgasm.

"Oh Luciano. It *was* better!" she whispered at last. "It was gorgeous!"

He grinned. "I couldn't let you go away with 'pretty good' now could I?" he asked.

Chapter Seventeen

When she got back to the *pensione* Clarissa was resting. She answered Lucy's knock with a loud 'come in'. The room was darkened, the shutters closed which was just as well Lucy decided. She did not want Clarissa, who was nothing if not intuitive, giving her a hard time about Luciano, scrutinising her, asking questions.

"I don't feel at all well Lucy. My tummy is like a roller-coaster. I've taken some Immodium and I'm going to rest this evening. You go and have dinner with the crowd."

"Oh I'm sorry Clarissa. Is there anything I can do?"

A little martyred sigh came from the bed. "No dear, thank you." A sniff.

"Any work to type?"

"No Lucy, I haven't worked today. I haven't been *able* to! I thought that would have been obvious to you!" Then a wail. "Oh Lucy, this is hopeless! I'll *never* get to see this man. I'm like a rat in a cage going around and around and around getting nowhere." She stared at Lucy in the gloom. "Good

God Lucy, this will be the first time in my career that I've failed so abjectly. So *feebly*. Dear heaven I'm slipping! Getting too old."

"No. Don't say that. Of course you're not." Lucy felt awful sitting there, on her secret, not telling, seeing Clarissa's despondency.

"I think we'll go home," Clarissa announced in a determined voice. "I'm not at all happy here. I cannot find Conrad Morheim and I'm missing good English food: roasts and potatoes and puddings. And I *hate* that desiccated woman Risa and that silly fool, half-baked exile Buffy. Atrophied has-beens! So I think I'll just pack it in."

Lucy's heart sank. She could not bear to go home, not just now. She was learning so much, finding things out about herself, the world and others. She could not, would not leave now.

"Just hang on until after the Diva's party," she suggested. "It seems a pity to just give up, especially when you are very likely to meet him there." She knew Clarissa hated people who 'gave up'. Feeble she called them.

"All right," Clarissa sighed. "The party is the day after tomorrow. I suppose I better stay till then." She smiled at Lucy. "Oh I'm so selfish." Lucy thought briefly that sickness did that to people. "How did you do today without me? How did the sitting go?"

"Oh fine." Lucy caught the piercingly intent eyes on her face and hurried on, "Luciano told me all about Leah, Conrad Morheim's daughter. He knows her. Are you interested?"

Ask a cat if it is interested in cream! Clarissa hoisted herself up in the bed. "What did he say Lucy? Tell me, at once."

Lucy told her. Her employer grabbed her ever-present notebook and biro and began jotting down every now and then, in her peculiar shorthand that Lucy, for some obscure reason found *easy* to decipher. When they had exhausted the topic of Leah, Clarissa began to flag.

"Now off you go Lucy. Leave me. I want to be alone."

Lucy did not go down to the Piazzetta that night. The last people she wanted to see were the Contessa, Cliff and Buffy, but most of all she wanted to avoid Nucio's knowing eyes.

She set out in the opposite direction, walking on the cliff road around the island. Meandering along she came suddenly upon a little *trattoria* perched on the side of a sheer drop into the sea. One of the great charms of the island were these delightful little places tucked into glorious nooks and crannies. She sat at one of the tables on the terrace where the wisteria was entwined in the lattice overhead and vine leaves and bunches of grapes in bounteous profusion, though still not ripe, shaded the scented space. There were flickering candles on the tables and the waiters moved languidly as if infected by the opium-dreamy quality of the air.

Lucy ordered and ate her antipasto, her home-made ravioli and her *dolci* in leisurely fashion. She felt totally at ease, at peace, at one with everything around her. She had never before felt so relaxed, so untense. Always alert, constantly at the ready all her life, she now felt utterly unwound, a calm happiness enveloping her.

She did not think of Luciano except to feel a warm gratitude for his beauty, his gift to her body, his ability to kiss her and make love to her until she had awakened. Like the Sleeping Beauty. She did not think of England or the fact that her home had been sold, or about the deaths of her mother and Barry. She did not think of Errol or Adrian or Clarissa and her friends here. She did not speculate on what she would do if Clarissa carried out her threat and went home. She was utterly, totally, intensely in the *now*. In the moment. At peace with herself and the universe.

Under the star-studded sky, under the scented canopy of fruit and leaves and blossoms, listening to the shush-shush of the sea below her on the rocks, the distant sound of pop music on a radio; not loud enough to be interfering, far enough away to be evocative, she felt part of the vastness of the sky, grounded on the pleasant earth, part of the sea and the flowers, warmly happy and complete.

She was sipping her coffee in utter contentment when a voice startled her.

"Mind if I join you?"

She looked up in disbelief. Conrad Morheim stood over her looking down at her, smiling. Dear God! Clarissa was combing the island, chasing all over the place in pursuit of this man, desperately trying to catch up with him while she, Lucy Leighton, kept bumping into him everywhere she went. She shook her head.

"No, of course not. Please do."

"Only you look so wrapped up in your thoughts. You looked very private."

She nodded. "I was. But I'm happy for you to break in."

He sat beside her. The candlelight threw shadows over his face and his dark hair fell over his brow. There was a sprinkling of grey through it. Lucy could not guess what he was thinking.

"You look like a contented woman," he said.

"You find that strange?"

"Yes. As a matter of fact I do," he replied. "Most women are not content. They are greedy."

"You don't like women?" she asked, surprised by his remark.

"I don't like most *people*," he said. "We are a rotten species. We foul our nest. We rape the earth that nurtures us. We kill and maim and judge each other. We torment and torture. We dislike those not identical to ourselves. Oh we are not at all nice."

"How sad you should feel like that," she whispered.

"Don't you?"

"No," she said. "No."

"Do you have good reason?" he asked.

She shook her head. "No, but I think what you put out you get back. You must have at some time put out something horrible to make you feel like that."

He rose abruptly from the chair and went to the balustrade of the balcony. He leaned over it. The radio was playing the Beatles, 'Love, love me do'. Lucy hummed it. His departure from the table had not disconcerted her. She felt he was like that. Moody and unpredictable.

She said, "Everywhere I look I see beauty."

He turned. "But that's nature. That's not man."

"Men and women are capable of great goodness, courage, gallantry, and artistic genius," she protested. She did not want this discussion. It disturbed her serenity.

"Ah yes," he said. "Luciano!" Then he added, "You know why I came over to you?"

She shook her head again.

"I was sitting over there," he nodded to the other side of the terrace. She could see the remains of a meal, a crumpled napkin, a half-full wine-glass. "I saw you and I suddenly knew who you reminded me of." He smiled at her and his smile was sad. "Once, long ago when the future still held hope, when I trusted, when I believed in people's goodness, like you, I went to the theatre. I saw an actress called Mercedes Marchant who enchanted me. She was . . ." he kissed his fingers and waved the kiss into the air in a very un-English gesture, "radiant! She seemed to glide across the stage, not touching the ground, moving with infinite grace. She was not of this world. She gave off a kind of luminescence. I knew that night that magic was possible. I fell totally under her spell. I did not realise then that it was all an illusion! Play-acting!" He had been looking out over the sea, remembering. Now he came back to her and sat again. "You have exactly her face. Her look."

"Oh no! I will never have what she had." She shook her head vehemently. "No. She was beautiful. I am pretty," her tone was matter-of-fact. Then she added, "She was my mother."

"She's dead then?"

"Yes. Recently. She had Multiple Sclerosis."

He leaned back in his chair. "How cruel. For a creature of grace and light and air to be so blighted. How tragic!"

Lucy remained silent. She felt somehow that he had hijacked her mother's death and neatly pigeon-holed it and her illness and that made her angry.

"I don't think you know anything about it," she said at last.

"Of course not. Sorry," he glanced at her grimacing, "I'm always doing that. It's one of my least likeable traits."

They fell silent gazing out over the moon-drenched scene.

"God can be very cruel," he said. "That is if you believe in him. I'm not sure that I do."

"How can you see all this beauty spread before you and *not* believe in God?" Lucy asked.

"Nature," he said, "I believe in nature. And nature is unbelievably cruel. She will, *is* biting back. Our cavalier treatment of her will not go unpunished. We will live to regret it."

It irritated Lucy, this negative attitude. Clarissa had said he was fed up with the world, but she was not. She resented her mood being spoiled. She found his pessimism warped her spirit, soured her content. It was because she felt distaste for what he said that she found the courage to speak about Clarissa. She took a deep breath.

"Do you know Clarissa Bourke-Rathbone?"

"No," he shook his head, "but I know *of* her. I believe she is looking for me. I intend to avoid her." His eyes narrowed and he stared at her. "Why? Why do you ask?"

"I'm her secretary," she said and watched him digest this information.

"I see."

"Why don't you talk to her?" she asked. "She's a very good journalist. You could share your pessimism with her. You could share your bleak thoughts about people. Tell her about it. Clear the slate."

"Clear the slate?" he asked frowning.

"As I understand it, you left the cosmopolitan world, the world stage, because you were disenchanted with the politicians, with the unacceptable behaviour of greedy people. So Clarissa told me. A lot of what you predicted came true, she said. Why not review your beliefs and tell us what you feel about it all."

"I had not thought about it like that," he said. "I hadn't thought about being *right*. That did not occur to me. I am just appalled by the way the human race makes the same mistakes again, and again, and again. It is senseless. I've just felt more and more disgusted by what the species gets up to, the indiscriminate *carelessness*. I take no pleasure in being *right*."

"Well, why don't you tell her that. You never know, it may do some good, reach some people. Think about it. Give Clarissa her interview."

Then we can stay a little longer in paradise. How awful I am, she thought, Conrad Morheim would despise me if he knew how self-interest drives me.

"Well . . . put that way . . ." he hesitated. "I thought of her as a vulture trying to pick my bones, but you make it sound not too uninteresting."

"I look on the bright side of things," Lucy said. "The positive side. But you must not let on you know me. You must promise me that."

"You mean you did not tell her our paths have crossed? You continue to surprise me Lucy."

"No. I didn't tell her." Lucy gave him a straight look. "We're going to the Diva's party on Saturday. Will you be there?"

"At Bebe Gianocco's? Well I wasn't going to, but," he stared at her, "I will now if that is what you want." He gave her a wistful smile. "I would do a lot to make you happy little Lucy. Keep that look on your face, the look you had before I broke in on your reverie."

She blushed and said hurriedly, "You'll give Clarissa her interview?"

"Yes, yes, don't hassle me please. There's only so much of this I can take."

"Oh I'm so glad."

"Why not? I can put the record straight. Though who'll be interested in reading such an interview I can't imagine. I should think most people have forgotten me."

"Look here Mr Morheim—"

"Conrad please." He looked at her amused. "Am I that formidable?"

She ignored his comment and continued, "Conrad. You haven't lived in England for a long time. No matter what you think most people there want to keep this world a beautiful place. They'll be interested in what you say, what you think, how you were right a decade ago. And," she glanced up as a waiter passed, "*Il conto per favore* . . . and I think you are like a small belligerent boy sulking in a corner to permit all the damage to happen and not try to *stop* it. You are crying ''S'not fair!' but you are making no effort to rise up and protest."

"I did. Long ago. It got me nowhere."

"That is not true." Two spots of red had appeared on Lucy's cheeks. "It got you branded the most unpopular man in England! So Clarissa says. That is a triumph after all when you think about it, isn't it? Galileo was not popular. Darwin was not popular. Freud was not popular. Who wants popular?"

He threw back his head and laughed. It changed his face and he suddenly looked quite young. "You know you're right! You are quite a little lady Lucy Leighton and you've shaken up this grouchy old war-horse. All right. You've swung it. I'll be at Bebe's on Saturday."

The waiter came with the bill. Conrad said, "Let me," but Lucy shook her head.

"No. I'd rather take care of it myself." Then leaving the *lire* on the table she stood. "Saturday then. And remember don't let on you know me."

"All right. Though why you don't want to tell her we met here tonight by accident and you persuaded me to give her an interview I can't think. After all, it's true and think how grateful she'd be."

"Clarissa is afraid she's getting old. Maybe she is. But if she can believe she managed to get to you by herself she'll gain a whole lot more confidence. Don't you see?"

"Oh yes I do, sweet Lucy. She's a lucky woman, having someone like you around." There was admiration in his eyes and she felt herself drawn to him as if she had no control and might drown in those troubled depths.

"There are a lot like me Conrad," she remarked, pulling her cardigan over her shoulders, holding out her hand.

"I doubt it Lucy. I doubt it. When it comes to cash or the good of the environment I have always found that people take the cash."

He took her hand in both of his, bent his head and kissed it. Her hand quivered in his, like a captured bird that wanted to flutter away. She looked at him, startled. The dark eyes looked into hers. She was aware suddenly of his masculinity, of the texture of his skin, the scent of it. He was male and tough; grown-up she thought. A man to Luciano's boy. He is fully developed, she reflected, and therefore scary.

"Let me walk you back," he offered.

"No. No thank you Conrad. I'd prefer to meet you Saturday," she said firmly.

She felt she had to get away from this magnetism. Escape. She almost ran down the narrow path, waving back to him, heart thumping crazily. What on earth was the matter with her that she should be fearful of this man?

Outside the hotel she stopped a moment to collect herself. Then straightening up she went in. She peeped into Clarissa's room but her employer was fast asleep. She went to her own room and throwing open the windows went out on the balcony.

A mosquito-repellent candle in a terracotta pot flickered and gutted, sending up blasts of strange perfume that fought valiantly with the sweet scents of the night. She leaned out looking over the parapet. Down on the Piazzetta the lights twinkled and danced and people milled around and every now and then laughter floated up on the air. In the harbour, little boats bobbed and out at sea, past the Faraglioni, a yacht lay at anchor. She could see people in evening dress on the deck lit by strings of fairy lights. Women in glittering garments and men in white dinner-jackets sipping drinks. Music floated over the water, old-fashioned music, sentimental and sad.

Night-scented jasmine in the garden below exuded its glorious perfume, vying with the mosquito candle. Santo Stefano looked like a marble palace and the moon washed everything in silver.

"So this is life," Lucy whispered, her heart still beating violently. "So this is *living*." Then smiling, wrapping her arms around her body she whispered again to herself, "I like it! I *love* it!"

Chapter Eighteen

The party at Bebe Gianocco's was strangely surrealistic. Everyone there seemed to Lucy a survivor from another time, another era. She felt she had been catapulted into an early movie by Dreyer, Fritz Lang or Cocteau.

The villa had the vastness of the nineteen-thirties. It was reminiscent of the Villa Azura and all the other villas on the island, inhabited or uninhabited. It was marble-floored, Roman statues abundant, flowers and greenery everywhere. The hall led directly to a huge room that had a terrace running its length and off it through an arch a smaller room where a buffet was laid out. In the main room a Steiner grand piano stood in a position of prominence, open with sheet music on its stand.

The Diva did not put herself out to make sure Lucy and Clarissa were introduced to people. Instead she left her guests very much to their own devices and sat on her sofa and received them in the manner of Madame Recamier. A white-jacketed butler and a house-boy served champagne.

During the buffet the groups of guests gathered

around the long trestle table, white damask clothed, groaning with aspiced chicken and fish, *foie gras*, caviar and fruit. They ate as if there might be a famine next day.

Buffy sat in a chair and smoked and drank copiously but did not eat. Cliff chatted to a very twitchy Clarissa who jumped at every new arrival, alert for Conrad Morheim's entrance.

The Contessa whispered to her, "He's *promised* he'd be here. I telephoned him and he gave his word. Relax Clarissa *cherie*. Don't worry," and she hurried off to greet her friends. She seemed in her element here among these people.

They were waxwork-like, strange and gallant little men and women carved from the same mould; shrunken in stature, pretending they were still in the first flush of youth, reassured by each other. They were, to Lucy, both tragic and touching. They stood or sat about in groups, chattering meaninglessly, drinking their wine, brightly determined to enjoy themselves.

Dressed to the nines, the women's wrinkled chests revealed by low-cut *décolletage* were decorated with amazing jewels, scraggy arms left bare, red nails on clawlike hands, they flirted coyly with white-haired men whose parchment faces, dyed eyebrows and uneasy teeth revealed a vanity both foolish and endearing. There was something grotesque about the gathering and only Clarissa and Nucio, the Diva and Lucy bore any resemblance to your average *homo sapiens*.

And of course Conrad Morheim, when he arrived.

When he entered the room there was a stir. Clarissa clutched Lucy's arm as if she could not believe her eyes. There he actually was, in the flesh.

Women fluttered like chickens at the approach of someone near their coop; high, excited chirping and squawking, and when he pulled over a small gilt chair and sat near Bebe, speaking softly to her, there was a general female sigh of regret. They were not the chosen ones this evening.

The men glared at him. They did not like him. He was against everything they stood for and they resented and feared him for that. He wanted their world to topple, thought them pirates and vandalisers and they wondered by what right he condemned them.

Most of the people there had, once upon a time, been important. They had belonged to outmoded monarchies, Princes of Moldavia or Ruritania, never-never lands long ago left behind, forgotten grandeur in palaces that were now museums in countries subsequently erased from the map. They were used to a way of life that they were trying, with the aid of their wealth, to perpetuate. It was a way of life considered gross now in the austere Nineties.

Some others were businessmen who had made it big but were found out in peculiar scams, insider trading, arms deals. They had had to leave their own lands to escape prison and disgrace in a past era when dishonour meant ostracisation.

Today no one cared; honour was out of fashion.

They had come to Capri, out of reach of the laws of their own lands and formed their own elite little ex-pat society. All the playgrounds of the rich: South of France, Marbella, Majorca, Sardinia, Barbados, Turkey and South America had similar colonies where these exiles spent the money so dishonestly acquired and sat out their remaining days in a style as nearly magnificent as they had been used to at home. Their clothes were the best, beautifully tailored, perfectly crafted. Their wives' scrawny necks and wrists were be decked in jewels and they were draped in Valentino and St Laurent with Gucci belts and Hermès scarves and Ferragamo shoes. They all looked as if they were out of some weird *dance macabre*.

Lucy shivered. She had been surrounded by lush beauty, fecundity and ripeness. She had been filled with a sensation of the blossoming of the world and herself. Now she was aware of the decay that follows ripeness and it brought her up sharply and unpleasantly. Perhaps this was what Conrad saw.

Clarissa was thrilled to see Conrad. Her face had lit up at his entrance and hope dawned in her eyes. She glanced at Lucy and whispered, "Bingo!"

It was after the meal and they had all settled down to hear the Diva sing. Conrad was delaying her.

At last he stood. He kept faith with Lucy and showed no sign of recognition, which was as well for Lucy was having great difficulty controlling her nerves. The sight of him in his tuxedo, his elegant length, his sombre eyes, his lean face activated her pulse-rate, her heart bounded, her throat became suddenly dry and she had difficulty swallowing.

The Diva had waved him away and there was an excited little flutter as the women guests made room for him.

Bebe prepared to perform, rising from her couch and smoothing down her skirts.

Conrad chose to sit beside Clarissa, between her and Lucy on a sofa, and as he sat he turned his face to Lucy and winked. He took care that no one else saw. She giggled and Clarissa glared at her and introduced herself to Conrad who greeted her gravely.

The Diva stood beside the grand piano, her large bulk resting on tiny feet. She opened her mouth and began.

It was like listening to angels. From that large woman a series of notes of such purity and spirituality poured that Lucy felt a huge lump in her throat and tears sprang to her eyes. She could *feel* the glorious sound sink into the depths of her soul. Around the room, listening to the arias of Verdi, Puccini and Donizetti, the ancient guests were obviously moved. Tired eyes sparkled suddenly with hope, old faces, inspired from within, revealed the boy or girl that had once inhabited that exhausted and ageing skin. Lucy seeing Cliff, tears rolling unheeded down his face felt suddenly ashamed. She had been contemptuous of these people and, she thought suddenly, none of us have the right to judge. She realised that, one day that will be me.

She sat breathless, listening to the glorious music. At the piano the accompanist, a thin little man with dyed patent-leather-look black hair played with passion while the Diva poured her heart out in divine song.

As Lucy listened she felt Conrad's breath on her cheek, the smell of his skin again near her. It was musky and fresh, like the trees and the sea and she felt intoxicated. His hand lay across the back of the sofa, tanned, fine dark hairs, square-cut nails. She wanted to stroke it and her insides clenched with the violence of her feelings. She glanced at him, his strong thick neck, brown against his white evening shirt, the slant of his cheek, the sensitive curve of his mouth.

He must have felt her gaze for he turned suddenly and looked at her. His eyes stared into hers and she gulped. The look was naked. Desire, pain and anger struggled there, staring into her soft gaze. For some reason she thought of her mother, her mother's eyes. Then, as quickly, Conrad turned away, leaving her shaken.

Eventually the Diva stopped amid protests. The last note she sang hung for minutes on the enchanted air, trembling, then died away.

No one applauded. For a moment all were silent. *Then* they clapped. "Brava!" "Bellissima!" "Magnifico!" "Brava!" It was all anyone could desire and the Diva accepted the homage with a wide smile and a gracious nod of her head.

"Dear, dear Conrad," Clarissa exclaimed as soon as she possibly could, as soon as the clapping died down. "I have been searching for you *everywhere*. At last I find you!"

Lucy stood and moved away from them. She felt as if she was suffocating. The room was open to the stars and she went out alone on to the verandah and sat in one of the wicker chairs there. No one missed her.

They all knew each other, the little band of socialites, multi-racial exiles hanging out together, desperately trying to pretend that the world where once they shone had not, after all, vanished.

Lucy felt her beating heart. It seemed it would burst from her breast and fly to him across the room. She wondered suddenly why Luciano was not there. She would have been grateful for his company. He was so reassuring.

She had avoided him the previous day. She had had a lot of work to do for Clarissa who had spent the Thursday doing research and had a huge pile of notes for Lucy to type. Lucy had not minded at all. She had wanted that Friday to herself, to rest within herself and absorb what was happening to her. She did not want to see anyone at all.

Luciano had telephoned several times but she had told them at the desk to say she was busy working and would phone back when she could. After all, Luciano knew she was not here on a holiday; she had to work.

She had found the typing just what she needed and

had made up her mind to call him next day, Saturday, but Clarissa had dragged her across to Anacapri to look at the tomb where Conrad Morheim's wife was buried, and she had never got around to phoning Luciano.

The headstone was marble. A simple message read:

'Mara. Wife of Conrad. I will never forget.'

"How strange!" Clarissa murmured. Lucy had been puzzled too. An extraordinary message. A literary man. An intellectual man, and the cryptic message. *'I will never forget.'*

"Perhaps," Lucy said to Clarissa, "it was a special message, a private meaning for him that people like us, outsiders, could not be expected to understand."

Clarissa shrugged. "Still seems strange," she said. "'I will never forget'."

I will never forget. Lucy thought about it now as she sat in the dark and idly let time slip by, content to be alone.

"You OK?"

It was Cliff, leaning over the verandah, puffing a cigarette.

"Me? I'm fine!" She liked Cliff. She felt sorry for him. His writer's block seemed to her an excuse. She felt that Cliff had gotten out of the habit of work and just couldn't be bothered to sit at his desk and discipline himself to create. The three books he had written decades ago were classics, but the last, published in nineteen sixty-seven seemed to have sucked him dry and he whiled away the hours on Capri where he had come to avoid taxes (everyone knew that in Italy no one paid any taxes), sipping wine, flirting, listening and watching. But never picking up his pen.

When Buffy laughed gently at Cliff's sloth Clarissa had tapped her nose with her finger and said, "Wait and see. Wait and see. I think Cliff is *absorbing*. He's taking things in. He'll suddenly produce and we'll all be taken aback."

When she said this Cliff smiled fatuously and remained silent. Lucy smiled up at him now.

"Clarissa says it's your first trip out of dear old England," he said.

"Yes."

"Be careful! It is very seductive down around the Med," he told her. "It uses you up. It takes the edge off."

"I gather that." She could think of nothing to say. The night was velvety blue, the air still, the sounds of the fabulous voice of their hostess echoing in her head, so that words seemed superfluous.

"I remember your mother." Cliff glanced over his shoulder at her. His face was pink and puffy but his eyes were kind. "She was something else."

"Yes. She was."

At that moment there was a disturbance. Lucy could hear voices raised in argument. She and Cliff exchanged glances. There was a pause, then one of the servants emerged on to the verandah and came up to Lucy.

"There is someone at the door for you Miss Leighton," he told her.

It could only be Luciano. Everyone else she knew was here. Embarrassed, she rose, said her excuses to Cliff, then walked through the suddenly silent room, everyone's eyes following her progress. She went into the marble hall where she found she was right. Luciano paced up and down smoking furiously.

"What are you doing here?" she asked in a whisper, acutely aware of the expectant silence in the other room where ears were straining to hear what was being said. They could see her there with Luciano and she felt horribly spotlit.

"I phone you, I phone you, you don' answer. I call and call, you are not available. Why do you act like this? After . . ."

"Shush!" She put her finger to her lips. "Luciano hush. Before you say something you regret." Luciano's face was a study in conflicting emotions, but mainly anger wrestled with hurt pride and distress. Lucy was confused by his emotions. She had not yet learned that two people who share an experience may not feel the same way about it.

"Oh! So that's it. You are regretting it! Regretting me!"

"No, no Luciano. Keep your voice down! This is not the place—"

"Not where your friends can hear! Oh I am so sorry! I do not mean to disturb you . . . what do you say? . . . butt in. I do not mean to butt in. I suppose I wait until you *condescend* to talk to me again, return my calls." He looked at her and to her horror she saw tears in his eyes. "You have *used* me Lucy. That is what you have done. Used me."

He turned from her in disgust and stormed out, past the expressionless butler into the night.

Lucy sat down abruptly on a marble seat in an alcove. She was shaken by what had just happened, shaken and confused. She had not realised Luciano might not feel as she did, might not appreciate her need to be alone. It had not entered her mind that he might feel let down; betrayed. She had been moving through the days and nights since he had made love to her self-obsessed, in a daze of physical and mental well-being. But she had been, she realised now, thinking only of herself, self-absorbed, unconcerned about him and how he might be feeling. A tear slid down her cheek.

Conversation had broken out once more in the next room. Chatter, laughter, the clink of glasses, the buzz of a party. She looked up. The butler still stood by the door as if he suspected she might need to leave and he must be at the ready. It was what she wanted to do most. Run away. She did not know what to think, how to cope, what she was supposed to do now. She had no previous experience to go by. She felt insensitive and clumsy.

"Are you all right?" Conrad Morheim stood before her, glass in hand, intent eyes upon her.

"No I'm not," she whispered, voice breaking,

glancing into thc other room, terrified in case someone saw her.

"Don't worry. It will pass. Everything does."

It helped. His calm voice. She didn't know why, but it helped. He sounded so reassuring.

"You'll look back on this one day, probably one day soon and it will appear trivial. You'll say, I wonder why it seemed so important then."

"You don't understand," she said.

"Oh yes I do. Someone, I imagine in this case Luciano," (Oh why did this have to happen, why, why, why? He'd think her in love with the painter. He'd think . . . he'd think . . .) "has done or said something you don't like. It is hurt pride. We all get angry when people don't behave as we want them to. Or expect them to. Am I right?" She nodded, reluctantly. "Well then. Sleep is best. Tomorrow all will seem a little better. Next week it will be gone. Next year you'll have completely forgotten the whole incident."

"Did everyone hear?"

He laughed. "No. It was just voices raised. But is that so important? What they think?" She looked doubtful.

"I suppose not."

"I'm always rescuing you from something or another." He smiled at her. "Little Lucy. Innocent Lucy."

"I am not!" She protested, surprised at the vehemence in her voice.

"Oh no. I forgot. Luciano!" She wanted to object,

deny even *knowing* Luciano, but at that moment Clarissa sailed into the hall.

"Ah there you are Lucy. What on earth was that all about?"

By now Lucy wanted to die. She wanted to disappear.

Conrad turned to Clarissa. "Your secretary forgot an appointment with her portraitist. You know how sensitive and volatile artists can be. Luciano is annoyed. Your secretary is distressed."

"Oh dear, dear, dear. Don't mind him Lucy. You mustn't allow him to upset you. Gosh Lucy, sometimes I deplore your guilelessness."

"It is enchanting though," Conrad remarked and Clarissa gave him a sharp glance. "I'll see you both tomorrow?"

"I thought I would interview you alone." Clarissa pursed her lips primly and frowned. It was obvious she was puzzled by Conrad's interest, however casual, in Lucy.

"No," he replied, his tone definite. "No! I would like your secretary to be present."

Clarissa raised an eyebrow. "It is not usual," she said.

"I know. But then *I* am not usual." He gave Clarissa a charming smile. "I want a third party there as a precaution." He looked squarely at Clarissa. "I am quite sure you would never *intentionally* misrepresent or misquote me. However, it is better to have an independent witness in case there is any dispute." He cocked his head. "Don't you agree?"

"I suppose so." Clarissa was not going to jeopardise her chances of the interview with him.

At this moment Bebe came into the hall. "Conrad, darling, surely you are not leaving?"

"I'm off," Clarissa said, then turning to Lucy, "I said your goodbyes for you Lucy. I thought you'd prefer it."

Conrad said, "I must go. Perhaps I can accompany you ladies some of the way?"

Clarissa was delighted. Anything that brought her nearer to Conrad excited her.

"All's well," she whispered to Lucy. "Perhaps we won't have to leave Capri just yet after all."

Chapter Nineteen

Lucy sat in the shadows of the large marble-floored room in the Villa Azura, looking through an arch as if at a picture through a frame into the sun-drenched world outside: the hillside, the luxuriant gardens, the sparkling sea below. She felt cool in the shade as she watched the sweat roll down the gardener's naked back as he bent over the hydrangeas. He was an old man and his wiry body was burnt toffee-brown. He wore faded blue jeans and a battered straw hat on his head and he toiled over the plants, occasionally straightening up and stretching himself as if his limbs had locked. She thought he looked younger than the men she had met at the Diva's party, yet she felt sure he was actually older.

This was the third day she had sat staring out at the endlessly beautiful and fascinating scene. The routine was always the same. They arrived, Clarissa with notebooks flying everywhere and a tape-recorder that always ran out of tape so that when Lucy was typing later that evening she had to yo-yo between Clarissa's notes and the recordings and make sense of it all. She always saw to it that

Clarissa had extra tapes but the journalist invariably got so caught up in what Conrad was saying that she would not take the time to change it.

They were ushered into this room every morning by the oriental servant, Han Su, forever flanked by his huge black dogs. They would wait, Clarissa busily revising what they had already covered, rehearsing questions she wanted to ask. Lucy would stare at the lovely statues resting serenely in their alcoves, and the tapestry that covered one wall of the room. It depicted a medieval hunting scene and was full of fascinating detail. She tried to identify falcons, hawks and sparrow-hawks, the species of dogs and flowers woven there.

Conrad would arrive. He sat in the same high-backed winged chair also in shadow. He brought with him a contained energy and a gloom and he spoke to Clarissa softly so Lucy had to strain to hear him. The words came from him reluctantly.

Lucy listened intently and though Clarissa had given her a jotter she never had any call to use it. She could never make up her mind what to write down. She did not know what she was doing there but was glad she was included. Just being in his presence made her happy. She sat with the jotter in her lap and listened as Conrad spoke.

Conrad always greeted Lucy impartially. He was off-hand with her as if they had never spoken to each other before; as if she was indeed merely Clarissa's secretary and a stranger. She did not know what to make of his attitude. She knew Clarissa was here because she, Lucy, had prevailed upon Conrad to give the interview but not by a glance did he betray that this was so. Lucy felt disappointed, desperately lonely, excluded as if she had been shut out.

She knew her attitude was unreasonable. After all what could he do? What did she expect him to do? She had asked for secrecy and that was precisely what he was giving her, yet she was suffering like a child from a strong sense that it was not fair.

He talked about his childhood, a lonely little boy growing up without a mother in a large gloomy rectory in Leeds. His father had been a devout and holy man with little love in him. A severe man. "He preached Christianity, paraded his Christianity but I don't think he *understood* it," Conrad said. "Lots of people don't, you know. They miss the whole point of Christ's message. *He* missed out all the bits about love which when you think about it, is most of it. He fed the poor, he gave away his money and worldly goods, he was principled, honest and kind but there was no laughter in him, no enjoyment, no love. He despised the people he helped. He was a perfectionist and thought that anyone who did not measure up was deficient in holiness. I was his son, his only child, so I too had to be perfect."

"He did not understand Christianity yet he was a rector?"

"He made Christianity selective. He *excluded* a lot of people, in fact most people were, in his opinion, unworthy. Especially the marginalised ones that if I read the gospels correctly Christ took particular care to include in his entourage. My father believed in a vengeful God who hated the sinner, the odd-man-out, the homosexual, the divorced, the illegitimate, the *mother* of the illegitimate. He hated them too as he believed God must. He believed God would reject all these, cast them out into darkness. I asked him what about the thief on the cross and he dodged that one. I asked him had not God come to *save* sinners and you know what he said?"

"No."

"He said, 'There are some Conrad beyond the pale. They do not deserve to be saved.' That's what my father preached. Charming isn't it?"

"Your mother died?" Clarissa, Lucy thought, was a brilliant interviewer. She always let Conrad run on until he was obviously exhausting that particular avenue, then she would gently prompt him, ask a question softly, never expressing an opinion of her own, always sympathetic.

"Yes. She died before I knew her. She was always fragile and I don't think living with my father helped. She became ill when I was about two years old. I think my father sapped her will to live and she died that year. I do not remember her at all." There was infinite sadness in his voice and Lucy ached to put her arms around him and comfort him.

"So your father brought you up?"

"Yes. I got my deeply negative view of the world from him." He smiled bitterly. "It has never left me, this awareness of the evil in mankind. The awareness of the division between the rich and the poor. The comfortable and the uncomfortable. Life is a bitch. Unreasonably unfair. There is a poem by William Blake . . ." Here he paused, then quoted softly in his deep baritone, the words echoing in the room:

"'Every night and every morn,
Some to misery are born,
Every morn and every night,
Some are born to sweet delight,
Some are born to sweet delight,
Some are born to endless night.'"

He thought a moment, then said, "It is cruel that. This world. No reason given. Arbitrary and unfair. Simple chance decides whether we fall into the lap of luxury or into deepest poverty."

Clarissa scribbled and there was silence in the room. A bluebottle buzzed, circling the ceiling then droned its way back outside.

"You went to University?"

"First time I laughed was in college. Really laughed, you know belly-laughed."

Lucy could not see him, his face was in shadow, but there was pain in his voice. "I remember discovering Peter Cook and Dudley Moore. I remember *That Was The Week That Was* and being incensed about injustice. I began to write. It was a time of protest. Young people rising up against the old tenets, against injustice and blind acceptance of an old order. I got published easily. Everyone was terribly passionate in those days about injustice." He paused. "Today all the energy and anger of youth seems directed towards self. *Me. My survival. My job situation.* In those days even the poor cared about others."

"What disillusioned you?"

"Haven't you been listening," his voice was harsh. Clarissa had boobed. "My father encouraged me to see the dark side of life."

"And afterwards?"

"Thatcherism. Thatcherism disillusioned, or rather confirmed my opinion of people. The cult of 'I'm all right Jack' and step over the bodies of your friends and the poor to get what you want. The cruelty of 'Get on your bikes', the birth of the incentive to cheat and swindle but don't get found out. That government made greed fashionable." He sighed. "But this is old stuff. It's boring."

"Where it's led to is not boring."

"No. You are right. It has led us to where we are now in a world that is being destroyed by us because of the greed of governments and industrialists. Money, money, money is the anthem. Oh it sickens me. We are the architects of our own destruction and slowly but surely we are beginning to take stock of what we've done . . . are doing."

It was the third day when Clarissa reached this point in the talks. She nodded, then looked up and asked, "And then you married Mara?" There was silence. After a few moments Clarissa asked, "How did you two meet?" She was persisting, her first mistake in Lucy's opinion.

Conrad stood and left the room.

For a moment Clarissa thought he had simply gone to get something, photographs or a drink, but Lucy knew he was not coming back. He did not want to talk about his wife.

They waited but nothing happened. Lucy could hear the gardener talking in Italian to someone below them; a woman. No one came to tell them the interview was over.

At length Clarissa rose. "Well, that's all for today I suppose," she sighed.

He never asked them to stay for lunch which Clarissa thought was very rude and unfeeling. "The least he could do, offer us luncheon. Heavens we come all this way and all he offers us is a drink."

"You forget Clarissa, he does not really *want* this interview," Lucy said.

They had lunch in the Piazzetta with the crowd. They were all fascinated and wanted every detail of what was going on in the Villa Azura, but Clarissa proved herself discreet and gave them titbits but no real information.

"He left the room today when I asked him about his wife," she said to Cliff.

"He was mad about her," Cliff said. "Adored her. When she died his friends said he lost his will to live. Since then he has shut himself away from everyone and everything and only comes out when the Diva gives a party. You are very lucky to get to see him at all." He smiled at Clarissa. "But then, how could he refuse such a charming lady as you? Eh?"

Clarissa smirked, glanced coyly up at Cliff under her eyelashes.

Lucy's heart sank. All she knew was that it upset her when anyone said Conrad Morheim adored his wife, and people said it all the time.

"He was depressed about the world *before* she died. Afterwards it amounted to a loathing. He rejected life itself," Cliff added.

"How could he? In a place like this?" Lucy cried.

"It is not the place Lucy. It is how he *sees* it. What *you* see and what *he* sees are two different things."

"Did you know her Cliff?" Lucy asked. Cliff knew who she meant.

He nodded. "Sure. She was gorgeous. Typical Italian beauty."

"Yes but what was she *like*?"

"Smouldering. That was how the papers described her. Masses of dark hair. Big passionate brown eyes. Wide mouth. Fabulous body. A real glamour girl."

Lucy sighed. The exact opposite of me, she thought.

"If you want to know what she was like get the video of *La Via della Rosa*. It's been reissued. It was the movie that made her famous."

Clarissa pounced on this. "Get it Lucy. Get it at once."

There was a video recorder in the lounge of the *pensione*. The proprietor said they could use it any time but they had so far no cause.

Lucy got the video. That afternoon, instead of a

siesta, Clarissa watched the video. Lucy watched it too. Clarissa impressed on her that she need not, that there was no call for her to waste her time and Lucy said she loved Italian films. It was a lie and she was surprised to hear herself announcing this but she wanted an end to the fuss. She had told Clarissa over and over that anyone who watched television or videos in this glorious place had to be an idiot. But this, for her, was different. She *had* to find out what Mara looked like.

Mara was exactly as Cliff described her. A dark voluptuous siren flaunting spectacular good looks and a magnificent body. She was the type of woman men lusted after. She had a body a cartoonist might sketch, an elongated eighteen-inch waist which eventually swelled into large upstanding breasts and generous hips. Long legs with plump calves and long narrow ankles in high heels. Her mouth, bee-stung lips, was sulky, her huge dark eyes challenged. This was Lucy's impression of her.

When she came on the screen Clarissa drew in a breath. "I can't quite see her with Conrad," she mused. "I'd thought of a more classical type, more romantic, less earthy. More Alida Valli, or Isabella Rossellini. This one is so obvious. Ah well, I hate to say it, but all men Lucy, seem to be governed by their willies."

"*Clarissa*! Shush!"

Lucy watched the movie with narrowed eyes. It was not a great film, not quality, not comparable with Visconti, De Sica or Antonioni. It was about a family barely surviving in a Rome slum, their loves, their hates. Mara played the daughter, working in a factory plagued by the unwanted attentions of a particularly ugly and unpleasant landlord whom she ultimately kills. He tries to rape her and in the struggle she pushes him over the rail from the sixth floor of the block. He dies and when the *carabinieri* arrive the neighbours cover for the girl, swearing she had nothing to do with it. She gets away with it, walking away from the camera with her boyfriend into the country and a new life. The End.

When it was over Lucy sighed. Clarissa said, "Exactly!" Then she asked, "What did you think of her Lucy?"

Lucy frowned. "Well, either she was a very great actress and put on all that peasant provocative stuff—"

"Which I doubt," Clarissa interpolated.

"Or she was a bitch."

"My sentiments exactly." Clarissa sounded triumphant. "I don't care what anyone says it looks to me like a terrible mismatch. I cannot see that woman and Conrad in love, not for the life of me. But I can see them crazy about each other in a destructive death-struggle kind of way. That I *can* see."

"What do you mean Clarissa?" Lucy asked, bewildered.

"Love can be as destructive as it can be nurturing Lucy. Sadly too, men get totally besotted by bitches. They do much better in the passion stakes than so-called nice girls. Tomorrow, when we go to the

Villa Azura I think I know the right question to ask. Tomorrow I think Conrad will tell us the truth."

"If he sees us at all."

"If he sees us," Clarissa agreed. "We'll just have to hope he does."

Lucy had not seen Luciano since the Diva's party. It was not because she did not wish to, rather because she was uncertain how to approach him. When she had time to think she realised how insensitive her behaviour was. She did the thing her mother always urged her to do: put herself in his place. If the roles had been reversed she could see how hurtful her refusal to answer calls or see him must be. Reluctantly she admitted she had not behaved very well but she had no clue how to mend matters. Nevertheless she decided that evening to go and see him.

Luciano's hurt proved short-lived. He had a sunny temperament and did not harbour resentments. He'd got caught up in his work and the painting was finished.

"You see! Is it not *perfecto*!" He pulled her into the studio, his face excited. "Look . . . what do you think?"

She caught her breath. The portrait was a mirror-image of herself. But it was more, much more. He had managed to convey her innocence, her vulnerability, but underneath he showed a wisdom, a tiredness, a sort of ancient knowledge. There she was, young, pretty, untried and deep in the eyes the experience of ages.

"My eyes look *old*," she said.

He nodded. "I know. Something in your past, but *not* men, not sex, taught you about suffering, pain and death."

"Are you still angry with me Luciano?" she asked.

"No. Not now. I was at first. We have a nice time together. I don't understand why you cut me out. It was hurtful."

"It was such a big thing for me Luciano. I wanted to think about it all. I . . ." she shrugged, "I wanted to understand how I felt."

"And you gave no thought to how *I* felt?"

She looked at him squarely. "No," she admitted, "I didn't. I'm sorry."

"Oh it is all right," he responded, "it is not important." Then he looked at the painting. "You like it?"

"It is superb," she told him truthfully. "I'd prefer to be prettier, but it is wonderful."

"Thank you."

They sat in the window drinking wine and talked, relaxed with each other.

"Did you know Mara Morheim?" she asked when the subject of the portrait was exhausted and he had ordered Lucy to stop apologising for her selfishness and her silence these last days.

"The English apologise all the time, so stop. Understand?"

"Yes," Lucy replied obediently.

"Yes, I knew Mara. Why do you ask?"

"I saw a movie of hers today."

"So?"

"So, I did not like her," she said.

"Women did not like Mara. But men did."

"Why?"

He laughed. "Lucy you are innocent! Mara was everything men fantasise about. She was *trouble*. A little exaggerated in the places men like: big boobs, big lips. Plump but firm backside. All curves. Provocative. She was provocative. All that hair. And the eyes promised sin."

"Gosh!"

"Mara looked at you and you knew she would be trouble but you wanted her anyway. She would be worth it."

"Did you?"

"All the men did."

"That's not answering the question. Did *you*?"

"I thought I had answered the question. I said *all* men. Not *some*. Yes, I did."

He pulled her to him then and began to kiss her. His lips tasted of wine. She melted into him, this time knowing what she wanted, ready for the experience, her body languid and pliable with desire.

They made love in a softly erotic pleasurable way. They helped each other, excited each other, touched, titillated and responded to each other until moving together, pushing into each other's sweet wet warmth they came together, a shuddering long and exquisite climax that went on and on until they fell exhausted in each other's arms.

Afterwards, in her own bed in the hotel, Lucy

acknowledged that it was the experience she thought about most, not the person she had shared it with. Oh she *cared* about Luciano but he was not her prime preoccupation; her body was. She did not think: Luciano, oh my darling Luciano, that was wonderful. She thought: That was wonderful. That was stupendous. Thank you Luciano.

How strange that was. She supposed she should be ashamed but her body felt too relaxed and she felt too drowsy and replete and she fell into a deep untroubled sleep deciding she would sort it all out tomorrow.

But tomorrow brought Conrad and his story into her life again and cast out all thoughts of Luciano.

Chapter Twenty

They went next day to the Villa Azura. As usual Han Su let them in. As usual Clarissa sat on the sofa opposite the winged chair and Lucy sat apart in the embrasure. As usual Conrad entered a short time later. He announced, "Let me make one thing clear: I will not talk about my wife."

"You never loved her did you?" Clarissa said it softly, so softly it seemed like a whisper from something else; some wraith or ghost in the room.

Conrad drew a shuddering breath and walked over to another arch that looked out over the harbour below. The sun was hot and flood-lit the scene with iridescent light. Everything outside was brilliantly technicoloured, everything inside was in shadow. Did he cast so dark a gloom? Lucy wondered. There was a pause.

"How did you guess?" he asked at last.

"I saw, *La Via della Rosa*." Clarissa told him. "It does not take much insight to realise that you have little in common with the woman in that film. I can believe that you fell passionately for her but not that you loved her."

There was another pause and when he at last moved Lucy thought, that like the day before, he was going to leave the room. But he did not. He came and sat in his chair.

"Everyone wants to talk about our *love*. Our ideal *love*. And I cannot."

"Why can't you simply tell the truth?" Clarissa asked.

"You don't understand," he replied.

"It's simple. The world thought you loved Mara. Everyone believed the story. But it was not true. Why not say so? It's no big deal . . ."

"You don't understand," he repeated, his voice weary.

"What don't I understand?" Clarissa sounded gentle, prompting softly.

"You see, I killed her. I murdered her."

Everything was still, not a leaf stirred, no bird sang. Lucy held her breath. Clarissa did not move a muscle.

"Oh God, why did I tell you that! You see, I *have* to perpetuate the myth. I killed her."

"And?" Clarissa whispered.

"Isn't that enough!" His voice was bitter. "I'm so tired. So tired. I've lived with it for so long. So long!"

There was another silence. Clarissa waited. "I was obsessed with her," he whispered, "I *hated* her. She was poison." His voice shook and once again he rose and this time paced the room, up and down, up and down. "She tormented me. She piled humiliation on humiliation. She was a fiend and a temptress and she used me."

Lucy thought of Luciano and shivered. Playing with another's feelings was not a trivial matter and could lead to tragedy.

"No one suspected. Everyone believed I adored her, was blind to her indiscretions. I was the envy of all. No one would have believed I did not want Mara. You possess the woman every man desires and you gain the envy of the world. Everyone believed I doted on her. How often people said to me, 'Jeez, you possess the number one sex symbol of the world' and then they would growl, you know make that sexist noise in their throats, 'Grrr . . .' 'Corr . . .' You know. I grew to hate it so. Then they would tell me how lucky I was and all the time she . . ."

He sat down in his chair and clasped his hands between his knees. Lucy could see by the whiteness of his knuckles how tightly they were clenched.

"It's all been done before," he continued. "We know all about it in this enlightened day and age. Infidelity. We are all experts. Plays, films have all trivialised unfaithfulness. There is nothing shocking about it any more. Forgive and forget. 'I will stand beside my husband' who has been screwing his secretary, bonking some little wanna-be. It is all thought to be eminently get-overable. We are trying to prove ourselves an open-minded society, a tolerant society. We make excuses and tell ourselves that we all make mistakes, no one is perfect. And the experts council us to accept and forgive. What we *don't* do is take into account our primitive emotions when it happens to us. How the tide of that emotion overwhelms us. How violent our feelings are. Under our sophisticated and tolerant façade a volcano bubbles ready to erupt. I was shaken to the core with terrible passions. When I read in a book that old-fashioned phrase, 'he saw red' I knew *exactly* what it meant. I knew what it felt like. How often a red mist clouded my vision. How often I was consumed by an uncontrollable fury that invaded my very heart and soul. Hurt pride is an earth-shattering emotion, and betrayal is devastating."

Clarissa let him talk. She did not prompt him or ask questions. In the dimness of the shadowed room his voice droned on and Lucy felt relief flood her and felt ashamed. All she could think of was that he did not love Mara, had not loved her. He was not grieving over her memory for he had never cared for her. The great love never was.

"I never loved her," he said to Clarissa. "You were right. I lusted after her though. I was besotted with her. It was first love for me you see. Oh I'd had my share of lovers. In Uni there was a set, I suppose you'd call it of angry young people. We hung out together and had affairs. We fell for the one, then the other. I had a fling with two of the girls. It was nice, cosy, friendly, but no big deal."

Like me and Luciano, Lucy thought.

"Our main purpose was protesting," he continued. "That came before anything else, before love or sex."

There was a pause, then he said, "Do you mind if I stop there today? I'm tired."

He stood. He looked tired in a world-weary sort of way. "I'm trusting you Clarissa," he said as she too rose. "This could get me into a lot of trouble."

Clarissa nodded. "I won't print anything that would jeopardise your freedom," she said.

He turned and looked at them. "You know, I don't really care any more. I don't know why I blurted that out and I will probably regret it but at this moment I feel so very relieved. I've carried so much guilt around with me, like a pile of heavy luggage on my back, and getting rid of it, dumping it, is relief beyond anything you can imagine. See you tomorrow." And he was gone.

They went out into the simmering heat. Clarissa turned to Lucy. "Well! That was quite a revelation," she said. "I'm not sure what exactly I'll do with it yet. Wow!" Then she said, "I want you to *promise* you'll not repeat a *word* of this to *anyone*."

"I promise," Lucy said fervently.

"No I mean it. Do you hear me Lucy?" Lucy nodded vehemently.

"I *said* I promise. Lord, don't you trust me?" she asked in disgust.

"Not even your precious Luciano."

Lucy's eyes widened. "Oh!"

Clarissa smiled. "Thought I hadn't guessed? I knew. From the first moment. I knew. You show it all in your face Lucy."

Lucy was embarrassed. She turned and walked

down the drive saying, "I *said* I wouldn't say anything and I *don't* break my word."

Clarissa had to huff and puff along beside her to keep up with her. "I know. And I'm sorry. I do trust you Lucy, I just had to be sure."

"*He* didn't have to ask me to keep his trust I notice," Lucy cried.

"He forgot you were there," Clarissa protested. "He didn't even *see* you." Lucy flinched. Perhaps that was true. Oh God, perhaps that was true. "You see, this is very important to me. That's all. It's the most exciting piece of news I've had in all my career."

A terrible thought nudged itself into Lucy's head. "You're not going to use it, are you?" she asked incredulously. "You're not going to actually print that? Destroy him?"

Clarissa hastened to reassure Lucy but she did not meet the girl's eyes. "Of course not, what do you think I am?"

"Well you need not worry on my account," Lucy told her tartly. "*I'm* not in the habit of betraying confidences."

"I *said* I'm sorry Lucy, I had to be sure."

Lucy suddenly halted and Clarissa, brought up short behind her, nearly bumped into her.

"What's wrong?" Clarissa asked.

"Does *everyone* know?" she enquired. "About me and Luciano?"

Clarissa looked uncomfortable. Her eyes travelled to the blue horizon. "Well . . . yes," she said at last. Then, as Lucy blushed under her tan Clarissa added,

"Well, what do you expect? This is a small island. People gossip. We all know each other, what we get up to."

Lucy remembered Conrad's words, "Do you really care what they think of you?" and she took a deep breath.

"Oh I suppose it doesn't matter," she said.

"Come on, let's eat," Clarissa urged them on. "I'm starving."

Lucy thought of Conrad, alone in his cool, dim villa and wondered what he was doing. Alone with his fury. Alone with his anger.

What would it be like to be eaten up with jealousy? she wondered. Well, she thought, tomorrow we'll find out. He was not going to stop now. That much she was sure of. He would tell them everything. He needed to.

Chapter Twenty-One

That evening Clarissa told Lucy that Cliff was taking her to a little restaurant he knew on Anacapri. Perhaps they could all meet for a drink in the Piazzetta later? She sounded coy and glanced at Lucy shyly as she imparted this information. Lucy said nothing.

Clarissa, in her chiffon and scarves looked very pretty and feminine and when Cliff called, starched and crisp in his seersucker jacket, his brick-coloured face glowing from a liberal application of Lynx aftershave, Lucy thought they looked very sweet together and having seen them off went to do her work. She noticed that Clarissa had not made any notes about Conrad's startling confession. She had put nothing down on paper and had obviously switched off the tape recorder while he was talking. She had all the information about him not loving Mara, but nothing else.

Luciano arrived later and they all met in the Piazzetta for drinks and watched the sunset.

There were just the four of them. Cliff said Buffy was out for the count having overdone it at lunchtime and the Contessa was wearing poor Nucio out.

"She's voracious!" he said. "Women appear to me to need sex more and more the older they get instead of the other way around."

Clarissa said nothing to that but smiled softly to herself and then looked at Cliff who met her glance, winked at her, then poured more wine.

Luciano was gazing out at the golden sunset, his eyes half-shut.

"Buffy should cut down on his drinking," Clarissa said. "It's taking charge of him. He's not in control any more."

Cliff nodded. "I know. It's very worrying. But he won't admit it. He refuses to acknowledge that he has a problem. It's hard to know what to do."

Some gypsies playing mandolins strolled into the Piozzetta, plucking their instruments and singing southern Italian songs through their noses. They were a gaudily-dressed group and in spite of their brightly coloured clothes and trinkets, hinted at grubbiness underneath.

There was something intimidating about them Lucy thought, something vaguely threatening. They *invaded* the Piazzetta, the brilliant dye of their attire and the raucous tones of their singing taking charge, dominating everything.

A girl in a red and yellow dirndl dotted with tiny mirrors no bigger than Lucy's little fingernail, a bolero of embroidered velvet, her abundant black hair held in check by a purple bandana, jingling ear-rings in her ears and a faint moustache over ripe raspberry-coloured lips, grabbed Lucy's hand while the leader of the group twanged 'O Sole Mio', singing the familiar words in harsh sawlike tones.

"Fortune. I-a tell you fortune." It was a statement not a request.

"No, no!" Lucy tried to pull away.

The girl's nails were rimmed with black and her teeth were bad. "Yes. I tell you." The girl insisted, holding Lucy's hand firmly in her own. Her eyes were menacing and contemptuous at the same time and Lucy gave in.

"Oh Lucy, it's all tosh!" Clarissa exclaimed and was rewarded by a venomous glance from the gypsy girl.

She stared at Lucy's hand. "Cross with-a money," she demanded.

"Oh it's *money* now, is it?" Cliff remarked. "It used to be silver. Is silver no longer enough?"

The girl did not reply and Lucy obediently took some money from the pocket of her jeans and gave it to the girl.

The sun had vanished below the horizon, leaving a sliver of crimson across the rim of the sea. The moon hung over Santo Stefano and the girl bent over Lucy's hand.

"You com-a from over the sea," she announced.

Clarissa snorted. "That much I would have thought is obvious," she remarked acidly.

"You-a have lost someone. Someone you love," she continued unperturbed by Clarissa's interruption.

Lucy gasped. "How did you know?" she asked.
"Oh Lucy, that's easy!" Cliff said. "Everyone has someone who's dead. Everyone."
"There is-a love here," the girl continued staring into Lucy's palm and glancing slyly at Luciano. "You meet an Italian, you like-a him a lot. Is good, yes?"
Lucy pulled her hand away. "Oh it's all nonsense, nonsense!" she said.
The girl rose. She had her money. She was satisfied. She laughed at them. "*Va fan culo*!" she taunted and giving a twirl, skirts flaring out, the moon catching the tiny mirrors and glancing off them in shards of light she made an obscene gesture and ran to where the others were trawling the customers sitting at the tables for tips.
"They come from Naples," Luciano informed them. "They're horrible!"
"Ah no. I wouldn't say that," Cliff cried.
"Well I find them scary," Clarissa admitted.
The relaxed mood of the party had been broken.
"You two run along," Cliff said, looking at Lucy meaningfully, "I want to talk to Clarissa. Ask her advice."
Lucy looked at the two of them and thought to herself what a nice couple they would make. She jumped up and Luciano went to get the bill but Cliff insisted on paying it.
When they left the square Luciano turned to Lucy. "Come back with me Lucy. Let's make love. It's a beautiful night."

But Lucy shook her head. “Mind if I don’t Luciano?” she asked, looking at him, troubled, hoping he’d understand. “I’m very tired. I’d like to go home.”

“To the *pensione*?”

“Yes.”

“Not to England?”

He had hit the nail on the head. She had thought, for the first time since she had come to Italy, longingly of home, of England. She shook her head again. Luciano laughed. “A worm in the apple Lucy. Mosquitoes in paradise. You have discovered that there is an underside to everything beautiful.”

“I suppose.”

They strolled along the tiny street of boutiques. “What was it about them that upset you Lucy? It’s not as if you don’t have beggars in England. They were only gypsies.”

Lucy frowned. “They were . . . menacing. They seemed to be *allowing* us to sit there enjoying ourselves. They seemed to threaten that at any moment they might erupt into violence, or . . . something frightening.”

He nodded. “Know what you mean. But Lucy, sweet Lucy, everywhere you go there is the dark as well as the light, the evil as well as the good. You cannot avoid it.”

She sighed. “I suppose not. Still I wish . . .”

“What *bella* Lucy, what do you wish *belissima mia*.”

"That the evil would stay away," she said, aware that it was a silly thing to say.

To her surprise he agreed. "Don't we all!" he murmured.

The moon spangled the sea with sparkling pin-points of light and the rocks thrusting upwards from the sighing tide looked shiny and coal black. They too looked menacing. The air was heavy with night-scented jasmine.

"It would be nice if Clarissa and Cliff got together," Lucy said. Luciano threw back his head and guffawed.

"What is it?" she asked puzzled by his reaction. "What's so funny?"

"But Lucy, Cliff's gay! Oh how innocent you are. Cliff and Buffy live together. They are a couple."

Lucy digested this. Then she asked, "Does Clarissa know?"

Luciano frowned. "I don't know. Now you ask me, I'm not sure. Oh Lucy you don't think . . . you don't imagine . . ."

They had reached the courtyard of the little hotel. They sat on the bench there overlooking the sea. "Poor Clarissa! The more I think about it the more I am afraid that she was flirting with him," Lucy volunteered.

"*Pianissimo*!" Luciano turned and looked over his shoulder towards the driveway. "I think she is coming . . . is not that . . ."

"Yes. Yes. Go, go Luciano," Lucy began but he shrugged.

"It's too late," he said. "She's here."

Clarissa arrived in the courtyard. She looked distressed. "The man's gay!" she cried in agitated tones as she came upon them. "Oh God, I feel such a fool. You knew Luciano! You *knew*!" she cried reproachfully, "and you never told me. You are a . . ."

Luciano, not in the least sympathetic, was laughing. "No, don't say it Clarissa. I did not imagine you fancied him. I would have told you if I thought . . . but I did not."

"Stop laughing Luciano! Don't be so mean," Lucy admonished, slapping his hand gently in an effort to shut him up.

"I'm sorry," he laughed, but he did not sound sorry.

"Clear off Luciano," Clarissa commanded with as much dignity as she could muster. "Clear off. I want to talk to Lucy."

Luciano shrugged and took his leave, kissing their hands with elaborate courtesy, giggling all the time. He turned away and they could hear his soft laughter as he walked from them down the hill.

Clarissa sat beside Lucy. It was very quiet, very still. "Have I been a stupid old cow?" Clarissa asked. Lucy shook her head.

"Oh no. Of course not. Clarissa, even I know we all do that sometimes."

"Do what? Make complete idiots of ourselves?" Clarissa asked in piteous tones.

"Yes," Lucy nodded, then added, "I could

kill Luciano. He had no right to laugh like that."

"Oh I didn't mind Luciano. You know Lucy, he is a very rare bird indeed. There is no malice in him at all."

"I hope you don't mean that there is some in me?" Lucy asked.

"Oh no. No, you are another. How odd. Two very rare people together in one place. Two people without animosity. Very rare indeed." She smiled at Lucy. "Do you love him Lucy?"

Lucy shook her head. "No. I *care* about him, but I'm not in love with him if that's what you mean."

"Good. Play with him if you will, but do not fall in love with him. He would not be faithful."

Lucy wrinkled her nose. "What a funny thing to say. I'm not sure if fidelity is the most important thing to me," she said.

"Don't underestimate it Lucy. Listen to what Conrad says. You would be amazed at what you are capable of feeling, the forces you can unleash."

Lucy remembered the violence of her emotions when Conrad was around. The unpredictability of them, the fact that they swamped her, ignoring her efforts to control them. She shivered. Clarissa stood.

"Let's go in Lucy. We've had a long day." She stared at the moon, sighed and whispered, "God, what an old fool I am. For a while there I felt young again."

Lucy slipped her hand into Clarissa's and squeezed it gently. "No. You're not a fool," she said softly, "only human." And together they went inside.

Chapter Twenty-Two

The next morning on arrival at the Villa Azura they found, unusually, Conrad waiting for them, already in his winged chair. It seemed that once started he could not wait to finish. He looked tired, as if he had not slept the previous night.

He greeted them cordially, then plunged almost immediately into his story throwing Clarissa into a flurry. She had to rev up instantly, go into high gear, bustling about setting up her recorder and pulling her notebooks and pens out, settling herself opposite him. Lucy sat in her usual place quiet and breathless, waiting.

"I met Mara on a visit to Rome. Those were heady days. The Italian film business was booming, the Via Venito seemed the hub of the world.

"I was nobody there. Oh I'd been a big noise in England but here I was unknown. The top people were film stars and politicians and they mingled there on the sidewalk at the cafes in the balmy twilights.

"A selective few intellectuals knew of me, knew my work, but not many. Not many were concerned with my burning rage at that time, my anger at how we were treating this planet; the direction we were taking. Italians live in the present, they are careless about such things; lazy, some might say. And so I lurked on the periphery where the glamorous collected, tolerated only because someone famous had invited me. Because I had been put on a list. It was the way it worked; still does. You have an introduction to some celebrity. He does his duty and asks you to an opening, a première and you go. You are now on a guest list, but no one really *knows* you. You talk to people who pay no attention to what you are saying because you are not famous. Then you stop trying to engage anyone in conversation. Then you stop accepting these invitations, which is what they wanted in the first place.

"It was quite a come-down for me and although at the time I would have denied it, I was in fact missing my audience. Missing the people who listened to what I said; to whom my words were important. So I was ripe for her. I had a bruised ego. I was a tiny minnow in a pool of sharks and I was about to meet the largest shark of all. What balm to the spirit!

"I was in the Cafe Greco on the Via Condotti one morning when I saw her come in. I knew who she was of course. The whole cafe acknowledged her entrance and she accepted their admiration as her due.

"She was tall. Those legs were long, very long. They were not thin legs; they curved, swelling out into softly rounded calves that tapered into the longest ankles I have ever seen. And she wore high heels. Black patent, with ankle straps. Guaranteed to drive a boy like me wild. Her hair fanned out over her shoulders and she looked the personification of a macho man's fantasy: all soft, curvaceous femininity. Remember Women's Lib was big at this time and men were uncertain and fearful. They were not quite sure of their role any more. Women were changing, or rather they were not trying any more to disguise their strength, the strength they had hidden for so many decades. They had stopped doing the little girl lost act and were letting us know what they wanted. And a lot of men were terrified that they would not be able to come up to scratch.

"Except Mara. She was, or appeared to be, what every man dreamed of: a soft pliant biddable woman who aimed only to please you. What a joke! What a misconception!

"She stopped at my table, all hesitancy, batting her lashes, dimpling, did I tell you she was covered head to toe in dimples? and she said, 'I have seen you with Visconti? Yes?'

"I have to tell you I had been in the great man's company twice in Doney's on the Via Venito. I had been introduced with a bunch of others and I doubt if he would remember my face or my name. I literally rubbed shoulders with him but we never exchanged a word. However, I told her, yes, she had seen me with Visconti.

"I often wonder what would have happened if I had been more truthful. She might have left me there in peace, drinking my espresso and none of the rest would have happened. I would have watched enviously as she spoke to another, bestowed her attentions on someone else. I would have gone home to England and perhaps found a nice girl, married and settled down. But even as I say that, aware of the tragedy that resulted, I do not think I would have chosen to live my life any other way. Fate or destiny prompted me and I said that fatal yes and she asked if she could join me. Every man in that little place envied me and I felt big-shot again, proud of being chosen by her.

"Afterwards she taunted me with it. 'I only sat with you because I thought you were a friend of Visconti,' she told me. 'You lied to me!' I would contradict her saying, 'No. I *misled* you, I did not lie.' Splitting hairs. And we would fight. God those fights! Like animals in the zoo. Fierce, passionate and lethal.

"But that was later. Those first weeks with her were a revelation. I had had my affairs with my sweet little fellow students, that was all. This woman was a maneater. I never stood a chance. She consumed me, right from the start. She gobbled me up and I was utterly enslaved.

"No matter what she said later she was mad about me then. I was so young. So innocent. She moulded me. She introduced me to depravity and I have to tell you I revelled in every minute, every deviant sexual practice; I was drunk on it all. Physical experiences that had nothing to do with love. Sometimes I think she destroyed me. There was no *real* love there but we were crazy about each other, like two animals on heat. We could not eat. My knees went weak when I saw her and she could not keep her hands off me. It was like being sick.

"We married. It was a scandal in Rome because she was a Catholic and we did not marry in the church. The papers had a field day. I had come to Italy to escape bad press but I had managed only to sink deeper and deeper into the mire. You see, I am a destroyer. I attract trouble."

Lucy remembered what they had heard about him; that Conrad Morheim destroyed all he came in to contact with.

"That is why," he said now, softly, "I have removed myself from the world. I will not cause any more damage."

For the first time Lucy interrupted. She had not spoken a word before on their visits to the Villa Azura except to say hello or goodbye, but now she spoke.

"It seems to me," she blurted out, "that it was *others* who destroyed you."

He looked at her, startled, then shook his head. "Oh no," he said, "I brought it all on myself. I participated in it. You'll not turn me into more of a victim than I actually was. I could choose. There was always a way out."

Clarissa glared at Lucy then turned back to Conrad, looking at him expectantly but saying nothing. He continued. "We honeymooned in Como with the world press in the hotel gardens. There was excitement in that, hiding, making love when any moment you may be interrupted. A sort of madness. We returned to Rome and the trouble started. The rows started.

"At first they were, I won't say fun exactly, but exciting. We would scream at each other but end up in bed together making love.

"But the rows became more and more vicious. I had never hit a woman. I thought I *could* not. I believed I was physically incapable of it. But she goaded me. She hit me, and her blows, her attacks, sometimes with knives or scissors were ferocious. When we quarrelled she would use whatever was to hand and use it ruthlessly and damn the consequences.

"It was soon obvious to me that she was unfaithful. I could accept her ill-humour, her violence. These things could be contained between ourselves, but infidelity . . . no! I was horrified. I was disgusted. And I was jealous.

"Oh my God how that emotion devoured me, consumed me. I had recovered from those incestuous battles, those vicious fights, but from her unfaithfulness, no! Never!

"I could not sleep. She was in my head, trapped with the demons of jealousy, hatred and revenge. They turned and turned in my mind, twisting and coiling in my dreams, in my every waking moment, a record played over and over and over in my brain until I thought I would go mad.

"I began to follow her. I stalked her. Oh it was a heinous game we played. We were both trapped. I thought of nothing else, no one else but her. Morning, noon and night she fuelled my being with a poisonous desire to inflict pain.

"Whether or not she chose her lovers deliberately to hurt me I do not know. It sounds conceited to say so, but I really believe that she did. We were engaged in a life and death struggle and everything she did, at that time, was aimed to make me suffer.

"What I find surprising is that none of her lovers told the *paparazzi*. I don't know whether this was lack of foresight on their part, disbelief on the part of the press (we were after all their chosen golden couple), or the terror of a lawsuit when they had no hard evidence, or the fear of Mara herself. She was very threatening and it was always obvious she meant what she said. She did not know the meaning of the word prudence, or discretion, or caution.

"And all this time we were the darlings of the social scene. Arm in arm at previews, at charity dos we were the most glamorous twosome around and everyone informed us, told us in no uncertain terms, that we were deliriously happy. You smile, the papers say you're happy.

"I felt dirty. I felt debased. How can I explain the bad taste in my mouth, the private hell I found myself in?

"It ended for me when I returned one night to our apartment in Rome and found Mara in our bed with the cook's son. He was fifteen, sixteen, thereabouts. She had planned for me to find them. She knew I was bringing a guest home for lunch and I left this man downstairs and ran up to the bedroom and opened the door and saw her like some lascivious Beardsley drawing, disgusting and obscene.

"She seemed to enjoy the situation. My guest was a member of the Academia Italiana, a distinguished philosopher and thinker who wanted to query me about my theories and I don't know what he must have thought. I haven't seen him from that day on.

"I left the bedroom, the boy on top of her, panting, frightened out of his wits, and joined my guest. I was shaking and physically ill and he asked me what was the matter. A few moments later Mara, in a short slip and no underwear burst in on us. Can you imagine how embarrassing that was? My wife, nearly naked, dishevelled, having obviously just got out of bed and the distinguished man of letters bewildered by her presence.

"Oh he was very gallant, but he did not stay to lunch, remembering an important appointment he had apparently known nothing of ten minutes before. Oh it was gross. I was half-crazy with fury and jealousy. I had to leave soon after my guest departed, leave her there laughing, saying the cook's son was a better lover than I, I had to go or I would have killed her then."

There was a pause, then Conrad said in a whisper, "I tried and tried to find out why she was like this. So destructive, so angry. She aimed to spoil everything. She was hell-bent on causing havoc. She could not bear to see anyone else happy. If one of her co-stars or fellow-workers was happily married she could not rest until she had seduced him.

"But the parts were getting fewer and fewer. Directors did not want her in their films. She sowed dissent. She created discord. And she seemed to know that not only was she spoiling things for others, she was spoiling things for herself as well. But she was incapable of stopping.

"By this time we had had Leah," he buried his face in his hands, then sighing, continued, "I am utterly appalled by my daughter, by what I did or didn't do for her. She was the real loser in all this. She came a distinct third in our lives. Poor little child. Sad little girl." He fell silent again and this time it stretched on for so long that finally Clarissa, much against her instinct, broke it.

"What happened?" she asked. He straightened himself slowly.

"One night Mara asked me to come away with her. On a break to Capri. She seemed subdued. She said she was fed up with the life we were living. She said she wanted a truce, wanted to make peace, wanted us to try again. I was delighted. I agreed and we left Rome and came here. Here to the Villa Azura. It was to be a haven, a retreat for us." He rose suddenly. "But now, I'm tired. He faltered, his face paling under his tan. He seemed distracted, overwhelmed. Let's leave it there for today. I'll finish tomorrow," he said.

It had been a short session. Lucy sitting in her alcove, although presenting a tranquil front to the room was, in fact, in turmoil.

Her heart bled for him. It ached at his every confidence.

Listening to him, yearning inside to comfort him, her sympathy went out to him. She wanted desperately to hold and comfort him, tell him it was all right, the nightmare was over, she would console and cherish him.

She had to tell him how deeply sympathetic she was, how she ached to heal his troubled spirit. He had to know, she had to talk to him.

Up to now there had been no opportunity. Clarissa was omnipresent at all their meetings so far and she had never been alone with him in the Villa Azura. Lucy felt sick with emotion. Her stomach churned, her heart pounded and she could not breathe. Her hand was gripping the notebook Clarissa had given her, and, as she listened, some overwhelming impulse made her scribble a simple message.

'Please meet me this evening after dinner in the Marina Piccola.' And she signed it 'L'.

As they were leaving she pressed the note into Conrad's hand. He looked faintly surprised and she had to hurry Clarissa out in case he made an incautious remark.

As the day passed she was thrown into utter confusion. Why had she done it? She figured he would meet her but she was pitched into total consternation at the thought of what she'd say to him, what she'd do. Had she been nuts? What had possessed her?

She toyed with the idea of not turning up but

decided that would be feeble and craven. She knew Clarissa was tired and would be happy to retire early and leave her to her own devices. Clarissa had become subdued since she discovered Cliff's true proclivities. Also she was preoccupied with her work and secretive about it the last few days, giving ambiguous replies to Lucy's queries. She explained that she was not going to commit anything to paper until she could figure out exactly what Conrad was leading up to.

"I don't know where this is going Lucy. I've got my reservations about how I should slant it. So I want you to wait until Conrad has said his say and I can make a decision."

"You're not going to sell him out Clarissa, are you?" Lucy asked anxiously.

"Don't be silly Lucy," Clarissa said tight-lipped, and Lucy knew it was pointless to pursue the topic.

Lucy made her way down to the Marina Piccola after an almost silent dinner of light pasta. She told Clarissa that she was going to do some shopping. The boutiques stayed open late, usually until after ten p.m. Clarissa accepted her excuses with equanimity, almost relief, and told her to run along and enjoy herself.

She went to her room and changed into her one pretty floral dress. It was button through and she left the top and bottom buttons undone on the pretext that it would reveal more of her tan. The reality was that she wanted to look sexy.

Conrad was not there when she arrived. She had

pictured him waiting for her anxiously, looking up and down, but he was nowhere to be seen. The little square was decked with fairy-lights. The air was balmy and smelled of the sea.

Lucy sat down at a table and ordered a cappucino. She sat sipping it, watching the moon, listening to the quiet murmurings of the sea and the chatter of conversation all around her and wondered what the hell she thought she was up to.

Ten o'clock came and went. People at the next table were drinking wine and laughing. He's not coming, she decided and finished her drink. She felt curiously relieved, almost glad he had not shown, that she would not have to face him.

As she rose to leave she felt a hand on her shoulder and she turned and looked up into his face.

Her heart stood still. She'd read the phrase, despised it, thought it a writer's fiction, but it happened. Her heart stopped. Then it leapt, fluttering like a bird and began to race.

"Come. We can't stay here."

She followed him obediently. She did not know why they could not have a coffee, here, on the Marina Piccola, but she obeyed him slavishly.

He led her away. They walked up the hill together, through a passageway of trees. He held her hand. She felt she might die of happiness. She wanted this moment to last forever and never to stop. She felt small and infinitely precious because her hand was in his. Out of all the women in the world she was beside him and he was touching her.

The moon seemed an enchanted light illuminating their path, the stars, lanterns glittering for their pleasure.

She sighed. He looked down at her. "Sad?" he asked.

She shook her head. "Oh no! No. It's . . . everything's perfect. Don't you feel it too Conrad? You and me and the night." She spoke spontaneously, without thinking. He stopped. There were trees and a broken stone statue, cypresses and a piece of sculpture chisled long ago for a Roman consulate or senator whose summer home it graced.

"Lucy I want you to understand . . ."

"What Conrad?" She stared up at him. His face was pale in the moonlight.

"You can't . . . I can't . . ." he faltered, then continued firmly, "I have not the right to influence your mood."

"Oh Conrad," she sighed looking at him ardently, expectantly. "You can't help it."

"No Lucy. Stop it," his voice was firmer still. "You are a romantic child," he cried impatiently. "Listen! I don't want to hurt you. I don't want you to feel . . . rejected. You are a lovely girl; I don't deserve you. But I took a vow long ago. No women. No sex. And I will not become involved in a casual affair with a visitor to Capri." She gasped. "I cannot and will not be so irresponsible. It would, *could* destroy you and me both."

He had turned away from her and she circled

around him to face him. "Why? Why would it Conrad? I love you—"

"Stop it Lucy—"

"You can see that. You *know* that I do. I *adore* you—"

"I said stop it!" He grabbed her arms, almost shaking her. "I'm bad news Lucy. Not for you. Out of your league. What you need is a nice young man. Like Luciano." She shook her head impatiently. "Oh don't dismiss him. One day he'll be a formidable painter, a celebrity and he'll handle it all a lot better than I."

"Don't Conrad. Please don't talk like that. I love you. You *must* feel it."

She stood on tiptoe and took his face between her hands. She pressed her lips to his, feeling his mouth responding to her kiss instantly. He cannot have had sex for a long time she thought, then, I'll get him that way. I'll snare him with my body.

She pressed herself against him and he groaned. She could feel him hardening against her almost immediately.

"No, no," he whispered, but his mouth now drank hers in, voraciously, like a thirsty man in a desert drinking his first drink after a long drought. His hands were pushing her dress away from her firm young breasts and she was urging him down on her, on the carpet of pine needles and cypress leaves on to the moss beneath them. She pushed her dress up over her thighs, aiding him, as if she had done this a million times, her body dictating what to do instinctively in the urgency of the moment.

"No, no Lucy." He sprang suddenly to his feet. "We cannot do this for an instant of gratification. No Lucy. It was the mistake I made before. I cannot allow our bodies to take over like that. I won't!"

She lay dishevelled on the ground, feeling sudden shame. She had not felt this ever before; had never been in this position. She covered herself hurriedly as if her naked body was debauched.

"Don't you see?" he asked her though he was not looking at her. "It's disgusting. It's degrading!"

She got unsteadily to her feet. She felt debased and utterly humiliated.

He put his arm around her. "Don't be upset Lucy," he said and she shrugged his arm away.

"You *did* love her really, didn't you?" she asked softly. "You lied to us when you said you didn't. Oh you're so fond of the truth, but you lied. You love her, always loved her, beyond all else, beyond the grave."

"I don't know," his voice sounded weary. "I simply don't know." He walked through the trees to look down on the twinkling lights below. "I only know that she's in my blood, my bones, my soul. I hate her but she never leaves me alone. She *haunts* me. If you call that love, then yes, I did love her. Still do."

Lucy felt the pain shoot through her. She was growing up fast. Was life always as agonising as this? If this was what teenagers went through then no wonder they were difficult. She had side-stepped all these overwhelming emotions, avoided experiencing them. Then her mother died and it was no longer possible to escape her feelings. She wondered idly if she could bear the humiliation, the hurt.

"Sweet little Lucy. I'm sorry," he said and strode away into the night leaving her alone under the trees.

Chapter Twenty-Three

There was someone sitting on the bench in the clearing in front of the hotel when she returned. She hoped she could circumvent whoever it was, circle around and creep indoors without being seen, but she discovered it was impossible to be silent on gravel and the person turned and she saw it was Adrian.

"Lucy! How nice to see you," his voice was warm and reassuring. "Come over here and sit down and tell me all the news."

She obeyed. She always followed a command instantly, but no sooner had she sat down beside him than the dam to her emotions burst and she dissolved into a storm of tears. Adrian put his arm around her. It felt very comforting.

"There, there," he soothed. "Is it that awful? I knew Ma was a hard taskmaster but not as bad as this!"

"Oh no, no, no! It's not your mother Adrian. No. She's been wonderful. It's just . . ."

"Then it must be love," he said. "Oh dear, dear, dear! Console yourself Lucy. *Everyone* does it."

"Does what?" she hiccuped. She needed to blow her nose and wipe her eyes but to do that she'd have to sit up and she did not want to leave the security of his embrace. "Everyone does what?" she sobbed.

"Falls in love with a handsome foreigner the first time they go abroad," he said. "Don't worry. It's painful but you'll recover."

She didn't bother to enlighten him, tell him it was an Englishman she had been besotted with, that she had made a complete fool of herself over him and that she wished she were dead. She felt protected and safe for the moment, her face pressed against his warm chest, the soft cotton of his shirt absorbing her tears and becoming damper by the minute, his arms holding her in a firm and masterful grip.

At last he moved. He foraged in his pocket and produced a handkerchief.

"Here," he gave it to her, "wipe your face Lucy. You look terrible!" His blue eyes were amused and to her horror she thought she might begin to cry again at his words.

"Oh dear," she was flustered, "I'm sorry."

"What for? You're still pretty even when you look terrible." He stood up smiling at her. "Poor Lucy. I did so hope I'd made an impression on you and that you'd compare me with the local talent and that I might somehow win! Fancy that! I suppose it was conceited of me. How could I compete against romantic Italians?" He touched her cheek with his hand. "Dry your eyes Lucy and go to bed. Tears tend to exhaust, don't they."

She did not take in the full import of what he said until the next day. She went to bed, tossed and turned all night reliving her humiliation, drowning in her mortifying memories. The horror was magnified in the dark. How ignominious it had been, how degrading. She squirmed in her shame, blushing in the shadowy room, hugging her defeat to herself.

It was nearly dawn when her embarrassment turned to anger. How dare he make her feel like this! What had she done, how had she behaved that he should make her feel this shame? All she had done was offer herself to him. Her gestures of willingness, her approach to him could hardly be considered shocking in this day and age. And he had been clumsy and cruel in his response, or lack of it. He could have handled it much better, much more tactfully.

Had it really been so shameful? What had he called it? Disgusting! Degrading! She covered her face with her hands when she relived the moment, picturing herself lying on the ground, skirts about her waist.

Then she pushed the image aside as another thought struck her. She tried to remember exactly; piece it together. He'd said first that he'd taken a vow. Did he mean a vow of celibacy? Like a priest? Then he'd recoiled from her, from sex, as if it had been something unspeakably dirty. Yes, that was it, it was not her it was *sex* he found disgusting. In that case the problem was his, not hers.

She sat up in bed. The Rector she thought had

won! Conrad Morheim did not like sex; thought it shameful, sinful. She thought of Luciano, his lovely body, the excitement and beauty, the sheer joy of their coupling. What light, she wondered, did Conrad's attitude about sex have on his relationship with Mara? Perhaps the whole story should be looked at through different spectacles. When exactly had Mara become aware that her husband thought that what they did in bed was disgraceful?

How could she convey this fascinating development to Clarissa? And how could she face Conrad tomorrow?

At last, in the early dawn she fell into a deep slumber and did not awaken until the sun filled her room and she heard Clarissa's voice calling her from her balcony to tell her that Adrian had arrived. For some reason this drove all Lucy's cares away.

Chapter Twenty-Four

Lucy had been petrified at the thought of coming face to face with Conrad again, but in the event he did not even glance in her direction.

Han Su showed them in and they were seated and waiting for quite a few minutes before Conrad arrived. When he came upon them he came quietly, taking his place in his winged chair silently, and waiting until Clarissa asked him, "And you came here, to the Villa Azura. What then?"

Lucy's heart had begun to thump uncomfortably against her side when he appeared but to her surprise it very soon quieted down and resumed its usual slow steady beat as Conrad began to speak.

"Why the hell am I doing this!" he appealed rhetorically, as if to himself.

"You *want* to," Clarissa said, "you're dying to. You've held all this stuff inside you for years, you *need* to get rid of it."

"Conscience," he said, "I wonder. If only we didn't have it."

"Then there would be mayhem. Crime. No justice."

"Is there justice?" he asked and as Clarissa laughed he insisted, "No, really, I want to know. Is there? *I* seem to have evaded it, wouldn't you say? In our cockeyed world what justice is there I would like to know. Money, as they say, talks. Do you know why I got clean away with it? Money, that's why." His disgust was obvious. "Hands greased. Dues paid. Wink, wink, nod, nod, nothing said, the right questions not asked. Doing all the stuff I had condemned others for doing."

"Tell me about it," Clarissa insisted softly.

Lucy listened and as they talked she felt the sudden impulse again and she scribbled on her jotter a question:

'*Ask him what he thinks about sex.*'

She tore the page out and folded it. There was a pause. Conrad was obviously thinking deeply, his head sunk on his chest, his eyes half closed. He seemed a stranger to her today; remote and alien. She moved across the room, quiet as a shadow and leaning over Clarissa's shoulder slipped her the folded piece of paper. She took it, hardly changing position, keeping her eyes fixed on Conrad. Lucy moved silently back to her place in the alcove. It seemed for a moment that Conrad dozed. Then he shook himself and sat up straight.

"I thought we would be quieter living here in the Villa Azura, more relaxed," he told Clarissa. "But that was not to be. The first two weeks were blissful. Like Como, our honeymoon. So romantic. Walking together hand in hand. Dreaming together. Talking of love. Then slowly but surely her demands, her perverted demands accelerated. Romance went. Passion ruled. She was slipping back.

"Leah joined us. We tried to pretend, for her sake. It was useless though, it always is. Don't ever think for a moment you can fool children. You can't. The terrible rows began again. It was agonising." He paused. He rose and walked to the arch and stood staring out as he had done the previous day.

"One night after we had dined in the Marina Piccola near the place Lucy met . . ." he glanced over his shoulder at Lucy, then recalling himself, glanced away out to sea and the sun and the flowers, so bright out there, a brilliantly coloured world while in here it was black and white.

Clarissa glanced back sharply at Lucy, then returned her concentration to Conrad as he began to speak again. Lucy felt sure that Clarissa had sussed that she had met Conrad on the sly and hoped she would not be too angry.

"We quarrelled all evening. It was that kind of vicious in-fighting in undertones, slashing each other verbally, ruthlessly. Leah had gone back to school in Paris and I remember thinking that I was glad she was not here. I also remember thinking that Mara would not have been so unrestrained if she had. I wished Mara dead. She said things that should never be said, thoughtless of the pain inflicted she lashed out mindlessly destructive, fierce and cruel.

"I got the feeling that she was goading me. I tried not to rise to the bait and I managed. For a while.

"We went home. She turned on me in earnest there, insulting me unbearably so that in the end I hit her." He shook his head as if bewildered. He returned to his chair. He sat down, rubbed his forehead and sighed.

"I have gone over it and over it a thousand times. How I could have done that. It is all a blur now. She had thrown a heavy cut-glass vase at me. She was screaming obscenities. She stooped and picked up a huge hunk of the thick glass she had broken, and you know how difficult it is to break cut-glass. She came at me, slashing at my face. I was so angry and I dived at her and punched her.

"I punched her hard. I put my full weight behind the blow, my fist clenched. She fell there . . ." he pointed at the marble floor near the alcove. There was a pillar with a fluted base and Lucy thought she could detect a darker stain there, then decided she was being hyper-imaginative. For some reason she kept thinking, Adrian would never behave like that. Never. You could taunt him, goad him, scream at him, but he'd never do that.

"She cracked her skull against that pillar. It killed her." He lifted his hands in a gesture of helplessness. "All that vibrant life extinguished in a minute. It was gruesome."

Not as gruesome as it must have been for Mara,

Lucy thought, and perhaps that dark stain *was* her blood.

More and more as she listened, Lucy decided that there was something missing in all this, some slant not quite right. Conrad broke the silence.

"I sent for the *carabinieri*. They took their time coming. I sent for her doctor. He got here first. Dr McLeash was Scottish and an alcoholic living on the island. He had been struck off the register in England for malpractice and he had no money. Which was awkward for him for he needed to feed his habit. I shamelessly gave him the equivalent of ten thousand pounds in *lire*, a fortune to him, but I was in a state of shock and by the time the police arrived Dr McLeash was committed to presenting the facts slanted in my favour.

"I hasten to add the facts were true, but truth can be selective. It can be emphasised, it can be manipulated. Dr McLeash testified to *her* violence, *her* abuse, *her* affairs and described me in a saintly fashion. It has always fascinated me how the truth can be two different things to two different people and still remain the truth. And then the good doctor came out with the clincher.

"What he told me shocked me. She was lying there, on the floor. I was sitting here, shocked, dazed. He came and examined her. Then he stood and said, 'You knew she was dying?' Then he saw my face and he said, 'No one could believe you had intent when you knew she was riddled with cancer and had only a short time to live. It was terminal you see.'

"I couldn't believe it. I told him exactly what had happened, how she had goaded me, driven me wild, attacked me. He said that she had probably done it deliberately, that she *wanted* to die. He was concerned, he said, about me. She'd said to him when she'd last seen him that she was going to take everything down with her. 'I'll destroy it all!' she said.

"He repeated it all at the hearing, at the inquest. I walked. They let me go without a stain. It seemed they believed I acted in a crazed state and that she had caused that state. That was what the doctor said: I was a man driven beyond the bounds of reason and she had planned to incite me to murder because she knew she was dying of cancer. I was, according to the Neapolitan court, an innocent man. Not at all what Mara had wanted.

"At first I was relieved. I could not have borne an Italian prison. I didn't want to be shut up, incarcerated in some horrible place. But I'd reckoned without the price I would have to pay. There is always a price to pay. Fine if you have no conscience, horrendous if you have. My father had refined mine to an exquisite sharpness and there was no escape. Surely, I said to myself, if they did not find me guilty, then I was innocent. But I did not *feel* innocent. I felt guilty as hell no matter what they said. They did not know what was in my mind. They did not know how I hated her, how I *wanted her dead*!"

He looked up, his eyes dark pools. "I have lived . . . existed here ever since. I have been eaten up with remorse and hatred and the fact that in my heart I know I'd do the same thing again. That's what's so terrible. I'd do it again. My choice would still be the same: to rid myself of her.

"Then the doubts started. Terrible doubts that tore me apart. Was what Dr McLeash said about Mara true? Did she really have cancer? Was she really dying? Or was it all a ploy to get me off, so that he would not lose the money. And you know, I'll never be sure. I'll never find out. That's the terrible thing. Dr McLeash wouldn't discuss it, refused to talk about it and the money I gave him did him no good. He drank himself to death and was buried a year later, the money mostly gone. He took the secret with him. Maybe he too could not bear the guilt. Maybe he too was haunted.

"I have never been able to shake off her memory. She is with me all the time. Sometimes I think she is still alive. Sometimes when I'm alone here, and I am mostly alone, I talk to her. I think she hears me." He paused, then amended, "I *know* she hears me. I am a poisoned man."

He buried his face in his hands and his shoulders shook. Lucy realised she felt no sympathy at all. He had, after all, brought it all on himself. He could have left. At any time he could have walked away from Mara. But he chose not to. Lucy reflected wryly that he had run from *her* fast enough and wondered if she was jealous. Or angry. Probably both. She acknowledged that she did not understand Conrad's obsession, but then she did not *want* to. She did not want to drown in that particular emotional morass.

Clarissa asked her question. "What do you think about sex?" she queried with a slight backward glance at Lucy.

Conrad looked perplexed. He shook his head and obviously puzzled asked, "What? What do you mean?"

"What I said. What do you think about sex?"

He frowned and stammered a little. "I . . . I don't . . . I don't know! Why do you ask? What are you talking about?"

"It's a simple enough question. Not at all shocking for this day and age. What do you think about sex Conrad?"

"I suppose it is . . . it is a biological necessity. A requirement. It's something you have to do, like eating and drinking." His voice was irritable and tense. He shook his head again. "But what it has to do with anything I don't know."

"I would have thought it had everything to do with everything." Clarissa had the bit between her teeth. "Sex, after all, is a fundamental energy. It infiltrates everything." Conrad said nothing, made no reply, so Clarissa asked, "Did Mara like sex?"

"I've *told* you. She was almost a sex maniac! She was into all sorts of things, perverted . . ." He stopped.

"What do you mean by perverted Conrad?" she asked.

He glared at her. "Everyone knows what perverted

is. I'm not going to draw a diagram." He sounded disgusted. "She was . . . she liked to experiment. Now, is that enough?"

Clarissa, however, was not to be fobbed off. Lucy suddenly knew she had been right; before he had answered she knew the missing element. It was that. Conrad's attitude to sex. He hated it. His father had taught him well.

"Let me understand this Conrad. Do you mean that anything other than the missionary position, as it is laughingly called, you on top of the woman, is perverted?"

"Of course!" He seemed surprised that she should have to ask. "The Bible spells it out. It is clear that sex, a degrading act in itself, is for procreation, is the insemination by a man into a woman for the making of babies. As I say, it is necessary."

Lucy shuddered. It was horrible, she thought, and looking at his tortured face she could see mirrored there revulsion and distaste. It was the same expression he had worn under the trees with her when he looked at her lying on the leaves and pine needles. Poor Mara, she thought. Poor, poor Mara. Vibrant, passionate Mara.

"Sex is like death. It is a giving away of yourself. It is diminishing."

"Is that what you really think?"

"Of course." He shrugged.

"Your father's teaching never really left you, did it?" Clarissa asked. "You never really broke away."

"No. I suppose I didn't," he said softly. "Was I wrong to think like this?" he appealed, looking up at Clarissa.

"That's not for me to say," Clarissa answered.

"I always thought that God, in his infinite wisdom should have been able to think of a better way to perpetuate the human race. A more decorous way. Why only *that* part of the body? Why does it have to be so gross?" He grimaced.

"I have always thought it beautiful," Clarissa murmured.

"Look around at all the beauty," he continued, glancing out over the sun-drenched mountain, the sparkling sea, the azure sky. "Nature is gorgeous. *We're* the blight. *We're* the destroyers. The nearness of rape to what they call 'making love' is like hate to love; too close for comfort." He shook his head. "It's all too difficult for me now. Once I was so clear. Everything was black and white. Our moral duty. Our culpability. Then Mara came and whispered such obscenities, saying they turned her on. Did things. Now I just don't know any more."

"I'll let you see what I write. It will be ambiguous." Clarissa glanced at him, her eyes gentle. She did not tell him he'd have no say if he did not like what she wrote. She added, "It would not serve my purpose to destroy you Conrad, though I doubt even if I told all, anyone could prove anything against you now, after all this time.

"I'm afraid you are condemned to live, like the Ancient Mariner, with your guilt forever. You are trapped in it and there is no way to make restitution or ease your conscience. The law will not accommodate you. Any advocate worth his salt would get you off scott-free. On the grounds of insanity." Clarissa smiled wryly. "He could prove, quite easily, that since Mara died you've lived here, alone, reclusive and isolated and it would be odd indeed if you had not become deranged and imaginative, that your guilt had not become obsessive. And remember, you cannot be tried for the same crime twice. So you'll just have to put up with it."

Conrad nodded. He seemed defeated. Clarissa turned to go. At the entrance she stopped. "I think you should leave this place," she said briskly. "It can't be good for you living here."

"What do you suggest I do?" he asked, spreading his hands helplessly. "Where could I go?"

Clarissa tutted quite openly. "Well now Conrad, given your history *I* think you should take up a cause. Join Greenpeace. Help Oxfam or the Red Cross. Do a course. Go to a trouble-spot and help out, empty bedpans. Something like that. Eh?"

She left the room and Lucy slid out of her alcove and hurried across the marble floor to say goodbye. His eyes were blank, dark troubled orbs with no acknowledgement of her at all. He was blind to her presence, lost in his own thoughts. She could have been a complete stranger. She took his outstretched hand. It was limp. She could think of nothing to say. "Goodbye," she whispered. He did not reply. His glance slid away from her and, bemused, he stared now into space.

She followed Clarissa out into the hot sunshine, out into life, out into the present.

"You talked with him Lucy?" Clarissa asked. "Alone?"

Lucy knew what she was referring to. "Yes," she said sadly, "I wanted to see him. Tell him I loved him."

"Nonsense," Clarissa said firmly. "You were infatuated with a myth. A mystery. Don't fall into the trap of becoming involved with someone needy, like your mother. Old habits die hard Lucy. It won't do. Won't do at all." She gave Lucy one of her radiant smiles. "No. What I think, I think you love my son though you don't seem aware of it yet."

Lucy stood stock still on the driveway, blinking in the sun. Adrian! She thought, Adrian. The niceness of him. The gentleness of him, the sweetness of his smile, his blue, blue eyes. How attractive he was. How she already knew his kiss would be heady as wine and making love with him would be wonderful and fun and, yes, sacred. Adrian. English and safe and home. She giggled. "You old witch," she cried.

"Not so much of the old," Clarissa snorted.

As they walked to the gates Lucy asked, "What will you say about him? About Conrad?"

"I'll tell the truth. I'll paint the picture of his childhood; that awful father. I'll relate his views on people, nature, the world. And sex. I'll outline his meeting and stormy life with Mara. I'll report her infidelity, her death, give the doctor's testimony, report the court case and its findings. I'll leave the reader to draw his or her own conclusions. Like a good reporter should. I'll be clear as a bell but noncommittal, I'll not take sides. That's what I shall do. All right Lucy, come along, there's work to be done."

Chapter Twenty-Five

The next morning Lucy found Clarissa as usual on her balcony eating breakfast. The *pensione* had become used to their routine and the proprietor had informed Lucy that it was not necessary to order breakfast each evening and she need only let them know if there was any change.

He was a dapper little man, proud of his titled antecedents. He always dressed formally in a neat grey or navy gabardine suit, a pink or red tie on a crisply starched and ironed cotton shirt, a flower in his buttonhole. His manner was a mixture of benevolent condescension, amusement and exuberant friendliness when he forgot his superiority.

"We are used to you now," he told Lucy smiling, showing his neat white teeth. "We know what you like."

Adrian was there and it settled Lucy to see him, calmed her and reassured her. If Adrian was there everything would be all right.

She had gone the previous day (fled would be a better word), to Luciano after a hard afternoon's work with Clarissa. She dined with him in Anacapri, trying to sort out her feelings and incidentally rid herself of the nasty taste in her mouth.

She had not liked what she had heard in the Villa Azura and was in some ways shocked by it. What Conrad *did*, did not offend her as much as his attitude which seemed to her craven. His acts did not appal her so much as his view of those acts. She had spent years of her life looking after her mother. She had learned that she either did it cheerfully, accepting her role with equanimity, ruthlessly giving up regrets, yearnings and comparisons or she should walk away, desert her mother. Either put up or shut up was her motto and she was disgusted that Conrad should indulge himself so endlessly in the self-pity of regrets, yearnings and comparisons.

Why didn't he just leave instead of hanging around someone he hated for so long, playing a perverted game. 'Let the dead past bury its dead,' the poet said and to live the way Conrad did, one foot in the past, wallowing in old mistakes, long-forgotten rows and death seemed to her a crime against the one thing he admired: the laws of nature.

She talked about it to Luciano whose hedonistic life made the whole argument a nonsense, incomprehensible to him. He simply did not understand how anyone could be like that and was not really interested in finding out. She lost his attention early on and found herself talking to herself.

They laughed though, and drank wine, but when he wanted to make love to her she fobbed him off, reluctant for some reason to give in to her body's inclination and went home early.

As she strolled along the little road above the Piazzetta she could see Clarissa and the gang there at their usual table: Cliff and Buffy, the Contessa, Chi-Chi and Nucio. Adrian was with them, staring out to sea, looking bored. Lucy stopped and stared at him a moment. What was this feeling he gave her? Security. Content. Rest and, what? Could it be love? She was not sure. She knew only that he was the one person she never wanted to get away from. He was the one person she absolutely knew she could count on. He was the one person she could envisage spending her life with.

She shook her head. This was nonsense. He turned then and seemed to search the darkness beyond the table for something, someone. She knew he could not see her but he was gazing in her direction as if he knew she was there. He did not fit into the landscape as the others did. He was not part of the scene. He was a visitor, anyone could see that. Oh, the others looked like travellers and certainly were not natives, but they were comfortable there, familiar with the place. Only Adrian exuded a lack of ease, a restlessness in the relaxed company. She smiled in the dark. He had stopped searching and looked once more to sea.

No, she thought, Adrian did not fit in here. He would be more at home sitting by a cricket match on a Sunday afternoon. He would look more at ease feeding the ducks in Hyde Park or under an umbrella in the rain, coming out of the Barbican or the National Theatre. He would be right at home in a pub or at the Savoy for tea.

He was a lovely man, she thought, and for a moment she wanted more than anything to be down there with him holding his hand. His skin would be soft to touch, his lips soft to kiss and the look in his eyes when they met hers would be soft too. So soft.

She turned away. She did not want to rush. She'd been through emotional turmoil in such a short space of time. Yet subliminally she *knew* what she wanted, subconsciously she had come to terms with her desires. She simply did not want to accept it all yet, the responsibility of her decision, the finality of it. She wanted to be utterly free for just a little longer.

She sat on the bench in front of the hotel when she reached it, sat and thought and enjoyed the view. She had never in her life been so content, so at peace. What a beautiful place the world is, she thought. And people, if you don't expect them to be perfect, people were, in the main, nice. Selfish but kind.

She had not had that much experience with men but they had proved themselves mostly lovely people. Luciano brought a smile to her lips. He was a wonderful lover, an amusing companion. But his priority was his painting. He'd desert without a thought his mother, his mistress, his wife, even his children if necessary to paint, to create, to work.

Against his art no one had a chance. Someone would find that acceptable, some other woman would make the journey to fame and fortune with him, sacrificing herself, making excuses for his selfishness, sharing his success.

But not her. Not Lucy. She liked him tremendously. She loved his body, she found his company delightful but that was not enough for her, she required more, much more. Luciano could not give her what she knew she needed; the depths and soul of him would not be with her but with his painting.

She thought of Conrad, and her weak-kneed reaction to him, her increased pulse-rate, her dry mouth. It had been a sickness with little reference to her mind, her reason. With Conrad and the macabre ghost of Mara she would revert constantly to the past. It would be comparable to when her mother was dying. She would become sucked into an illness that was totally destructive, she would be trapped in a tragedy that was long gone and abscessed in the mind of the man she had desired.

It had become essential for her to be healthy with healthy people now. When she thought of health Adrian sprang instantly to her mind.

She went to bed and slept soundly all night. No dreams disturbed her, no debate took place in her subconscious. She knew what she wanted now and all it needed was for her to accept it on a conscious level.

Now, sitting at the breakfast table with Clarissa

and Adrian, listening as they mulled over the information received the previous day she felt a wonderful peace descend on her soul.

"If you wrote everything, all we've learned, could Conrad go to prison?" Lucy asked.

"Not for murder," Clarissa said. "But if I reveal that he greased the doctor's palm, he could be tried for that. Perverting the course of justice. Tampering with the evidence." She smiled at Lucy, patting her hand. "However, I won't. It is not worth it. To destroy him I mean. He suffers enough. He has made his own prison."

"Hi! Hi there!" The voice called up from below. They looked down and saw on the gravel driveway the slight form of a young girl. She was as thin as a matchstick, her face painted white, her lips vivid carmine. Her eyes were heavily ringed with black kohl and almost every protuberence was pierced by rings. Silver rings. She had rings through her nose, rings through her eyebrows as well as rings through her ears. There were rings on each and every finger and one through her bottom lip. She wore black jeans and a black turtle-necked T-shirt and her arms were liberally tattooed with repulsive likenesses of snakes, devils, gargoyles and skulls. She was waving to them, shading her eyes with her hand, a tote-bag on her back.

"Hi! Hi!"

Clarissa leaned over the rail. "Hello," she returned. "Who are you?"

"I'm Leah Morheim," the urchin replied.

"Comc on up," Clarissa beckoned. "Second floor. Room nine. Come right in."

She did just that. She seemed even tinior than before.

"I heard what you were at," she told Clarissa, plonking herself down on the chair vacated by her hostess. "Writing something about my Papa. I wanted to make sure you got it right."

"Got what right?" Clarissa asked innocently.

"Got the fact my father is a shit right," the girl said. She had the bad skin of drug users and her lips were cracked and dry under the scarlet stain, the tiny ring looked discoloured. Her manner was belligerent as if she thought that they were all her enemies.

"Well, we gathered that," Clarissa said calmly, not in the least disconcerted. "Although it seems to me all the blame cannot be pinned on your father. It takes two to tango you know."

Leah took out a crumpled pack of cigarettes, lit one and squinting up her eyes said, "Don't give me that crap. There's no excuse for murder, no way, no how. Bet he didn't tell you that."

"As a matter of fact he did." If she had hoped to shock Clarissa she failed miserably. Unperturbed Clarissa continued, "Your father was upfront with us. Perfectly frank. He held nothing back. But Leah my dear, I'm not in this to apportion blame. I shall simply place the facts before the reader and let them make their judgement. And I've decided, as well as the interview, I'm going to write a book about Conrad."

She glanced at Lucy. "Yes Lucy. Isn't that good news. I'm going to need your help for a long time to come." She turned back to the waif. "Oh by the way, this is my secretary Lucy Leighton, and my son Adrian."

But Leah Morheim was not interested in Lucy and Adrian. She barely acknowledged their greeting. "Bet he didn't tell you about Dr McLeash," she said.

"Yes. 'Fraid so. As I said, he was very frank."

This time the girl looked disconcerted. She had the restlessness of the addict, continually plucking at her nails, pulling her hair, scratching at her arms.

"You know something Leah? You are very like your father. He too is very critical and unforgiving. Maybe that is why you hate him."

Leah glared at her. Adrian stood up so that his mother could sit down and he went into the bedroom and pulled out another chair. They sat around the girl in a circle watching her.

"I'm not at all like that shit," she protested. "I wanted to explain to you, make you see my mother was OK. I didn't want you to get the wrong idea. He bitches her so much. He never says a good word about her. Mamma was wonderful. She was talented. She was *fun.*"

She sighed and shook her head. "He could never see that though. He thought he was right and moral. She didn't stand a chance. He'd cast her in the role of scarlet woman and she couldn't get out. He used to bitch about his Papa too but he was doing *exactly* what he complained his Papa did. Being judgemental." She stared at them, "Always criticising her. Saying she was a whore. She *wasn't*. She just wanted to be normal. Have fun. Laugh a lot. Live and love."

"She told me he should have married the Virgin Mary. He wanted someone, she said, to put on a pedestal and worship. Not flesh and blood like Mamma. He drove her *mad*. He criticised her all the time. He called her the whore of Babylon. I liked that. I thought it sophisticated . . . cool! He caught me once in my bedroom, dressed up, wearing Mamma's high heels and lipstick and he lost it. I thought he was going to have a fit. I was terrified. He shut me in the wardrobe for the day. It was the longest day of my life. He let me out when it was dark."

She looked out over the sea, her voice a whisper. "I've never been able to sleep without a light since then." She was silent a moment, then continued, "He told me once, 'If you're not careful you'll grow up to be like your mother!'" She appealed to them. "Didn't he see that that was *exactly* what I wanted: to be like her. I *adored* her. She shone. She was dazzling. I wish . . . I wish . . ." Her lips trembled and she squeezed them together. "I wish I had *half* of what she had."

Lucy covered the restless, ringed hands with hers. "I know. I know," she murmured fervently, filled with unbearable sympathy.

Leah snatched her hands away. "No you *don't*. How could you? I hate it when people say that."

"But she *does* know," Adrian insisted gently. "Her mother was a dazzling actress herself, a star.

Mercedes Marchant lit up the London stage for two decades. She was before your time."

Leah was taken aback. "Gee, I'm sorry. Oh hell, I always think I'm unique."

"You are," Clarissa said promptly, "but not in *every* way. Everyone we meet, there are always differences *and* similarities."

Leah looked tentatively at Lucy. "You had it too? Everyone comparing, seeing you don't measure up? Expecting something, you don't know what . . . maybe even *they* don't know what. Shit, it's awful!"

Lucy nodded. It was too complicated to discuss. There were points of reference but she also felt there were enormous differences. It was much simpler for her, Lucy felt, so simple that it would seem stupid. Infantile and unhip. For Lucy had accepted her mother's position in her life, accepted it, had come to terms with it and acceptance is all. There was no point in trying to change a situation that was cast in stone.

"Just as long as you don't make my Mamma out to be a whore. That's why I'm here. It's what Papa does. I'll take you to court. I'll sue you for millions . . ."

"Hang on Leah. There's no need to threaten me. I don't take kindly to blackmail. I've told you. I've no intention of making your mother out to be a whore."

"It was what Papa called her. She couldn't help being beautiful and sexy. She couldn't help other men wanting her." She was crying now but she did not seem to be aware of her tears. The kohl was streaking her face as she sobbed and she suddenly appeared very young to Clarissa. "She couldn't help that he criticised her all the time for being what she was, being herself. She couldn't help that he was a puritan through and through." She looked at Lucy as if only she could understand, "There is no joy in my Papa. No laughter. Did Jesus ban laughter?" she asked.

Lucy shook her head. "No!" she cried. "Oh no!"

"My mother was a naturally joyous creature and my father killed that joy. It was the worst thing he did to her."

She tightened her lips again and looked over the sea. "Why did he do that? It is as much a crime as killing her body. The worst thing was killing her spirit, not the murder. But he doesn't understand that." She glanced up. "He told me, his daughter all about that. Can you believe it? He wanted forgiveness." She snorted. "Some hope. Oh it came as no surprise. I'd felt it. I read the papers, put two and two together. But forgive him? Never! He'll have to stew forever in his guilt. All I care!" The tears splashed unheeded on her cheeks and her voice was defiant.

"I think you should try to forgive him Leah. For your own sake," Clarissa said. "You'll wear yourself out, hating him like this. You're only hurting yourself. It will eat you up, like your father's guilt is eating him up."

Leah tossed her head. Her make-up was slipping

in the heat, what was left of it now that her tears had streaked the kohl. She looked a mess. She stood suddenly. "I gotta go," she said, "Luciano is expecting me. I'm staying with him for the moment." Luciano didn't like her very much, Lucy knew that, but, she thought, that would not worry him. He had his painting and Leah would be a mere peripheral irritation.

"Thank you for coming Leah," Clarissa said. "And for what it is worth I was going to paint your mother as I see her: a glamorous and beautiful star that poor Conrad just couldn't handle. I never had any intention of painting her as a whore. Far from it. I think I got an accurate picture of both of them."

"Good!" Leah replied.

"And Leah. They were both good people at heart. They were just very bad for each other."

Leah looked at Clarissa and nodded. Then she was gone leaving a faint smell of grass behind her.

"Well!" Clarissa sighed, then looking at Lucy suggested, "Why don't you take Adrian to the Belvedere and show him the view from there." She smiled at Adrian. "It's unbelievable. You'll think you've died and gone to heaven."

"But the work—" Lucy began.

"I've nothing at the moment for you Lucy. I have to edit some of the stuff before you type it up for me."

Adrian stood. "Come on Lucy. You're stuck with me. Show me this view, then I'll buy you lunch."

"Off you go children and enjoy yourselves,"

Clarissa urged them, a little smile on her lips. "And don't hurry back," she called after them, smiling more broadly as she watched them disappear down the driveway, Adrian holding Lucy's hand.

Chapter Twenty-Six

They were alone in the Belvedere. Capri spread her bounty at their feet. The sea heaved, swollen and indigo shot with clear emerald-green currents. The flowers around them opened their petals and exuded a scent that went straight to their heads.

"You know what Ma is up to Lucy, don't you?" Adrian asked standing close to her. She nodded. "Do you mind?" he persisted.

She turned and looked at him. "No," she whispered hesitantly. "No. I don't mind at all."

"You see Lucy, from the first moment I saw you, standing at the top of the stairs in the Savoy, I've loved you."

Her eyes widened, "You did? But . . ."

"Oh I know. It's not supposed to be like that. But it was, for me. There you stood, everything you felt on that beautiful face of yours—"

"*Pretty*. Not beautiful. Pretty."

"*Beautiful!* You hear me, beautiful. You are beautiful Lucy, inside as well as out. You are beautiful, beautiful, beautiful and I can't live without you."

She stared at him and for the first time in her

life everything, absolutely everything was right. In place. Harmonious. No regrets about the past, no yearnings for the future.

"Oh Adrian!"

She had felt happy before, at peace before, but there had always been something at the edge of her mind, some anxiety unresolved, some happening she would not be up to, some achievement she could not attain. Now all that melted away and her trust was firmly handed over to him. A sacred gift. He understood.

He took her in his arms. She just reached his heart. He held her close and she was home. Sheltered and safe.

She could lay down her burdens now; share them with someone else. She felt a huge wave of love sweep over her like the water below over the rocks.

"Ma is a wily old bird, isn't she?" he commented, smiling.

Lucy giggled. "Sure is," she said burying her face in his chest. She could feel his lips in her hair and his hands held her tight.

"I want to get to know you Lucy, everything about you. It's going to be fun. Such fun."

Yes, Lucy knew it would be fun with Adrian. Building a life. Sharing a life. Yes, it would be fun. She smiled a secret little smile and whispered, "Am I really beautiful Adrian?"

He tilted her face up to his. "Oh yes!" he assured her. "You're *very* beautiful my darling. Very beautiful indeed. And I intend to spend the rest of my life telling you that you are." Then he looked out to sea and said, "I think the time has come to go home, don't you?"

She said yes, and she meant it. This time she didn't mind at all.

Epilogue

Adrian and Lucy were on their way to the opera when it happened. Every so often Clarissa asked them to join her at the Royal Opera House to hear a favourite piece and they always accepted her invitation with alacrity. Both of them loved the Garden but even more than that they loved her company. A babysitter would be duly employed, they would dress up and make a night of it.

They lived in a pretty little mews house off the Moscow Road. It was not smothered in bourgainvillea and there was no hibiscus or wisteria but Lucy had put two tubs outside the brightly painted front door and planted them with geraniums and ivy, and each window had a windowbox planted seasonally. They were empty at the moment because it was winter.

Adrian shivered in his raincoat. He wore it over his dinner-jacket though it was no real protection against the wind from the north.

They got into the black London taxi relieved because it was so warm and they were out of the cold.

The mews house was small and Adrian had been discussing with Lucy and his mother the need to move to a larger house. Their two children, Mercedes aged four and Dominick aged two, would soon need separate rooms, and to their joint delight Lucy was pregnant again.

Clarissa had written a biography of Conrad Morheim and it had been a huge success so she could afford to help them. Why these things happened no one could predict but the story of Conrad Morheim had shot to the top of the bestseller list and was proving a nice little earner for Clarissa. The time was right, Clarissa's publisher had told her, the public were terribly interested in ecology; it was the flavour of the year and the book capitalised on the public's interest.

Conrad was nowhere to be found. He appeared to have vanished off the face of the earth. The *paparazzi* had descended on the Villa Azura only to be met by Han Su and the black dogs with the information that Signor Morheim had gone away and no matter how much they searched the island no one could find him. Bebe lamented his disappearance and the Contessa wrote a stinging letter of condemnation to Clarissa saying she thought her unkind biography must have driven him mad. '*He's left all his friends and it is your fault,*' she wrote, as if Conrad had ever been friends with Risa, Clarissa snorted.

The book had actually been a portrait of an obsessed writer, disillusioned by society, unable to shake off the teachings of his childhood and utterly under the spell of his wife. People loved it, and Clarissa felt that Conrad would agree her assessment had been fair. Her conscience was clear.

Lucy glanced at Adrian, at his dear profile, his kind face. He was so good, so gentle and she loved him so much. And he was such fun. He had been right about that.

She could not imagine life without him. He was the star that guided her in the dark, the friend she had never had, the good companion she had always longed for, the lover who completed her, the beloved father of her children.

She thought of the girl she had been at her mother's funeral six years ago. So much had happened to change her and when she thought about it she knew that she had everything she truly wanted.

Errol Armitage had said as much at dinner the other night. They had become good friends. He had tracked her down after her return from Capri and she had introduced him to Adrian who had taken to him as she had known he would. At all events they often dined together either in his apartments or in the little mews and Clarissa often joined them.

Lucy thought they were very compatible and she tried her hand at matchmaking but they both confided in Lucy that they were used to living alone and did not feel at this late stage that they wanted to change their way of life. But they saw a lot of each other, went to the theatre together, to concerts and openings, shared cosy little dinners in the best restaurants in London and generally enjoyed each other's company enormously. Lucy, however, lived in hope. She wanted everyone to be as happy as she and believed that the only way to such happiness was marriage.

Errol was godfather to little Dom. Unfortunately Anthony had to be content in being an avuncular godfather to Mercedes, as Davina still remained reluctant to breed. Anthony had been best man at Lucy and Adrian's wedding. Adrian had said afterwards that it had taken every ounce of restraint to stop himself from wiping the self-satisfied grin off Anthony's face.

"He's taking complete credit," he informed Lucy who laughed and told her new husband that he deserved to.

"If it had not been for Anthony's kind idea I would never have met your mother and therefore I would never have met you. Think what a disaster that would have been." She gazed at him with tenderness and he began to kiss her. He always began to kiss her when she had that look in her eyes.

The taxi got stuck in Long Acre and then waited in Floral Street. It was nose to nose for at least ten minutes and showed no sign of moving so Lucy suggested that as they were so near the Opera House they should get out and walk. "You'll be cold darling," Adrian protested, but Lucy insisted. Adrian paid off the driver and they got out and walked down Floral Street.

Lucy noticed the little group. A man and a girl were helping a vagrant off the ground. There was a battered old van and it seemed to Lucy that the couple were trying to help the vagrant into it. He was obviously worried about some stuff in a black bin bag which was in the corner of the doorway he had been occupying. He was a pitiful sight, holding his sleeping bag to his chest as if it was infinitely precious, which, Lucy supposed, it must be to him.

"Poor sod." Adrian had noticed the direction of her attention. "Poor bastard. Anyone who says they *choose* to live like that is an insensitive idiot. Come along Lucy, he's being looked after. I don't want you to catch cold. God help him. How could he sleep out tonight? It's freezing!"

But Lucy's knees had turned to jelly and her heart thumped in her breast as if it would burst her rib-cage. She grabbed the street-lamp and prayed that she would not fall.

She had seen the face of the helper. The man was carefully striving to retrieve the bin-liner full of who knows what, and put the vagrant into the back of the car. He seemed to be trying to reassure the man that the bag was going to follow.

It was Conrad Morheim.

Lucy had not expected her reaction to this figure from the past. His hair she saw was greyer, the eyes hollow, the expression grim. Typical Conrad.

"Darling are you all right?" Adrian had stopped because she had. She leaned against a parked car her hand against her breast. She hoped Adrian would not see him.

"Yes, yes. Just a dizzy turn." She glanced up at Adrian, at his anxious face peering down at her.

Then she looked across the narrow street and at that moment Conrad looked at her. Their eyes met. He stared at her and gave an infinitesimal shake of his head, as if to say: no, don't recognise me. Pretend I'm not here. The glance was piercing but was soon over. He had looked at her for a mere second yet she felt her whole being in chaos.

"Darling, would you like to go home?"

She shook her head. "No. No."

"I don't want you . . . you must take care . . . the baby . . ."

"I'm fine. Really I am."

Lucy looked at the girl with Conrad. It was Leah. She looked exactly the same. They had the vagrant in the car now and they both got into it, into the front seats. The car had 'St Clements' Help For The Homeless' written on the side. Lucy read it as Conrad drove past them and out into the main thoroughfare in Long Acre. His face was illuminated briefly in the light spilt from the street-lamp. His cheeks were hollow but his face was more relaxed than she remembered.

"I'm fine," she told Adrian, feeling normal again.

Why had she reacted that way she wondered, her heart leaping like a salmon, her knees rubber? Was this how Conrad had felt about Mara? This emotional violence? This internal chaos? She could only thank heaven that she did not have to put up with such overwhelming onslaughts of confused feeling. She could not have sustained it. I'd die, she thought. Like Mara, I'd die.

So Conrad had taken Clarissa's advice. She'd tell Clarissa at an appropriate time and wouldn't she be pleased. She might add a codicil to her book. A footnote.

Lucy smiled up at Adrian. His look of concern touched her heart as Conrad Morheim never could. Tenderness, she decided. That was what was so absent in Conrad and Mara's relationship, tenderness. She wouldn't trade all the weak-kneed passion, heart-thumping emotion in the world for one moment of Adrian's tenderness. She decided, as she looked up at her husband, smiling tremulously, that all the heartbeats of the glamorous were not worth one look of tenderness from his blue eyes.

"It's what separates the men from the boys. The women from the girls," she told Adrian, laughing. His face cleared.

"Oh, you're all right Lucy. I was worried. What are you talking about?"

"Nothing," she smiled at him, "nothing. Except I love you."

"I know sweetness." He kissed her cheek. "And I love you." Then he looked up. "There's Mother," he told her, "and Errol. Come on darling, I'm dying for a drink."

Lucy took the proffered arm. She thought of

Conrad and Leah tending the destitute. A man of extremes.

She decided she was a moderate person. She decided the journey was over.

PERDITA'S PASSION

PERDITA'S PASSION

Genevieve Lyons

PAN BOOKS

This edition published 1999 by Pan Books
an imprint of Macmillan Publishers Ltd
25 Eccleston Place, London SW1W 9NF
Basingstoke and Oxford
Associated companies throughout the world
www.macmillan.co.uk

This first world edition published in Great Britain 1997 by
SEVERN HOUSE PUBLISHERS LTD of
9-15 High Street, Sutton, Surrey SM1 1DF
First published in the USA 1998 by
SEVERN HOUSE PUBLISHERS INC of
595 Madison Avenue, New York, NY 10022.

British Library Cataloguing in Publication Data

Lyons, Genevieve
Perdita's passion
1. Love stories
1. Title
823.9'14 [F]

ISBN 0 330 39651 X

Typeset by Hewer Text Composition Services Limited,
Edinburgh, Scotland.
Printed and bound in Great Britain by
Mackays of Chatham plc, Chatham, Kent

This book is for my lovely friend Barbara Westerberg who introduced me to the Brooke Hospital for Animals upon whom the Cooke Hospital in this book is based. They do the most wonderful work in Egypt and Petra and all around the Middle East. I would like to thank them for their help and wish them well for the future in their wonderful work.
And to my beloved daughter Michele.

Chapter One

As the clergyman said the words, "I now pronounce you man and wife," Perdita saw Larry turn away from his bride and look over his shoulder directly at her.

She was just behind the bride and groom, decked out in her finery. "Like a bloody Christmas tree," she thought.

Posy had chosen the dress, a frilly pink number that was not at all Perdita's style. She felt uncomfortably aware that neither the colour nor the cut suited her. She looked, she decided, like part of the wedding cake.

She stood rooted to the spot clutching the bride's bouquet, white-knuckled as if she was in the dentist's waiting room.

Larry had to turn quite awkwardly to see her. Why had he done that? It embarrassed and excited her. Struggling as she was with her feelings, trying so very hard to accept the fact that he was marrying someone else, she had psyched herself up for this day. Since last he held her in his arms, she had relegated him to another compartment of her mind; a sealed compartment. She had demoted him from passionate lover to friend and that was so difficult, and very, very painful.

It was odd, she thought, how she could go on doing

normal things even when momentous things were happening. Even while her heart was breaking she ate, blew her nose, coughed, swallowed.

She was a spunky girl. She was a survivor; someone who struggled to conquer her emotions, not allow them to dominate her. She was used to doing these things, managing herself, and even though her heart was broken her stern upbringing prevented her from what her mother described contemptuously as 'going to pieces'.

It had to be faced and she faced it bravely, full-on, even though the pain in her chest threatened to overwhelm her. The man she loved so passionately, the only man she had ever loved, would ever love and whom she had thought loved her was marrying Posy Gore, her best friend. How could that be? Why had he deserted her? What had she done? Where had she gone so wrong that he was marrying someone else?

And Posy? What was Posy thinking of? Were they really in love? Did Larry love Posy, then, more than he had loved her? It seemed impossible, yet at the moment when he had uttered the most sacred words, the clincher words, the binding-together words, he had turned around in the church and looked at *her*.

Had Posy noticed? Perdita was not sure, it had happened so quickly, was over in a flash.

The church was full of light. The sun shone as if a film director had arranged it, in shimmering rays slanting directly on to the bride and groom, spotlighting them. Perdita heard Larry's cousin, Leonard Dalton, a photographer by profession, murmur, "Lovely, lovely, oh boy that's perfect, perfect, perfect!" as he snapped the event for posterity. There was another professional somewhere with a camcorder whirring away.

The church was packed with well-dressed, stylish people with happy, smiling faces. Some of the women, mainly the married ones, were dabbing their eyes with tissues or handkerchiefs, depending on their ages, very careful of their make-up. Each recalling, sentimentally, their own wedding day, those days in their lives when everything seemed perfect, when the world was full of hope, their hearts full of love and the future stretched before them, unrealistically trouble-free. Only Perdita struggled. "Oh God, help me to stop loving him," she prayed as the organ crashed out Mendelssohn's *Wedding March* in triumphant crescendo.

Posy's veil was back now and as she turned she smiled radiantly at Perdita, accepting the return of her bouquet from her friend's outstretched hands. Was there a hint of victory in Posy's eyes as she smiled at Perdita?

Larry was not looking at her now, but he was not looking at Posy either. He was looking at Leonard who was snapping away, dancing backwards down the aisle. The 'someone else' who was capturing it all on video whirred away just behind him and Perdita flinched as his lens pointed towards her face. She did not want to be captured forever on tape looking pained and tense, her eyes full of anguish. To be frozen like that forever, with her feelings naked on her face, would be awful.

They went out into the sun, the organ music ringing in their ears. Rice and confetti were thrown. People laughed and squealed excitedly. Everyone seemed happy, full of good humour, only Perdita ached for it all to be over.

She thought, despondently, that she would have to

sit at the wedding feast, keep smiling, keep up the act for another couple of hours at least. Was she capable of that? The pain inside her twisted her heart, tightened her throat and made her head throb unmercifully. It was the first time she had seen Larry in months and she had not known it would be so agonising. Every lovely curve of his face, every precious bone in his body was so very dear to her, so familiar, so beloved. How could she live without him? I know every inch of you, she thought, I love every tiny bit of you, so how did this happen? I thought you loved me. Oh God, Larry, I believed you loved me with the same passion that I loved you. Well, she thought, I was wrong. So wrong.

The village church was very old, chosen for its quaintness. Posy was not a very religious person. She stood under the apple trees by the lych-gate, her arm through her new husband's, smiling up into his face and Perdita hoped vindictively that an apple would fall, plonk on top of the bride's head. But it didn't. Her wish went unanswered and Leonard and some of the camera-mad crowd click-clicked at Posy's laughing face.

Then she too turned and looked over her shoulder at her friend, at Perdita. The russet leaves drifted down like the confetti all around her and this time there was no mistaking the look of triumph she shot at Perdita, no mistaking it at all. "I've got him," her expression said, "You haven't!"

As Perdita stared at her friend, her father came up behind her. The sound of his voice in her ear startled her.

"Let him slip through your fingers, eh Perdy?" he remarked. "Bloody careless of you!" Perdita shivered.

How was it he always managed to hurt her, always managed to say the one thing that would pain her most. "You do not look your best, my dear, in pink," he continued. "You shouldn't have allowed Posy to put you in that particular colour, and that dress makes you look like a cream-puff!"

Perdita squeezed back her tears. He could still do it. Still hurt her, his words slicing through her, cutting, cruel. I should be used to it by now, she thought, I should, after twenty-five years, have developed some kind of immunity.

And I thought I had. But I'm so vulnerable today, so very raw. Perhaps I should not have come.

And where's David? she wondered. And Fern? Surely they should be here too.

She blinked her eyes rapidly and swallowed. She could see the glamorous figure of her mother talking to Leonard Dalton near the ancient church porch. He was snapping her and she was laughing, saying something flattering to him no doubt, but she had one eye on Perdita's father, Lucas. She too seemed vulnerable, Perdita thought. Distressed. There was a wild look in her eye that was quite out of character. She wants him to notice her, Perdita decided, but he won't be impressed. He'll disappoint as usual. Her parents were often not on speaking terms.

Her mother did look beautiful. Stunning really. She always made Perdita feel awkward and unworthy. She wore black and white, a huge-brimmed black straw hat, like a halo in a Byzantine icon. It had a white grosgrain ribbon around the crown. She wore a white silk dress with a black rose print and a black silk swagger coat, short and fluid over it. So chic!

Perdita did not reply and her father moved away. He was flirting with Vicky Mendel, a girl who used to be at school with Posy and Perdita. Vicky had blossomed, there was no other word for it; bloomed and blossomed.

In the dim and distant past Vicky had been overweight and spotty, thick-bodied and unattractive and she had, naturally or by dint of ruthless dedication, Perdita was not sure which, turned herself into a page three girl. Literally. Perdita's eyes had nearly popped out of her head when, over a commuter's shoulder on the tube one day, she caught sight of a near-naked babe, full page in his newspaper and thought there was something familiar about her. The man was drooling over the photo of the topless girl and, craning to see the name, Perdita had instantly remembered. How could she ever forget? Vicky Mendel the ugly bully had turned into this curvaceous chick. The ugly duckling had become a swan. Well, maybe not a swan, Perdita reflected, a pouter pigeon might be nearer the mark. There she was in the paper, re-packaged, bare breasts proudly aimed at the reader, a saucy grin on her face.

Perdita had told Posy the awesome news, that Vicky Mendel was a page three girl, but Posy took the information calmly saying, yes, she thought everyone knew.

"How'd you expect me to know?" Perdita had asked crossly, "I don't read that paper!"

And Posy had said, "Well, neither do I, but it didn't surprise me!" and Perdita realised that Posy had not known about Vicky but for some reason had pretended she did.

She looked now with distaste at her father preening before the sexy, big-breasted girl. A contemporary of his daughter. The fact did not seem to bother or deter Lucas Hastings. He wore on his face that buccaneer grin that made him what the BBC called 'the thinking woman's crumpet'. Not that Vicky Mendel could by any stretch of the imagination be called a thinking woman.

"Your father's playing true to form," her mother's voice in her ear made Perdita jump. "Who's the girl?" she asked.

"Vicky Mendel. From school," she replied reluctantly.

"You mean that chunky little bully you and Posy hated so much? The one who didn't get to go to see Lucas on his programme?" Perdita nodded. "Well, well, well. She did finally get to meet him," her mother's voice was waspish. "She looks like a tart and is behaving like a tart, so she probably *is* a tart!"

"Oh Mother!" Perdita's tone was resigned. She was used to her mother's caustic comments, her father's put-downs yet they always affected her. She wished she could develop a thick hide, that what her parents said would cease to hurt so badly, that so many relatively unimportant things would cease to *matter* to her so much. The smallest thing, she reflected, threw her, building up real or imagined slights into agonizing facts.

They were piling into the cars now. Leonard took Perdita's arm. "Come with me," he invited, "you look quite lost there, all alone."

"Oh Leonard!" she felt herself wilting before him, her brave facade crumbling.

"That bad?" he asked. She nodded. "Larry?"

"Oh yes," she breathed in painfully.
"Your dad?"
"Mmmm."
"Your mother?"
"Mmm. Oh, everything. Everyone."

She looked up into Leonard's kind sympathetic face. "It's awful! Life sucks!"

Leonard smiled. He had a nice smile. She wondered why she could not fall in love with him. Why, oh why did it have to be Larry Burton?

Leonard took her arm. "Come on," he said. "It will pass. I promise." He cocked his head. "I'll drive you to the Savoy. You can cry as much as you like in the car."

The wedding party was to be held in the Savoy, in the River Room overlooking the Thames. Perdita was only too happy to go with Leonard. It removed her a little from the main protagonists, gave her a little space.

Leonard's car was around the side of the church. Green velvet fields stretched away to the horizon and here and there little cottages snuggled into the land looking serene and somehow reassuring. They had been there for so long, surviving wars, love, hate, family tragedies and dramas and celebration. The message was, as Leonard said, that everything passes. Except property. She thought of Oak Wood Court and sighed.

Perdita smiled at Leonard. "I'm grateful," she said as they got into the car and fastened their belts.

"It's okay," he replied turning the key in the ignition, glancing at her. "You still love Larry, don't you? Even though . . ."

"Oh yes, I still love him, Leonard," she turned away

from him, looking out of the window, "I didn't know till today how much."

"What went wrong?" he asked. She shrugged.

"I don't *know* what happened. It's a mystery."

"You don't, eh?" He sounded disbelieving. He backed the car out of the lane and began to drive towards the motorway.

She stared at him. "Do *you* know, Leonard?" she asked.

"Well, I think . . . See I tried to guess. I've written the scenario. You fell out of love with him . . ."

"Oh no. No, no, no!" There was pain in her protests.

"Well, I thought maybe you'd thrown him over, and then, obviously Posy moved in. I didn't believe that Larry would be such a fool not to get wise to Posy. She's so transparent. But Larry is old fashioned."

"What do you mean, Leonard? I don't understand."

"What a perfect couple you and Larry would make. You're as innocent as he is. How two such bright people can be so naïve I don't know!"

"What do you mean?"

"Oh, Perdita, everyone knows it except you. And maybe Larry. Posy wants to *be you*." He bit his lip and glanced sideways at Perdita. "I think she's pregnant," he said.

Perdita frowned, digesting this. "Larry's baby?" she asked in a choked voice. "Ah, Jesus!"

Leonard swung the car around the corner leading to the motorway. That would do it, she knew, for Larry. He was so chivalrous, so conscientious. He would insist on being responsible. But she couldn't believe it. That meant he'd had sex with Posy when he was supposed to be loving her. But Leonard continued. "I wouldn't put anything past her. She may be lying."

"Oh, Leonard, don't be so unkind," she protested but it was automatic.

"Well, it's true. Little Posy gets what little Posy wants come hell or high water, haven't you noticed?"

"Not particularly. She's always been a good friend to me," Perdita had said this so often it sounded like a mantra. "When I was lonely and had no one . . ." her voice trailed off.

"You are *too* loyal Perdita," Leonard said, and then, frowning, "Now shut up and let me concentrate on my driving."

They were on the motorway. Perdita could see the large black limousine with the white ribbons fluttering from the bonnet ahead of them. It was going to be a long day.

She sat back and lapsed into silence and allowed Leonard to get on with it. She thought, remembering their lives together, so entwined, that Posy had indeed always been there. Always.

Chapter Two

Perdita remembered when she first saw Posy Gore, the very first time she had really noticed her.

Posy was sitting on the low bench in the school changing room clutching a shoe-bag. She was staring at the milling throng of uniformed teenagers around her with wide, frightened eyes.

They were changing for gym and Perdita felt a tug of pity for the small girl sitting there as if frozen to the spot.

"Hey, you new?" she asked. The girl looked up, nodding. She had scared eyes and a hungry expression.

"She left me here," she whispered and Perdita could see she was scared. "And I don't know, I don't know . . . what . . . where . . ."

"Here, let me help. You must have Anna Dent's locker. She left. Her parents are in the Dip Service. Most of the girls here have parents overseas." Then, seeing the bewilderment on the girl's face she explained. "Diplomatic Service," she said.

The stranger nodded. "I know. My father is ambassador to Mhulendi," she stared at Perdita. "It's in Africa. He doesn't want me there because he says the schools are not up to scratch. Is your father in the . . ." she paused, glanced shyly at Perdita, "the, er, Dip Service too?"

They giggled together at this and Perdita shook her head. "No, my father is a TV presenter. Lucas Hastings." She always sighed when she imparted this piece of information, expecting the awed response. Posy did not disappoint. "God! You mean *Lucas Hastings*! On the BBC? *Lucas Hastings* is your *father*?"

"Yeah."

"Holy mackerel!"

The girl introduced herself as Posy Gore and latched onto Perdita instantly and forever. It seemed natural for Perdita, after their meeting, to show the newcomer around, explain the routine of the school to her. She showed the new girl the ropes and found that Posy clung to her like ivy.

Perdita did not mind and they became friends. Indeed she was grateful for she had no friends of her own anyway.

St Catherine's was a fashionable private boarding school. Most of the girls there had parents abroad. Perdita's parents, however, had sent her there not because they travelled but because they did not really want her around.

"Father says it's for my good, that this is the best school in England," she told Posy, "but he can't fool me. He just doesn't like me much. He *hates* my mother."

"I can't wait to meet him," Posy said. Perdita looked at her, puzzled. "Oh, I don't think you will," she told her new friend, "*I* hardly ever see him myself."

Posy smiled and did not argue. They lay in the dorm whispering, the curtain between their beds pulled back.

Perdita had wondered at the chance that had taken Jessie Lomax out of that bed and into Anna Dent's now vacant one down at the bottom of the dormitory. When she asked Jessie the girl giggled and said, "That new girl, Posy, gave me a gold chain if I'd move. She must have a pash on you, to think you're worth a gold chain."

"Oh, don't talk rot," Perdita had retorted sharply, but it made her think. Then she forgot about it.

"It's a bit thick though," she told Posy, "knowing you irritate your father and your mother hardly knows you're alive. We have a house in Berkshire but my father is hardly ever there. Mother is an interior decorator and she has a *pied à terre* in Kensington. Father practically *lives* in the studios. He has a poky little place in Shepherd's Bush." She shrugged. "He says he chose it deliberately with no room for anyone except himself."

"My dad is *always* preoccupied," Posy told her. "He's got no time for me. I don't irritate him like you said you irritate your father. That at least would be *something*. He's just *worried* all the time. But he smiles. He's always smiling, never stops no matter what upsets we have. Always has this grin on his face, but his eyes are desperate."

"And your mother?" Perdita asked.

"Oh, Mother is scared too. It's contagious, fear is. Ever notice? If one person is afraid it *infects* others. She doesn't sort of have *time* to be anything but worried. She *says* she worries about me all the time but I don't believe she does. I think she just worries out of habit. She never writes and seldom phones. When I call her she's never there and if she is she only talks for a minute, then says she has to go." Posy was silent for a moment, then she said "But I'm going to change my life, see if I don't. I'm going to get everything I want."

"Oh dear, what a right pair we are!" Perdita laughed. She pulled the curtain across.

"Night, Posy."

"Night, Perdy." Silence, then, "Perdita?"

"Yeah?"

"We're friends, aren't we?"

"Sure," Perdita was drowsy, wanting to sleep.

"Best, best friends. Friends till death," Posy insisted.

"Sure."

"Till death us do part." Posy's voice was intense.

"Of course. Now let me sleep," Perdita yawned and drifted off into oblivion.

It was nice to have a friend. Perdita was a lonely girl. Neglected by her parents, until Posy came on the scene she had spent most of her time by herself. She did not make friends easily and being Lucas Hastings's daughter did not help.

She had inherited her mother's beauty and her father's intelligence and a lot of the girls were jealous of her. Though she did not impress or startle at first glance, hers was a beauty for the connoisseur. Wonderful bones, elegant lines, a Filippo Lippi Madonna. She was tall and rangy and, horror of horrors, could eat what she liked without putting on weight. It was perhaps this more than anything else that made the others reject her and hold her in suspicion.

She got firsts in her exams without too much swotting and that did not help either. So, in spite of the fact that such a girl was, in books, the favourite, the leader, in real life Perdita found she aroused only resentment and envy.

Another thing that aroused their animosity was the fact that all the girls wanted her to get them tickets for various TV shows; chat shows to meet their favourite pop stars, game shows to win big prizes and make an impression, and simply to be invited into the glamour (as they thought) of the studios and the media people. They could see no reason other than sheer meanness why she wouldn't accommodate them. Her father had the number one show on telly, and they simply did not believe her when she told them that her father wouldn't oblige.

Lucas Hastings refused point blank to get tickets for anyone, ever. He was adamant. So Perdita had to tell her fellow students and classmates that her father did not go in for that sort of thing, but they didn't believe her.

"If he once started," she told them, "he says the demand would never end. He decided he wouldn't ever make an exception for anyone, ever."

The girls refused to understand and it did nothing to help Perdita's popularity.

Perdita herself did not help matters herself by not appearing to care. A little display of vulnerability or need might have softened hearts which were intrinsically hard, but she was fiercely proud and refused to stoop to subterfuge to gain friendship and acceptance. Besides, she had been rebuffed by her parents and knew the hurt of rejection, and so she guarded herself against it.

Posy filled an empty space in her life and if she was not the ideal companion, someone Perdita would have chosen for herself, nevertheless Perdita was glad of her friendship.

There was one girl, large, unattractive and a bully, who hated the tall leggy blonde and who relentlessly played tricks on Perdita, generally endeavouring to make as much mischief for her as possible. Perdita tried not to allow Vicky Mendel to get to her. Underneath, Vicky, like all bullies, was weak and had an inferiority complex.

Perdita was stronger both mentally and physically but she was incapable of using the sort of tactics, the show of strength needed to stop Vicky and her little set.

Besides she was so used to her father and mother verbally abusing her to be able to ignore the girl's vicious tongue. But until Posy's arrival at St Catherine's Perdita had combated Vicky Mendel's persecution, taunts and tricks with the same method she used on her father and mother: by pretending nothing was happening. She simply did not react.

Just suffered. Suffered dreadfully. Most nights she lay crying into her pillow, careful that no one heard her, loneliness engulfing her in waves. But she would not crack. When Posy came she had someone to share her suffering with and it made a huge difference. And Posy chose to remain staunchly at her side against the crowd. Perdita could not understand why, but she was very grateful.

Vicky had a gang and after Posy's arrival it seemed her sole purpose was to torment the two friends. Their schemes became outrageous and, angered that Perdita had an ally, the gang poured gallons of water on the friends' beds so that they had to sleep in wet beds for weeks. They filled the lockers beside their beds with new-born mice from the lab and their gym shoes with the contents of a jar of sauce from the kitchen.

It infuriated and frustrated Vicky that neither Posy nor Perdita were intimidated. They did not respond or let their taunts appear to hurt, treating the pranks and insults with lofty disdain. The girls did not seem to care if everyone thought them chicken when they refused dares. And all the time Posy was there, by Perdita's side, together with her in unpopularity.

Posy wanted to go to Oak Wood Court, the vast estate that old Jack Armstrong had left to his daughter, Perdita's mother.

"I've read all about it in *Hello*! magazine," she told Perdita, "Oh please, please, please invite me! I'm your best friend, aren't I?" She nagged and nagged until eventually Perdita asked her mother if she could bring her friend for the weekend.

"Of course, darling. But I do hope she'll know how to conduct herself. Who are her people?" This was the kind of remark that made Perdita reluctant to have Posy stay with her. Her mother, and her father, could make a person feel very awkward indeed. Perdita, however, had underestimated Posy.

"The Gores. Her father is Ambassador in Africa," Perdita told her mother.

"The South African Ambassador? White I presume?" and without waiting for a reply, "Oh, that's fine. I'll be there this weekend. I have to check up on the drapes in the library and Bates says the Persian carpet has caught the sun in the music room and there's a faded patch. Some silly maid forgot to close the shutters. So I'll see you then. Graham will pick you up in the car."

* * *

The school was not too far from Oak Wood Court, both being in Berkshire, and to Perdita's great embarrassment, Posy squealed in excitement when she saw the Rolls in front of the school entrance awaiting them, and Graham in full uniform holding the back door of the car open.

"Oooh Perdy! This is style! This is so cool!"

"Don't, Posy, *please*! It's too *gross*. It's *not* cool to go ballistic about a *car*. Unless it's a Lambourgini." She sighed. "Mother insists that they'll treat me better in the school if she flashes a bit of money about." Perdita rolled her eyes to heaven. "If only she knew! It makes them *hate* me. It's trashy to flash. Not the thing at all!"

Posy never oohed again in Perdita's presence, even though the grandeur of Oak Wood Court far exceeded her expectations.

They sat in the rear of the Rolls as it bore them smoothly up the driveway to the mansion surrounded by the wonderful hundred-year-old trees the place was named after. Posy could not restrain a gasp when the house hove into view. It was a gracious building: Corinthian pillars fronting a terrace that looked out over the lawns; the dolphin fountain in the middle; the rose garden to the right and the oak wood to the left. It conveyed a sense of permanence, an indifference to time, serene and classic, impervious to the hassles of the world.

"It's beautiful, Perdita," Posy breathed. She felt nervous now with the reality of wealth and privilege palpable in front of her, and she felt the stirrings of misgivings.

Melinda met them on the terrace. A man servant took

their cases from Graham and and disappeared with them into the great marble hall Posy could glimpse through the open front doors.

It was June and warm for the time of year and Melinda sat at the table on the terrace. Her greeting for her daughter was coolly distant and she welcomed Posy graciously but without warmth. She was, Posy thought, the most elegant and sophisticated woman she had ever seen in her beige Armani trouser suit and cream satin shirt, her grooming impeccable.

They sipped tea and nibbled cucumber sandwiches in silence. Melinda made absolutely no attempt at conversation. Posy, it seemed to Perdita, dwindled visibly in her mother's presence and she did not blame her friend. Posy seemed to shrink into her chair as if she wanted desperately to disappear and shook her head every time she was offered anything by the immaculately uniformed Filipina maid.

"Well, if you are finished Maria will show you your room, em, Posy," Melinda said at last, not really looking at her guest and Posy squirmed in her chair, wishing now she had never asked to come here, wishing she was a hundred miles away. "She's in the Yellow Room, Perdita." Then Melinda suddenly stared at the guest. "Maria will have unpacked for you. You'll find everything ready."

Melinda pressed a bell beside her on the white damask clothed table and Posy thought about her jumble of packing, and the state of her underwear and felt herself shrink under the stare.

In moments another Filipina maid appeared from the house.

"Take Miss Gore to her room, Maria." Melinda

glanced at Posy again. "I don't suppose you have appropriate clothes to dress for dinner," Melinda said calmly, looking her guest over, "but we do dress for dinner here so do your best. Perdita will lend you something. Everett Nash is dining with us and Lydia Beckworth."

"Oh, Mother, Lady Beckworth is absolutely *horrible!*" Perdita cried, "Why did you have to ask her? You know I hate her."

"Well, you'll have to put up with her this evening. That's what society is all about. Putting up with people you don't like and never allowing them to suspect it. Shows how well-bred you are." She sipped her tea and Posy did not know whether to rise or stay seated. She was acutely self-conscious and felt as if she was six times larger than normal.

Melinda's perfect face was without feeling. There was no shadow of joy or warmth to be found there, no glimmer of a smile broke the severity of her expression.

"Doctor Lovette is coming too, Perdita. Try to entertain him," she looked at Perdita, then Posy. "Perdita is not at her best entertaining," she said, "she does not have the social graces and I'm sure I don't know *where* I went wrong. My husband says it's all my fault! I hope you are more gifted, Posy, in that direction." She sighed. "Well, perhaps Perdita will improve when she gets out of these terrible teens."

She beckoned with a slim white hand and the maid drew near. "Maria," she said then turned to Posy. "They are *all* called Maria. It's an obsession with them." Then turning back to the maid, she said, "Please take Miss Gore to her room. Be down at seven-thirty for eight, Posy, please. Drinks in the library. All right, off you go."

"You never *told* me," Posy said when Perdita came to her room half-an-hour later carrying an evening dress over her arm.

"I *did.* I did, I did!" Perdita cried, "I told you over and over and over but you didn't *listen*!"

"It's so unfriendly! The house is a mausoleum." Posy shuddered. "It's scary."

"Well, I warned you but you *would* come."

"I thought your Mum and Dad might be a bit stand-offish, like in *Murder on the Orient Express* or *Death on the Nile*, but this is . . ."

"Well, I live with it," Perdita said tartly. "Here's a dress of mine you can borrow. Don't thank me either, I'm cross." She went to the door and turned. "This weekend is going to be a disaster, I can feel it in my bones. But then, all my weekends are disastrous, so what's new?" And she left Posy alone.

The rooms were coldly austere, Posy discovered. They were as unwelcoming as the hostess and Posy found the great house intimidating. But she was impressed and determined to fit in. She decided she could get used to the grandeur and formality of Oak Wood Court and decided to become a constant visitor there.

Perdita told her that her mother insisted on keeping everything as Grandfather Jack had had it, refusing to change anything. "It's a shrine," she told Posy, "and that's why I think Father is uncomfortable here."

Posy succeeded in her plan. She cultivated Melinda who was not impervious to her outrageous flattery. Posy instinctively knew how to ingratiate herself when she wanted. She had that social ability that Melinda derided her daughter for lacking, and that Perdita was too straightforward to manage. Posy knew how to please those who might be useful to her, aware of their unspoken needs from a light for a cigarette, a refilled glass to the right thing to say and when to listen and murmur assent. She was adept at massaging egos and persuading people of their own importance.

Perdita was not so gifted and often fell foul of her mother's acid tongue. There, too, Posy was sympathetic. She consoled Perdita often when her friend was reduced to tears at some carelessly cruel criticism made by Melinda.

So Posy overcame her nerves and often visited Oak Wood Court. She was very disappointed, however, that Lucas Hastings was never there.

"Doesn't Mr Hastings ever come down here?" she asked one evening when they were dining, just the three of them alone. They were in the library sipping sherry, Melinda was of the school that believed young people should be broken in to the social graces as soon as possible. Perdita had been allowed small quantities of alcohol since she turned twelve. "A sip of wine or champagne never hurt anyone," Melinda said. "Nobody *likes* the taste at first so best to get used to it early on."

Posy had never had alcohol before she came to Oak Wood Court and she loved the taste from her first sip. But she did not tell Melinda that. She was far too clever.

There were usually dinner guests at Oak Wood Court and sometimes house guests and Posy liked that too, although Perdita hated it. Posy had to pretend to her friend that she too was put out by the visitors, but in fact she adored the challenge of winning them over, of getting them to notice and like her.

And they did. They liked her because she made herself useful to them. She agreed with them. She flattered them.

But that night there were no visitors. Melinda had not expected to be there and was not in a good mood.

Losey, the gardener had told Bates the major-domo who had informed his mistress by fax to London that a strange sickness had attacked her roses and they needed specific treatment.

"I need her to see for herself. Decide which way to go. Won't take the responsibility on my own," Losey said.

If Melinda cared for anything apart from Lucas it was her roses. She loved that garden, its bowers, its arbours, the overwhelming scent, the beauty of the blooms. So she had come down to make her choice of cure for her darlings' sickness. She was worried more about their health than she would have been if Perdita had been ailing, and Perdita was aware of this.

Melinda was also cross for now she would miss the first performance of a new production of *Aida* at Covent Garden. Perhaps the Vicky Mendel situation would never have been resolved for Posy and Perdita if Melinda Hastings had not been so angry.

"No he doesn't, the stupid man," she replied to Posy's question about Lucas not coming to Oak Wood Court. She sounded more acerbic than usual. "Don't sit like that, Perdita, you look like a farm labourer."

"Sorry, Mother." Perdita sat up straight on the leather chair.

Her mother always asked her to sit there and she

always slid down and her mother always corrected her.

"How many times must I tell you?" Melinda asked rhetorically. "No, Lucas does not come to Oak Wood Court very often which is funny because it was one of the reasons he married me," she said bitterly.

"Mother, please!"

"Everyone *knows* Perdita. Besides Posy is almost one of the family. I only wish you had half her social graces."

"It's so sad I've never met him," Posy interpolated hastily. She was thrilled at Melinda's words but anxious not to upset Perdita. The last thing she wanted was for Perdita to go off her.

"Oh! Celebrity hunting, Posy?" Melinda hit out, accurately, to Posy's discomfiture. But Posy shook her head vehemently.

"Oh no! It's just that," she leaned confidingly towards Melinda, assessing her anger and the perfect climate for her plan, "remember how we told you about Vicky Mendel?"

Melinda nodded, "She sounds very ill-bred," she remarked, "not at all the thing." But she was not very interested.

Posy said, "Well, she's getting worse. She's doing filthy things now. Tell your mother, Perdy."

"Oh, it doesn't matter," Perdita said briskly. The last thing she wanted was to get her mother involved in school upsets. She only managed to make things worse. Melinda had an awkward habit of marching into the school, throwing her weight about, metaphorically speaking, and threatening Mrs Pollock and making everything impossible.

"Tell me, Posy, if my daughter won't."

"I just think it is best ignored. We are not reacting to her disgusting tricks so she'll get tired. Eventually."

"Yes. And maybe she'll have really hurt us by then," Posy said, "who knows what she'll think up next? See, Mrs Hastings," Posy turned to Melinda, "she put urine in Perdita's water. The glass we have beside our beds at night." Perdita looked out of the window, her face stony. Melinda looked horrified.

"But that's revolting! And dangerous. Outrageous. Why didn't you tell me, Perdita? I'll go back with you tomorrow and speak to this girl. And Mrs Pollock. I'll get Lucas to sue. I'll create such a scandal. I'll make a real stink . . ." Perdita sighed. "I told you," she whispered. But Posy protested aloud.

"That would only make it worse," she said, shaking her head. "No, Mrs Hastings, I have the perfect answer. Settle it all peacefully. No trouble. Only I don't think you could manage it," she said slyly.

Melinda's eyes glittered. It was a challange that Posy could not have put better. Perdita stared at her in admiration. Posy launched into her master plan. "*All* the girls want to see the TV studios. The BBC. They would *adore* to see your husband's show. It would be *educational* too. So, if Mr Hastings could let Perdy and me bring our friends, that is all the class *except* Vicky Mendel and her cronies, then I can guarantee they'd never bother us again."

"*I'll* get you tickets," Melinda said firmly.

"But Father will be—"

"Your father need not know anything about it. I'm his *wife* after all. I'll tell them it's to be a surprise. His daughter's class. Sure." Melinda sounded as if she would enjoy it, but Perdita sat horrified at the scenario that flitted through her mind. Her father would be furious and her mother would not be there.

"I wonder, could you get *two* sets?"

"Why two?"

"Oh, Perdy, don't be dense! We'll only ask our friends the first time. But we'll let it be known that Vicky could persuade us the second time . . . the carrot, see?"

"Dangle the possibility of a later visit to the Beeb depending on behaviour? You are a clever minx, Posy. I think I'd rather have you as a friend than an enemy," Melinda said dryly.

"But I'm not hurting anyone. I'm being a peace-maker," Posy said virtuously.

"But Mother, Father will be—"

"Don't worry about your father, Perdita," Melinda said, the light of battle in her eyes. "Leave him to me."

Melinda was, if the truth be known, delighted to have this opportunity to spite her husband. She had suffered so many slights, smarted under his indifference so acutely that she looked on this as a heaven-sent situation; a chance to get at him whilst helping her daughter. She got two sets of tickets behind her husband's back. She sent them to St Catherine's with instructions to allow Perdita and her chosen friends to go to the show.

Lucas's programme was a mixture of political cut and thrust, investigative reporting and interviews with the current names in Government, the literary world, the arts, film and pop worlds. It was presented in front of a live audience and Mrs Pollock, the headmistress, decided in her wisdom that the show would be an educational experience for her pupils.

Suddenly Perdita was the most popular girl in the school. She gave the list of names of the people she was inviting to the headmistress and noticed the flicker of understanding cross her face as her eyes travelled down the names. She knows, Perdita thought. She knows something has been going on and she hasn't done anything about it. She stared at the headmistress in disgust until the latter said, "Fine, Perdita. This is fine."

"Everyone's going from my class, except Vicky Mendel," Perdita said pointedly. But Mrs Pollock did not pick her up on it. "Vicky Mendel is not invited," Perdita added.

"Very well, the choice is yours, Perdita," Mrs Pollock replied and that was that. "You may go, Perdita, and remember I expect you all to behave like ladies."

Fifteen girls went to the show. Lucas was infuriated but, daunted by the horde of teenagers, he simply ignored them, leaving them to the ministrations of the hospitality staff.

The girls had a ball. They met a politician, which bored them, but Mrs Pollock would be pleased to hear about it. They met a superstar promoting her latest film who was delighted to spend a little time with them. Their obvious admiration repaired somewhat the damage Lucas's abrasive questioning had done. Last of all they met their dream-boat, Oggy Vac Two from the Hot Bed Bash, the very, very latest cool pop group. They gawped and sighed and he signed their autograph books, for he too felt a little squashed after his interview with Lucas Hastings, though unlike the film star he was not bright enough to fully comprehend the derision and contempt that he had been held up to.

After that, Vicky Mendel lost her gang. The other girls blamed her for their lack of invitation. The second tickets were never used, for Lucas Hastings issued a ban on anyone under eighteen being allowed into the audience. He announced that he was concerned about the morals of the young and his show, he insisted, was adult and sometimes contained unsuitable language. "A load of crap," was how his daughter summed it up.

"See," Posy said, "she knows now she's no match for you." She was referring to Vicky.

Perdita shrugged. "She never was," she replied calmly, "she was never worth bothering about. All her pranks were so *feeble*."

Posy said, "I think you're wonderful!"

Perdita said nothing. She did not want to be thought wonderful but it seemed ungracious to say so. She knew the truth; that she *wasn't* wonderful. Posy had this weird idea about her that she was special. But Perdita knew better. Her mother and father were really clever people and they found her a big disappointment. They could not be wrong. Posy, after all, was immature. What did she know?

She had taken Posy very much for granted and now, sitting in Leonard's car she thought about her in a detached way for the first time. Had she really thought Perdita was so wonderful? Why on earth had she invited Perdita to be her bridesmaid? To the wedding at all?

And Vicky? Why had she invited Vicky to her wedding? Perdita recalled that after the visit to the *Lucas Hastings Hour* Vicky had sucked up to the friends and, whereas Perdita had kept her at the usual arm's length, Posy had basked in being wooed by the girl.

Now Vicky was flirting with Lucas. Well, Perdita thought, she'll suffer for that. Lucas will flirt back and then, without conscience, he'll discard her. No matter what happened, Vicky would suffer. Her father made everyone suffer.

Vicky was someone else now, not the girl who bullied herself and Posy. That was another time, another world.

Leonard drove in silence, the car rolling smoothly towards London and the Savoy and Perdita took off the horrid little bunch of organza flowers and rested her head on the back of the seat, and remembered.

Chapter Three

She wondered when it was that Posy had begun to copy her. Posy's hair was wild and fluffy and dark but she had at some time cut it, had it straightened and dyed blonde. It did not suit her. The shoulder-length cloud of dark hair had haloed her small face, given it definition, while the flat blonde bob diminished her. When she came to think about it, Perdita realised that Posy wore her uniform the same length, wore her cardigan over her shoulders the way Perdita did, oh, and lots of other things. She wondered now why she had not thought it odd before.

Posy insisted on flattering her even though Perdita would shake her head and deny the compliment. "Oh don't talk tosh, Posy. I'm *not* beautiful. You know I'm not. Lucas says I'm the ugly duckling that *won't* turn into a swan."

"Oh, your father's an artist. He's creative," Posy told Perdita earnestly, "it's to be expected from him. Creative people are difficult. And destructive." She nodded wisely.

"And you would know, would you? Well, let me tell you, not all of them are, not by a long chalk. I can count—"

"Well, he *is*!" Posy interrupted firmly, "so you must forgive him. But that's not the point. The thing is, you are beautiful and the others are jealous. Why else do you think they're so cool with you?"

"I don't *know* Posy, and I don't *care*. Let's leave it. Okay?"

The uniform thing seemed silly at the time. Perdita's uniform was short on her because her legs were so long. Posy had hers taken up to thigh-length and Vicky Mendel had pointed it out to her one day after choir. "Your friend looks like your clone," she whispered in Perdita's ear on the way out. "Same uniform, same hair." And then, some weeks later, after Posy had read an Andrew Marvell poem aloud in class, Vicky had mouthed, "Same voice!" Posy had finished so Perdita didn't think about it, brushing it off. She felt it necessary to stand up for her friend against the enemy, as she then thought of Vicky, denying any accusations she made, even to herself. She would always be loyal.

"Why doesn't your mother divorce your father if she hates him so?" Posy asked after the show when they had all seen Lucas Hastings at his most vitriolic about his wife.

"You got the tickets from *whom*?" he had shouted, and when Perdita told him he yelled in disbelief, "From *her*! Bitch! She'll pay for this. Your mother, Perdita, is a shit of the first order, a harridan and a trollop. Be warned! If you turn out like her you'll end up in the gutter. It is where she should be, would be only for me."

The girls all thought this outburst the artistic temperament in full flow and they shivered with excitement and wished that their dull, dreary fathers showed such spunk.

Perdita hated it and wished she were somewhere else, anywhere else. "My mother won't divorce him," Perdita said, "and she doesn't hate him, she loves him."

"Funny way of showing it," Posy said, bewildered.

"No, *he* hates *her*," Perdita tried to explain. She knew Posy would never understand the complicated relationship. "He won't divorce her because she has the money and the house." Posy would understand that. "But I think that underneath it all they really love each other. I think they *enjoy* fighting. I think they get a kick out of it." She frowned, and added, "It makes me sick, though."

It was her dream. She wanted so desperately to believe that the acrimony, the fights, the verbal abuse was a game, that Lucas and Melinda loved each other really and that they both loved her but had a funny way of showing it.

She had fantasies in which she would have, say, a car accident, or nearly drown. She would be doing something very brave, like swerving to avoid a child or rescuing a friend from drowning. She would come to in a hospital bed and there on one side would be her mother and on the other her father. Melinda would be weeping, concerned and devastated and Lucas, eyes full of tears, would smooth her damp hair back off her forehead, tenderly, lovingly. "You gave us such a fright, Perdita," Lucas would say and her mother would nod. "Don't ever do that to us again," Melinda would sob, "We love you so!" and Lucas would nod. It was her favourite dream, treasured, consoling, nurtured at twilight, and after it she always slept soundly.

Melinda was an interior decorator. Lucas said she was

an inspired amateur. "She has no training in design or at *anything* to qualify her for the job," he would say disdainfully. "I don't hear any of my clients complain," Melinda would reply tartly.

"That's because anyone who'd have you for a designer must *per se* be clueless," he'd retort triumphantly.

When Perdita left school her mother gave her a job in The Design Factory, her firm and Perdita got a tiny little flat in Chelsea. She was glad to get away from the quarrelling, the dissension, to be private, uncriticised, at peace. She didn't put much effort into the little two-roomed flat. She looked on it as a temporary place of peace, a break from Berkshire, from school, from Oak Wood Court and Kensington before she moved on somewhere else. She had this feeling that she was marking time, that something would turn up to change her life. The clouds would lift and she would suddenly know what she wanted to do, which direction her life would take.

When her mother asked her how she had decorated the flat Perdita tried to explain this feeling to her, but her mother said, "Nonsense, Perdita, you'll still be here in twenty years' time, wondering where your life has disappeared to. You have absolutely no ambition." Her mother did not bother to come and see the apartment and Perdita was just as pleased that she did not.

On one of the rare occasions that Lucas was at Oak Wood Court, Perdita had cause to think about her friendship with Posy analytically. She tended to accept the girl's presence without question, but Melinda, with her usual acidity, remarked, "Are you two joined at the hip, or what?" when Perdita pitched up with her friend for the weekend.

It was autumn and they sat around the long heavy mahogany table eating a salad lunch.

Posy was there as usual. Posy was always there. Perdita did not answer her mother but it started a train of thought. It was automatic now, Posy coming to Oak Wood Court, Posy keeping her company wherever she went. Perdita wondered now why.

She supposed she used Posy as a buffer between herself and her parents, yet very often Posy agreed with them. It was habit, Perdita decided, and what other choice had she? Posy admired her; or said she did.

Neither Lucas nor Melinda seemed surprised at the girl's constant presence, but although Posy's affection and admiration was balm to Perdita's deprived soul, it also irritated her and made her uncomfortable. It was as if she did not *deserve* Posy's friendship and also she did not completely trust it.

She was not sure if this disbelief sprang from her own insecurity or suspicion that maybe Posy was a sycophant, that she was as Lucas, cruel as ever, would say, arse-licking.

It was Lucas who brought to their attention the fact that Posy was utterly without family or friends.

"Seems strange," he muttered that autumn day over lunch in the dark, heavily Victorian room. "You'd think you could dredge up an uncle or an aunt, a cousin maybe. *Someone*!"

Posy shifted uncomfortably on her chair. Melinda often asked why she bothered to come to Oak Wood

Court and put up with the baiting that went on. Posy never replied.

"Well, I . . ."

"Her mother and father rarely come to London," Perdita said.

"They were both of them only children," Posy added.

Then Lucas looked down the table at his wife. "I believe," he said, "the Design Factory is not doing so well," he remarked with relish. The girls on either side of the table between them stared from one to the other.

"It's the Nineties, Lucas," Melinda replied tartly, "or haven't you noticed? I thought political commentators like yourself were supposed to notice social changes? When I started the business fifteen years ago people could *afford* to have their homes 'done over' as the Americans say."

Lucas threw a glance at the ceiling. "Ghastly American vernacular," he remarked.

"But they can't now. These are more frugal times, Lucas, and DIY is the thing these days." She smiled down the long table at him. "But I'm still doing reasonable business."

"And you have, my dear, enough money of your own to be able to afford not to worry about trivialities like lack of customers."

"Precisely!" Melinda went on smiling. "And," she announced, "With Perdita in the Factory alongside me—"

"You're working with your mother?" Lucas gasped. "Dear God, I knew I'd bred a dud but you really are proving a total wash-out Perdita if you settle for mindlessly titivating inanimate objects for tasteless clients in bourgeois houses."

"That kind of sentence *may*, I repeat *may* impress on your programme, Lucas but it leaves me totally unmoved," Melinda retorted, "I make a good living at it—"

"Huh! Your clientele has halved in the past five years."

"One exclusive client per year is enough to keep me busy," Melinda bit her words off, two spots of red on her cheeks.

"He's getting to her," Perdita mouthed at Posy across the table.

"Unlike you, Lucas, my work does not depend on ratings."

"Just as well for you, my dear, if it did you would have to shut up shop."

"My work has appeared in *House and Garden*, *and* in *Hello*! magazine!" There was a note of childish pride in her voice.

"Oh halleluiah! The zenith of style and artistic achievement. *House and Garden*! *Hello*! magazine! Oh, bully for you!" Then he glanced at Perdita. "I suppose you realise you'll be her slave labour. She can't find staff because she is an appalling boss so she'll pay you a pittance to be her gofer, run errands, be general bloody dogsbody."

"No, Father, I don't think so."

But Lucas was right. Melinda behaved as if Perdita was still in the nursery and she could order her about willy-nilly. She had her daughter doing errands that a child of ten could easily manage and although Perdita asked regularly, pleaded with heartfelt passion for more responsibility, Melinda promised but never fulfilled her pledges.

And so it went on and Perdita whispered to herself in the dark of the night, they really do love each other. They're just playing a game. They really do love me. I'm not a wash-out, someone to be despised, to be looked at with contempt, not worth knowing, not able to do much more than run errands.

And Posy told her she *was* worthwhile. She supported Perdita, bolstering her confidence, what little she had.

Then, that weekend Posy asked Melinda for a job in The Design Factory. And got it.

"I do hope you don't mind, Perdy. We're best friends and I want to be *with* you. It would be such fun, wouldn't it, working side by side? And I'm sure I could help you with your mother."

"You could have told me you were going to ask her." Perdita struggled with her feelings. She did not want Posy in the shop but she was sure her antipathy at the thought of working with her friend was based on jealousy and unworthy emotions and only a real bitch would mind her friend working alongside her.

"Well, I *was* going to tell you, Perdy, but then I thought, Mrs Hastings won't want *me*!" Posy laughed self-deprecatingly, "She'll turn me down flat, never let me work with Perdy. It's a wonderful dream that'll never come true. I'd've told you and then I wouldn't have got the job so we'd *both* be disappointed."

She assumes I want her to be there, Perdita thought, biting her lip, feeling like a louse. Oh God! I'm *horrible*!

Perdita had met Posy's parents only once. They had

visited London from Mhulendi when the girls were still at St Catherine's. They had taken the girls to tea in the Savoy. Mr Gore smiled all the time, just like Posy said he would and Mrs Gore stared at him, stared at Posy, and stared at her. It was very disconcerting. She seemed to be waiting for something all the time. Expectant.

"Posy says you are great friends," Mr Gore remarked. Conversation was stilted in the extreme. He seemed to be at a loss to know how to talk to his daughter which, Perdita reflected, was only to be expected. He never *saw* her. There were long silences in the Savoy lounge.

"Yes, we are Papa," Posy cried eagerly.

"Good, good." Another long pause.

"You happy about that?" Mr Gore asked Perdita who didn't know what to say so she nodded.

"Your father is Lucas Hastings?" Mrs Gore enquired.

Again Perdita nodded. "That's nice," Mrs Gore remarked then lapsed into a brown study of her husband's face.

Mr Gore suddenly said, "We called her Posy because she was so sweet. Like a bunch of flowers. When she was a baby."

Mrs Gore nodded eagerly, "Yes, yes. We didn't know what to call her for *weeks*. She had no name, poor little scrap. Then her father said, 'She's like a posy of flowers', and from then on it was Posy."

"Yes. Like a bunch of flowers when she was a baby. Then she grew up," Mr Gore said. "I suppose it's a silly name now," he smiled dryly. "Oh no!" Perdita protested. Another silence. "You like school, do you?" This from Mrs Gore. The girls nodded and Perdita gave up and looked around.

All the other people there seemed at ease with each other. They laughed while they nibbled their sandwiches and scones. The pianist in the arbour in the centre of the room played Cole Porter.

Thick carpets absorbed the sound of footsteps and waiters flipped efficiently about and the clink of china and the buzz of conversation made a pleasant background for the elegant crowd. But not for the Gores or Perdita. At their table the awkward silence persisted.

Perdita remembered that day now as she got out of Leonard's car on Posy's wedding day. That day so long ago when they emerged from the Savoy and waved the Gores goodbye, Perdita remembered Posy looking back over her shoulder at the gracious facade. "When I get married, Perdy, I'll have the reception here," she had affirmed. And she had been as good as her word.

Perdita remembered saying, "How do you know you'll get married, Posy?" and Posy's reply, equally firmly, "Oh, I will. I will."

Perdita had not thought about Posy's parents since that day when they had tea together. They were shadowy background figures, but, she suddenly realised, they should be here now, surely, on their daughter's wedding day? She had not noticed them in the church and she looked around but could not see them anywhere here either.

Lucas was sitting in a comfortable armchair, his nose almost buried in Vicky's cleavage. Staff were hovering over him as if he were royal or something. He always commanded this kind of attention and Vicky was obviously revelling in it. Perdita glared at him bitterly then, turning, noticed her mother doing exactly the same thing; glaring at Lucas.

Perdita frowned. Her mother looked as if she was going to cry, and Melinda was always so in charge of herself. Perdita's heart skipped a beat and for a moment she felt frightened and she didn't know why. Such naked pain on her mother's face took her aback.

Posy beckoned her over. She sat at the head of the table, Larry beside her. The wedding breakfast was about to be served. The table was covered in white napery, champagne bottles on ice, white flower arrangements, glimmering glass. Behind her, Perdita could see the slow, sinuous grey scarf of the Thames flowing past and in front of her the guests were taking their places, searching for the placements.

"Perdy, I wanted to thank you, thank you very, very much," Posy looked at her most sincerely.

"What for?" Perdita asked. She would not look at Larry. She could not bear to. He sat with his back half to them, speaking to Leonard.

"For everything. Your friendship. All those years. For everything you did for me, all your kindness."

"For Larry too?" Perdita could not resist asking coldly.

Posy's eyes widened and she drew in a sharp breath. A look of touching innocence settled on her face. "Why Perdita, what on earth do you mean?"

"You know exactly what I mean." Perdita wished she could stop. It was an inappropriate conversation at an inappropriate time.

"Sorry, but I don't! I'm surprised, Perdy, after all this time that you could be so, well, I hate to say it . . . bitchy!

This *is* my wedding day after all," Posy looked hurt and reproachful. "I was your friend all those years when no one else wanted your company . . ."

"What . . .?" Perdita's eyes widened. She stared at Posy, speechless.

"When no one wanted to be your friend," she repeated firmly. "I was loyal and faithful," she persisted. "And, Larry told me it was all over with you and him. *All over*. So . . ." She shrugged. "What you expect me to do?" She was whispering, she obviously didn't want anyone else to hear her. "You can't blame me, can you? He just got bored with you."

Sitting there in her white satin wedding-dress, the flowers in hair that was bleached and cut to look exactly the same as Perdita's, the innocent expression was gone and in its place, eyes narrowed, lips drawn back she looked for a moment feral, like an animal with bared fangs and Perdita shivered. She suddenly realised that perhaps she had always known Posy felt like that about her. That underneath it all she really hated Perdita, was jealous of her. The problem was, Perdita always deplored her thoughts when they took that turn, believing she was being, as Posy had just accused her, bitchy. Maybe she *was*. It was all so confusing.

Then as swiftly as the vicious expression had appeared, it vanished to be replaced by sweet serenity.

"We'll say no more about it, eh, Perdy?" Posy asked.

Larry was turning around and the wedding breakfast commenced. It passed, for Perdita, in a blur. She sat beside strangers, aunts and uncles of the groom. This should be my day, she thought, these people my new relations. She felt sorry for her breakfast companions for she was as awkward as the Gores and they laboured in vain to get her involved in the conversation.

Later, someone came to her with a pile of faxes, telegrams, goodwill messages. "Can you take these up to the top table?" a bright-faced male who was slightly drunk asked. "And why aren't you there? You're the bridesmaid, after all." For the first time she wondered about that, then decided it was not worth the bother. What did it matter anyway?

She rose and found her knees unsteady. She must have drunk more champagne than she had intended. She wasn't drunk exactly, but she wasn't sober either.

She moved as steadily as she could to the top table. She handed the pile of paper to Leonard.

"Wonder who they're from?" she said, leaving them on the table in front of him, "Posy's got no one but me. They'll be Larry's mates," she added. Leonard looked a bit startled.

"And where is David? And Fern? Where are they?" she heard herself ask, quite loudly. She did not look at Larry. She could not bear to. She wanted desperately to throw her arms around him and ask him what had happened. She wanted to tell him she adored him, that her heart was breaking, but as she opened her mouth someone drew her away quite firmly.

"I want to say . . . I want . . ." she was muttering, but whoever was steering her moved her purposefully from the top table. She turned to protest and saw the person who had hijacked – or saved – her was Larry's mother.

Chapter Four

If Perdita's parents battled and Posy's smiled remotely and seemed incapable of communication, Larry's mother, Anjelica Burton, epitomised to Perdita the perfect mother. Kindly, understanding and friendly, Perdita had looked on her as ideal. She had not seen Anjelica since the split with Larry. She had dodged her and not answered her calls. Perdita was not sure why she had acted like this except she believed that somehow she was to blame and that Anjelica would tell her it was all her own fault. Perdita had longed to talk to her lover's mother about the sudden collapse of their relationship, but kept putting it off, in the hopes of . . . what? She had no answer.

Larry's mother was drawing her away now from certain disaster and Perdita knew that she read the situation accurately and was saving her before she made a spectacle of herself.

"You don't want to do or say anything you might regret, Perdita," Anjelica whispered and sat her down at a table some way from the bride and groom. People were dancing and the band was playing 'I Just Called To Say I Love You.' They were alone at the table.

"What on earth happened between you and Larry?" Anjelica demanded. She leaned forward. "I've never seen a couple more perfectly suited than you two. Then suddenly . . . this!" she spread her hands and nodded towards the bride and groom.

She was a stout, homely woman with a wide smile and beautiful, kindly eyes. "That one," she said indicating Posy, "is trouble. I was so sure *you* were the one for him, Perdita. You seemed so happy together."

Tears filled Perdita's eyes. She never cried in public but the champagne seemed to have loosened her up and now she began to sob. Anjelica made her exchange places with her so that she had her back to the newly wedded pair. "Oh God, I'm sorry," Perdita blubbered, "what will you think of me?"

"Hold on, Perdita, I didn't mean to upset you," Anjelica looked about. "Calm down and tell me what's wrong. I thought you two were perfect together, and happy."

"So did I," Perdita cried, wiping her eyes. It was difficult to stem the flow once it started. "So did I. Oh, Anjelica, I don't know what happened. It was all fine, I thought. We had pledged ourselves to each other in Egypt. We came home and then suddenly, without a by-your-leave, Mother telephoned to tell me Posy and Larry were engaged. Well," she amended "David did first, I think."

Anjelica's brow furrowed. "It's so utterly unlike Larry. To behave irrationally, to change his mind. It's simply not his style." Her eyes hardened. "And I don't like this one at all." She indicated Posy, shaking her head, obviously perplexed. "And where *is* David?" she asked, "what happened to him?" She spread her hands and Perdita's heart missed a beat. "He should be best man. After all he's Larry's best friend. Always has been. Hector Davenport has never been that close to Larry. I can't understand any of it Perdita, I really can't."

"Have you asked Larry?" Perdita queried, not wanting to talk about David.

"Of course I have, but I cannot get any sense out of him." She took Perdita's hand between hers. "And I've never seen him so uncomfortable. Never. Larry is an honourable man, he *has* to be true to himself or he's on hot coals. Oh God, Perdita, what on earth's going on?"

Perdita shook her head and did not reply. She liked Anjelica holding her hand. She liked the touch. She wished her mother would make affectionate gestures like that but Melinda never did.

Perdita had a good idea why David was not there. He would not want to see her, or Lucas. She sighed. What a tangle it all was.

"I'm feeling very sleepy, Anjelica," she said.

"Here, have some coffee," Anjelica urged, letting go of her hand, filling a cup, giving it to Perdita who gulped it down like medicine. Anjelica refilled the cup. "Your nerves will be shot to pieces," she said, "but it's better than falling down."

Anjelica leaned back in her chair, staring up at the top table where her son sat with his bride. He was laughing, head back showing his fine teeth, sharing a joke with Hector and Leonard. Posy sat twirling a glass which was empty, staring into space.

"I've never liked that girl," Anjelica said, then glancing at Perdita, "Oh I know she's your friend, Perdita, but there's something, well, unpleasant about her."

Perdita said nothing. She was wondering how she could have been so blind all those past years.

"'Scuse me," she stood a trifle unsteadily, "got to pee."

"Let me go with you," Anjelica said, rising too.

"I'm okay really," Perdita smiled at Anjelica, "I won't disgrace myself. Don't worry." She took a deep breath and walked with great dignity towards the ladies.

She had the sense, when she reached the short flight of steps that led to the upper lounge to hold onto the banisters as she mounted them.

In the ladies she bumped into Vicky Mendel. Vicky avoided her eyes. "Don't worry about me Vicky, what my father does is of no interest to me," she told the girl, giggling. Vicky smiled tentatively back at her.

"It's nice to see you, Perdita," she said. Her eyes were anxious and Perdita realised suddenly that Vicky was in awe of her.

"Well, I don't know if I can return the compliment," Perdita replied, then seeing Vicky's crestfallen expression decided, what the hell? It seemed so unimportant now, so trivial. "After what you did to me in school," she finished. It sounded feeble to her and the accusation lacked force.

"You were so stuck-up," Vicky said, "you were like royalty, exclusive. You and Posy. She never let any of us near you."

"What do you mean?" Perdita, suddenly sober, stared at her erstwhile enemy.

"Well, like, she told us all about your . . . your . . . well, you know."

"No, Vicky, I don't."

"Well, like, oh come on Perdita, *you* know."

"No, I don't." Perdita was becoming more and more apprehensive. "Tell me."

"That you and she were . . . like a couple. *You* know. She said you loved her," Vicky sighed, took a deep breath and said, "that you were lesbians. But you *knew* that." she muttered defensively.

"No, I did not," Perdita said quietly, 'and for your information, Vicky, nothing like that went on. I am not a lesbian. I've never *loved*, as you call it, Posy Gore."

Vicky was staring at her, drying her hands in the towel. "You mean that . . . you mean she was lying?"

"Yes, Vicky. She was lying," Perdita said firmly.

"Je-sus! Cripes! We believed her," she gulped. "Christ, Perdita I'm sorry. We shouldn't have . . . thinking about it we really should not have taken any notice of what Posy Gore said. She boasted all the time . . ."

"About me?"

"Yeah. About you. She told us how your father and mother fought all the time. How your father made a pass at her one night but she knew you would be wildly jealous so she never told you. Gosh, Perdita, we didn't know she was lying."

"Okay, Vicky. Enough. I don't want to hear any more."

"I'm sorry, Perdita, I'm really sorry." Vicky came over to her and Perdita could see genuine regret in her eyes. "I was such a stupid cow. Still am. I was jealous of you. You are so beautiful, so . . . so . . . you had everything. I guess if we'd thought about it we'd have realised we were being given a line, but I guess we *wanted* to believe it."

"Masie Stokes and Jinny McAlister *were* a couple and you never hassled them," Perdita remarked.

"No. But we weren't looking to hassle them." Vicky shook her head. "God, I was a jealous bitch. I know you can't forgive me. I don't *expect* you to. Just the same, I'm sorry."

"Oh I do forgive you, Vicky. I really do. I was as stupid as you. Stupider in fact. Naïve. A dope."

"She takes people in," Vicky said with something like admiration in her voice. "She's a great con artist, when you think of it."

"Well, we've got her number now," Perdita said.

"Not before time."

They parted, if not friends exactly, at least at peace with each other. The champagne had dulled Perdita's responses and she was not up to piecing what Vicky had told her together and fitting it into the various incidents in their lives. What other lies had she told? And had she perhaps fabricated some fairy tale about her for Larry's consumption? If she had and he believed a slander then Larry was not worth having, not worth loving. But she doubted it very much.

Perdita tried to assimilate the information she had just received after Vicky left the ladies and she sat staring at herself in the mirror while the attendant fussed around her, wiping non-existent specks of dust off the vanity tables, looking at her apprehensively. She sat there until Anjelica, fearing the worst, came to find her.

Chapter Five

They had had good times together. Posy could always make her laugh. She was much better at the work in The Design Factory than Perdita was. Or so Melinda said. Regularly. "It's my turn now," Posy told her. "You were always helping me with my homework at school. Perdita was so clever, Mrs Hastings," she told Melinda.

"I doubt it," Melinda said.

Perdita believed she was clumsy and obtuse because her mother's constant criticisms made her that way. Her mother took away her confidence while at the same time she boosted Posy's. But then, Posy praised Melinda as much as Melinda praised her. It seemed to Perdita as if her friend and her mother were locked in a mutual admiration society and she was left out in the cold. She tried to be grown up about it, but when she tried to have a civilised conversation with her mother about it like they suggested on the talk shows Melinda said she was jealous and denied that she treated Posy any differently to the way she treated Perdita.

"I send Posy off to get me something and she comes back with exactly what I want. I send you . . . you never manage to do it right. Never. What do you expect me to do? Give you a medal for screwing up?"

Perdita had screwed up the day she met Fern and David for the first time. And Larry.

By this time Posy had her own tiny apartment. She had wanted to share with Perdita and had pleaded. "It would be cheaper all round, Perdy. We could get a much bigger flat if we shared." Then she begged. "We've been friends for so long, Perdy, why don't you want me to live with you? I've done so much for you, I was the only one who stuck by you all these years." Then she threatened to break off their friendship. "Oh, you are being so mean! How can you? I don't think I want to know you any more." But she did not mean this and it was about this time that she was deciding to ask Mrs Hastings for a job.

Perdita held her ground. She said she needed her privacy. "It's all you'll get, privacy," Posy cried, "you've never had anyone else but me. Never. Even your parents don't like you. You'll regret it, being all alone all the time and you'll change your mind. But don't think I'll come running. I won't."

They had never been close after that, although Posy kept up the appearance of affection for Perdita. They saw each other daily in The Design Factory, but whatever had tied them together had gone and they only tolerated each other because of their mutual past and because they were used to each other. And Perdita was not lonely in her tiny apartment.

Then the day came that was to change everything for Perdita.

It was a cold March day, sunny but windy. Perdita would never forget that day, the day she met Larry. She would never forget anything about it.

All of London was in bloom. Apple blossom, cherry blossom, the daffodils were everywhere. Trees heavy with magnolias, waxen pink and white flowers floating in the warm air and every tree bursting into verdant leaf.

Her mother had sent her to Colefax & Fowler on the Fulham Road to match some samples and swatches, and there in the window of a rather expensive but discreet Italian restaurant, she glimpsed her father.

She was going to rush across the street to greet him, something she always did when she saw him even though she knew she would be rebuffed, held at arm's length. She went on rushing into his arms and Melinda said she was a glutton for punishment. That March day she stalled. What stopped her was the fact that she had to wait for a break in the traffic. If the road had been clear she would have run across and the story of her life might have taken a completely different direction.

But the traffic was rushing past, horns honking, and when Perdita, hopping from foot to foot was able to get a clear view she saw her father emerge from the restaurant. And then she saw he was not alone. He had someone with him. It was a woman. A beautiful woman.

Perdita froze. She was used to seeing her father flirt with babes but this was no babe. Melinda was a beautiful woman but few would say she was soft. This woman was soft as butter. She was a curvaceous woman with a wonderfully sexy body. Perdita ran her hands over her own slim figure. She took after her mother, lean and rangy as a boy, a clothes hanger, enviably beanpole tall and flat. This woman was voluptuous. Red-haired, round faced, dimples probably, Perdita hazarded a guess. She looked as if her whole body would be dimpled. She had a tiny waist and inside her wool suit she swelled into curves above and below her belt. The wind blew her hair across her face and Lucas turned and gently lifted the red-gold strands and pushed them back. There was something in his gesture that stopped Perdita's second attempt to cross the road and made her want to hide from them. There was an expression in his face so tender, so loving, an expression that she had never seen there before. They looked as if they were locked in their own world. Very private.

This was not a colleague, no working lunch. And this was not lust, some casual fling with a bimbo. This woman was different.

Perdita got furtively back into her car hoping they would not see her. She hunched over the wheel trying to make herself invisible, heart beating a tattoo in her chest. She felt as if she had peeped into someone's bedroom and seen something she shouldn't. She felt guilty.

She watched them laughing together. Her father looked so handsome and charming when he laughed but it was not something she ever saw him do. This man was the father she had always dreamed about, the sarcastic droop gone from his mouth, the bitterness from his eyes. He was young, boyish and good-humoured as he stood there in the Fulham Road holding this woman's hand, hailing a taxi.

There were a lot of people around and the traffic flowed loudly by, screening her from the couple. She thought of them as a couple. A traffic warden on the prowl was approaching Perdita purposefully so she started the Audi and pulled away from the curb just as a taxi pulled up in front of Lucas and the woman. Perdita, turning the car, saw him help the woman in and they drove off.

She followed them. They turned towards the King's Road in the direction of Parson's Green. They ended up in front of an elegant house in a terrace of elegant houses, a house with window-boxes full of yellow and purple pansies. The taxi drew up and her father and the woman got out and went inside the house. She noticed that her father used a key from his keyring to let them in.

Perdita had drawn up a few cars behind the taxi. She stayed where she was, confident that neither her father nor the woman would notice her; they were too absorbed in each other. Another traffic warden was sauntering down the street, notebook in hand and Perdita moved the car forward past the house as a van that had been delivering stuff to another house drove away, leaving a convenient space. Perdita put the Audi in and sat there watching the house.

She waited a long time. Her mother would go ballistic waiting for her swatches but Perdita couldn't care less about that now. She's always *accusing* me of being incompetent so I bloody well will be, she muttered to herself as she sat there staring at the pansies.

Children came home from school, shrieking, shouting, roaring their exuberance to the sky. Mothers gathered young families close and shepherded them indoors with talk of tea and TV. They hauled prams and strollers up steps, bright women in shirts and jeans, shining hair and good teeth. Their men would be home later, barristers, doctors, businessmen. Comfortable.

Perdita sat very still for a long time until, at last,

Lucas emerged. He glanced to the right and the left, then turned and waved to a window upstairs. Perdita ducked down to see. It was the soft redhead and she was obviously *en déshabille*. A satin housecoat slid off one rounded shoulder and white marble breasts were almost revealed under gossamer lace. She looked wanton and infinitely desirable.

She waved back at Lucas and blew him a kiss. Lucas turned then and strode away.

Perdita sat there, uncertain what to do next, emotions churning within. She wanted to go, run away and hide, but also she wanted to stay, know the truth. Face the fear of what she would find out. What can of worms she was opening. But she knew too that she could not go back. It was too late for that.

A bunch of girls in school uniform sauntered down the street eating apples, chewing gum, shoving each other good humouredly. One of them, a redhead, came tripping down the street and, turning, ran up the steps, took a key from her pocket and let herself into the house Perdita's father had emerged from only a short time before.

Perdita waited for a while, then got out of the car. She crossed the road and went up the steps to the house, heart thumping. She looked at the bell but there was no name on it.

As she looked the door opened and the girl stood there. She had changed into tennis clothes: an aertex polo, white shorts, tennis shoes and socks. Her red hair was pushed off her forehead by a white bandeau. She was very like her mother.

"Hi," she said, bright-eyed and helpful, "Can I help you?"

"I'm looking for, for a person called . . ." Perdita couldn't think, saw a van down the street with the name McLeish and something about Tree Experts printed on the side and she swiftly said, "Tree. Mr Tree."

The girl laughed and shook her red hair, "Oh no! We're not Tree. We're Morrison."

"I'm so sorry."

"Not at all," the girl frowned, "And I don't think you'll find a family called Tree along here. Not that I've heard of, and we know most of our neighbours."

"I'm sorry."

"Don't apologise." Then she called back into the house, "Mom, we know anyone called Tree?" There was a reply but Perdita could not hear. "Sure it's not Parson's Lane? Or—"

"No, no. I'll check. Thank you." Perdita ran down the steps breathless suddenly. The girl closed the door behind herself as Perdita got into her car and she waved, and hurried down the road swinging her racket.

There was a paper shop just around the corner beside a pub and Perdita went in and bought a paper. There was no one in the shop except an aged Pakistani woman who was serving. She sat on a stool behind the counter fiddling with her sari, obviously bored. Perdita guessed this was a slack time for her, just after the schools had decanted the sweet-loving hordes and before the commuters returned home, popping in for fags and the newspaper.

"You know a family called Morrison?" she asked the woman.

She nodded. "Yes," she said, "we deliver papers. *Times* readers. And the *Independent*. *Vanity Fair*. Number sixty-seven. Very nice family." She shook her head. "Never see the husband though. It's not good. A man is the centre of a family. How can you call it a family without the head?" she appealed to Perdita, who shrugged. "You *can't*!" she said with finality. "People don't understand. If the man is not in charge all discipline vanishes. Society goes to the bad when you disturb the balance." This was obviously her favourite topic and Perdita wondered what her children had done to warrant her strong feelings.

"So it's Mrs Morrison and her daughter?" Perdita hazarded.

The woman frowned, "Oh, Mr Morrison is *there*. But not the *head*. It's wrong, don't you think? A woman controlling!"

It must be her daughter-in-law, Perdita decided, upsetting the balance for the woman. "The head of *that* house is Mrs Fern Morrison. She has a daughter Miranda and a son, David."

"Oh, she has a son too?"

"Sure. He is animal doctor. Though why people want doctors for their animals I dunno. Silly."

"A vet?"

"Yes that's it. A vet. National Health is in a mess. They need doctors, but he does *animals*." She clicked her teeth disapprovingly. "They have a practice down the King's Road. Not far." She looked curiously at Perdita. "Why you want to know?"

"Oh, just . . . are those the strongest mints you have?" she asked changing the subject.

"No, no, these are best." Perdita paid for them and left.

She was too far gone now to turn back. She wondered about Mr Morrison who was there and not there. She left her car where it was and walked to the King's Road, went up and down both sides of a couple of blocks and eventually found 'Morrison & Burton Veterinary Surgeons' on a brass plaque.

The entrance was smart; modern chairs that looked comfortable, a glass table in the centre piled with magazines and a bowl of flowers. There were notices on the cork board on the wall; people searching for lost pets, puppy breeders advertising, litters of puppies or kittens available with the stricture, *An Animal is for Life. Scooby Don't: a Frisky Dog means Unplanned Puppies. Have your dog neutered – the National Canine Defence League*. A sign said that David Morrison BVSc MRCVS Veterinary Surgeon and Laurence Burton BVSc MRCVS Veterinary Surgeon were the men to see if there was anything wrong with your pet. "Don't leave it until it is too late," you were warned.

A tall, red-haired young man came out of another room as Perdita spoke to the receptionist who sat behind a small partition where files were obviously kept.

The young man spoke as she opened her mouth. "Can I help you?" he asked.

"Mr Delsey to see you, Mr Morrison. His Betsy is poorly." The receptionist glared at Perdita and said loudly, "If you could wait your turn."

"All right, Rita," David Morrison glanced towards a little man with a cat carrier on his knee. There were angry sounds coming from within the cage, spitting and hissing. "Be with you in a mo," he said to the little man, then to Perdita, "Can I help you?" he said again.

The man with the spitting cat stood up and came towards the young red-haired man. "My Betsy is poorly," he announced, glaring at Perdita. "I was next, Mr Morrison."

David Morrison smiled at her. "Can I help you?" he repeated, looking at her with admiration in his eyes. Then, "Just a moment, Mr Delsey, I'll be with you in an instant."

Perdita shook her head. "I'm afraid I'm a fraud. I came here to find out . . ." she faltered. Mr Delsey and Rita the receptionist were staring unblinkingly at her. Colour flooded her face.

"Mr Morrison! Mr Delsey's been waiting a long time . . ."

"I'd like to talk to you . . . talk to you . . ." Perdita stammered.

"Look," he took her arm and led her to the door, "I finish here in five minutes . . ." He grinned ruefully, "or however long Mr Delsey's Betsy takes." He was whispering. "Maybe we could have a quick drink? There's a pub opposite. I'll see you there in five, ten minutes, okay?" She nodded and he raised his voice again. "All right, Mr Delsey, come with me."

She waited apprehensively in the pub. She ordered a lager and sat at a table in an alcove sipping it, picking absent-mindedly at a coaster advertising Guinness. There was a mock fire near her and it glowed redly. The pub was full of sunshine rays slanting onto the worn wood floor.

What would she say to him? She had no idea. She could not tell him the truth, could she? Your mother is sleeping with my father? In the name of heaven, what could she say? She nearly bolted, but something held her back.

He came into the pub, blocking the sunshine for a moment. There was a wonderful vitality about him and he went to the counter, ordered a beer and came and sat beside her. "You like another?" he pointed to the lager. She shook her head. "No, thank you."

He was very like his sister; thick red hair brushed back, bright green eyes flecked with brown. Good skin.

"Now, how can I help you?" he asked. She blushed and lowered her head. He smiled. "Oh Lord, it's not that bad, is it? What has happened? Your cat? Your dog? Passed away? Oh, don't look so upset," he cried, obviously concerned.

She nearly lied and nodded. She *could* pretend her pet had died, but truth telling was deeply ingrained in her and she could not bring herself to play a game.

"I don't mean to be flippant," he said.

"No, no. This is so awkward," she felt ashamed of her prying, unable to think what to say.

"Well, no use beating about the bush. Spit it out!"

"Look, maybe I'd better go," she stood up, "I think I've made a mistake . . ."

He rose and pressed her firmly back into her seat. "No. Tell me what this is all about. I'm a big boy, I can take it." He grinned. "Besides, I like looking at you. It's a long time since I've seen a girl as pretty . . ." he frowned, "no. Beautiful," he amended and leaned back, watching her.

"Well, you're going to hate me in a minute," she said.

"Then don't tell me!" he said. "I don't want to know. Let's just have this drink and enjoy ourselves." He held out his hand. "I'm David Morrison," he said.

"Perdita Hastings."

"What a lovely name. What do you do, Perdita Hastings?"

"My mother's an interior decorator. I work for her," she clapped her hands against her cheeks. "Oh gosh! She sent me to Colefax & Fowler ages ago to get stuff and I forgot. Oh help! She'll be furious!"

"Oh, I dare say she'll forgive you. Don't rush away. We've just met."

"So here you are!"

Someone stood over them, blocking the light. She looked up into still grey eyes, the gentlest eyes she'd ever seen, calm and compelling.

"Ah, Larry! You finished? This is Perdita Hastings. Lovely name, isn't it?"

Perdita was caught in his glance, trapped there in those grey pools of warmth. She could not remove her gaze from his. "Perdita this is Larry Burton, my colleague."

He gave her a feeling of peace, of reassurance, a feeling that everything was going to be all right. She'd never experienced such a feeling before. She'd heard other girls in school say their daddies made them feel safe but she had no experience of it up to now, up to this moment.

Confused and near tears suddenly, she glanced from one to the other, feeling like an intruder in the midst of goodness, an alien there. If they knew what I am really like, she thought, why I had come. To shatter their peace, sow doubt and dissension. She shivered as the two men stared at her. She stood up and picking up her bag she fled leaving them gazing after her.

Chapter Six

Her mother was furious with her, disproportionately angry. "I can't trust you to do the simplest errand without you making a mess of it," she cried. "Where have you been? Where's the stuff I wanted?"

"I didn't go!" Perdita said defiantly, flinching as her mother glared at her.

"You didn't *go*? Where the hell *were* you then? You're gormless, you know that, Perdita? Sometimes I think you are mentally challenged. That's what they call it now, but where I come from we call it soft in the head. And it's too late now. The shop will be closed."

"Let me zip over there, Melinda. I just might make it," Posy was bright and eager. She glanced sympathetically at Perdita, then raised her eyes to heaven behind Melinda's back, and when Melinda turned and flipped her the car keys Perdita mouthed, "thank you". Posy caught them and was gone.

Melinda stared at her and raised one eyebrow, shaking her head slowly as if in bewilderment. "Why can't you be more like Posy?" she asked in a tired voice. "What did I ever do to deserve a child like you!"

Perdita didn't reply. She was used to it. She tried to let the things her mother said flow over her but they never failed to sting. Her head drooped. Melinda came nearer and pushed Perdita's shoulder-length hair back from her face.

"Your hair's a mess dear. You'll have to do something about it. Get it cut properly. Go to Nigel. He's a genius."

Her mother's hair, the same colour as her own was cropped stylishly short. She fiddled with her daughter's hair a moment as if she had every right to paw it. "Oh leave me alone, Mother," Perdita cried.

"Now, now dear, don't be pettish with me." She wagged her finger under Perdita's nose. "I'm seriously thinking of sacking you," she said calmly, dropping the bombshell, "so you be careful, my girl. One more day like today . . ." she shook her head again and moved away, "and you are out!"

Perdita's heart sank. If her mother let her go she'd be jobless. Perdita didn't think she'd get another one, did not believe she was capable. There was so little she could do. She crept away as she often did, trying to avoid her mother's eyes. Melinda seemed to forget all about her when she was out of sight. It was when she was in her mother's presence that she was a constant irritant to her parent. So she slunk away

Never in her whole life had Perdita managed to surprise her mother. Melinda was always so composed, in charge of things and, Perdita had to admit to herself, she was so predictable. Why would her mother be surprised at anything she could do?

The following day, however, Perdita had the unique pleasure of seeing her mother's composure totally wrecked. Melinda came to find Perdita, who was lurking behind a pile of Peter Jones curtain material, and there was an expression of utter astonishment on her face. Gob-smacked was how Perdita described it to herself.

"It's for you," she said in disbelief, "the phone. A *man*!"

"Thank you, Mother." Perdita, though inwardly excited, managed to look calm and unruffled.

Her eyes wide, Melinda glanced at Posy. "Can you believe it?" she asked. She gaped at Perdita as she took the call.

It was David Morrison.

"Remember me?" he asked, "the fellow you ran out on yesterday?"

Melinda was standing right beside her, staring in amazement at her daughter.

"Hi, David. Yes, I remember."

"I got your name out of the book. Phoned you at home and got your message there that you were at work. You told me you worked with your mother, so it wasn't difficult." She could tell he was smiling. "Well, it struck me we had unfinished business."

"What do you mean?"

"I mean, lovely one," *Lovely one*! *Lovely one*! Perdita glanced at her mother. Melinda's blue eyes were boring into hers, puzzled, disbelieving. *Lovely one*. "I mean, I'd like to get to know you better, Perdita."

"But . . . but . . ."

"No. No buts. And don't sound alarmed. I'll be civilized. I can't think why you treat me as if I were Jack the Ripper and I promise hand on heart I'm *not* the big bad wolf! I'll not gobble you up. So, here's what I suggest . . ."

"No, no I can't . . ."

"*Listen*. Let's meet in the pub we were in yesterday for a drink and a chat. I promise I won't pry. *Please*, Perdita. About six? How does that grab you?"

Looking at her mother's incredulous face, Perdita suddenly thought, why not?

"Okay. Fine," she said.

"Good. And don't worry. You don't have to talk about anything you don't want to. Okay?"

"Sure. See you then." She put the phone down. Her mother went on staring at her.

"A date?" she asked. Perdita nodded.

"Who with? The Elephant Man?"

Perdita did not answer. Posy was contemplating some huge over-sized Chinese vases. Melinda called to her. "Hey, Posy, hear that? Perdita has a date!"

"Oh, jolly nice Perdy," Posy sounded sarcastic.

"Why don't you go too, Posy? Just for a while. Tell us what he's like. Check he's not blind!" Her mother watched as Perdita's head snapped up. "Oh no!" she cried in alarm, before she could stop herself.

"Only joking," her mother's eyes narrowed. "But it *might* be a good idea. You have no idea, Perdita, have you? You need protection."

Perdita did as she usually did and slid away into the shadows hoping her mother would forget about her altogether.

Perdita slipped out of the office surreptitously, by the back way, at five-thirty. She would not put it past her mother to have Posy spy on her. She looked right and left, decided to shake anyone who might be following her and took the longest route to the Fulham Road.

It was fun, pretending she was shaking off a tail, doubling back on herself, jumping on the eleven bus to Hammersmith, catching the tube to Knightsbridge, then the twenty-two to the Kings Road and the thirty-one to the Chelsea and Westminster Hospital on the Fulham Road, then walking back to the pub.

By the time she got there she knew there was no way Posy or anyone, no matter how skilled, could still be tailing her.

She hoped what she was wearing would be all right. She always wore the same outfit, it was her uniform. Blue jeans, a white shirt, a navy cashmere cardigan and a navy blazer. Her mother had tried to put her into power suits but she categorically refused to wear the tiny clinging skirts and ornate jackets, saying she felt damned uncomfortable. Melinda told her that to look good that was how you were supposed to feel. Posy, however, had no such scruples and she often wore Melinda's cast-offs. Neat little multi-coloured Christian Lacroix outfits, Karl Lagerfeld designs.

"Anyone else would be grateful," Melinda told her daughter. "*Posy* is grateful. But not you, Perdita. Oh no!"

She was late. David was waiting for her at the same table near the fire.

"Oh good," he said when he saw her, "I thought you'd shied away again. Stood me up."

"No."

"Sit down. What will you drink?"

"Lager please."

She was sitting alone at the table in the gloom when Larry came in. He saw her and her heart stood still and she felt as if she was suffocating. All the breath seemed to leave her body and her chest felt as if it was held in a vice.

"Hello! You're the girl from yesterday, aren't you? Um . . ." he wrinkled his brow. "Ah, Perdita, isn't it?"

She nodded. She couldn't speak. David returned with the drinks and when he saw his partner his face fell.

"Christ, Larry . . . don't tell me I'm wanted!"

"Sorry. Sorry old boy," Larry held his hands up in a gesture of surrender, "emergency! Mrs Nelson needs you. She says Prissy's had a bad turn. She said she tried to bleep you but . . ."

"That's because I turned the damn thing off. Because, guess what? I didn't want to be disturbed," David said crossly.

"Well, she called the surgery. Said you'd promised you would come when she called. No one else will do. Prissy is in pain." He turned to Perdita. "She has no one else in her life. She loves that animal like a child."

"Oh, damn Prissy!" David put Perdita's drink down in front of her. "Okay, okay. I'll go. Sorry Perdita. I *did* promise. Will you wait?"

"I'll keep Perdita company," Larry smiled at her and she smiled back. His smile enfolded her like a warm blanket on a cold day.

David left. "He likes you," Larry said, then leaning forward, "problem is . . . so do I."

"You didn't . . .?" She knew he hadn't set it up; he simply wasn't the type.

"Oh no!" he sounded shocked, "I wouldn't do that." Then he smiled again. "Not that I wouldn't be tempted. But David is my friend and partner and I wouldn't do anything . . . Mrs Nelson is kosher. Scout's honour," he glanced away into the fire. "But I could have sent Rita, our receptionist to deliver the message to David. But," he smiled at her again "I wanted to see you. See if you had the same effect on me."

"What effect?" How stupid I am to ask him that. I suppose I should know, she thought. But how could she know? The experience was totally new to her.

"Well," he leaned across the table, "when I see you my heart leaps into my throat. Like it used to do when I was a kid and the headmaster sent for me. I feel I might choke. It's not entirely pleasant." His expression was rueful. Was he making fun of her? "I have difficulty breathing," he added.

"Oh I *know*!" It was out before she could stop herself. It was naïve, she knew that but it seemed she had lost all reservation. That sturdy barrier she had so carefully built around herself, that wall she had erected between herself and the world seemed to have tumbled down like the walls of Jericho.

"You felt it too? Oh good. That settles that!" He sounded very businesslike. "Then I think you should tell David before he gets too interested. He is, you know. He's gone on and on about you and we can't see each other unless we are both up-front with him."

"Is that necessary?" she asked, not relishing the idea at all.

"Well, don't you see, once you started going out with him I wouldn't try to take you from him. It wouldn't be fair."

The idea of telling David anything at all appalled her. What would she, could she say? I'm interested in Larry not you? No. She would never be able to drum up enough courage to tell him that out of the blue. She had always found it impossible to be that straight with people, afraid she might hurt them as her parents hurt her.

"I can't," she said helplessly, twisting her fingers together.

She looked so distressed that Larry found the impulse to console her irresistible. He leaned forward and in the same gesture her mother had used, but oh so tenderly, he pushed the hair from her face. "Then I will," he told her. "Hey, it's not the end of the world. You haven't said you'd marry him or anything."

"Oh gosh, no!" Her eyes were huge pools of misery and he wondered who had managed to bruise her spirit so dreadfully. She was like the wounded animals he treated. She wrenched at his heart, touching him deeply and he wanted to ease the pain of her mute pleading.

"I'm very stupid," she told him. "You don't know how stupid I am."

"Don't ever say that again," he commanded seriously, his voice tinged with anger, "never, do you hear? You are certainly *not* stupid. What gave you that idea?"

"My mother is always telling me. And she's right."

He shook his head. "No she's not," he contradicted her firmly. "And what does your father have to say about it?"

She sighed. "Oh, he thinks so too. He agrees with her. It's about the only thing they *do* agree about. So you see . . ."

"I think *they* are the stupid ones."

"Oh no! My father is *very* clever. Everyone knows that."

"We had a saying in school Perdita, a silly childish taunt. But I've discovered it is true. When anyone teased us, calling us names, we'd shout back, you know, the way kids do, 'What you say is what you are!' "

"But my father is a brilliant man. You must have heard of him, Lucas Hastings?" His eyes narrowed. "Now, you see! You're shocked. He's a political commentator, a brilliant journalist. Everyone who knows me cannot believe I'm his daughter. He thinks I'm dumb. And Mother! She's so bright. So clever. Compared to them I'm a total slouch. They are both so successful."

"I didn't say they weren't successful. Or clever. I said they were stupid. You can be clever and stupid at the same time, you know. Clever at political commentary, at maths or physics, world affairs, facts, figures, everything, *but* stupid about human emotion, about feelings. About people. Your parents, Perdita, may be brilliant but they are utterly stupid about you."

"How do you know?" she asked wondering about how sure he was.

"It's obvious!" he said. "Now, that's all I have to say on the subject."

There had been few people around but now the pub was becoming crowded. Perdita did not mind. Truth to tell she did not notice. It seemed to her she was alone in the whole wide world with this wonderful person, the two of them the only people there. Isolated by their awareness of each other. His smile enchanted her, put a spell on her. She smiled back at him creating a warm intimacy between them.

"Now," he said. "From now on you are not to worry about *anything*. I'll talk to David and you and I will have dinner tomorrow evening after I've had a word with him. Okay?" She nodded. If he had asked her to go to Abu Dhabi on the morrow she would have happily obeyed.

"Will David mind?" She hated so much to displease anyone, hated anyone to think she had behaved badly.

Larry smiled sadly. "I guess he will," he answered. "I don't think he'll be at all pleased. After all, you are his discovery. But," he spread his hands, "thank God it's not a question of first come first served, Perdita. It won't kill him. Anyhow," he added briskly, "you cannot go out with someone when you fancy someone else. It's not honest."

"Is that what I feel? Fancying you?"

He looked at her and the expression in his eyes melted her heart. "Yes. Oh yes, I hope so," he breathed.

She rose. "I'd better go," she said.

"Yes. I'll call you tomorrow. What's your—"

"No. No, don't do that. I'll meet you here. Same time."

He nodded. "And Perdita," she looked down into his clear eyes, "don't believe what they tell you," he told her, "they are quite wrong." His heart swelled painfully at her expression, her trembling lip, her disbelief. She had been so hurt and as she returned his gaze steadily there was trust and gratitude in her eyes.

"Thank you," she whispered.

She left the pub on wings of joy. She felt as if she floated six inches above the ground. No one will spoil this for me, she decided. No one.

Chapter Seven

"So she's done another runner." David plonked himself down in the chair Perdita had just vacated. "What's the matter with the girl? I'm not gruesome, Larry, am I? Or are you simply not telling me that I'm really the Frankenstein monster?" David was laughing.

"She hasn't, David," Larry said calmly.

"Hasn't what?"

"Done a runner."

"Ladies?"

"Uh-uh!"

"Oh heck! She had someone else. That's it. She was meeting her boyfriend. And I really fell for her. Ah well! *C'est la vie!*"

"No, David. It's not that either."

"Let me get a drink. I can't bear this."

He fought his way to the counter, exchanging pleasantries with the barman, getting his beer. Larry sat waiting patiently, watching him, a worried frown creasing his brow.

When his friend returned he took a deep breath and said, "David, I've something to tell you and I don't think you are going to like it." He met David's enquiring look squarely, cleared his throat and continued, "Perdita and I have clicked. *Wham* – like that! That's the truth. Sorry."

Davis blinked. "But I . . . but we . . ."

"I don't know how or why it happened, David, but it did."

David glanced at his friend. "Oh, thanks a bunch! Since when have you descended to stealing your best mate's girlfriend?"

"She wasn't your girlfriend. You just fancied her. Well, she fancied me."

Larry felt relieved. David's reaction was irritated, slightly miffed, but certainly not heart-broken. He did not seem deeply resentful. Larry had been afraid that their friendship might be at risk and that was something he would not be happy about.

Larry valued their friendship. He was a loyal person and he did not make friends lightly. David had been his mate since university. They had set up a practice together and worked and travelled together peacefully ever since. They rarely had a disagreement.

They had the same interests in animal welfare, girls and Chelsea Football Club. Larry, much as he was drawn to Perdita, would not, at this point, have easily given up his friend for her. If David had been really disturbed, Larry decided, he would have backed off. If David had been very upset he would have phoned Perdita and, as unhappy as it would have made him, he would have cancelled their date on the morrow, swallowed his feelings about her and fled to Egypt until the pain subsided.

But David was all right about it and Larry smiled, relieved, and relaxed.

The two began to talk about Egypt and their work

there with the animals. Larry was trying, without much success, to organise a fund-raising event in Lambourne, Berkshire where his mother lived. They discussed the pros and cons of a garden fête, a pop concert or a pet competition. As evening lengthened into night-time they decided that the best idea would be an amalgamation of all three. "God, I wish we had a higher profile," Larry said, and David nodded.

"We can't afford a PR person," David said ruefully.

"Some day," Larry sighed, "Some day, mate."

Five years earlier the two vets had taken a trip to Egypt, a holiday, simply to sightsee, look at the Pyramids, the sphynx, the King Tut relics in the museum in Cairo. They were hoping to enjoy themselves, but the trip turned out quite differently.

What had happened was to change their whole lives. They had been sucked into a quite unexpected relationship with Egypt, her animals, her people. They became involved more deeply than either of them could have imagined. Instead of simply sightseeing the pair got embroiled, quite by accident, with an animal welfare organisation, although their friend Yasser Assam insisted it was not really an accident but the will of Allah.

Be that as it may, on that first trip they were visiting a souk, buying presents for the folks at home when Larry drew in his breath and clutched David's arm.

In front of them in the crowded bazaar a man was beating his donkey with such force that he had drawn blood. The donkey shrank under the blows, shivering in pain. He seemed worn out, too ill-nourished to try to avoid the violence, too exhausted to rear up or otherwise physically protest. No one paid any attention except the two Englishmen.

Outraged Larry ripped the whip from the man's hands and the man screamed back at him. A crowd was collecting and David became worried that they might find themselves in serious trouble. Such interference from outsiders was not appreciated here in Cairo. But Larry, incensed, was oblivious to the hostility he was arousing.

"This animal is in a bad condition!" he told the screaming man. "Not good. Sick."

The narrow street was littered with rubbish. An old man with a brown face criss-crossed with lines like a walnut, sucked on a hooka just inside his stall. He was used to turmoil in the bazaar, the shouts of vendors, the arguments, the haggling. It was all the same to him.

The crowd was mainly Egyptian in their long robes and head-dresses. There seemed to be no other Europeans around and Larry and David were very much alone.

The crowd clustered around the two friends, hostility growing as the man with the whip screamed at them, saliva collecting at the corners of his mouth and, leaning over, tried to retrieve the whip from Larry.

"The donkey is sick. Sick." Larry reiterated, undaunted, and quite furious. If there was anything guaranteed to anger Larry Burton it was the sight of the strong picking on the weak.

"He doesn't understand you." A cultured voice behind them made them turn. "It is his way."

"Well, his way is wrong!" Larry insisted, white-lipped.

"Peace, peace, my friend. We are on the same side."

The man who addressed them was an Egyptian. He wore Egyptian clothes, an ema over his head and worry beads threaded through his fingers. He was a small man with a good-humoured face and he was frowning.

"We are trying to teach them," he said. "Leave him be for the moment," he instructed, "it is no use here and now." He indicated the crowd. Then he held out his hand. "Let me explain. I am Yasser Assam and I run the Cooke Hospital for Sick Animals here in Cairo. Perhaps you have heard of us?" Larry and David shook their heads. "No, can't say we have." The man sighed. "Ah well, some day. Some day I hope you will."

Larry grasped the man's outstretched hand. "I'm Larry Burton and this is David Morrison. We are veterinary surgeons from London."

"Ah! That is why you stopped. Most tourists, when they see such a sight as this," he indicated the poor donkey staggering between the shafts of the cart, "they turn their heads away, condemn the whole Egyptian race without understanding the circumstances, the poverty, the ignorance. And they go home. Do nothing. Well, we are trying to improve the situation, here and in Jordan. As far as India the Cooke Hospital for Sick Animals is spreading and doing good work."

"It is appalling," Larry looked at the tottering animal, his eyes full of pity, "it is no way to treat an animal."

The Egyptian shrugged. "The man is poor. The animal is his only means of support," he explained. "You have no idea in the West. You are protected from the cradle to the grave. You do not understand when it is a matter of life and death. Literally. How can you? Well-fed bodies say I would die before I could harm my pet. But you have never felt *real* hunger. You have never been in the situation that man is in. He takes his anger, his frustration, his fear out on the animal because the donkey is his livelihood and it has let him down and the man is staring death in the face."

The donkey fell suddenly, in harness, pulling the man down off the cart after him. They watched in horror as the owner of the donkey screamed, jumped up and began to kick the dying donkey, yelling invective, exhorting it to get up. Then, when it became obvious to him that the donkey was dead he burst into tears and loud lamentations, calling on Allah, wringing his hands, moaning and shouting and waving his fists in the air.

"He has lost his livelihood," Yasser murmured and sighed. He looked at the two men beside him. "Come and have a coffee with me." He bowed to them, then indicated a coffee stall a little further into the souk. "There is nothing we can do here."

"What will he do now?" Larry asked. The Egyptian spread his hands. "Starve, unless he has another animal, which is doubtful. He wouldn't have been so violent with that one if he had."

"But Mr Assam . . ."

"Call me Yasser."

"Yasser. If the donkey was his only means of livelihood, then why did he beat it so?"

"Oh, to urge it on. To make it do the impossible. Make it young again. Fear makes him behave violently." He strolled through the bazaar, nodding to right and left, returning greetings, leading them to the coffee stall. "When the donkey or the pony, or ass or cow or whatever animal becomes old or lame or simply gets sick, they cannot *afford* either to release them for treatment or replace them. So they work them on and on, trying desperately to keep them going."

"But it should never happen. The animals need care," David said. "They have the wrong end of the stick."

"Do you think I don't know that?" The Egyptian's face was downcast. "It is a sad business," he said, then he brightened. "Perhaps you might be able to help us," he said, "perhaps Allah sent you here to the bazaar today for just that purpose. Here. Good morning, Amar. Sit here."

David and Larry sat on the small stools and sipped the thick black coffee out of tiny demitasse cups. People nodded and smiled at them now in the company of this man who was one of themselves, accepting the foreigners because Yasser had accepted them.

The Egyptians, David and Larry were to discover, were a good-natured people. Yasser told them all about his work with the Cooke Hospital in Cairo.

"It was an English lady who began it in the Twenties," he told them. "She was, like yourselves, outraged when she saw a similar sight as you did today, and she saw how the animals suffered. As I said, these people are poor. Desperately poor. There are no soup kitchens here, nowhere to go if you have no food, no Welfare State. Their animals are often their only means of support, their only means of transport, only means of income. Everything. They cannot afford to let them recover, give them the time and they are often kept working when they have crippling wounds, diseases or injuries. What we do, what the Cooke Hospital does, we provide free help and care for the maintenance and health of the animals." He was leaning towards the two vets, speaking earnestly. They could see how passionately he felt.

"We provide free treatment and, in the case where the animal is worn out and there is nothing more we can do, we put it down humanely and give the owner a small subsistence allowance while they are without their means of livelihood, and until the owner gets from us a contribution towards another beast of burden." He paused, then smiled at them. "Oh, how I hate that phrase," he said, shaking his head. "If the animal is in no pain we let it have a few peaceful days before we put it down, probably the only proper rest it has had in years."

Larry and David were moved. Yasser told them that the Cooke Hospital needed more help, more funds from the West to continue their work.

"We'll be glad to help," Larry told him impulsively, "won't we, David?"

His friend nodded emphatically. "Just let us know what to do, how best we can serve."

"Information and education. We need friends to pass on the message," Yasser told them. "Now you must come and see the hospital and, if you would do me the honour, please dine with me tonight."

They eagerly accepted the invitation. It was a productive meeting and they cemented a friendship. They kept in touch, participated, at first in small ways, then they became more and more involved in the life of the animal hospitals that spread across Egypt and Jordan. They raised funds for the cause, and at every available opportunity they helped out in the Middle East.

It became an obsession with Larry. It was his main interest. He only worked in the small practice off the King's Road in order to be able to afford to go to Egypt. He often flew to Cairo, Aswan or Luxor for the weekend to look in on the hospitals, give some practical help, dine with Yasser whenever possible and discuss ways and means to improve the situation. He gave lectures in Egypt and Jordan. And in London. The lectures helped enlighten people everywhere about the situation.

He discovered to his horror the full extent of the unconscious cruelty meted out to these overworked beasts, how they often laboured hour after hour in temperatures well over one hundred degrees Fahrenheit, with little opportunity of water or a rest in the shade.

As a Westerner he was appalled at the conditions prevalent in the Middle East, conditions inconceivable to people at home in Europe.

"What I cannot emphasise enough," Yasser told Larry, "is our *educational* work. We tell the owners, as you have seen, advise them on the future care of their animals which is after all in their own best interests."

Larry and David were both heavily involved in the cause, but with Larry it became a passion. Inspired by all he had seen he became more and more interested and began to want to spend as much time as was humanly possible in Egypt.

He loved Egypt, its ancient culture, the sweetness of the people, their generosity and good humour. The place, the task, the Egyptians, became part of his life, perhaps the most rewarding and important part.

Chapter Eight

Next evening Larry and Perdita had dinner in La Familia at the bottom of the King's Road. Although the food was superb: Taglitella Ortolano, salad, baked swordfish, followed by a fabulous chocolate mousse and coffee, they did not do the meal justice.

If they did not eat much they did not speak much either. They sat opposite each other, oblivious to the chattering diners around them, the Italian *dolce vita*, the laughter, and examined each other's faces intently, eyes travelling over every inch, like small caresses. Larry discovered a tiny mole near Perdita's right eyebrow and saw that her golden hair was platinum near her pretty ears.

Perdita's eyes roamed lovingly over the lines on his sun-tanned forehead and at the corners of his grey eyes. They both knew there would be time for talk, time for laughter, time to eat. It was not necessary yet.

Afterwards, they strolled up the King's Road together. Larry took her hand in his and she shivered with pleasure. His hand felt rough and strong, the palm velvety-soft against hers. She had never felt so secure in her life before.

They took their time getting to know each other. They both felt their relationship was too important to rush.

They went to the theatre together, and to concerts in the Albert Hall and the South Bank. They spent every evening in each other's company and Perdita, with passionate intensity, evaded her parents and Posy. She wanted to put off the inevitable meetings for as long as possible.

Larry brought her to meet his mother. His father had died of cancer when he was in his teens. "That brought me and David close," he told her. "His father has multiple sclerosis, you see and is very sick. Has been for years." The man of the house who was there, but not there . . .

When Larry's father had died his mother had bought a smallholding in the country, leaving, she said, the hubbub of London for the peace and serenity she found there. Her efforts had produced a wonderfully welcoming home, a delightfully old-fashioned cottage garden, an apple orchard at the back of the cottage beside a small running brook. It was picturesque and Anjelica Burton made no bones about enjoying her quiet existence buried deep in Berkshire.

Perdita was instantly drawn to her. She responded to the warmth and kindness she found in Larry's mother, the gentleness, the absence of the cruelty she was used to in her own home, the indifference she had seen in Posy's parents. She spent every weekend she could with Anjelica and Larry, getting to know them, basking and relaxing in their undemanding and uncritical acceptance of her.

The month of April came and went and on the last weekend in Meadow Cottage Larry kissed Perdita for the first time.

They were standing on the hump-backed bridge over

the bubbling little stream, staring down at the dancing wavelets. The sun was cowslip-yellow and the air perfumed with the scent of honeysuckle and hawthorn.

"It's perfect here, Larry. Like something out of an impossibly romantic movie," she said.

Larry turned to her and, taking her face between his hands, he leaned towards her and kissed her.

Perdita let the bunch of wild flowers she held in her hands drop and drew in her breath as his lips met hers. A shock like an electric current coursed through her. Her body melted then, as his arms circled her, she almost fell at the sweetness of it, overwhelmed by a longing to melt completely into him, become part of him. He held her against him, supporting her.

"I love you, Larry," she whispered as she raised a painfully exposed face to him, a face full of trust and hope and love, a face that reminded him yet again of the wounded animals that came to him to be healed.

"I know, my dear, I know," was what he said, smoothing her hair from her brow.

They held each other tenderly. They were not in any hurry. Passion could wait. Larry was not about to hustle Perdita. He understood her modesty, her need to grow slowly into love, and Perdita, shyly and tentatively allowed Larry to know her, but slowly, little by little. For the first time in her life she began to put her trust into someone else, completely, without reservation.

"When will I meet your parents?" he asked her. "It is usual, you know."

She drew away from him and he could see her fright.

"Soon. Soon," she said, turning her face so that he could not see her expression, could not meet her eyes. She stared down at a black swan sailing serenely on the water. And remembered her father's words: *You're the ugly duckling who does not turn into a swan!* And she shivered.

"Perdita, you must not be frightened. You must trust me."

"Oh I do. I do. But I don't trust *them*."

"They can't hurt you now," he protested.

She shook her head then turned to him. "You don't know them, Larry, what they are capable of. You have never been exposed to . . . to cruelty."

"My father died. That was cruel."

"Yes, but he was a kind man. And your mother is an angel. No, I mean the cruelty of *people*, not the cruelty of fate. You cannot imagine or understand what it is like."

"It can't be as bad as you make it sound, Perdita," Larry insisted, not understanding. "They can't hurt you if you don't let them. You're a big girl now. And I love you. Nothing can change that."

She said nothing. She did not tell him that old habits die hard. She did not try to explain that verbal abuse cows one, that you learn to duck, to avoid, but never to assert your rights. The price you had to pay was too high and, anyhow, her spirit was too bruised to be able to do that. And her family had been playing the game too long for her protest to be listened to or be taken seriously.

She wished with all her heart that she could avoid introducing her parents to Larry. It would be wonderful if they never met at all and she could keep her relationship with him a precious thing apart, away from their soiling fingers. But she was a realist and knew this was a vain hope, she would eventually have to face the music.

Chapter Nine

At the end of that April she met Fern Morrison. It was unexpected, and unplanned. She had no desire to meet her father's lover and she had avoided David as much as she could without arousing either of the friends' suspicions. They decided she kept out of David's way because she was sensitive to his feeling of disappointment because she cared for Larry and because she did not want to cause a rift between the friends. This was partly true, though her self-esteem was never very great and did not allow her to feel that important.

Larry wanted her all to himself and this was easy to manage because when he was on duty David was off and vice versa. So they did not tend to clash. All three of them worked hard not to get in each other's way.

However, one glorious day Perdita popped into the surgery to pick Larry up and found he had been called out on an emergency.

"We're shutting up shop here," David told her. "Larry said he'd pick you up at my place in about an hour. We couldn't, off-hand, think of anywhere else you might comfortably wait for him." He grinned at her. "I won't try to seduce you, I promise," he teased her, "though I have to admit, I'd like to." Perdita lowered her head, embarrassed. It was her own fault. Larry knew she felt self-conscious sitting alone in public places. He had teased her about it, but gently, tenderly.

"They stare," she said defensively, "probably thinking how awful I am, that I'm alone because no one wants to be with me."

"No. They are thinking how beautiful you are and they are probably wondering how they could meet you," he told her, and she blushed and smiled.

She went home with David. He drove her.

"Great, there's a place to park right outside," he said, easing the car smoothly in between a Jaguar and a Beetle. "You bring me luck, Perdita. There's almost never a space here." He cut the engine and looked across at her, his arm draped over the steering wheel. "Remember the day I went to see Prissy? The day Larry stole you away from me . . ."

"Oh no he didn't!" she protested, "He—"

"No. I know," he smiled, shame-faced. "That was unfair of me. But you remember that day? When I had to leave?" he asked again. She nodded. "Well, Prissy's owner was so grateful for what I did," he glanced at her sideways, "and I assure you it was nothing; Prissy had a bone in her throat and I . . ." he made a chopping motion with his hand. "It popped out," he said, then, glancing away, "She's written a cheque for the Cooke Hospital. A very large cheque. Larry has told you about the hospital and our involvement in it."

"Yes, yes," she cried. "He talks about it all the time. He wants to take me there."

"Well, so you see, you bring me luck," he said, "even if you don't love me."

She shook her head, "No," she said, "I don't, David. But I like you *so* much!" Then, hesitantly, "You don't mind, do you? About Larry and me?"

He stared at her for a moment, then nodded. "Yes I do," he said, then more firmly, "of course I do. You are the most beautiful—"

"I'm *not* beautiful!" she contradicted him, but felt a thrill of pleasure at the compliment just the same. "I may be to Larry because he loves me," she continued haltingly, "but I'm *not* . . ."

"Yes you are! You don't know, do you? You have no idea. You, Perdita, are *truly* beautiful. Like Ingrid Bergman was. You are not manufactured, mass-produced, a clone, a copy. You are completely naturally beautiful. You haven't had your hair coloured, your body is not starved and your nose is not bobbed . . ."

"Should I get it bobbed?" she began, and he shook his head angrily in contradiction.

"No, no, no, don't you *see*?" then he saw her face and realised she was teasing him, laughing to herself. "No, listen Perdita. I mean what I say. If ever you break with Larry . . ." He heard her gasp and an expression of consternation crossed her face. "*If* it doesn't work out for you two," he frowned, "Larry is so . . . so tied up in the Egypt thing. I mean . . . he's a very self-contained man, he isolates . . ." he faltered to a stop, seeing her expression was aghast. "Or maybe you just need a friend. Remember," he imitated Humphry Bogart, "you just have to whistle."

She smiled at him. "Thank you," she said.

He leaned over and kissed her cheek. "Thank *you*," he said, then moved to get out of the car. Perdita glanced up at that moment and saw the woman there. Fern Morrison stood in the same window as she had stood that day when Perdita watched Lucas walk away from the house. She stood in the same pose, looking down on them and Perdita knew she had seen her son kiss her. And because she had been conditioned to feel fear, she was frightened.

Chapter Ten

Fern came into the comfortable drawing room moments after David had settled Perdita on the sofa. The room was large and bright, and very comfortable. The sofa was old and sagged, covered, like the armchairs, in flowered chintz. There were bowls of flowers everywhere and French windows led out onto a paved patio, a walled garden full of cherry blossom, magnolias, camellias and lilac. There was wrought-iron garden furniture, brilliantly white with a striped green and white umbrella over the table. There was a jug of lemonade and glasses on the table. David went and poured some for both of them and as Perdita put the glass to her lips the door opened and David's mother came in.

She was unfashionably plump, but trim, deep-bosomed with a small waist. Her skin was alabaster white and her legs were long and shapely. She had been in a *robe-de-chambre* at the window but had obviously pulled on the long floral skirt and loose white cotton knit. Her red hair shone like a burnished halo about her head and she seemed very nervous, very tense.

"This is Perdita Hastings, Mother," David said, drinking his lemonade. His eyes were admiring as he looked at Perdita.

The woman frowned and her large green eyes were troubled. She had a voluptuous, pre-Raphaelite look about her that struck Perdita as very sexy and she thought how unlike Melinda she was. She also thought, she knows who I am and she does not like me being with her son, but what can she do? Perdita wanted to tell her not to worry, that she was Larry's girlfriend, not David's, but she didn't know how.

"I'm waiting for Larry, Mrs Morrison," she managed and the woman smiled. She had small even teeth and her lips were very red but she wore no lipstick.

"Call me Fern," she said, then stood with her back to them, looking out where the cherry blossom drifted like confetti over the small garden.

It was then that Perdita noticed the wheelchair half in and half out of an arbour at the bottom of the garden. She could just see the outline of legs under a tartan rug, two feet in hand-made leather loafers resting on a footrest. The arbour was draped in wistaria and the heavy clusters of mauve blossom hid the rest of the chair. It was obviously Mr Morrison, Perdita decided and wondered whether she would meet him. There was something faintly sinister about that chair, half-visible, protruding from the wistaria.

"Would you like a drink, Mother?" David asked.

Fern shook her head. "No, dear." Then, cocking her head, "Ah, here's Miranda."

There had been no sound, no warning, but moments later Perdita heard a clatter at the door and a girl's voice called, "Hello Ma! Hi, you home?"

"In here, dear," Fern called. David smiled at Perdita.

"Mother's radar," he said. "She always knows when we're home before we get here."

Perdita thought, that must be handy when my father is here. Jolly handy. Then she chided herself for being bitchy. She wondered, nevertheless, whether the man in the wheelchair waited there in the arbour while Lucas was visiting Fern.

Fern turned around as the girl who had opened the door to Perdita when she had first come to the house exploded into the room and threw herself at her mother, hugging her. Then, turning to David, she said, "Can you help me with my bike, Dave? The chain's gone funny." Then she noticed Perdita and she frowned, looking very like her mother.

"Hello! I've seen you before, haven't I?"

"No you haven't, brat," David said, laughing. "This is Perdita Hastings. My terrible sister Miranda."

"Yes I have. I remember," the girl was not going to be stopped.

"When?" Fern looked intently from Perdita to her daughter and back again. Perdita felt the blood rush to her cheeks. How could she explain what she had been doing at the door of their house?

"You rang the bell. Looking for someone called Tree," the girl said brightly, "last month. I thought it was a funny name at the time." Fern was watching Perdita, hawk-like

"Like Max Beerboam Tree. Sir Henry Tree. No, it's quite common." David was obviously puzzled and kept glancing from Miranda to Perdita and back, but he was trying too to be polite and charming and not upset Perdita.

The girl was sure of herself. "Oh yes, I remember you," she said, "I remember thinking how beautiful you were. I'm a painter you see. I look at people's faces. I register them."

"My sister, Perdita, is at *school*. She *hopes* to become a painter. But she has not yet."

"I am what I am, now. I was born a painter and will always be a painter, Dave. Don't show your ignorance. Artists are born not made."

"What is she talking about, Perdita?" David asked.

Perdita was saved by Fern. There was something in her eyes that told Perdita that she knew everything. She had guessed that Perdita had followed her father here and she did not want her children to know about any of this.

"David, go and see if you can fix Miranda's bicycle, there's a dear," she said firmly. "Your friend and I will sit a while in the garden and chat. Off you go." She shooed them out of the room, giving them no opportunity to disobey, then she shepherded Perdita into the small garden, indicating the wrought-iron chair as she spoke. "Sit there, do. There's a cushion. That's better." She settled Perdita in the chair, "It is nice here, don't you think? I know it's small but it's very pretty. The rhododendrons will be in bloom soon. They are a brilliant cerise and beside the white camellias and the mauve lilac they look wonderful."

Perdita could tell she was chattering on, deciding what she would say. Then she remarked, "Excuse me a moment," and she went down the small paved pathway to the arbour. Perdita saw her lean over the wheelchair, her head and shoulders disappearing behind the wistaria.

She could hear the murmur of voices, one dark, one light, but she was too far off to hear what they said. Then Fern tucked the rug in around the knees and Perdita could see a hand, thin, tapered fingers plucking at the checked material.

Fern returned and sat opposite her visitor. She glanced obliquely at her. "My husband," she said and Perdita saw her large green eyes were full of pain. "He's an invalid. Very sick."

"I'm sorry." Perdita did not know what else to say.

"Why did you come here?" Fern asked gently. "I saw you too, that day Miranda mentioned. You rang our bell and asked for a family called Tree? Why did you do that?" Perdita remained silent. "Now you come here as David's friend. He has spoken of you a lot over the last weeks. So unlike him. He has never spoken so much about any girl before."

"Oh, it's not David," Perdita bumbled, "it's Larry Burton. I'm . . . em, his girl-friend."

"But David *is* interested in you, though? Am I right?"

Perdita nodded. "But I've *told* you," she protested, "It's Larry I'm . . ."

Fern Morrison waved an elegant white hand for silence. She leaned forward, putting her elbows on the white iron table. "You followed your father here that day, didn't you?" she asked calmly. She had narrowed her eyes against the pale sunshine.

Perdita nodded. "Yes," she admitted reluctantly, "I saw you come out of the restaurant that day. Mother sent me to Colefax & Fowler . . ."

"So you thought . . . what? I'm curious to know."

"That you were his . . ." she could not think what to call her without sounding coarse and bitchy.

"Mistress?" Perdita nodded. "Why not his quick lay? His tart? It could have been a thing of the moment. Impulsive. Just for that afternoon."

A cloud passed over the sun, casting Fern Morrison's face in shadow. "No," Perdita insisted. "There was something about you both together that made me realise that you knew each other very well. You were familiar with each other. I could tell that. It was not the first time."

Fern stared at Perdita. She thought for a moment, then sighed. "It's difficult," she said. "I've agonised about this since the day I saw you down there in the street. I knew you would come back. Then David began to rhapsodise about you. I was frightened. Very frightened."

"But why? If my father chooses to have an affair with you, what's it got to do with me?" Perdita, although she could not blame her father for looking for love outside his home, could not keep the sarcasm out of her voice. "If it *was* David, which it isn't, what has it to do with you and Father?"

Then suddenly she went cold, for before Fern Morrison spoke she knew exactly what she was going to say.

"Because Lucas Hastings is David's and Miranda's father too. That's why I'm frightened. And I'm trusting you, Perdita, to keep this a secret . . ." She glanced at the arbour. "My husband does not know. Must never know. And David must never know." She squeezed her eyes together and her hands on the table were knotted in a fierce embrace. "My poor Paul," she whispered, staring down where the wheelchair protruded from the arbour. "He thinks they are his. We tried, you see, after he became ill. Up to then we thought we had plenty of time. We tried and it was agony. And useless, but he *thinks*, he believes . . ." She frowned. "We were selfish, you see, deciding not to have children until later. Then Paul was struck down. I tried to conceive with him but it didn't work. Couldn't have. And Lucas, your father . . . I got pregnant. At first I was terrified. I thought of abortion. It was an outrageous thought for me. I wanted children desperately. Then I thought, Paul need not know. It made him so happy. He did not feel useless any more. I decided on the lie I live now."

She turned and looked at Perdita. "I don't expect you to understand. I love Paul, you see. I love the man he was. He was my childhood sweetheart, only he never had the time or the opportunity to grow up. His pain put a stop to that. Like all invalids he is fretful and irritable. Difficult. But I'll never desert him. He would die without me. The children. His home." She turned away from Perdita. "I love Lucas too. It is a quite different love. Passionate. And he loves me, Perdita, and I'm sorry if that hurts you." She stood. "Oh why did you have to follow us? Why couldn't you have left things as they were? But I suppose that is unrealistic. It was bound to happen sooner or later." She shook her head sadly "I've been afraid, all these years."

"Afraid?"

"Yes, terrified would be more accurate."

"Of what?"

"Paul finding out. It would kill him. Some busybody discovering the liaison, Lucas and me and telling the press. Can you imagine their glee, the field day they would have? They don't exactly *love* your father, Perdita. He has been . . . em, *short* with them to put it mildly. They would make hay with a scandal about him." She sat down again, looking pleadingly at Perdita. "He think's he's above all that, that he is invincible. He is careless, pays no attention."

Perdita could well believe it. Her father would court danger arrogantly. "And if it all came out he'd be the first to suffer. And David and Miranda. Most of all my children. His children. We cannot hurt them. You can imagine how confused they'd be if they ever found out. Oh, it would be such a mess."

Perdita stared at Fern's hands, her fingers lacing and interlacing, her knuckles white and red.

"I was young, you see, so young. Madly in love. Lucas was famous. He said he did not love Melinda, she would never give him a divorce. And I knew I would never divorce Paul."

She was appealing to Perdita as if her life depended on it. Perdita supposed that, in a way, it actually did. She felt as if she was floating, as if she was up on a stage in a dramatic play. None of this was real. It was too theatrical. Yet she knew too that all of it *was* true.

"I was happy, Perdita, as well as being frightened. It was all pat. All perfect. Paul thought he had sired two healthy children. This gave him such solace. I was having a passionate affair with your father. I was, you might say, having my cake and eating it. Now that I'm older I know that I was wrong, that there's always a price to pay and the ones who pay most dearly are usually the innocent ones. David and Miranda. I know now that the truth will out, but please don't tell them,

Perdita, please." She glanced at Perdita. "I've never had the courage to break it off. Give up Lucas. You know your father, Perdita. He would never let me. He's not an easy man. And I love him. I would never do anything that might upset him and he won't let me go."

The door banged and there was the sound of laughter in the hall and David's and Miranda's voices raised in light-hearted banter. The figure at the bottom of the garden had not stirred.

Fern brushed at her skirt with nervous fingers. "I hope you won't say anything, Perdita. I had to talk to you about it. I saw David kissing you in the car, you see. He's your half-brother. I had to say something."

"I know. It's all right. I won't say anything," Perdita said, her head in a whirl.

"You won't tell David. Promise me." Fern's lip trembled. "I couldn't bear to lose him and I would, if he knew."

"I promise."

David shouted, "Just washing my hands, Mother. Won't be a mo." Then he popped his head round the door. "Larry's coming. His car just turned in off the King's Road. He'll be ages finding a parking space. Maybe you'd better go out to him, Perdita," and he disappeared.

"May I phone you?" Fern asked. "I'd like to meet you. Talk to you properly. Tell you about—"

"Yes. Yes please. I would appreciate that."

"All right." Fern seemed satisfied and she turned into the drawing room as Larry entered, followed by David.

"Ah, Larry, how nice to see you. You got a parking

space, then?" and without waiting for a reply Fern added, "Do have some lemonade, do. It's fresh." She was again the gracious hostess, welcoming her guests, holding up her cheek for Larry to kiss.

Perdita realised that no one had introduced her to Paul Morrison. She supposed they did not think her important enough to make the effort. Or perhaps he did not like company. But he had been at the bottom of the garden all that time. Still, she thought there was something faintly rude about it and wondered again where he was when Lucas called.

Perdita sat there feeling shell-shocked. She stared down to where the wheelchair was statue-still, then she too held up her face for Larry to kiss. But inside she was reeling from this avalanche that had hit her. She was trying to come to terms with the fact that she had a whole other family that up to now she had been completely ignorant of.

Chapter Eleven

That night in bed Perdita tossed and turned, fought with the pillow, was nearly strangled by her sheets and eventually gave up all attempts to sleep. She tried to sort out the whole tangle in her mind but failed to reach acceptance and therefore peace.

David was about the same age as herself and that meant her father and Fern had been lovers when Melinda was pregnant with Perdita. For some reason Perdita felt this was unfair. Not playing the game. Fairness was important to Perdita. She was a very fair person and she had to admit that for her father *not* to have had someone extra curricular in his life would have been almost an impossibility. Ditto Fern. She assumed the other women in his life had been red herrings to distract from the real situation and she reflected now that, in the main, her father seemed to behave outrageously publicly and she had often wondered whether he ever saw any of these dolly-birds privately. She had doubted it.

Perdita had not thought too much about it, but she doubted very much whether her father and mother ever made love. She had never seen any evidence of it. They never slept near each other at Oak Wood Court and lived separately in London. She had fancied that, like all young people who could not conceive of their parents 'at it' as they used to say in school, that her mother and father *must* have a sex life. But as she got older it became more and more obvious to her that Melinda and Lucas did not appear to. Apart from their obvious antipathy towards each other there was a lack of opportunity. A contrived lack of opportunity.

Since Perdita had fallen so passionately in love with Larry Burton she recognised physicality in others. It was easy to spot, that tactile response even between people who hated each other but still felt a sexual tug or were not entirely indifferent to each other. Lucas and Melinda seemed to their daughter supremely indifferent, uncomfortable even. It appeared as if they found each other distasteful. So it seemed to her naïve to suppose her father was leading a celibate life. And it was as unrealistic to imagine a woman as obviously ardent as Fern Morrison would give up sex for life because her husband was an invalid.

Eventually she slept. She had decided not to allow the puzzle of her parents and the Morrisons to interfere with her own happiness and her happiness was tied to Larry. What had any of them to do with him? Nothing. She did not have to tackle their motives, their complicated lives. She let it drop.

Larry spent the next week trying to persuade her to come to Egypt with him. He was scheduled to spend some time in Luxor at the end of May. He said he could not, would not, be separated from her.

"You've got to come with me, see what I do there. It's important."

She, bemused by his need, touched to the core by her

indispensibility, nevertheless hesitated. She had never been out of England. Her parents never thought to take her with them when they went abroad. However, Melinda had sorted out Perdita's passport, although she had no intention of taking her daughter anywhere. It was typical of her mother, but now Perdita was grateful.

It was natural that Perdita was a little scared at the prospect. Her love and trust was at war with a totally irrational fear. She fought it and love and trust won.

Fern phoned Perdita and suggested they have tea in the Savoy. Perdita was not at all sure she wanted to become involved with Fern Morrison. She had enough on her plate with the whole Egypt thing and Larry and she would have been happier to completely avoid the situation so fraught with emotion, but she had stumbled into it and she did not know how to extricate herself. So she agreed.

Perdita arrived first and waited awkwardly for David's mother to arrive. Fern wore a long skirt and a low-necked black top and gypsy earrings. Her red hair tumbled around her face, emphasising her pale skin. The waiters rushed to her assistance with great enthusiasm and Perdita could only reflect on the aura of sensuality Fern Morrison exuded. She sat on the sofa, indicating the armchair in front of her for Perdita, and Perdita nodded and obeyed. Fern waited in composed silence for the tea to arrive and poured without comment. Perdita found the silence unbearable and shifted in her chair restlessly.

When the waiter had brought the cake-rack with sandwiches, scones and finger cakes and they were both nibbling a cucumber sandwich and sipping their tea, Fern spoke at last.

"Well, Perdita, what do you think of me? Am I the woman you hate? Cruella de Vil? The Wicked Witch of the North? Or is it the East? I can never remember." She waited. The pianist was playing songs from another era. 'The Nearness of You'.

Perdita shook her head. "No. I don't hate you," she said at last. "I know I should. I think I must be an unnatural child, but you see I don't really like my father and I *hate* my mother. I expect I would hate you if I loved them, but I don't." She stared defiantly at Fern who met her gaze levelly.

"Really? Why?" she asked calmly.

To Perdita's horror, tears sprang to her eyes. The enormity of her mother's contempt for her suddenly seemed overwhelming. "She despises me. She thinks I'm useless. How can you love someone who doesn't care a rap for you?"

"Easily," Fern said.

Perdita blinked rapidly and the tears slid into the corners of her eyes then dropped onto her cheek and trembled there before sliding down to her chin. "Anyhow," she said, "she's right. I guess she must have hated having a daughter like me." She leaned forward putting her cup down on the silver tray. "You see, they're so talented. My mother is *perfect*. Her body is, well, perfect . . ."

"Yes. Lucas says she's a clothes horse," Fern muttered, but Perdita continued as if she had not heard.

"Everything about Mother is neat and glamorous and attended to. Never a hair astray, never a nail chipped." She glanced down at her own broad hands, the nails filed across, plain, almost antiseptic. Then she looked back at Fern. "Then there's her work. Every job she does is a success. Meticulous. That hotel she just did – everyone talks about it. Compared to her I'm talentless, stupid, clumsy and ugly. Or so she tells me." Perdita's voice was not self-pitying, simply matter-of-fact.

"Does Larry think you are ugly?" Fern asked.

"No, but—"

"Does David?"

"No, but Mother's standards are very high."

"Have you ever heard of jealousy?"

Perdita's eyes widened. "You don't imagine . . . that would be ridiculous!"

"Why, Perdita? It's quite common, you know, for a mother to be envious of a young daughter. And Melinda is in love with a man who does not love her. That makes for bitterness. Why not, Perdita?"

All Perdita's pat answers, all her deductions were thrown into confusion. She gasped, "Because . . . I've just told you. She's perfect! And I'm . . . why on earth would she be jealous of *me*?" she asked incredulously.

"You are young, Perdita, and very beautiful, no matter what you think, and she must be very lonely. And loveless. Listen, Perdita, for a moment." A frown creased the smooth white brow. "When I came here today I did not know how you felt about things, whether you . . ." she shrugged, bit her lip and continued. "What happened, long, long ago, warped your mother and reduced her life to a lie. She trapped Lucas into marriage and it did not work. I'm sure your mother thought it would. It was not her fault that she is the way she is. And she *is* jealous of you. Maybe she's not even aware of it but you are young, beautiful – oh yes you are. You have your whole life ahead of you and she is growing old and her whole life must appear a sham when she thinks about it. Loveless and so sad. She cannot change now. It's too late. She's made her bed so she must lie on it." Fern gave a wan smile. "Most of us do," she said.

"What happened? To make her the way she is? You said . . ."

"I'm not sure if I ought to tell you this, but, well . . . Do you remember your grandfather, Perdita?"

"Gramps Jack? Mother's father? Oh yes. He was always nice to me. Gave me chocolates when he shouldn't."

Fern nodded. "Yep. That sounds like him. Buying you. He bought everyone."

"Oh no! I'm sure . . ." But she wasn't. Not at all.

Grandfather Jack was always giving her things her mother did not approve of. Grandfather Jack treated her mother, Perdita suddenly realised now, exactly as Melinda treated *her*. Grandfather Jack ordered her mother about, ridiculed her, spoke contemptuously of everything she did and often reduced her to tears. But he had always been nice to Perdita, though it upset the little girl when he whispered, "Whatever you do don't grow up like your mother!"

"Your grandfather was a very big wheel in the BBC," Fern said.

"Mmm. I know."

"What you may not know is, he threatened to scupper your father's career, and believe me he was quite capable of doing so, if he did not marry your mother."

Perdita stared at her. This she had not known. Fern put a dollop of cream on her scone and topped it with a spoonful of blackberry jam. Melinda would be appalled at such indulgence.

"I was going out with your father at that time. He had finished with your mother. It had all been on her side in any event. She adored him and pursued him relentlessly. He broke it off and started to date me. Then Melinda found out she was pregnant, and all hell broke loose."

She bit into the scone, licked the cream off her lips and sighed. "Unfortunately, your father always put his career before anyone or anything. You can guess the rest. Jack Armstrong, when he found out his darling daughter was with child, as he insisted on phrasing it, went ballistic. He said if Lucas didn't marry his daughter, make an honest woman of her he'd make sure Lucas never worked in the business again. He'd have him black-listed. And he could do it. Jack Armstrong was quite capable of doing it." She smiled at Perdita, "Your mother was delighted. She was madly in love with Lucas, and unfortunately Lucas was career-mad." She wiped her lips with the napkin. She wore no lipstick yet her lips were red as berries. "You must understand, Perdita, that things were very different then. Not that many people used condoms. Sexual health was not the issue it is today." She shook her head. "Even today, with all the publicity, the warnings, people still take risks. Imagine what it was like then."

"So my father was forced to marry my mother?"

Fern nodded. "He needn't have, of course, he could have married me and lost his career. But he was seduced by Daddy Jack's power. Position. Marrying Melinda guaranteed a glittering career. He had immediate entry into the world of the high-flyers, the big names, the stars. He would inherit Oak Wood Court, have access to property, money and, most important, a father-in-law who could make or break him. Who could ruin him, make sure he never worked in his chosen field *or* who could push him forward, make him a household name. When I was going out with him, before he," she glanced at Perdita, "sold out," she said wryly, "he was very small potatoes. He was at the bottom of the ladder. After he married your mother he was propelled to the top. Yup! He betrayed himself. He loved me, but he wanted the power, the fame, the fortune. He paid a high price for it, Perdita. I've watched him grow bitter. I've watched him as he grew to hate his wife. I've watched him doubting his own success. He wonders constantly if he would have made it without Daddy Jack's ruthless pushing. He's a very unhappy man, your father."

"Then why did you . . . do you . . ."

"I love him. Don't you know yet that love tolerates all kinds of stupidity? And I'm still waiting for him to leave your mother." She lifted an eyebrow. "Do you mind?"

"No. No. They would be much better apart," Perdita said. "And you? Paul?"

"Paul had been madly in love with me for years. We were children together. He asked me to marry him when your father married Melinda and I did." She waved a pale hand. "Oh, it sounds complicated now, but it seemed so simple then. I was angry. Lucas had married another woman. Paul asked me and I seized the opportunity. How could I know he already had MS?" she averted her face but Perdita could see the pain mirrored there. "No one knew. I suppose it was my punishment," she said sadly.

"And what . . .?"

"Lucas came back to me almost at once. He left her bed after the honeymoon and ran to me with open arms and pleading eyes. He cried in my arms that night, Perdita, and deep inside he has been crying ever since. That night, David was conceived and Paul was told he had MS. What a tangle." She turned to Perdita. "I hope I haven't shocked you?"

Perdita shook her head. "No. You've made a lot I didn't understand clear," she replied.

"You see, what eats into your father is the knowledge of his own venality. She was the big man's daughter, his road to fame and fortune, and I was the daughter of a shop-keeper. No contest. But he hates the fact that he betrayed both himself and me for mercenary rewards. He likes to think of himself as an idealist. He's been at war with himself since he married your mother."

"How could you put up with it?" Perdita asked, "take him back?"

"I told you. I love him. I can't *not*."

"And David doesn't know who his father is?"

"No. We became very careful. Lucas became paranoid. No one must find out. Old Daddy Jack was watching all the time. After all he only died a few years ago. And people were very moral in those days. Not like now. I remember a religious broadcaster lost his job and was discredited forever because he had an extra-marital affair. So did the presenter of a children's programme. Scandal could finish you in those days. It's different now but Lucas is in the habit of secrecy. He says it gives spice to our relationship, but I think it is simply habit. And his fear of the inevitable emotional wrangles. Like when David and Miranda find out. *If* they find out.

And you of course. But," she sighed, "I live in hope."

"Why didn't he come clean when Grandpa Jack died?" Perdita asked.

"Well, habit, as I said. And," Fern poured more tea, delicately using the strainer, "Daddy Jack's will was clear and air-tight. If Lucas divorces your mother he forfeits all rights to the properties and the money."

"But he hardly ever uses Oak Wood Court and he doesn't need the money."

"It's fear, Perdita. Habit. He simply cannot trust. He visualises a catastrophic scenario. Totally unrealistic." She tut-tutted, then continued, "You see, he's never had to stand on his own two feet and realise he can survive. Hard times are wonderful teachers. When you survive you know you have it in you, the strength. He does not know that. Cheating is silly. It takes away confidence forever. Men! Dear Lord!"

They talked as the waiters removed the linen from the low tables and set them up for drinks. Tea-time was over. It was coming up to cocktail time and bowls of nuts and appetisers replaced the cake-racks and silver condiments. The piano player was having a break and the chandeliers were lighting up as evening fell. Dinner was being set in the River Room beyond them.

They talked and Perdita wished that Fern had been her mother. They parted, promises exchanged on both sides.

Fern said, "Don't blow your opportunities, Perdita. Seize whatever happiness you can. Don't waste your life like your mother and father have done. Time goes by so quickly and suddenly it is too late."

Perdita thought about her words and decided that, after all, she would go to Egypt with Larry.

Chapter Twelve

Before they went to Egypt, Larry insisted on meeting her parents. Lucas and Melinda behaved beautifully, thereby utterly confusing Perdita. Obviously they had decided for some devious reason that they would be on their best behaviour and Perdita did not know whether it was a joint decision or one reached independently.

Oak Wood Court lay bathed in spring sunshine as they drove silently up the long drive lined with oak trees, heavy and dark overhead, leading to the elegant entrance to the mansion.

Lucas and Melinda stood at the top of the steps waiting for them, welcoming smiles on their faces. They looked, Perdita thought, like a couple in a movie and she muttered, "Oh Jesus!" under her breath.

"Your parents?" Larry asked in disbelief. "I thought you said . . ."

Graham was waiting to take the car and park it and as Larry pulled up and got out of the Honda he took the keys from him. Perdita realised that she had made Lucas and Melinda sound like characters from a Stephen King novel and here they stood, side by side, the perfect couple. They never fail to hurt me, she thought, and wondered if she was totally mad for thinking such weird thoughts. Had she really wanted her parents to shout at each other in front of their guest? No, of course not. But this way made her seem a liar.

"Darlings!" Melinda cried, oozing charm, "welcome!"

Lucas smiled his famous smile and said, looking deeply and sincerely into Larry's eyes, remembering his name, a trick he learned long ago, "So nice to meet you, Larry. Come inside. I'm sure you'd like a drink after the drive."

The house had a formal atmosphere that Melinda had done nothing to change since her father died. Old Jack Armstrong liked to frighten his subordinates, so the place was intimidating. Melinda saw no reason to decorate the place, keeping it as a sort of shrine to Jack's memory.

They had drinks in the library, a sombre room with leather chairs and a huge log fire burning and Lucas waxed eloquent about ecology, how careless the man in the street was with regard to his habitat. He's done his homework, Perdita decided, and was not at all sure she appreciated the fact.

"It is appalling how indifferent we are to the way we are destroying the planet we live on," Lucas said, one beady eye on Larry. "It's disgraceful. I see a future where the mountains will be grotesque piles of discarded black plastic bags, the sea will be a sewer and the food will all taste of cotton wool, and," he paused, thinking, "what's that song? *Put 'em in a tree museum.* Like that! All the forests will be cut down and man will drowning in breathlessness. We may even have to buy oxygen in shops. Go around wearing masks. Having to purchase the air we breathe."

Perdita could see Larry warming to him. He had fallen

under that potent Lucas spell, just as she had feared. She could practically hear his brain ticking over; why did Perdita paint such a harsh picture? This guy is great. Feels just like I do. She wanted to shout out, "It's an act! It's all a sham!" But she remained silent.

She could not understand why this upset her. Wasn't it better that Larry liked her parents than not? She supposed that she wanted Larry on her side, understanding her, her frustrations.

Melinda was flirting now with Larry, drawing him out about his work in Egypt and he was responding to her charm like a plant to the sun.

They had lunch in the long dining room. The conversation, mainly between Larry and Lucas, was slightly provocative. It was the sort of repartee that Lucas was famous for in his interviews and Larry was holding his own beautifully. Perdita felt left out. Soured, her conversation uninvited, she realised with clarity that Lucas was showing her up. He was revealing to Larry his daughter's ineptitude. Her silence appeared sulky, and she supposed it was, but to Larry she must look clumsy, dull and uninteresting.

How she remained seated at that table she never knew. She wanted to run and hide, to leave Berkshire and flee back to London while her mother and father sparkled and shone. She yearned desperately to put miles between her father and mother and Larry. She knew she was being unreasonable. She despised herself for her awkwardness, her dullness, but could think of no way to change matters. She sat silently till her father remarked, "Are you all right, pet? You haven't said a word for hours!" Perdita nodded. He never called her *pet*.

Lucas smiled at Larry and winked, twirling the stem of his wineglass between strong fingers. "Perdita's being sulky again. She's a shy one, our Perdita. But I'll say this for her," he glanced at Larry, "she's got good taste."

Perdita blushed. She tried to think of something clever to say but could not.

It had begun to rain and they returned to the library to have their coffee, truffles and *petit fours*. The maid brought the tray and poured and served the coffee. She was handing Perdita the demitasse cup when the door burst open and Posy came hurtling in. Perdita glanced at her mother and saw the malice in Melinda's eyes. She's done this deliberately, she thought, and her heart sank.

Posy was wet and, with the exuberance of a puppy she shook herself in front of the fire. Keeping up a babble of chit-chat, she greeted Lucas, Melinda and Perdita and then stopped squarely in front of Larry and asked, "And who is this lovely man?" As if she didn't know! Perdita felt her cheeks glow redly and she admonished herself yet again for her evil assumptions.

From Perdita's point of view the afternoon went from bad to worse, though it seemed that the rest of the party found the time spent together delightfully entertaining. Larry and Posy laughed a lot. Lucas was witty and Melinda charming. Only Perdita, it seemed, was excessively quiet.

When the time came to return to London, Posy asked ever so prettily if Larry could give her a lift. Larry said, of course, very graciously and appeared only too happy to oblige. Perdita, intensely irritated at the intrusion, for she had planned to try to make Larry understand about how her parents appeared to him and how they treated her when there was no company on the way back, had no choice but to acquiesce and make the best of it.

Posy contrived to jump in the front seat of Larry's car leaving Perdita to climb in the back. On the drive home after Larry had shaken hands with Lucas and Melinda with assurances and reassurances that they would 'do it' again soon, much good-will all round, with many goodbyes littering the air, Posy began a subtle flirtation with Larry right under Perdita's nose.

Larry, partly preoccupied with his driving answered in kind, laughing and joking with Posy and Perdita sank into sullen silence in the back, certain now that she was totally uncivilised. She hated the fact that she felt as she did, envied her mother's and Posy's ability and despised herself for being a nerd.

When they reached Perdita's flat she was further upset when, instead of Larry joining her and Posy getting a taxi to her flat the latter pleaded with Larry, "Could you, would you give me a lift home, Larry? Please? Perdy won't mind, will you, Perdy?"

Perdita was too tired, too defeated to argue. Afterwards she wondered why she hadn't said she wanted to speak to Larry. She could have said, "If you don't mind Posy I'll call a cab for you." That would have been fine, but she simply did not have the heart. She hopped out of the car with a remark about being tired and having to make an early start, ran up the front steps and let herself into her apartment before Larry could reach her. She burst into tears as soon as she had closed the door behind her.

Chapter Thirteen

Posy spent most of her life feeling utterly frustrated. She could not understand why, when she got what she wanted, as she almost always did, she was not happy. Like resembling Perdita, like the job at The Design Factory, like meeting the Hastings, getting herself invited to Oak Wood Court. Before she achieved her purpose she was confident that when she got there it would be over the rainbow time. It never was.

She wanted Larry. She knew she had to pounce or he would slip away and she would become, to him, merely Perdita's friend.

Posy never worked out why she desired the things, people, fashions, jobs that she did, all of them Perdita's. She never sat down and thought it through. She never consciously realised, *I want this because Perdita has it*. Her craving, her ambition overwhelmed her, blinded her to all else and she knew that person, place, thing or style was what she wanted more than anything else and she went after it with frightening determination.

Her plan that evening was quite clear and simple; she would get Larry into bed. She had divined he was an honourable man so she knew she'd have to be careful. But being honourable, she reasoned, would force him afterwards to drop Perdita in favour of her. *Then* she would be happy.

Perdita would recover. After all, they were not sleeping together. Perdita, when Posy had asked her, had blushed and shaken her head and Posy knew her friend well enough to understand that they had not as yet had sex. So, Posy reasoned, Perdita and Larry were still not, in her book, hooked up. Love was a free-for-all. Like war the victor took it all and all was fair. And Larry was, after all, a man and men were ruled by the equipment in their pants.

How she was going to get the honourable Larry into bed with her was another matter. It was a challenge. She would have to be very careful, she realised that, and shivered with sexual excitement as she asked him to carry her weekend case up to her door.

She had made sure the case was heavy. She had put a candlestick that weighed a ton in the bottom of her Samsonite carry-all. The iron candlestick was one of a pile of odds and ends Melinda had bought locally, from a house near Oak Wood Court and was going to use in a chic residence she was decorating in Maida Vale. Posy had shoved it into her soft case smiling at how heavy it made the carry-all. She looked up at Larry, helplessly appealing to his chivalry. As well as being honourable she knew that Larry would be chivalrous. Obvious. She also guessed that he responded to vulnerability and she looked up at him with practised eyes, utterly submissive and helpless.

Once in the small apartment it became easier. She told him to put the case down in the living room and went swiftly into the kitchen, leaving him standing awkwardly in the middle of the room, aware that it would be rude to just go. She poured him a brandy. She kicked off her panties and went back into the living room. She gave him the brandy and it seemed to him churlish to refuse. Inevitably, he downed it in one. He was, after all, about to leave. She, with the bottle in her hand, re-filled it instantly.

"No, no, not for me, Posy. I'm off now." He looked around for somewhere to put the glass but there was nowhere and she did not take it from him.

"Oh, drink it up," she said, and he quaffed it obediently.

"Hell, I'm driving," he said and she watched him relax. He was not the type to drink very much and the quick brandies would take the edge off him, diminish those honourable instincts just a little. All this time she kept up a light chatter.

He was talking to her now about Perdita.

"It's funny how she paints her mother and father as unkind. Villains even," he said.

"Well," she shrugged, "Perdita does . . . exaggerate. She lives in another world, does Perdita," she told him,

What happened next left him perplexed for the rest of his life. He was never able to explain how it happened. Afterwards he thought it would – could – be classed as rape. If the situation was reversed and he was the woman it certainly would.

She crossed the room swiftly and sat astride him. The action took him aback but his limbs responded almost automatically to her sudden proximity. She pushed him against the back of the armchair and kissed him; her body gyrating against his.

It was lust. The brandy had weakened Larry's resistance and his manhood reacted eagerly to the onslaught so that he found himself deprived of the ability to resist. She had her hands all over him. She was undoing his pants, she was exciting him, arousing him, and he was aware only of the sensations in his groin.

She was thorough. Her busy hands, her soft lips, her body against his, weakened him and he was putty in her hands. His mind was numb, all his feelings were centered elsewhere.

She got him free and pushed him into her expertly, with such force that he gasped. He felt the excitement down his legs and an unbearable erotic energy washing over him.

She impaled him and worked her body against his, moving faster and faster against him as the rising crescendo thundered in his ears then exploded as he came fiercely into her.

It all took five minutes. He sat there in the armchair dazed, unable to grasp exactly what had happened, still shaken by the force and intensity of the encounter. He had never experienced anything like it before in his life and could not grasp now how it had happened, or if it had really happened at all. Perhaps it had been an hallucination, a figment of his imagination, bizarre and frightening.

Posy left him there, picking up his glass, returning to the kitchen. She smiled to herself, a secret, satisfied smile. It was all right now. She wanted nothing more just yet. She had accomplished her purpose. All was well.

It had been easier than she had anticipated, much easier. After a moment or two, time for Larry to have recovered his equilibrium, she returned to the living room. She felt confident, in charge of the situation. She walked up to him. He was standing in front of the mantelpiece, a puzzled, worried look on his face. She kissed his lips softly. He recoiled.

"Was that good for you?" she asked, deliberately arch.

"What?" He was still frowning, perplexed.

"It was wonderful for me," she said. "Oh, thank you, Larry."

"I must go . . . I must . . ."

"You'll call me, Larry, won't you?" She touched his cheek.

"Em . . ."

"I'm not the type of girl you can have a quickie with, you know. But you are not the wham-bam-thank-you-mam type, are you, who'll have his wicked way and then just leave."

"It was more like you having your way . . . I'm sorry . . ." He could not wait to get out.

"It's no use you saying you're sorry." Her voice was becoming harsh.

"I didn't ask you to . . . well . . . you know. What we did . . ." he stammered.

"What do you mean?" she cried, "what are you suggesting? That I *forced* you? That I *made* you do it against your will?"

He wanted to say yes, but in his heart he knew it would not be completely true. He had, after the surprise, those initial reluctant moments, not pulled away. He should have, he knew that, but he didn't. If he had not exactly enjoyed the experience it had certainly excited him unbearably, so much so that he had not wanted her to stop.

He wanted more than anything now to leave, to get out of here. He was thoroughly upset and angry. His head was in a whirl as he ran the film of what they had done over in his mind. He thought he could chart their every move, their every word, how it had happened, but with everything she said he became more and more unsure. She was twisting things. Had he behaved inappropriately without even realising it? Had he sent signals, unaware he was doing so?

Larry, a calm, cerebral man, had never before experienced anything like this. He had had his share of amorous encounters and had felt guilt in some cases, and in some not. He'd made love to his high-school sweetheart and parted from her regretfully when she fell in love with another. But it had been straightforward and uncomplicated. He had never before been in a situation like this and he was desperate to escape it.

He stared at Posy for a moment and in that moment she was suddenly afraid. His face was pale, his lips tight, his eyes hard.

"I'm in love with Perdita," he said.

"After that show of passion, I doubt it," she contradicted him sweetly.

"I wouldn't call it passion," he said, "I'd call it lust."

"I didn't do it on my own," she said.

He cleared his throat. "I've got to go," he announced firmly. "This thing has become . . ."

"Don't worry, Larry. I won't breathe a word to Perdy."

"Don't call her that!" It was out before he could stop himself.

"I've always called her that! I've known her longer than you have."

She was looking at him intently. Her eyes were very clear and he had a sudden realisation that she was far cleverer than he had given her credit for.

Perdita had warned him about her family, and about Posy and perhaps he should have listened. He had not taken her seriously enough, believing, especially after he had met them, that she was ultra-sensitive and they were not really such monsters after all. Now he was not so sure. She had told him how they made her feel and he had seen for himself her insecurity, her lack of confidence. He had chosen not to accept the fact that she had not been born that way, that someone had taken those qualities from her, had torn her down. He had allowed himself to be seduced by her father's brilliance, her mother's charm and her friend's duplicity. He cursed himself for a fool. It was all superficial, their brilliance, their charm, their deviousness, all insubstantial.

Afterwards, full of self-disgust, the actual happenings of that night changed subtly in his mind. He blamed himself. He decided he had had a mental aberration, was horrified at his venality, his weakness, his appalling lack of moral fibre. What a shit he had been. But, he felt he had learned his lesson. It would never happen again.

He flew to Egypt next morning, faxing Perdita at The Design Factory. He told her he had been called away suddenly. *I have been asked to go to Aswan urgently*, he said in the fax. *See you when I get back.*

Melinda pulled the paper out of the machine, reading it aloud. "Oh dear, I hope we didn't frighten him off," she remarked and Posy smiled.

Chapter Fourteen

Perdita decided to fly to Aswan and join Larry. His fax had made up her mind and suddenly it all seemed very clear to her.

She loved him and he loved her. Why then should she hang back?

She packed a case and without telling anyone hopped on a BA plane from Heathrow the morning after Larry left, two days after his visit to Oak Wood Court. She left a message on her answerphone to the effect that she had gone away and for the caller to leave a message. She faxed the Old Cataract Hotel where Larry had told her he always stayed and went to Heathrow at the crack of dawn. She closed her eyes, crossed her fingers and gave herself over to the heady sensation of leaving England for unknown and foreign shores.

Egypt, Land of the Pharaohs. She was dazzled when she landed for the sun was fiercer than she had ever known it. She found herself surrounded by robed Arabs in an unfamiliar atmosphere and the heat fell on her like a blanket.

She had thought she would be intimidated, but like the redoubtable Victorian Englishwomen who had preceeded her here to the shores of the Nile she felt only a surge of excited confidence. I'm free, she thought, I'm a free agent. There is nothing to be afraid of.

She took a taxi to the hotel and gave herself over to the totally alien atmosphere of the place. Camels, only seen before in her ancient Bible in school. Children, barefoot, begging. The Eastern buildings and the men arguing, chatting, telling their beads, sitting in the shade outside their shops. The dusty palms and above all the bustle around the huge ships on the waters of the Nile.

Entering the hotel she felt she was entering another era. The large Victorian rooms, the ceiling fans, the calm servants, the atmosphere of age-old tranquility soothed her and she went to the desk, relinquishing her case and her carryall to willing hands.

"Has Mr Burton checked in?" she asked the smiling face behind the desk at reception.

"Yes, but he is not in at the moment."

"There is no hurry," she told him, her voice echoing in the vast marble hall.

Her room was delightful and before she unpacked her few things, her chinos and shirts and toiletries, her black Jean Muir dress, she ordered a pot of coffee and sat at her window looking out over the Nile, sipping contentedly.

It was an amazing sight. The fellucas, their sails gleaming against the sun, the big pleasure ships that sailed the river taking passengers up and down the fertile banks. From Cairo to Luxor, Edfu and Kom Ombo to Aswan and on to Abu Simbel.

The crowds below her moved slowly but were the noisiest she had ever seen. They shouted, gesticulated, hurried on their bicycles, pulling the carts, the motley crowd ebbed and flowed like a tide past the hotel.

Why hadn't she travelled before? Why had she shut herself up, boxed herself in, close-minded, restricted, caged in her own little world, dominated by others?

She had never before felt this sense of freedom, this wild excitement in her breast. Here she was, a stranger in a strange land, utterly content and alone. She lifted her arms over her head and stretched and yawned happily and felt herself relax. "I didn't know," she murmured. "I did not know that this was possible."

Larry burst into her room a little later and swept her into his arms and kissed her and held her for dear life.

"Oh my darling, my love. Oh you don't know how good it is to see you."

"Hey, hey," She laughed with delight at his warm welcome. "Easy. I'm here. I'm not going to run away."

"Oh, my precious one," He buried his face in her hair, then kissed her passionately and she responded as never before, all restraint gone, eager for him.

Larry's love-making was urgent and intense. Guilty and disgusted with his last performance, he wanted only to wipe away the memory of Posy and that weird erotic interlude. He loved Perdita and his love was pure and passionate and he gave her his heart as well as his body as he caressed her and urged her to release.

Perdita kept her eyes open so as not to miss one second of these wondrous moments. The man she loved, inside her, every limb entwined, utterly his. She could see the stars through the window as she came. As the sensations climaxed and her whole body shook she had her eyes wide open and she stared at the stars. There seemed to be thousands, millions very near, bright gold pinpricks blazing in the ice-cold desert night.

She thought, if I died now I would have reached Nirvana. So this is the fulfillment of love. This is what the poets rhapsodise about. This is why people die, this is why lovers are speechless or utter the old, old phrases again and again.

This is what my mother waits for from my father waiting so hopelessly, in vain. This is why my father lives a lie and this is why Fern Morrison has been prepared to live a life of concealment, gambling with the well-being of her children.

And Perdita understood. Yes, she thought, this is worth searching the world for, dying for. This is love.

Chapter Fifteen

'I want to know about all the women in your life ›efore me."

"No you don't!" He thought fleetingly of Posy then ismissed that tiny cloud. It seemed a dream to him ow, another world.

"Did you love any of them like you love me?"

"No. I didn't. And stop this inquisition, Perdita. It ; pure insecurity and I don't want you to be insecure ver again."

She sighed happily. "I won't be," she whispered, "not fter this time with you."

They stayed in their room for two days, sending down or food. The minion who delivered their various meals niled knowingly at them, but benignly, like an indulgent arent.

Life became unreal for Perdita. She felt herself isolated ith Larry in a strange and beautiful place of the senses, wondrous place of foreign scents and exotic foods and ›unds, a place where her inner self was revealed to her, ıowing her to be a woman passionate and generously ving, able to give and receive. The discovery was tonishing and her ardent soul glowed as she blossomed ith the fabulous acceptance of her newly found beauty.

I am desired and desirable, her heart sang. I am cherishe
and lovely. It was amazing, and after years of believin
herself unworthy to be loved the gift he gave her of h
own unique beauty was a pearl beyond price.

When they eventually left the hotel they strolled alon
the banks of the Nile, pestered by vendors trying to pus
at them beads, bangles, chains, miniature sphinx, ston
pyramids, King Tut masks in glorious blue and gol
but Larry and Perdita were oblivious to their pesterin
Hand in hand, as lovers always are, they had eyes onl
for each other.

He introduced her to Yasser and they got on immed
ately. The Egyptian liked her total lack of artifice, h
naturalness and her real interest in their work. She wa
outraged as he explained their work to her and becan
instantly converted to the cause. Larry's passion woul
be her passion too. But she had a natural affinit
with wounded, helpless beings and her warm hea
was instantly anxious to help.

"Something will have to be done, Larry," Yasser sai
as they dined in the hotel one night, "we are running o
of money. We've got a huge overdraft and I'm afraid we'
have to close the refuge here in Aswan if we don't get a
immediate infusion of cash."

"Hold on, Yasser. We'll get it somehow."

"Little dribs and drabs are no use, Larry. We nee
real money."

"Tell me about it," Perdita asked, "explain."

Yasser waxed eloquent over dinner and Perdita pledge
her help and support. It seemed to her a wonderf
opportunity to share Larry's life and interests, an
something she herself was terribly interested in.

"Do you think we could get your father interested?" Larry asked casually and she did not even flinch. She realised suddenly that she no longer feared her father. Her awe of him, her sense of inferiority was gone, just like that.

"Why not?" she asked lightly. "But it would have to come from you, Larry. He won't listen to me."

"Can you set it up?" he inquired.

"Sure. I'll try. Nothing to lose."

They watched the molten sun go down over the hills, the fellucas outlined darkly against the sky. They went into the desert and he took her to visit the wonderful temples, at Philae and up the river to Abu Simbel. The magnificence took her breath away. It was awe inspiring and she could only marvel at her ignorance. The world was so full of wonders, stupendous man-made creations that defied time, yet revealed man's mortality as nothing else could. Humans aspiring to be God, trying to out-do the Creator.

But in the end God always won. No temple was grander than the desert itself, no ancient monument could outshine the Nile. No wonder could compare with a rose, a palm tree, no artist could match a sunset.

She said as much to Larry, who agreed with her.

"It's what your father was saying," he said.

"Oh, him again!"

"It *was* what he said."

"I know. Sorry, Larry. It's just that he is different with me. I don't expect you to understand."

He thought of Posy and shuddered. "But I do," he contradicted her, "I really do. However, in the context of the hospital he might be very useful to us. Let us play him at his own game, Perdita. He might find it very convenient for his image to be seen to help us. Animal welfare is a popular cause in England. Look at David Attenborough. Rolf Harris. Put it this way, Perdita, it won't hurt his image one little bit."

"And that is very important to my father."

"I know."

They stayed on. Larry explained that they had a locum when either of them were away from the practice.

"I get more and more absorbed here, Perdita," he said, and she got the feeling that this was where his spiritual home was.

Perdita phoned her mother. "Where are you, Perdita, in God's name? Why haven't you been at work? I'm sorry, but at this rate I'll have to fire you. Posy has been pleading with me not to do anything drastic . . ."

Not are you all right? Are you ill?

"I'm in Aswan, Mother." Her voice was cool.

"Wha . . .?" Astonishment. Melinda deprived of words.

"Egypt, Mother."

Silence. She could almost see her mother's bewilderment and she giggled, then said, "It's okay for you to fire me. I'm not coming back to The Design Factory."

"What?" She could hear the utter disbelief in her mother's voice. "Are you . . .? What is happening?" Incredulity.

"I'm here with Larry, Mother. I don't want to work for you any more." She kept her voice light. "I've got other things to do now." She replaced the receiver.

She had decided to work for Larry in whatever

capacity he needed her and he was enthusiastic. They talked it over.

"At the moment, from what I can see, it's hit or miss," she said, heart beating fast, "it's amateur. Now I know amateur means you do it for love, but you need organising. I could do that, I know I could."

"You're absolutely right," he agreed. "We've registered, done stuff like that but both David and myself, *and* Yasser are more interested in the veterinary work than in the fund raising at which we're all hopeless." He told her she would be very good at PR, and his belief in her did wonders for her morale.

"You would be terrific at it, Perdita. You have a natural shy, persuasive manner that disarms and I think you would be an asset. It is what we have lacked and I have been looking for." He frowned and she stared at his face, taking in every line and curve in a loving gaze. *I adore you*, she thought, *I worship the ground you walk on.* His hairline was beaded with sweat and she wanted desperately to lick every drop away, but she sat opposite him in the large Victorian lounge sipping her tea decorously and no one would have guessed her lascivious thoughts. She was utterly content, like those bees drunk on nectar she used to see lurching about the rosebushes in Oak Wood Court, she felt dizzy with love. Her body was so relaxed it felt liquid, and she marvelled at how she'd grown.

She telephoned her father at the studio at a time when she knew he'd be available. She had never before in her life phoned him. She was quite calm as she talked to him, outlining the programme, the Cooke Hospital work, its aims, its usefulness and, above all, its appeal.

"You'll tug at the hearts of the British," she said, "you know how they love animals and how they respond to people actively involved in helping them."

"Why do you need me?" he asked calmly. Listening to her, he was all business.

"We need funds. You are high profile. Your name would be invaluable to us. Could you give us a mention in the *Hastings Hour*? It's a bit hopeless when we have to rely on garden parties arranged by Larry's mum and local events haphazardly put on to raise funds."

"Mmmm."

"At the moment only people in the know, and that's not too many, are organising events to raise money. Your name would uplift the whole undertaking to national status."

"Really, Perdita, I never knew you had such a high opinion of me."

She did not get hurt or angry, did not stammer or stutter, simply said calmly. "I don't. We're not talking about my opinion of you. I'm simply stating the fact that you are a public figure with immense pull. So was Hitler!" She heard him laugh loudly. "Will you help?" she asked.

"Yes," he said incisively, much to her surprise. "You let me know what you have. Send me the bumph. A video would be helpful. Get Larry to do interviews. I remember thinking he would be camera-friendly. He's got a good, strong face. Have him talk to us about it. You know, shirt unbuttoned, sleeves rolled up, hair tousled, that sort of thing. Heart-wrenching, animals in pitiful states. I'll give you a five, ten minute profile on the programme."

"When?"

"About June? Okay?"

"Sure."

"And be here to take the feedback. When I do something there's a hell of a lot of feedback and I'm bloody well not dealing with it. 'Bye."

They whooped. They danced around the hotel room like dervishes. He lifted her up, twirled her, whirled her about in his arms and they made love.

They spent the next month filming the Cooke Hospital: its work, the people, the animals there. What Perdita saw impressed her and the video was remarkable.

"It's very good, Larry. Not at all sentimental. It should shock and move people but it is not sensationalist or gratuitous. And you've done what my father wanted. You look great presenting it."

"You'd think that anyhow because you're mad about me." He turned, laughing, but pleased too, she could see.

"Is David okay about us being here so long?" she asked.

"Sure." He smiled. "He's a bit jealous. Thinks you've taken his place a bit."

"Oh gosh, Larry I . . ."

"It was bound to happen. But he'll get over it. I've suggested he do a video and you try to get Rolf Harris or David Attenborough to front it."

Perdita frowned. "I'm afraid not, Larry. This has nothing to do with the fact that I love you, but you are perfect fronting the video we've done and I want people to associate you with the project. We don't want them muddled. As my father said, you are camera-friendly.

You come over great. You'll have them opening their wallets. Putting David Attenborough or other big names in now would only confuse the issue."

"David's not going to be over the moon about all this, but I reasoned with him and I'm afraid he'll just have to accept what's best for the hospital." He stared into space, a worried frown on his face, then glanced back at her, smiling suddenly. "Well, it can't be helped. I'll sort him out when we get back."

She did not want to leave Egypt. Never in her life had she been as happy as she was in Aswan.

They dined with Yasser that last night in the Old Cataract Hotel, in the fading grandeur of the lofty, chandelier-lit dining room. They were a joyful party, celebrating the end of their most pressing problem, the beginning of new hope. They toasted each other and their commitment to the Cooke's Hospital with new optimism and when Larry and Perdita went to bed that night they were a little tipsy, and oh so happy.

"Will all this change in London?" she asked a little tremulously.

He took her face between his hands and smiled at her anxiety. "Of course not, my darling," he assured her, "I love you, I always will. And we have a lot to do, you and I."

But it did change. It changed drastically in a way neither of them could have forseen.

Chapter Sixteen

The programme went out and the response was overwhelming, exceeding their wildest dreams.

Perdita had returned to the flat. She had expected Larry to move in with her, or that she would move in with him, but he explained that she would be uncomfortable in his one-room pad over the surgery and suggested they look for a place together.

"But let's wait until after the programme goes out, my love, we've got too much on our plates before then. Besides, I have to involve David, spend a little time with him. Placate him. After all, we've left him out completely. He has no function in the project so he'll be miffed and I don't blame him."

"If it had been the other way around I cannot see you being upset. I think you'd only be interested in what was best for the hospitals."

"Well, he's younger than I am." Larry shrugged. "Maybe I'm overdoing it. I would have been glad he was getting the hospital help. Yes."

The project, once rolling, took all their time. There was so much to be done, more than either of them realised. Lucas was gleeful. "Now you know how hard I work," he crowed to a harassed Perdita, "people think my job is simply standing in front of the camera. Well, now you know it's not!"

Larry had to film an interview with Lucas and Perdita, who provided the data and the history of Cooke's Hospital for Animals, had not only to familiarise herself with everything about the project, but she spent a great deal of time faxing, phoning and writing this information for the studio.

"How many times do I have to tell them?" she asked Larry on one of the few occasions they were able to get together, albeit in a crowded studio with a full crew looking on.

"As many times as it takes," he told her, smiling at her, adding in a whisper, "I miss you so. How I miss you!"

"Do they lose my faxes or something?" she asked, murmuring back, "Me too. Oh, Larry, you're starving me, why?"

"I dunno whether they lose them or not, but it's worth it. Oh, it's worth it." He took her hands in his. "We'll be together soon, my dearest. At the moment this is my priority. I don't know whether you realise how grateful I am," he told her earnestly, "This is my life's work. My dream. My *raison d'etre*."

"But it isn't only gratitude, that you feel for me, is it?" she inquired anxiously.

"Oh, my darling, how can you think that?"

"I don't. Not really."

"You've got to learn to trust me."

"I do. I do."

And then there was silence and a great void.

Perdita was busy night and day with the overwhelming response to the programme. Letters, faxes, receipts to be sent, phonecalls, correspondence to people as far as Penzance and Edinburgh, from all over the British Isles stuff kept pouring in. Lucas was right, the feedback was astonishing. She had queries to reply to, informative leaflets to send out and sometimes she had to research questions and find accurate answers. The e-mail, the faxes, the phone calls, the questions, the donations, all had to be dealt with and Perdita was too new at the business, too anxious to get it right to delegate, and Larry was nowhere in sight.

At first it did not worry her. There was so much going on. Worn to a frazzle, yet exhilarated and excited, she phoned him once or twice after she got home but there was no reply, only his answerphone taking messages.

She could not seem to reach him on his bleeper either, nor his mobile and God knows she tried. Still not alarmed she sent faxes to the surgery informing him of the fabulous amounts donated, sure he was thrilled by the public's generosity, needing his congratulations. Each night she fell into a dreamless sleep, too tired to miss him too much, trusting him as he had asked her to.

It was the beginning of the second week after the programme and things were starting to slow down a little when she began to worry and it suddenly seemed distinctly odd that there had been no word from him, no response to her messages. No communication at all.

Then David came to see her and dropped the bombshell.

She had thought it was Larry when the knock came to her door. She rushed to open it, her heart skipping at the thought of seeing him, hearing his voice, feeling his arms around her. So she was surprised to see David there, but not alarmed. He was probably going to have a little moan to her and maybe ask her to give him a look-in to the Cooke Hospital thing. After all it was his project as much as Larry's. He was entitled.

He stood in her little living room looking awkward and ill at ease. She decided she was right and he was going to talk about the project and how he'd been overlooked when he said, "There's no easy way to say this Perdita . . ." he paused. She knew then that Larry was dead. He'd had an accident. He was hurt, needed her.

"It's Larry," she cried, everything in her shaking in anguish, "he's . . . he's . . ."

"Oh God, my dear, he's going to marry Posy."

She giggled, relief flooding her. "Don't be daft, David. They hardly know each other." Then she saw his face and felt her heart stop a second. She sat down abruptly. "That was sick!" she whispered through lips that were suddenly dry. "You sick bastard. How could you joke like that? Play such a trick on me? What a foul thing to say."

"It's true, Perdita. I wish it wasn't. I promise you I'd never do that to you. Unfortunately it is true."

"It's a lie! It's a lie!" she shouted.

"Why would I lie to you?"

"Because you're jealous of Larry. The publicity he's getting. You're jealous because I love him. You want to spoil . . ." Even as she spoke she knew what she was saying wasn't true.

"No, my dear. You know that's not true. You know this thing is not a competition. It's about helping the animals. I don't really care how or who gets it done as long as it *is* done. Anyhow, you know I wouldn't do something like that."

Then she said helplessly, "Why? How?" accepting it, wanting to understand.

"I don't know. He won't say. He can't. He doesn't want to see you. He says he couldn't bear it."

She shook her head, her world crumbling around her, falling down, crashing down, breaking up into little pieces. "No, no. It's not true! It can't be!"

All those nights in Egypt, in that bed, wrapped in his arms. All that love, that passion. She had heard that when drowning your past flashes through your mind and now all she could see were pictures of the past running through her head like a television screen. Her father's face: "You look awful in that colour Perdita, but then not many colours suit you." Her mother: "You must get something done with your hair, Perdita, it's so straggly." Her father: "Your skin is not your best asset, Perdita." Her mother again: "You're so clumsy, Perdita, do you have to drop *everything*?" Her father; "I don't know where we got you, Perdita, I really don't. You have nothing in common with either of us."

And then Larry: "You're perfect!" "I love you." "You are beautiful!" "Never say that again! I won't have you put yourself down."

She shivered. David had made a mistake, a terrible mistake. "Where is he? I want to see him." She stood up and started for the door.

"He does not want to see you." David stopped her. "Here."

"What's this?"

"He said to give you this."

It was a sheet of notepaper. No envelope. It was his handwriting and the distinctive signature. It said:

> 'I can never see you again as my love. I cannot explain, don't ask me to. I have no choice, my dear. Just forget about me. I don't deserve you. Please do not get in touch, it would not change things and would only cause you pain.
>
> Larry Burton.'

She read it three times, maybe four. The blood rushed to her head, then ebbed away and she fainted, slipping unconscious to the ground before David could catch her.

Chapter Seventeen

David stayed with her for the next week. He was always there. He gave her a sedative at night and slept on the sofa in the living room.

Afterwards he told her he was afraid she would try to kill herself and she replied she had wanted to, wanted to badly, desperately wanted to leave this planet, turn out the light on her life, feel nothing more. Time was a blur, a nightmare. Engulfed by an unbearable loneliness and pain, a feeling of complete betrayal, the days passed infinitely slowly. Deep, deep, heavy-footed moment by lingering moment, time ticked slowly by, an eternity of long drawn out, agonising seconds passing leadenly.

Her mother phoned. Listlessly she took the mobile rom David. "I hear your chap has got engaged to Posy," her mother's voice held a note of vindication as if, Perdita thought she had warned her daughter of ome perfidity, some calamity.

"Yes," Perdita said.

"Oh, Perdita, when will you learn . . ." Perdita witched the phone off abruptly. She did the same hing on Posy.

She could not believe that Posy would ring her, but her friend did, bubbling over, excited.

"I'm so happy, Perdita. I'm only sorry about you if you are upset . . ." *Upset*! Her heart was breaking *Upset*! "I know you two were seeing each other . . ." *Seeing each other*! Bodies entwined in the silver light o an Egyptian night, the golden warmth of an Egyptiar day. Kisses sweeter than wine. Nights and days o passion. *Seeing each other*! Perdita shook with angry tension. ". . . but Larry tells me it is over so I movec in. I can't say I'm proud, Perdy, of what I've done, bu I love him." You *want* him, you mean, Perdita thought "I don't want to lose your friendship, Perdy, I really don't . . ."

Perdita cut her off. *Click*. Like that. End of friendship If it had ever been one. She wondered about that now She hated Posy, hated what she had done, wanting he to be dead.

Had Posy ever been her friend? Perdita, in those dark nights and days deplored her own weakness, her naïvety She had, she realised given permission to others to abuse her, use her, prey on her. But she had been brought up like that. It had been the crucible of her existence. She had known no better.

"I've no backbone, David," she sobbed one nigh when tears eventually came, like a benediction, dis solving the knot in her chest. "I'm so weak. I *hate* saying no to anyone, particularly those close to me."

She wept, cried, wailed and wallowed for twenty-fou hours, sobbing away her hatred, her fury, her resentment leaving only an enormous regret.

"I know," David had answered her.

"No you don't!" she cried angrily. "You haven't a

clue what it's like to love and have that love rejected. I lived in hope, all my life, hoping I'd get the love I so much needed from my parents and I waited in vain. I *longed* for them to love me. Ached. They never did. Fern adores you, anyone can see that. And what's more she *approves* of you."

"Yes she does. And it is hard that yours didn't, Perdita. But you'll have to get over it. Move on. Not let them defeat you."

"*They* didn't defeat me, David. Larry did," she told him helplessly.

"Have some brandy, it will relax you."

"Don't like brandy," she replied stubbornly.

"Nevertheless, have some."

She looked up at him with tear-washed eyes. "You've been so good to me, David, over these weeks," she told him.

"Oh I've got an ulterior motive," he said jokingly, but seriously too, making her nervous.

"Like a brother," she said, then asked because she wanted to know, "Who is doing your work, David? You've been with me here most of the time these last weeks. Is Larry in the surgery?"

David turned his back and poured the drink. "Yes, he is. Well, he had that long break in Egypt, didn't he? So now he's at the practice with the locum and I'm here."

Perdita smiled sadly. "That long break! Was that what it was to him? A break in Egypt?" The pain returned like knives in her breast. "Oh, David, where did I go wrong?"

He shook his head helplessly. They had been over

and over this so many times. "I don't *know*," he sai
and gave her the brandy.

"Is she so much more desirable than I am?"

He knew whom she meant. "No. She's a bitch. It'
partly your own fault Perdita, for letting her int
your life."

"I couldn't say no." She smiled sadly, then gulpe
the brandy down. "I see now that she wanted what
had. Though why anyone would want that I canno
understand."

"She only saw the appearence of what you had, no
the actuality," he said.

"She took from me all those years, took from m
mother and my father and from me."

"She took your confidence, Perdita. She tried to stea
your soul."

"Well, she's succeeded. She's broken my heart, m
soul, my spirit. I have nothing left."

"No, Perdita, as you said, Larry did that."

She let out a long, jagged breath and nodded. "Ye
I suppose so," she said.

"You mustn't let them destroy you, Perdita. What yo
have to do now is to put it all behind you. It's difficult
know but you must."

She stared at him, eyes wide. "You think it's tha
easy?" she cried.

"No," he sighed, "no I don't, but you have to *tr*
For the first time in your life, Perdita, you have t
stop bowing down in defeat. It's habit, Perdita, *habi*
You must try, a day at a time to evict Larry and Pos
out of your head." He pulled her around to face hin
"Listen, Perdita, you think it's the end of the worl

now, well, it is not! Larry and Posy are filling your mind. They are living there at the moment. You have given them space. House-room. Now is the time to put them out. It will take time, hard work. I never said it would be easy, but it gives you something to do. A task."

"How do you know so much about it?" she asked.

He smiled. "Oh, I've had experience," he said. "Every time they come into your head . . ."

"Which is *all* the time,"

"Change the disc. Push them out. Otherwise they'll haunt you. Come between you and your work, your sleep, your every waking thought. You have to be ruthless with yourself and start at once."

She nodded. It made sense but only because Posy was in there with Larry, in her head. She'd never have wanted to evict Larry. Posy was, however, another matter and she knew those thoughts of Posy and Larry would drive her mad. Posy doing things with him that she had done. Posy in his arms. No, that was torture. Pure hell. She would do anything to pluck that out, give herself respite from that particular agony.

"What am I going to do, David?" she asked him piteously, "what's going to happen to me? I don't think I can bear it."

"You're going to survive, Perdita. Start by taking my advice. Get them out and free yourself. This won't last forever, believe it or not."

"A bit of me wants to," she looked at him appealingly, "A bit of me nurtures the pain. It means he's still *there*. Part of me. When it goes it really will be over. I'll be desolate then. Empty. Maybe forever."

"No. You'll be ready for a refill. Ready for a new love. And I'll be there. Waiting. Oh Perdita, you know how I feel . . ."

She shook her head vehemently. "No! No, David, you must never . . . you must not think . . ."

"I'm sorry. Oh God, Perdita, how awfully crass of me. So soon. Oh forgive me. But I will wait. I mean it. I'll wait for you."

"No, listen, David, you must listen. It's not possible. It's *never* going to be possible." She was adamant. He looked at her, frowning. "But why? Why not, for Pete's sake?"

"I can't tell you. I can't."

He left it at that for the moment deciding it was much too soon after her break with Larry, that he was rushing things, being insensitive.

He took her out regularly to dinner and entertained her with his stories of the practice. She winced every time he mentioned Larry but it was inevitable that he should figure largely in David's tales of animal adventures and amusing anecdotes. After all, he was the partner and David did not want to avoid any mention of him completely because he hoped she'd gradually accept the idea of Larry and Posy and the wound would heal leaving the path open and clear for him.

After all, he'd seen her first. She had been his choice. Then Larry with his brilliant smile, his charm, his shy manner, that manner that seduced all their female clients and made him, inevitably, their first choice, had stepped in and led her astray for a short, oh so short a time. Couple of months. What was that in the long years of a life? Nothing.

She had begun to rely on him, he could see that. Sometimes he coaxed a smile from her and sometimes as the weeks passed, a laugh.

He told her they wanted her to continue her PR work for Cooke's Hospital. At first, in her shock and despair, she rejected the idea out of hand, but David talked her round. "You have to learn to face the situation, Perdita. Larry is still on this planet. Pretending he doesn't exist will not do you any good. In order to recover you have to come to terms with it." He smiled at her over the rim of his glass, "And it is a job you are very good at."

She nodded. "I loved it," she agreed.

"You did fantastic work for us. The cheques are still coming in."

"That was my father," she said.

"There you go again!" He shook his head, exasperated. "Running your contribution down. Another habit you'll have to break." He leaned forward over the table. "Look, Perdita, this job really excites you. I can see that. It would be cutting off your nose to spite your face to quit now. You can keep out of Larry's way. He'll be anxious not to confront you anyhow. He'll not be too happy to have you in his face and so much of your work can be done alone." He grinned at her though her heart was crying at his words. "Or with me," he said.

She knew it was dangerous. Both men were dangerous to her, but she loved the job. It made her feel successful, something she had never felt before, and she felt at last she was doing something worthwhile. The Cooke Hospital really mattered to her. It inspired her.

But it was not only that. Her motives were not strictly

pure. She wanted to have *something* to do with Larry, his job if not his bed. She needed, in spite of what David said, some connection, a tie she did not want to sever.

There was a mountain of work awaiting her. She clocked in at the BBC to clear up the last of the correspondence and met her father quite by accident. He seemed surprised to see her.

"Posy's been looking for you," he said without preamble.

"Oh!" she kept her voice calm and the fact that she achieved even this gave her confidence. "What on earth for?"

"To be her bridesmaid. She wants you to be bridesmaid at her wedding." There was a malicious gleam in his eyes that angered Perdita and she managed to reply lightly, "Sure! Tell her I'd be glad. Delighted." She was rewarded by his surprise. "But I'm busy, Father, can't talk now. Got to go."

"I didn't think you'd want to go on working on the project," he persisted, "after Larry dumped you."

Again, that terrible pain, fierce and stabbing in her chest. "Why on earth not?" she asked airily, wide-eyed, puzzled. I'm doing okay, she thought. David was right. He'd told her to act until it became real. "I like this job much better than the one I had in The Design Factory with Mother ordering me about all the time. And I'm bloody good at it," she retorted. She could see the astonishment on his face again as she breezed away from him, crying, "Hi Benny," to the man on the desk and waving her hand. "Hi Babs," she called to the girl at reception.

She allowed the job to take her over and working hard occupied all her time and what little emotion she had left was spent on the distressed animals in the Cooke Hospital. A lot of her grieving was channelled into their plight. She also took a crash course in the RSPCA First Aid for animals and general knowledge about how to care for and treat them.

She threw herself into the project, organising parties, flag days, sorting out a calendar timetable, promoting publicity and fund-raising events. She was careful with the money they'd received, sending Yasser a hefty cheque to support the Aswan hospital and organising a video of him, taking the viewer around the hospital, showing how the money was being spent, the work to be done and what was needed.

Perdita rail-roaded her father into doing a follow-up on *Hastings' Hour*, thanking the viewers, showing the video of Yasser and giving a detailed report of where their money went and how it had helped. They showed the viewers the hospitals in Cairo and Luxor as well as the one that had been threatened in Aswan.

"It's the donkeys that do it every time," Lucas said. "Poor, overworked, starving creatures. They look cute and pathetic at the same time. Show them a poor starving snake or ant-eater and they wouldn't give you a penny!"

"I don't know whether this job's made you callous beyond belief, Father, or were you always like that?" Perdita asked coldly.

"Don't tell me you really give a shit about those creatures, Perdita," he said, one eye on her.

"As a matter of fact, Father, I do."

"Oh! And I thought it was a ploy to get back at your mother and me." He laughed. "And maybe retrieve Larry from Posy."

"No, Father. None of you are that important in my life any more," she retorted.

"Wow! The kitten has grown into a cat that can scratch," he said laughing. She met his eyes and saw a spark of admiration there. "And what about Larry? Maybe you don't want to sever the tie," he remarked shrewdly.

But she tossed her head, "Larry chose Posy. His bad luck!" she cried and Lucas threw back his head and guffawed.

She didn't see Larry. He kept well away. Now and again she got a fax relating to the project from him, but nothing personal.

Bit by bit the initial pain receeded. Little by little the shock of rejection, of love spurned waned. Life, her job, being so busy helped to heal her. But though the immediacy of the hurt was soothed, underneath it all Larry stayed firmly fixed deep in her heart, lodged there, beloved and cherished, hurting her constantly and the awful ache of her love for him never really disappeared.

She presented a cheerful face to the world. She took David's advice and practised replacing her anger and pain, her sadness and frustration with work. She was galvanised into action, sorting out the problems, solving the puzzles, and it worked. After her orgy of self-pity and grieving it all slipped away and the pain and anger diminished. Nothing lasts at an acute level for ever.

But Larry stayed. She did not seem able to dislodge him and much as she wanted to she could not hate him.

He was her love. He would always be.

but [illegible], she did not [illegible]
[illegible] want to [illegible]
[illegible]
[illegible] her [illegible]

Chapter Eighteen

Perdita began to be aware that in a way she was doing to David what Larry had done to her. She was dining with him, going to the theatre with him, for walks or [illegible] drinking [illegible] villages [illegible] the pubs on the river [illegible] about the [illegible] Hospital. She was sharing a lot of her time with him and, to her [illegible], she realised that he was becoming her closest [illegible]. Much too close.

She did not really think of him as a brother – well [illegible]

[illegible] Romance with a capital R?' She was being flippant. [illegible] she meant it nevertheless. Also, she wanted to get away from David for a while. He was getting to be a habit, becoming an essential part of her life. It would have been okay if they could have simply remained friends, but she knew David would not be content with that for long. She dreaded having to break

Chapter Eighteen

Perdita began to be aware that, in a way she was doing to David what Larry had done to her. She was dining with him, going to the theatre with him, for walks or just sitting in cafes drinking cappucino or idling in the cool dimness of the pubs on the river he loved, sipping lager and talking, mainly about the Cooke Hospital. She was sharing a lot of her time with him and to her horror she realised that he was becoming too close for comfort. Much too close.

She did not really think of him as a brother – well, half-brother – but when he looked at her there was passion in his eyes, and desire.

She had decided to go back to Egypt again. "I want to lay the ghost," she told David, "and it's important for the work that I know exactly what's going on there. But for my own sake too. I don't want to turn what happened there into an idyll. Romance with a capital R." She was being flippant, but she meant it nevertheless. Also, she wanted to get away from David for a while. He was getting to be a habit, becoming an essential part of her life. It would have been okay if they could have simply remained friends, but she knew David would not be content with that for long. She dreaded having to break with him and she was apprehensive about how she would cope without him. So she decided to go to Egypt.

Yasser wrote. He told her not to come to Karnak as he would be in Luxor. He said the heat was intense.

> It's too hot for you, try to come in October or November. In the meantime I will, on Larry's instructions send a precise rendering of exactly where every penny has gone, how much has been sent to Alexandria, to Cairo and to Karnak and Luxor. They will send you videos of progress made. I cannot express my gratitude for all that you are doing to aid the cause. I have to say, dear Perdita, that whatever went wrong between you and Larry should be righted. You were a radiant couple, so suited, in my humble opinion, to each other and when Larry wrote me it was over between you I was very sad. I hope you find a way to, how do you say in English? Bury your differences.

The letter made her cry. The paper seemed to smell of the desert, of sand and the Nile. Those precious memories rushed back and she could see the thick and sparkling inlay of stars and feel her body respond so ardently to the man she loved.

Things came to a head in August. The summer in London may not have scorched like the Egyptian one, but it too was unbearably hot. Perdita felt prickly and irritable and at odds with herself. She felt as if she was waiting, for what she did not know, but *something* to happen. Posy had sent Perdita a wedding invitation with a note that read,

'Your father says you'll be my bridesmaid, Perdy, and I'm so happy. We do after all go back a long way. It would not be the same without my dearest and best friend. I'll send you the dress – don't worry, I know your measurements.'

David said, "Don't go, Perdita. You don't have to do this."

He sat in the armchair he always sat in when he came to her flat. He would arrive and plonk himself down in it automatically, reminding her of his assumption of intimacy, and her permission. But how could she discourage him yet still keep his friendship while he remained in ignorance of their true relationship?

She shook her head. "Oh, but I must go," she told him, "It's like an end, David. The End. *Finito*. I *have* to see them tie the knot with my own eyes."

"Don't be bitter, Perdita. It will corrode your soul."

"I'm not," she contradicted him, "I'm being realistic. When I see them exchange their vows I'll be sure the whole thing is over for me forever."

She was curled up on the sofa, the Cooke Hospital correspondence littered the floor and the table all around her and there was a half drunk glass of white wine beside her.

"You told me to face up to it and I have. I feel a lot better about it now, David, but I won't believe in the *reality* of it until I see with my own eyes the two of them saying 'I do'."

"Then there'll be hope for me?" His voice shook a little and she bit her lip. "No, David," she cried, exasperated, "I *told* you and told you. No. There can never be anything between us."

"Why, Perdy, why?" he persisted. "I know I'm not Larry. I don't expect that 'first fine careless rapture' to repeat itself for you, but a more solid relationship built on loving kindness, surely that should be possible? Give it a try at least. Come on, Perdita," he coaxed, "consideration. Faithfulness. We have the same interests. We're never short of conversation. Our tastes are similar, haven't you noticed? All this time and we've never quarrelled. We are always in tune."

"Like brother and sister," she said softly.

"Oh no! What I feel for you is not brotherly. I adore you, Perdita and I think we'd make the perfect couple."

"No, David. It's impossible. Put it out of your mind forever."

He rose swiftly and in an instant was beside her kissing her, his lips tender on her cheek, then on her mouth, his ardour deepening into passion.

She pushed him away violently, shrinking back, her eyes horror-filled.

"No, David, *no*!" she gasped.

Surprised at how appalled she was he cried, "Hey! I'm not Frankenstein's monster, for God's sake. I'm just a chap who loves you. What's *wrong*, Perdita?"

"*We are*!" It was out before she could stop herself. "We *are* brother and sister, David. Well, half-brother and sister." She jumped up off the sofa as he recoiled in shocked surprise at her words. "Oh, David, I never meant to tell you. I promised your mother . . ."

"My *mother*?"

"Yes. She doesn't want your father to know. He thinks he's your father, but he isn't. Lucas Hastings, my father is. You and Miranda. Now you see why . . ." She wrung her hands together in distress. "Oh, I didn't mean to say anything about it, but—"

"Jesus, Perdita, have you gone *mad?* What the hell are you talking about?" He sounded so angry, and she was suddenly frightened. She had expected him to be upset, yes, but he was raging. His eyes were blazing, murderous. She twisted her hands together in anguish and cried out to him, "It's true, David. Oh, I'm sorry, so sorry. Don't let your mother know I told you."

She knew it was a stupid demand and she was babbling. How could he obey her? He was much too close to his mother for there to be deception. He was bound to confront her with this shocking revelation.

"Oh, I didn't want to tell you," she cried contritely, "break my word. But I *had* to, don't you see? You were going to make love to me." Distressed she went on twisting her fingers together, wringing her hands, unable to think how to make things better.

"Jesus, I'm not surprised Larry broke off with you. I couldn't think why he behaved the way he did, but now I know. What a fertile imagination you've got. Of all the sick, *sick* jokes . . ."

"It's *not* a joke."

"It's sick!" he hissed at her, "sick. *You* must be sick. My God, how could you invent such an evil story? How could you even *think* such a thing. It really takes a weird person to dream up such a lot of garbage."

He was so furious. She had never seen him as angry. He stood over her, towering, his body shaking. There was a white line around his mouth and his skin had lost its colour. His red hair flamed and his eyes were wild.

"It's the truth," she insisted.

"No way!" he shouted and grunting in disgust he left the apartment abruptly, slamming the door behind him.

Where would he go? she wondered. Then she decided he would, of course, go to his mother. In a panic she phoned Fern but there was no reply.

Perdita sat, arms around her legs, wringing her hands endlessly, shaking her head, whispering to herself, "What have I done, oh what have I done?" and finding no answer at all.

Chapter Nineteen

David hurried home, his head in a whirl. He was certain Perdita, for whatever reason, was lying. Was she mentally disturbed? Had Larry discovered it and broken with her? Was she insane? She was obviously lying, but why? Maybe she'd invented this horrible story to get back at Larry, as some sort of elaborate excuse so that he wouldn't make love to her? Why on earth would she think of such a thing? Why on earth would she mind that much, him making love to her? She would know he would not force her to do anything she didn't want to do, so why this terrible lie? It was such a far-fetched *foul* story and had to be, simply had to be, the product of a weird mind.

Had they mis-read her completely? David thought of all those stories about her mother and father being monsters. But Larry had said they were charming and her father had gone out of his way to help her with the Cooke Hospital project. Perhaps Perdita was warped, mentally twisted. Was that why Larry had run from her like a scalded cat?

And yet. And yet.

It fitted. In some strange way it was almost as if he'd been aware that for years there had been some secret, something not quite true about the happy families they played. He'd never wanted to dig, never wanted to enquire about certain things at home.

Like why he had never felt an ounce of identification with his father. He had assumed that it was because of his illness, an illness now so far advanced as to make his father uncommunicable. He knew his mother had someone else but he had been very careful not to find out who it was. It had not however occurred to him that he might not be Paul Morrison's son, that this other man in his mother's life might have fathered him. He had never considered that at all and, even if he had, he would not have wanted to know.

But Lucas Hastings! Dear God, Lucas Hastings.

He drove recklessly, double-parked outside the house. He opened the front door quietly. There was no one in the living-room. His father, bedridden now, would be in his own room.

David leapt up the stairs two at a time and, knocking gently at the door of his mother's bedroom, opened it.

There was his mother, in bed, naked in the filtered light through the slatted Venetian blinds. It striped her like a golden zebra. And in her arms lay the equally naked Lucas Hastings.

For a moment all was absolutely still, frozen. Nothing moved. Then David gasped as if his chest would burst and Fern raised her arms over her face as if to hide it. "Oh no!" she whispered softly, "oh, please God, no." Lucas rolled over on his side and stared at David as if his interruption was just an inconvenience.

"Shit," Lucas muttered. "Oh damn!"

The anger David felt throbbed in his temples but no

words came. Huge, overpowering waves of fury shook his body like a palsy and he knew that if there had been a gun nearby he would have used it. It was as if the David he knew, the pacifist David, the body he lived inside, had inhabited all these years, had vanished and he had been taken over by some powerfully dark and evil presence. He knew now how people could kill.

Shaking, he closed the door. He knew that the scene would never be erased from his mind. He knew that his life had been changed forever. He knew that something, a purity, an innocence, a spontaneous gaiety and trust had been killed that day and was lost forever. From now on everything would be coloured by the events of that day. Every memory was tainted by what had happened. Everything he did or said, everything he remembered, every assumption he made, every word his mother had ever spoken to him had been based on a lie, on misinformation, on adultery and lust. How could he ever trust anyone ever again?

How long he stood outside the door, shaking, watching fond memories die one by one like the leaves in autumn, he did not know. He went to his father's room. The door was ajar and his father lay in bed propped up with pillows. There was spittle on his chin and the nurse who came to look after him wiped it carefully away. Did she know what was going on down the corridor? She was a lovely, compassionate Irish girl, thick bodied, patient and slow-moving. Did she know all about his mother's love in the afternoon? No, he contradicted himself, no, *sex* in the afternoon. It wasn't love. He wouldn't dignify it with the name of love. It was not what he felt for . . . Oh, Jesus! Perdita! No, no!

"He's quiet, sir." The girl looked around and smiled at him and suddenly David wanted desperately to make love to her, to forget himself completely in an erotic encounter with her motherly breasts and swelling hips that would dull his senses, kill the pain if only for a moment, give him surcease. The girl had pale skin and freckles all across her nose and her hair was coarse and black. He wanted to touch it, kiss her wide generous mouth, to affirm something. Make a statement. Reassert himself. He wanted to lose himself in the sex act with this soft Irish girl with the sympathetic eyes as if by so doing he would wash away his father's sickness, his mother's guilt and Perdita's involvement in it all. Horrified by these thoughts he left the room.

His father was incapable of helping him. It did not occur to him that the same truth applied to his mother.

Chapter Twenty

What had happened forced Perdita to push the past away. She had no choice, it was sink or swim time. She took stock.

David and Larry no longer loved her. That was certain. Posy had never really been her friend, she saw that clearly now. Her mother actually disliked her. She would not use the word hate, it was too strong, too close to love to be applied to what Melinda felt for her daughter.

That left only Lucas and she believed that her father had always resented her, blamed her for his forced separation from Fern, David and Miranda where his true love lay. If it hadn't been for her he would not be with Melinda now, he would be with them.

So, she told herself realistically, she had no one. There was no one. And it had to be her fault. She was somehow incapable of having a relationship, of being loved. She faced the fact, doing what David had told her to do. Being firm with herself and unsentimental.

She had a job. An inspiring job. A job she loved and the animals did not reject her. She had a niche, a path to follow and that was what she decided to do. Pull yourself together girl, she told herself, get on with it.

She threw herself into her work with energy, vigour

and all the pent-up love she had a surplus of and no one seemed to want. Despite the heat, she went to Egypt. Despite Yassar's warnings. She went to Cairo and Alexandria, to Luxor and Edfu and, crossing the Sinai desert, to Jordan, Amman and Petra. There were branches of the Cooke Hospital for Animals everywhere.

It was a gruelling journey in the heat, on overcrowded planes and on horseback, in uncomfortable and rickety jeeps and all without Yassar's help. She sweated in the shade, drank gallons of bottled water, doggedly ploughed on and on in a kind of daze, determined to get firsthand knowledge, to understand, to give herself body and soul to this mission.

The desert was unrelentingly demanding. It sucked her dry then filled her with a sort of spiritual fulfilment that changed her. It forced her to look at herself calmly, almost clinically. Under a carpet of stars so brilliant that they lit up the landscape so that the desert looked like a shimmering day, she sat, cross-legged and did not dislike what she saw inside herself. Her faults were ones of humanity, abundance of love, ardour and passion. She was not disgusted by herself, saw no meaness there and did not, as she had done previously, turn away in disgust. Eventually, she began to like herself and admire the spirit within herself, her soul, her centre.

She was excited too, in spite of the heat, the insect bites and her gippy tummy, excited by the hospitals, the work done there.

She was greeted with delight by the veterinary surgeons who met her and who introduced her to their assistants, farriers and supporting staffs. These people made a great fuss of her, delighted by her interest and eager to educate her. They also pleaded for more money which she was able to promise them.

She got quite expert at diagnosis and travelled in the mobile clinic with them, wise enough not to interfere, ready to stand back and watch and learn from the experts.

She loved the animals – mainly horses, donkeys and mules – that they treated. But there were dogs too, and cats. Sometimes she nursed a gazelle in her arms. Hurt and frightened, in need of her compassion, separated from their mother she embraced all the poor, wounded frightened creatures they cared for.

All of the people with Cooke's had a single aim. To help and heal and try to make the plight of these maimed creatures easier, better and educate their owners.

There were examples of unbelievable cruelty that shocked her but she learned to keep the tears back and get on with the job. Do what she could and leave the rest.

She met kindness and gratitude everywhere she went. She helped out with a mare foaling and assisted at the humane putting to sleep of a donkey beaten half to death and covered in sores.

They called her Golden Isis, after the goddess of love and divine power. She grew bone-lean and tanned, her skin hardening under the relentless sun. She toughened up inside too and as the time passed and Posy's autumn wedding day neared, it became clearer and clearer to her what her aims were, where her priorities lay. No longer tentative, no longer doubtful, no longer needing the approval of others, she decided she would return to England for Posy's and Larry's nuptials, then she would come back here to Egypt. Return to work, to labour in this, her chosen field because it inspired her. She was impervious to heat and dust, the flies and discomfort, and she realised slowly and with relief that whatever cards life had dealt her up to now, however unloving, harsh, cruel even, her parents had been, however badly Larry had treated her, however thoughtlessly cruel, inconsiderate, clumsy and feeble she had been with David and, lastly, however badly she had suffered at Posy's hands, all of it, all the components had brought her to this point, had been her preparation for this pathway that she wanted so badly to tread. Her life, if lived another way, might not have readied her for this most precious experience. The cruelty she had suffered had given her the compassion needed for the job, the eyes to see and the ears to hear the requirements. She had needed it all, the people close to her, their behaviour, their indifference, their carelessness of her feelings, and eventually Larry's introduction to Yasser and the Cooke Hospital for Animals. The events of her life were all needed to get her here where she wanted to be, here where she could find fulfilment and peace within herself and, most of all, a sweet content in her purpose.

She wiped her forehead with her arm, then holding the end of her white cotton shirt flapped it in and out to try to circulate some air around her burning body. She took off her hat and shook out her damp hair. And she smiled.

The Egyptians were all around an exhausted mare who had just given birth. The foal was staggering about on shaking legs. They had been at it all night.

She had stroked the mare's forehead, soothing it with soft words. The beast had been worked near death and now the owner nagged them asking over and over when she would be ready to work again. "If she don't work, I starve. My family starve." The Egyptian vet, ably assisted by a slim Pakistani man on leave from his own country, interested in setting up a similar operation there, said in Arabic, "Look, we will give you a small subsistence allowance. Some dinari." The man's face lit up and he grabbed the vet's hand and kissed it. "Thank you. Thank you," he cried.

"But you must do as we tell you," the vet insisted, "otherwise no dinari."

"Oh yes. Oh yes."

"She must rest in the shade." He indicated the mare and the man looked blank, bewildered. If he did not take a rest why should the horse? What nonsense was this? "We insist. Otherwise no dinari."

The man sighed, looked wildly about as if for help, then giving up to these crazy people he nodded. "Right. Right."

"Do you not see?" the Egyptian vet called Suliman asked. "She will be more use to you, be able to do more work, give you more foals if she is well and strong? Do you not see?" The man nodded but did not look at all sure.

They were packing up to go, cleaning up, putting equipment into the mobile van.

"Did you understand?" the vet asked Perdita and the Pakistani. They nodded. Both had picked up a smattering of the language. "I never know whether they intend to do as I ask or not," the Egyptian told Perdita, shaking his head. "Sometimes they put the unfortunate animal to work directly our back is turned. Sometimes they obey us simply for the money. Then sometimes, Allah be praised, they get the message. They actually see the sense in what I am telling them."

The foal was greedily sucking from a plastic bottle with a teat the Pakistani was holding out.

"The mother has hardly any milk," the Egyptian said. "You'll have to give the foal this." He gave a box of supplies to the owner.

"Is more than I have for me," the man said.

"The foal will not live otherwise," the Egyptian warned the smiling man. "And it's got stuff in it not right for humans to have," he added. The man went on smiling. "He's happy," the Egyptian remarked laconically to Perdita. "He thinks he has had great good fortune. It's quite possible he'll use the food for the animals for himself and his family. The money will go, and then . . ." he shrugged, "who knows?"

"Can't we come back? Monitor him?" Perdita asked.

"We will when we can afford to. That we will leave to you. You have to arrange the money for us to buy the vans and the equipment," he smiled at her and threw his bag into the back of the van. "Raising funds so that we can do the job properly." He too wiped his forehead with his arm, "Come on. Let's pack it up here. We've done all we can."

She would delegate. In the summer, in the hot season she would nag the rich, get princes and princesses interested, do the social thing. She would use her father mercilessly. She would get tennis stars, hot from Wimbledon, to open fêtes, opera stars from

Glyndebourne and Covent Garden to sing their hearts out at soirées in the gardens of aristocratic houses, and pop singers to rock and roll in the grounds of stately homes. She would get fashion designers to contribute to charity shows on catwalks in grand hotels and top models to give their time free. After all, as her father had said, show them a picture of a wounded animal and they'll give you the moon.

Then in the autumn she would return here, to Egypt and help out, work hard. Winter and spring she would spend here, where her heart was.

Perhaps that was the purpose of Larry Burton in her life. The reason she had met him. To bring her here, to show her a way of life that she responded to, that she loved. Give her a purpose. If so it had been worth it, all the pain, all the hurt, all the agony.

The others were in the truck. The horse owner was nodding and still smiling at them. She jumped in after them. "All aboard," she cried banging the side of the vehicle with her fist. "C'mon. Let's go, go, go!"

Chapter Twenty-One

She got back just in time, two days before the wedding in fact. She suffered through the ceremony, decked out in pink frills. She felt acutely uncomfortable.

She saw it done. Pledges were made and all she could hope to do was get over it and get on with her life.

The final irony that day was when Posy threw her bouquet and Perdita was the one who caught it. It was reflex action, her catching it, she didn't mean to, but there it was in her hands and she could only stand looking silly in the unsuitable fluffy dress.

And David was not there. Nor Fern. She had supper with Leonard that evening, after the feast where she didn't eat anything at all and got tipsy. Leonard said some solid food in her stomach would fix her, so after the speeches, after the toasts, after the bride had thrown the bouquet over her shoulder and the happy couple had departed on their honeymoon, Leonard took her to supper.

"Where are they going, Leonard?" she asked. She held her breath. She could not have borne it if he said Egypt.

"Paris, I think," he replied. He had brought her to a big noisy restaurant, the latest craze, designed like the Pompidou centre, all steel girders and funnels, scaffolding and tables. Waiters rushed about, good-looking young men, most of them drama students waiting for their big chance, a spot on *The Bill* or a bit in *London Bridge*. They ordered bruschetta and a green salad. Perdita said she could not manage more but Leonard urged her to eat.

"It will soak up the booze," he said.

"I'm not drunk!" she protested. "Well, only a bit sloshed."

She was absent-minded, chewing on the ciabatta bread.

"You still love him, don't you?" Leonard asked, glancing at her quizzically.

"You asked me that before," she told him. "Yes I do! I can't help it."

"I guess love cannot be turned on and off like a tap," he remarked, then, without a pause, "Do you think you could get your dad to use a video I made in Slovenia?" he asked slyly.

She sighed. She thought, *here we go again*. "Oh, Leonard I can try. I need him now, though, for the Cooke Hospital project. But I tell you what, why don't you come to Aswan, or Karnak with me next trip and make a video there? Father will definitely use that, then you can ask him about the other."

Leonard nodded eagerly. "Great idea. When do you go?"

"I've got to see Father first. As soon as possible, Leonard. Can you leave at the drop of a hat?"

"I'm ready when you are. I've had my shots so I'm okay there. I'm trying to break into film reporting. My photography has gone as far as it will go."

"You've got a show coming up," she said.

"No, Perdita. You missed it. It was on when you were away."

"Oops! Sorry!"

"It's okay. So I'm ready when you are."

"All I need is to see Father and get him to remain involved."

Chapter Twenty-Two

Perdita found it was quite easy to draw her father into her schemes. She was not stupid enough to imagine that he did it for her sake, or out of compassion for the animals. He did it because after the transmissions about the workings of the hospitals his ratings had soared.

She had made a video of her own emphasising the English origins of the hospital and how it was the British love of animals that saved the situation. Lucas said it was a good psychological move.

"Inspired, my dear. Let the British public feel they are superior to others and they'll shell out quick enough. Forget the hunt meets, the dog fights, the fact that grown men go out in their health and strength and shoot pretty little birds. Forget the fact that the RSPCA is overworked and understaffed and working all the hours God sends. Oh yes!"

"Oh, Father! Don't be such a cynic," she admonished.

They were lunching in the Groucho. Lucas was attracting a lot of attention. A few brave people came to his table and he introduced her, quite proudly she thought, as his daughter. The one who was raising the profile of the Cooke Hospitals for Animals.

To her surprise he had phoned her and asked her to lunch soon after her return, a few days after the wedding. She had been going to phone him but his call came first. "Didn't have time to talk to you at Posy's bash," he said on the phone. She was about to say, no you were too busy! She wondered whether he had screwed Vicky that day or if all those bimbos were red herrings to distract from Fern and his liaison with her. "I got your letters and your video," he said, not waiting for her comment, "but I need a better quality of film. Your video is all very well but it reeks amateur. There are some questions I need to ask you for follow-up, so will you have lunch with me?"

She readily agreed. He was waiting at the table. He rose when she entered and stared at her as if seeing her for the first time. She thought he was going to whistle, his admiration was that obvious.

"God, you look great." She nodded coolly and sat down, unfazed. She was delighted by his reaction but was not about to let him see that she was.

"The tan suits you," he said, "but not when you are decked out in pink frills."

"The climate played havoc with my skin," she said. But she knew she looked great. She still wore the same uniform: designer jeans, a sea-island Ralph Lauren cotton shirt the collar turned up near her tanned face and a Hermes scarf knotted at her throat. The sun had bleached her hair platinum and she had a navy cashmere cardigan, its arms tied over her shoulders.

"I want you on the show with me," he stated baldly, forking green salad into his mouth. She giggled. "What's so funny?" he asked her suspiciously.

"You look like the cows on the hills," she laughed, conscious she was annoying him, "your mouth full of green, chewing!"

He licked it all in glaring at her, but he said nothing.

"Why do you want me on the programme with you?" she asked. "Aren't you afraid I'll steal the limelight?"

He laughed, genuinely amused. The idea was absurd. No one could steal Lucas Hastings's limelight. "Because it would be great. Don't you see? Lucas Hastings's daughter following in the footsteps of her old man, up to her ears in social causes, just like him. Noble family, intent on doing good."

"*A* cause, Father. One!"

"Sure. Animal rights. Flavour of the month. Women's Rights, Ethnic Minorities and Animal Rights. They are the buzz topics of the moment."

"So you'll use me as a career asset?" she queried.

He nodded. "Sure," he replied, unconcerned, "suits both of us."

She had to agree.

They talked about a format, surprised that they seemed so much in agreement. When they had finished their rack of lamb, new potatoes and peas, Lucas, not bothering to ask her if she'd like pudding, ordered coffee, sat back and said suddenly, his face serious, not meeting her eyes, "I think you ought to go and see your mother."

Surprised, she asked, "Why?"

"David's been busy while you've been away," he replied dryly, "that's why."

"Da-vid?" she stammered.

"Yes, David! You know. The chap you told I was his father." He glared at her now, mood quite different, brows drawn together fiercely. "Chatty, aren't you? Couldn't keep your trap shut. That's why he wasn't at the wedding. He knew I'd be there."

"I'm sorry, Father. I didn't mean to tell him, truly I didn't. But he was making a move on me. I *had* to." She kept her voice calm and reasonable.

His eyes widened. "Oh! Jesus!" Obviously the thought had not struck him before, that such an eventuality was possible. Lucas Hastings was fazed. "Oh, Christ!"

"Yes, Father. Oh Christ! What was I to do?"

"Lie," he said briskly.

"Lies don't come so easily to me," she retorted. He made a face.

"Miss Goodie-two-shoes."

"No, I'm not. Liars, in my experience reap what they sow and the truth almost always comes out in the end."

"How true," he replied sarcastically. "I suppose you are thinking of me and Fern."

"Among others!"

"Ah, yes. Posy and Larry. What a to-do, eh?"

"Is David very upset?" she asked, not wanting to talk about Larry.

"David?" he cried as if David's feelings were of little importance in the scheme of things. "The thing is, yes, David *is* upset. But more important he's rampaging all over town mouthing off, telling all who'll listen about me and Fern Morrison."

"Can you blame him?"

"Well, yes I can. More diplomacy is needed. After all

it is his mother we're talking about here. She's taking it quite well. You see, Paul is dying. He's out of it. Doesn't know day from night and that was her main concern, not to hurt him."

"Really? Then she should have stopped screwing you all those years."

"Don't be coarse, Perdita. Much you know of love!"

"Oh but I do, Father, I do."

He looked at her keenly narrowing his eyes. Then he continued. "When Paul . . . goes . . ." he hesitated.

"*Dies*, Father. When he dies. Why can't you say it? *When he dies*."

"I'll move in with her. David shot his bolt, coming the high and mighty, blabbing judgementally all over the place. He's given us the courage to go ahead. It's not what he intended at all but there's nothing to lose now." He stared at her, then continued. "I'm not apologising to you or anyone, Perdita." He paused, stirring his coffee. "The thing is, with David spewing forth the gutter press are bound to get wind of it and start digging, so I decided to go to them before they 'did' me." He took a deep breath. "I gave the *Echo* the full exclusive. Shock-horror details. You're not going to like it Perdita but it can't be helped. I slanted it obviously in my favour and I'm afraid your mother and grandfather don't come out of it too well. After all, I've loved Fern for a very long time. I wanted to tell you before they publish."

"Well, how thoughtful of you!"

"I didn't want you to read it. Not that you'd read that rag, but, well someone would have been sure to show it to you."

"Why do you suddenly want me to see Mother?"

she asked, suddenly realising where this was all leading.

"Ah, yes! Well, Perdita, your mother is very upset. As I said she doesn't come out of it too well," he looked shifty.

"You mean you told them she got pregnant with me and you *had* to marry her. Oh, Father!" Her voice dripped contempt.

"So she's very upset," he pressed on, "very, very upset. I hoped you could talk to her. Console her. I've never hated Melinda, I just don't love her."

"You could have fooled me! And my mother, in case you hadn't noticed, Father, doesn't *like* me so I can't think she'd be glad to see me. But I'll give it a go." She stared at him a moment. "I suppose this is why you want me on the programme? Because the story is about to break. You want me to appear as the loving daughter. Win support. Make you look good."

He had the grace to look embarrassed, squirming a little. She smiled.

"Don't worry, Father. I'll do it. But not to save your hide. Not for your further glory but because it suits me. I need your help for this thing, otherwise you could go whistle."

"I said you were a chip." He grinned at her appreciatively, but she contradicted him.

"No, Father, I'm not. This is not self-interest. This is a cause I'm deeply committed to."

"Don't kid yourself, honey. I started that way too. And I'm interested in every issue I take up. I could not, *would* not come across believably if I was not. The camera *knows*. But I'm not hypocritical enough to lie and say I don't enjoy what I do, or pretend I'm so lacking in selfishness that I care only about the subject matter. I'll do everything and anything to further my career."

"How's Miranda taking it?" Perdita asked.

"Surprisingly enough she's fine. She's absorbed in her art. She wants to be a painter. She's good too. I think she guessed about me and her mother a long time ago. Girls are much more practical about things like this."

"Really?"

"It doesn't seem that important to her, but you never can tell. She's in France at the moment on an art course in Provence. We'll know more when she comes back."

"Okay, Father, when do you want to do this?"

"Next week. On the programme. We'll use bits of the video you brought back. But you know, Perdita, at some point I'd like a professional film of it all out there . . ."

It gave her great pleasure to announce, "I have that lined up already."

"Have you now? Who have you lined up pray?" He looked surprised.

"Leonard Dalton. The photographer."

"I know who he is. Well done, Perdita. He's a talented chap. That sounds very interesting. Very." He looked at her. "You know Perdita, sometimes you amaze me.

"I know."

"I've been a lousy father, haven't I?" he asked ruefully.

"Yes," she said.

"Mmm. Not in my nature. I haven't been any better to David and Miranda." He made a face. "I don't like kids," he said, "I'm awkward with them." Then he smiled deprecatingly at her. "Sorry."

"It's all right, Father."

"I must have done something right. You've turned out okay!"

She rose. "Well, Father, thanks for lunch. I'll be in touch." She turned to go but he called her and looking back at him over her shoulder she caught his appreciative, buccaneer smile. "And Perdita, you've turned into a stunner. I though you ought to know."

She grinned back at him. "I do know," she said. "It's a little late though, Father. You should have told me that years ago, no matter whether it was true or not. But you never really saw me, did you?"

"No, and I was a fool," he said and watched her as she walked away head held high.

Perdita went to see her mother. Melinda was not at the Design Factory. They said there that she was 'at home' and Perdita took that to mean the apartment in Kensington. However, her mother was not there either, so Perdita drove to Oak Wood Court.

She felt curiously calm and cheerful as she sped along the motorway. Autumn was in full and gloriously strident colour, the red and gold, burnt umber and copper of the leaves glowing warmly in the burnished sunlight. She thought of the many journeys she had made down this road in fear and apprehension, nervous and unsure. Well, not any more. Her parents no longer had the power to hurt her. She had advanced out of their reach.

Oak Wood Court was ablaze with amber glory and she could see the gardener and the handyman busy collecting the fallen leaves. Everything must be tidy for Melinda,

Perdita thought. If it was me I'd like to leave them scattered over the earth for a while. She said so to her mother. "It would be like an exotic carpet."

Her mother was sipping a hot chocolate on the terrace. She looked pale but immaculate as usual. She was wrapped in a cashmere housecoat, blue as her eyes.

"Well, when all this is yours you can do what you like, Perdita," she told her daughter tartly, "but until then neatness and order is the name of the game, I'm afraid. Your grandfather dinned it into me. Neatness and order." Then she examined her daughter. "You look different," she remarked.

"Father said I looked stunning," Perdita said.

"Did he now! Oh well, I don't think for a moment he realises what you have done to your skin. You'll look a hundred soon, I wouldn't wonder. Like a crocodile."

"Thank you, Mother."

Melinda drummed her fingers, long nails perfectly manicured. "I suppose you know he's broken my heart," she stated dramatically. Perdita burst out laughing.

"Oh, Mother!" she cried, "you're not serious!"

"Don't you *dare* laugh at me," Melinda said glaring at her angrily. "He has publicly humiliated and made a complete fool of me before the whole world." She stared out over the lawn, pulling the robe closer around her. She tapped a newspaper that lay on the table in disarray. The *Echo*.

"Have you seen this?" she asked.

"Yes," Perdita said, "I have seen that. But Mother, humiliation and being made a fool of are not the same things as having your heart broken." I should know, she thought.

Her mother held up the silver pot. "Some chocolate?" she asked and Perdita nodded. "Sit down, Perdita. Don't *hover*. It makes me nervous."

She poured the drink for her daughter and offered Perdita an almond tuille. "I have lived with your father all these years pretending I didn't know about *her*. It's been a terrible strain."

Perdita gasped and put her cup down abruptly. Her mother glanced at her.

"You thought I didn't know? You thought I was that stupid? Well, I did know about Fern Morrison." She spat out the name. "She's haunted me all my married life. Oh God, Perdita, you have no idea what it is like, three in a marriage. Your lover loving someone else."

Oh yes I do. Dear God, I do. Perdita sipped her drink. It warmed her. She felt very cold inside.

"Why did you trap him into marriage, Mother? You should have known it wouldn't work."

"I thought it *would*. I was very young. My father brought me up to believe he could get me anything, make anything I wanted happen. And he could, everything except your father. Oh he got him for me all right. *Purchased* him for me. But he left out the fact that you cannot manipulate human emotions. You can *get* someone but you cannot make them love you. I thought your father would forget Fern and begin to love me. After all I was bringing him so much. This place. A guaranteed career. Young people always believe the impossible. It is hope. I was so crazy about him, you see. I waited and waited and it never happened. I waited until this," she tapped the paper, "hoping, endlessly hoping." There were tears in her eyes. "I was so much in love. I would have done anything, gone anywhere, followed him to the ends of the earth for one kindness, one endearment."

I know, oh I know, Mother, Perdita thought, but remained silent.

"But all I brought him made him resent me. The very gifts I brought him poisoned him against me."

"I think you have to face the fact, Mother, that no matter what you did he wouldn't have been in love with you. You cannot force a man to love you." As I know. As I know so well.

Melinda sighed, looking out at the massed red-gold trees and a tear fell on her cheek and ran down leaving a little pathway in her make-up. Perdita stared at it. She had never before seen her mother's make-up flawed.

"Oh, but he did love me," she whispered. "I had one night of passion with him. One night when he loved me, was all mine. And you were conceived, and so he had to marry me. Father said. He'd have blacklisted him else. He had that power."

Perdita shook her head. "I think you are mixing sex up with love, Mother." Then thought, I don't think she knows the difference. "But Mother, to trap him like that . . . it wasn't fair."

"I didn't *care*," Melinda cried. "And that one night that he loved me was worth it all, everything I suffered." I know, Perdita thought, I feel the same about Larry. Oh God, it was worth it.

Melinda turned back to Perdita, "This will all be yours when I die. I don't want Lucas involved."

It had never before occurred to Perdita that eventually

she would be mistress of Oak Wood Court and she was not at all sure she wanted to be. It had never felt like home to her. It was not a place she felt comfortable in.

"Don't, Mother. For Goodness' sake, that shouldn't be an issue for a long long time."

"Oh yes it is. I've got cancer Perdita. I've a year at most."

Perdita's eyes widened. Her mother had never been close to her but *death*! Unable to absorb the implications of this information she listened in silence as her mother continued, "I filed for divorce while you were away. I'll get it very soon. It will come through any day now. And I've made a will. It's airtight, says *everything* of mine, this house, this land, my money, is all yours and Lucas can't touch a penny. My lawyers assure me he has no claim. Not since he went into print about his unfaithfulness."

"Mother, I don't *want* it. Don't you see?" Perdita looked earnestly at her mother. "It would be a repetition of your mistake."

"What?" Melinda looked puzzled.

"Don't you understand, Mother? You've led a life of bitterness and frustration. For years and years now, decades you have destroyed yourself, been eaten up, doing what? Waiting. Waiting for something to change. My father married you only because of me and because of all this," she swept her arm around indicating the land, the mansion behind them. "And you and he both suffered because your priorities were all wrong. Suffered endlessly. Because of this place. Without all this you would both have broken away. Father would have gone to Fern, lived with her and his family there. He'll be so happy, doing that."

"Well, I don't want him to be happy."

"Then you don't love him, Mother. It's what made him so bitter and hateful, all those years loving someone else. Not being able to love her publicly, not being able to acknowledge the kids. And you, Mother, who knows? You might have found another love. Another life."

Melinda stubbornly shook her head. "No. I've always been mad about Lucas. There would never have been another man for me."

"That's being close-minded. You don't *know*. People change. In any event you could have had a happier life. Even alone. Free to do as you wished, Mother, not mentally tied to a man who did not love you." She thought, I could be talking about myself. This could be me if I hadn't got the project. Am I so like her then? We are both one-man women. "And I don't want that legacy, Mother. I don't want all these accoutrements. Not knowing if the one I loved loved me for myself or all this *stuff*! Look at Posy Gore. It took me so long to realise all she fell for was what we had." Perdita shook her head, narrowing her eyes against the glare of the autumn sun, sipping her chocolate. "I was never popular in school, Mother. And it was because of this. I wish, I just wish I had been ordinary. Not hampered by too many possessions and parents so much in the spotlight. You have to be very strong to survive that. And you flaunted the possessions. So did Gramps." She looked at Melinda, shrinking deeper into her housecoat. Her mother looked suddenly frail. "There was a poem we did at school Mother. William Henry Davies. End of term concert. You and Father were supposed to be there when I recited it all by myself up on the stage. But you never came." She closed her eyes, remembering that small figure, red knees, scanning the audience, hoping, praying, then realising no one of hers was there. Other girls waved surreptitiously to loved and familiar faces, but there was no one there for her to wave to. Vicky Mendel whispering, "Your dad so high and mighty he thinks school concerts beneath him?"

Had Miss Davenport deliberately chosen that particular poem for her to recite? Or had it been the luck of the draw, a haphazard choice? She recited it again now, not caring any more whether her mother listened or not.

> "When I had money, money, O!
> I knew no joy till I was poor;
> For many a false man as a friend
> Came knocking all day at my door."

"Posy," her mother interjected, "I never liked that girl."

> "Much have I thought of life, and seen
> How poor men's hearts are ever light,
> And how their wives do hum like bees
> About their work from morn till night."

"Well, I don't know about *that* Perdita!"

"It was the time Mother, the period. I *know* what it means. Listen,

> 'So, when I hear these poor ones laugh,
> And see the rich ones coldly frown—

Poor men, think I, need not go up
So much as rich men should come down.

When I had money, money, O!
My many friends proved all untrue;
But now I have no money, O!
My friends are real, though very few.'

"That's what I feel, Mother. So let Lucas have it. Heaven knows he's paid for it. Over and over again. He deserves it, and quite frankly Father doesn't really care if his friends are true or not."

"That's a terrible thing to say, Perdita!"

"Well, Mother, I'm afraid it's true."

Nothing Melinda could say would change her daughter's mind. When Melinda told her she would leave the will as it was and Perdita would, willy-nilly, inherit, Perdita said, "If you do that Mother, I'll sell up, everything and give it to the hospital. Cooke's needs the money more than I do. We could build a whole new hospital in Nepal for what this place would fetch."

"Oh my God, Perdita, no! That would be terrible."

"Well, it's your choice, Mother."

"At the wedding, I was so . . . Oh Perdita, I'm so unhappy. My life's been such a mess."

For the life of her Perdita could muster no sympathy. Her heart felt dry and cold. She was sorry for her mother, but it was like reading a book. She was not touched.

"Yes, Mother. It has and I don't intend to follow in your footsteps. At least Father grabbed a little joy on the side. Let him have the damned place."

Perdita stayed with her mother, talking to her, being

supportive, but more like a nurse than a daughter. She did not, could not pretend a love she did not feel.

Although Melinda clung to her and obviously needed her now it was too late for Perdita. And it was too late for Melinda to change. She remained self-absorbed, never thinking to ask Perdita about her work, the Cooke Hospital, her daughter's interests.

During the last year of her mother's life Perdita was mainly in Egypt. When she came home she spent as much time as she could with Melinda. She was dutiful, sometimes flying from Egypt to spend a long weekend with her mother. But she did not pretend a grief she did not feel and when Melinda died the following autumn at Oak Wood Court her daughter was at her side. But she did not cry at the funeral.

By then Perdita's life had changed completely and as she gazed at her mother's coffin being lowered into the earth she was engulfed by a great sadness at the waste of a life, a life that repelled love, rejected affection and died waiting for something that could not, never would happen.

Chapter Twenty-Three

Leonard went with her to Karnak. She had done the show with her father and the studio had been inundated with phone calls and overwhelmed with letters, faxes, e-mail and cheques. It was a huge success.

Perdita advertised for a secretary and gave the job to a young man called Malcolm Radcliffe. He had been accountant for the NSPCA, was passionate about animals and was very rich. A minor member of the aristocracy, he was inhibited, had a stammer and was painfully shy. Perdita warmed to him instantly. He was very like what she had been.

The Cooke Hospital project was perfect for him as it had been for her and, unlike her, Malcolm had spent his whole life with animals.

"I like them better than humans," he told her, "they're reliable. They don't desert you, don't make fun of you, and they never let you down. No, they're much better people than people."

Perdita laughed. "I do know what you mean, Malcolm, but I only ever had a dog and a cat. You've farmed."

"My father farmed," he told her, "and the farm went to my big brother. I spent all my life fighting fox-hunting. All the excuses are a total lie. It is cruel beyond belief.

As Oscar Wilde said, 'The unspeakable in pursuit of the uneatable'."

Perdita left all the book-keeping to him, "It's not glamorous, your side of the business, doing the accounts," she said.

"I don't mind. Anything that helps. Only too glad."

"You can come out and see our operations for yourself when you've finished that lot." She pointed to the racks of mail to be answered, the faxes, the cheques to be acknowledged and receipted, the thank-yous to everybody.

"Oh gosh! Golly! Good. I'd love that."

"We are a small, dedicated team," she told him, not informing him that the small dedicated team had two members not on speaking terms, who communicated by fax and who spent a great deal of energy avoiding each other.

"That suits me fine," he said and gave his neighing laugh and Perdita thought, not for the first time that he was exactly like a horse.

Leonard said, "I think his Mater had an affair with a stallion and Malcolm is the result," and Perdita told him to try to be sensitive to the newcomer.

"He's been scarred," she told him. "Takes one to know one."

"Yeah! I know the sort. His Mater threw him into boarding school when he was six and . . ."

"Yes, Leonard. So watch what you say. No taking the mickey, okay."

"Okay. You're the boss!"

"I like him," she added, watching Malcolm sorting the mail with precise efficiency.

"Yeah, so do I. But he's just like a horse. Equine. Tosses his head. Laughs like a nag and moves like a colt. He's probably gay."

Perdita did not care whether he was or not. He did a superb job and was a thoughtful employee, always available, always enthusiastic.

In Egypt she laboured. She worked until she dropped. Yasser was a constant support and help and together they not only made the units in Karnak, Edfu and Luxor solvent, but where there had been only one hospital on the outskirts of Cairo, there was now the beginnings of what would be, as the funds came in, another quite large one in the centre of the city.

She kept out of Larry's way. Yasser told her he was in Luxor three weeks after his wedding day.

"Is he alone?" she asked.

He nodded. "Yes. His wife is not with him."

"What does he propose to do?"

"He wants to go to Jordan. He asked me if you were going there. He said if you were he would come here to Cairo instead. I told him I would ask you." Yasser looked at her, his large brown eyes reproachful. "I told him I did not like being used like this. As a go-between," he spread his hands. "It's not dignified."

"I'm sorry, Yasser, and you are quite right. We cannot avoid each other forever."

Yasser paused, then glanced at her under his bushy brows. "He asked, like you did, if you were alone."

"What did you say?"

He smiled wickedly. "I said you had Leonard with you."

She giggled. "Oh, Yasser, you are naughty!" But she worried about meeting him.

Sometimes it was too hot to sleep and she lay awake all night listening to the night noises, the constant hum of activity on the banks of the Nile, the sound of the overhead fan in her room purring softly, until eventually the high, harsh call to prayer from the mezzuin came from the minarets announced that it was dawn. It was a record now, not a person anymore and she thought sadly that progress left many casualties.

She thought about Larry all the time. It was as if he'd left her for a while and would be back any minute to take her in his arms and kiss her and make love to her and she thought, I'm exactly like Mother. If I'm not careful I'll waste my life marking time. Dreaming instead of living.

Leonard made a magnificent documentary about the animal hospitals in Egypt. Full of poignant images and wonderful enthusiasm he had brought all his skill as a photographer to bear and the result was stunning. He used both herself and Larry, but separately and although they never met, on tape it appeared they did.

Lucas was delighted with Leonard's work and predicted it would be nominated for awards.

Paul Morrison mercifully died and, after the funeral, Lucas moved into the house with Fern. Miranda seemed unconcerned, accepting her mother's behaviour with absent-minded indulgence. Utterly absorbed in her own life, she behaved as if Lucas was simply another lodger in place of Paul. She seemed to care little who was *in situ*.

"The young are so preoccupied with themselves, their own lives, their own affairs," Lucas told Perdita, "it amazes me."

"Does it, Father? I think your statement applies to the older generation as well." Her tone was caustic.

"Oh, Perdita, you enchant me! You are developing a witty style all your own."

He was proud of her, she realised and in her long and affectionless life it was better than nothing. A distinct change for the better.

She pondered the fact that when she ceased to need their love, both parents had developed an affection for her.

David had not taken the situation as calmly as his sister. He was angry and hurt and Perdita hoped that Larry was helping him.

He had moved into Larry's rooms over the surgery and although Perdita tried to talk to him on the phone he brushed her off briskly and made it obvious he did not want to have any more to do with her than he had to.

In the spring before her mother died Perdita, flying home from Egypt for the weekend to see her, found Posy Burton at Oak Wood Court. Perdita was tired, dusty and hungry, not at all pleased when on running up the steps to the terrace where she could see her mother swathed in her cashmere shawls, sipping tea, she realised Melinda was not alone. There was someone else sitting in the pristine-white high-backed wicker chair in the shadows. As she kissed her mother the shadow rose and Perdita, turning, saw it was Posy.

"Hello Perdy."

Perdita was silent a moment, collecting herself. She had not seen Posy since her wedding day.

Posy looked slim and svelte. She had an elegance about her, a well-groomed, pampered patina that made the viewer look twice. She had stopped bleaching and flattening her hair to look like Perdita and it was her natural soft brown colour springing out in a cloud about her face, making her features look small and dainty. She looked very pretty and all Perdita could feel was a terrible resentment.

She must be happy with Larry, she thought angrily. Then, sadly, he must love her. She has the look of a woman in love. That look had not been there on her wedding day. Strange.

Perdita nodded to her friend. "Hi Posy!" she said a trifle sullenly. "Mother, how are you? You mustn't tire yourself."

"I won't tire her Perdy," Posy said.

"I'm *not* tired," her mother protested peevishly, "I'm full of drugs and I'm feeling no pain. For the moment."

Melinda's face was egg-shell pale, her cheeks sunken, her eyes panda-circled. She wore a turban to hide her hair, thinning now from the chemotherapy.

"Mother, I . . ."

"No go! Go walk with Posy. She wants to talk to you." Melinda lay back on the reclining canvas chair they had got for her.

"Oh, does she? About what may I ask?" Perdita knew she sounded childishly sarcastic but she could not help herself.

"About Larry," Posy said tranquilly.

"Well, I've nothing to say to you on that score, Posy, so you can save your breath."

"I think you might have," Melinda waved a hand aimlessly in the air. "Go on. Go to the cherry orchard. See the trees in bloom. They are a wonderful sight."

Reluctantly, Perdita went. Posy walked beside her but did not take her arm as she used to in the old days. The trees were shedding clouds of moon-silver petals and the glittering shower like snow peppered the girls' hair. The pale spring sun glimmered through the trees.

"When all the world was young, Perdy, we used to walk like this. Under these trees."

Perdita closed her eyes, then said, "I was a fool ever to trust you Posy. You sucked me dry."

To her surprise, Posy nodded. "I know," she said, "and I'm sorry."

"Bit late for that. Everyone is sorry all of a sudden. Father, Mother. Now you. And it's too late, Posy. It's too late."

Posy shook her head. "It's never too late, Perdy." She stopped and turned, looking around. "There used to be a bench here somewhere." Spotting it, she said, "Ah, here it is. Let's sit."

She sat down, seemingly not worried about the seat of her beige suit. Perdita stood over her. "Look here, Posy, I'm tired and travel-stained. I need a shower and something to eat. This is not a good time to exchange reminiscences. If you think I'm going to park myself here and natter to you about the past and your marriage you are very much mistaken." I sound exactly like Father, she thought.

"Oh, sit down, Perdy and shut up and listen," Posy

commanded irritably. "God, you can be very uppity. Arrogant. You always were. Making it impossible for people to get near you."

She was probably right, Perdita decided ruefully and sat. Her jeans had protected her from much worse than the lichen-encrusted bench.

"I'm in love, Perdy. For the first time in my life. Truly in love."

Oh God! Oh God! Perdita's heart sank and she felt suddenly sick and faint. "I don't want to hear this, Posy," she almost begged.

"Oh yes you do!"

"Why are you being so cruel?" she whispered helplessly.

"Ah! So you do still love him?"

Perdita did not reply, she did not have to. Posy smiled at her. "This is the first decent thing I've ever done for you, isn't it?"

"I don't understand."

"Larry is yours, Perdita. He always was, always will be."

"But you love him."

"No. Not Larry. Listen, Perdy, I confess. I've always been envious of you, of what you had. All this." She looked at the blossom-laden branches of the cherry trees laced overhead, the outline of Oak Wood Court in the shimmering distance. "A distinguished and famous father. A fun mother . . ."

"Fun!" Perdita echoed in disbelief, but her mind was trying to get around those sentences Posy had just uttered: *Larry is yours*. How could he be? He was married to Posy. She had been at the ceremony, a witness.

"And you were beautiful," Posy was saying, "the other girls were so jealous. So was I."

"This is all in the past, Posy. Over and forgotten."

"No, it's not. I wanted to be like you Perdy, *be* you, so I changed my hair colour and copied your clothes. I wormed my way into your mother's affections and then into a job with her company. It was so easy."

"I never could. Worm my way into her affections, I mean."

"No. You couldn't, could you?"

"Where's all this leading, Posy? You're not telling me anything I don't already know."

"It's leading me to telling you that I stole Larry too. I lied to him. Said I was pregnant when I wasn't. I seduced him, Perdy, told him I was going to have his baby."

"And he fell for it?" Perdita's voice was bitter.

"You know Larry, Perdita. An honourable man. There are not many of his kind left. He would never leave a child of his without a proper and legitimate father, and of course he believed me. He *would.* I was very persuasive. And Larry is not the sort of chap to go about suspicious of people. Like you, he *trusts*. Stupid, if you ask me."

Perdita stared at her. "He realised his mistake almost at once." Posy bit her lip. "I was so disgusted with myself. Copying your clothes, your hair was one thing. Stealing from you was another." Perdita looked at her in surprise. "Oh yes, I took things from you too," she said, "I took lots of things without telling you. Cardigans. Perfume. Soap. Scarves."

"I thought I was careless, always losing things."

"I let you think that. And coaxing your mother, well, it was childish at best. But Larry was another matter altogether and I regretted it almost at once."

"You seemed to enjoy your wedding," Perdita could not keep the bitterness out of her voice.

"Yes I did. I would be lying if I said I didn't. It was great, sitting there on the top table, all in white, the cynosure of all eyes. I had achieved what I had set out to do. I had *won.*" She laughed. "You looked so silly in that pink and suddenly for the first time in my life I felt equal. I had a man *you* wanted. I was the star attraction. I looked as good as you."

She turned away. "Then we were alone together and it all collapsed. It was shocking and sordid."

She paused and Perdita could see her chewing her lip. She used to do that in school when she was upset and Perdita used to tell her to stop but she never did.

"We arrived that night in Paris. Larry had been so silent on the plane. He couldn't make love to me, Perdy. He just couldn't bring himself to. He tried, but it was no use. The same sense of honour that forced him to marry me when he thought I was pregnant, the morality that insisted he give his child a stable home, that very virtue forbade him having sex with someone he did not love. He could not be unfaithful to you."

She paused then, "You see when he'd . . . no, he *didn't* make love to me that time, before. When we came back from Oak Wood Court. Remember the night? I insisted on cadging a lift? I made love to *him*, took him by storm. But that was before you two were *really* serious, before you went to Egypt. After he had pledged himself to you it became impossible for him." She paused again. "It was a farce. We were strangers. He was fair and said he'd make a stab at some kind of life together. For the child's sake. But I wasn't pregnant. I felt degraded. No triumph now. So I told him the truth."

Another pause. Then, "We were sitting at a sidewalk café. You know those Parisian cafés? It was autumn, remember. The trees were glorious and there was a snap in the air, like energy. Exciting. All around us people were talking. You know the way they do in France, gesticulating, waving their arms about, fluttering their hands, chatting nineteen to the dozen, laughing, being affectionate, touching each other. Smooching. Oh, everyone seemed to me to be in love. And Larry and I sat silent as the grave. Nothing to say. Nothing at all. We sat at either side of the table, silently sipping our *café au lait*, staring into space. There was no victory there, just boredom. So I told him the truth. That I'd planned it. The seduction. That I wanted what you had. That I wasn't pregnant." She glanced at Perdita. "I'll never forget his face, the way he looked at me. The loathing. The contempt. I was lower than the lowest in his eyes. That honourable man could not comprehend such perfidity, not in a million years. To him I was a malignant and worthless sub-human. He stared at me for a long moment, that look upon his face, then he left. Stood up, put some francs on the table and went. I never saw him again."

They sat in silence while Perdita tried to sort out her feelings. At first she had briefly decided that if he was weak enough to be seduced by Posy and silly enough to believe she was pregnant, then he did not deserve her love. She was too good for him. But it was typical of Larry that he would feel that if he fathered a child he must marry the mother, and it was his utterly chivalrous and noble character, his very old-fashioned morals that had made her love him so much. She could not blame him then if he acted in character.

Posy was right. He was an honourable man and not many women in these times thought that admirable. But she did. Oh yes, she did.

Posy said, 'When I got back to the hotel his clothes, his suitcases were there. He never retrieved them. Couldn't bear to. He'd paid the hotel by credit card. They said he'd phoned through. He vanished from my life, Perdita. All over."

"That was . . . when?" Perdita asked.

"Autumn last year. I thought he might come back to me. Get over his disgust. Also I did not want to admit I'd been dumped." A smile broke, like sun coming out from behind a cloud and her face softened. "Then last month something happened to me to change everything."

"You said you were in love. I thought you meant . . ."

"Oh God, no!" Posy laughed, "no. It's David. David Morrison, Larry's partner. And from what the papers say, your half-brother. He consoled me when I tried to find Larry. He was so good to me."

"He seems to make a habit of that," Perdita muttered. She rose and paced about trying to work it out, thinking.

"Well," Posy asked eventually, "what do you think, Perdy?"

"It's another part of me, Posy. Just another part of *me*. Don't you see that? You seem unable to go outside my family. It's the same old pattern."

"But I love him. It is different, Perdy. When I came back from Paris alone I was miserable for a while. I couldn't go to you and I had no one else. Mother and Father are in Columbia. I think Father's been demoted. He's in a terribly nervous state and my mother is off the walls. Well, anyhow I decided to sue for divorce."

"It was too soon surely?"

Posy shook her head. "No. On the grounds of non-consumation. He's never made love to me, had sex with me *after* the ceremony. I went to the surgery to try and talk to Larry about it, ask his forgiveness and I met David. Well, we talked. About you. About Larry. We were both angry and we found it a relief to share our resentments. Well, the long and the short of it is, Perdy, we plan to marry as soon as my divorce comes through."

"So where has David been all this time?" Perdita asked.

"Why, with me!"

Perdita stared at her friend. No matter how hard she tried she could find no affection in her heart for Posy. But she had no hatred either, she simply felt sorry for her. Posy doing the same immature things as she had always done.

"So I'll be Lucas Hastings's daughter-in-law," she said now, smiling at Perdita.

"Yes, Posy, you will." She was glowingly happy, that was obvious.

She rose and took Perdita's hand. "And everything is okay now? I've made amends. And we're truly sisters at last, Perdy. Isn't that grand?"

Perdita didn't reply.

"And I'll help you with the project, Perdy. I've seen it on *Hastings Hour*. I'll get into it with David and we'll be a team."

Perdita thought for a moment. Her first reaction was dread. Posy interfering again, perhaps making trouble. But on second thoughts she realised such a thing was impossible. Posy had no power over her any longer and she had so alienated Larry as to make herself obnoxious to him. She could imagine his reaction and how he now felt about Posy. Perdita had, by now, authority enough in the organisation to control what Posy did. She would not enjoy the field work in Egypt, that was certain. Posy was not one to tolerate the harsh conditions Perdita accepted as part of the job. No, she would give Posy to Malcolm and, knowing Malcolm, he would put Posy to work slaving over a hot computer, answering letters and phone calls. It was not Posy's style. She was too ambitious for Cooke's Animal Hospital. She'd love to appear on TV but would be in the bar hob-nobbing with the media names, not at all interested in the results of the transmission. That part of the operation would bore her to death. So would the heat, the flies, the medical requirements. No, Perdita reflected, Posy could not, would not disturb her any more. She had no power over her and, Perdita thought, I'm free. At last I'm really free. And she smiled to herself as Posy rambled on.

She rose and, gently removing Posy's hand from her arm, she walked beside her back to the house.

Perdita was lying on her bed in the Old Cataract Hotel, drenched in sweat. The dark wood fan overhead turned swiftly and silently trying to circulate the stagnant air. She stared at it mindlessly.

She was very tired. A lot had happened to occupy

her mind. The new hospital in Cairo was well under way but more money was needed. It would probably always be like that.

Leonard was working on another programme to be shown before Christmas. She was in daily communication with Malcolm and Posy who had settled down obediently under David's wing. Lucas said he'd work in the latest video because, he said, in January and February people did not want to spend. "We'll have to show it before Christmas. People are more disposed then to spend. With Christmas over generosity flies out the window."

Her father seemed younger, more boyish and certainly more cheerful during the past year. He had stood beside her at Melinda's funeral. "Poor cow!" he'd whispered. "Poor sad cow. What a drag she was."

"Father, don't be unkind. Not now," she'd whispered back and he'd lapsed into silence.

He was happy with Fern and Perdita had formed a tentative friendship with her father's mistress, soon to be wife. She liked Fern and got on well with her when the emotional baggage was unpacked, discussed and sorted.

She remained close, too, to Anjelica Burton. Larry's mother had called her and invited her to stay at the cottage. Perdita had confided everything to her and she had sighed and quoted, "'Oh what a tangled web we weave when first we practise to deceive'! Oh, my dear, I hope you will not allow my son's old-fashioned morals to keep you two apart. You are so very right for each other." She leaned over to the girl. "And you know, Perdita, if you had been in Larry's shoes you'd have done the same. You too are honourable. When you are discrediting your mother and father remember we have the morals we are given and it seems to me that, difficult as it may be to credit it, they did not do so bad a job." When she saw Perdita's surprise she said, "Oh yes, my dear, they did. And, if you'd got pregnant by, say Leonard even though you loved Larry, you would have felt honour-bound to marry the photographer, wouldn't you? Peas in a pod, oh yes you are, so like each other."

David and Posy announced they were engaged. Fern was mildly troubled, but she had Lucas there to support her now and it was Lucas who said, "Don't worry, I'll keep that young lady in line. I have her working her guts out in the studios. I know what makes her tick. Just throw a big name at her for ten minutes every now and then and she's happy. I'll see David comes to no harm." And both Perdita and Fern believed him.

In the meantime there was her work. It occupied her thoughts, took all her energy. Gave her all her energy.

And now, in the hotel in Egypt she decided it was useless trying to sleep. She got up, showered and slipping into a loose silk wrap, she opened the French windows, went out on the balcony and looked up at the sky.

She never ceased to marvel at the density of the stars here in the desert. There seemed to be so many more visible here than in England. Clotted together in massy brilliance, they danced in and out in glittering splendour. The sky looked like a dark cloak trailing diamonds.

Everything was quiet now, between the night and the dawning, the world hesitating between night and day.

She stretched her arms wide and drew in a breath of cold morning air. She could smell the desert, that dry hot smell and the fragrance of the fig trees, the olive groves near the banks of the Nile. She sniffed the ancient river itself, sour and salty. She thought of Cleopatra and Nefertari, Hatshepsut and the fabled beauty of the women of Egypt. They must have stared as she was doing at the slow green waters and the twinkling stars.

"You take my breath away."

The soft voice came from under the palm tree in the midian that divided the toing and froing traffic on the street. But she knew that voice. That voice had never been far from her heart.

Her heart leapt within her and she dared not breathe. The figure detached itself. "Larry," she cried, leaning down, her face illuminated by the stars and her love. "Wait," she called, "wait there."

She ran inside, got the hotel key with the room number on it. She leaned over the balcony and threw the key to him. A drowsy driver with his donkey and trap looked at them sleepily, then laughed.

Larry caught the key and disappeared. She went inside and closed the windows.

There would be no recriminations. There would be no hashing and rehashing of the past. Their love was stronger than that, purer and more enduring.

As the door opened she too opened her arms to receive her love, her passion. Larry.